EMPTY ROOMS

EMPTY ROOMS

Jeffrey J. Mariotte

WordFire Press
Colorado Springs, Colorado

DEDICATION

This book is dedicated to the survivors.

Acknowledgements

A number of people helped me see this book to the end. These people generously showed me their Michigan: Michael LaVean, Paul Storrie, Jodi Riggins, Rose Ann Stewart, Nancy Hart, Liz Seelye, and Noah Seifullah. Anything I got right is thanks to them, and anything I didn't is on me. I also owe great thanks to Marsheila (Marcy) Rockwell, Howard Morhaim, Kevin J. Anderson, Rebecca Moesta, and the whole crew at WordFire Press, and my family.

> *The awful daring of a moment's surrender*
>
> *Which an age of prudence can never retract*
>
> *By this, and this only, we have existed*
>
> *Which is not to be found in our obituaries*
>
> *Or in memories draped by the beneficent spider*
>
> *Or under seals broken by the lean solicitor*
>
> *In our empty rooms*

The Wasteland, T.S. Eliot

1

The Morton house squatted on the edge of its corner lot, as if it had tiptoed over while nobody was watching and waited there, trying to decide which way to spring. When Richie Krebs first saw it he said to his wife, "That place looks haunted."

Wendy didn't even glance his way, just stared out the side window of the borrowed red pickup, its bed piled high with their belongings. Checking out their new neighborhood. "Babe, this is Detroit," she said. "Every third house looks haunted."

Wendy was overstating the situation, and yet she wasn't. Their city's condition varied neighborhood by neighborhood, street by street, sometimes block by block. Native Detroiters, Wendy and Richie weren't immune to the impact of ruin porn, those inescapable photo essays focusing on the city's vacant homes, abandoned factories, and boarded-up storefronts. They had friends who bucked the trend, whose property values clung tenaciously to life. But they had given up on their own place, surrendered to foreclosure, and walked out on their mortgage. Their former neighborhood looked like it had barely survived nuclear war. By contrast, the one they were moving into was a vast improvement, as if it had suffered only a moderately bad pandemic.

The whole situation was depressing. One more layer of bad news, adding to the sedimentary crust of it that had been building for the past thirteen months. Their marriage seemed the only thing decent left in Richie's life, and it, too, creaked under the strain. He hoped moving to a new home, paid for with cash saved up by not paying their mortgage for several months, would improve things. Hope, however, was a scarce commodity these days, something he could only bring himself to parcel out in limited rations.

His worst times were the evenings, when he rose, unrested from daytime sleep, and got ready for work, donning the uniform he despised so much he hated to look in the mirror when he wore it. The provided shirts were a quarter-inch too short in the sleeves, frayed at the cuffs, and too tight across his broad shoulders. The tan shirts and brown pants, with their ridiculous, stiff gold stripes down the outer seams, were vaguely reminiscent of Nazi apparel. And all of it, especially the badge, reminded him of his own greatest failure: the shield he no longer wore.

He didn't believe he was suicidal; just the same, he was glad he no longer owned a gun. He remembered an instructor at the Detroit police academy he had attended, a burly man wearing a white shirt that strained at the shoulders and barely closed around his bull neck. The man had a silver buzz-cut and a fighter's nose, cocked to the right like a cabinet door with a busted upper hinge. "Never surrender your weapon," he had said. "If you give up your weapon, in ninety-nine cases out of a hundred, it'll be used against you. The last thing you want is to be shot with a bullet you loaded."

Turned out, that wasn't last on Richie's list, after all.

What didn't occur to Richie, in those optimistic rookie days, was that when the DPD fired you, they not only took away your badge but they reclaimed your department-issued firearm. Richie also got rid of the backup piece that his training officer had insisted he carry. Guns weren't hard for cops to unload. Some kept small arsenals at home or stashed in the trunks of their personal vehicles, and were always up for a bargain. Richie sold his backup to a rookie with a glow like an expectant mother's. He reminded Richie so much of himself, at that fledgling point in his career, that the conversation was literally painful.

The next time he paid any attention to the Morton house—though he didn't yet know it by that name—two minutes after he pulled out of his driveway on a cool April night, he briefly wished that he had kept at least one of those weapons.

His encounter on that night led to a different sort of education, one they couldn't provide at the academy. Safety is a comforting lie, he learned. What a person takes from life can't be given back, and what's given away is not easily reclaimed. He wished he could forget those lessons, wished they could be discarded as easily as steel and springs and gun oil. But forgetting is an illusion; once something is tucked into a pocket of memory, he found, it's there forever, and the more horrible it is the closer to the front it remains, easy to slip out and worry at, like a scrap of familiar fabric rubbed soft and ragged over time.

On the night Richie's lessons began, under a bright three-quarter moon, his headlights scraped past abandoned houses, empty windows gazing blankly across neglected lawns toward the cracked and crumbling street.

As Richie made a left at the corner, he braked for an old dog hobbling across the road, and slowed with those headlights aimed at the big corner house. A scraggly elm stood in the front yard. Richie was already looking away when he noticed a black kid with a crowbar heading toward the house. A black kid in Detroit was no more surprising than a foreclosure sign; one bearing a crowbar, still not entirely foreign. But it was eleven-thirty at night. The kid hadn't come to make any owner-approved modifications.

Richie had passed that vacant house at least twice a day for three weeks. It was easy to distinguish a newly vacant one from a long-time empty. Recent ones still had landscaping, the boards nailed over their windows were new, often bearing orange stickers from a lumberyard. Graffiti hadn't yet turned them into primitive message boards.

This house's yard was thick with knee-high weeds. Its windows were covered in wood that had taken on the gray patina of the siding, age and weather scraping and dulling its paint and providing a neutral background for the urban art decorating it.

As Richie watched, the kid cut along the side of the house, toward the back. Richie was no longer a cop—for a lifelong dream, that had been a brief and ill-fated adventure, six years and done—but he still wore a uniform with a badge on it. He braked his aging Ford Tempo and got out, clutching a Mag-lite in lieu of a gun.

Weeds brushed his uniform pants. There was a fence around the backyard but the gate dangled from a single hinge, wide open. Richie played his flashlight beam over the gate and beyond, lighting more of the same miniature jungle. He paused just inside the gate. "Hello?"

No answer, but he heard a quick, ragged intake of breath from around the corner. The kid had probably been headed for a back door. Richie wondered if he had a gun. So many did, these days.

"Security!" Richie said. "Come on out. Let me see your hands."

Another sharp breath. Hugging the wall, Richie rounded the corner.

The crowbar flashed in the Maglite's beam, spinning end over end toward him. Instinct shoved Richie back behind the corner as the bar slammed into the wall, spraying wood chips. By the time the crowbar thumped down in the weeds, the kid was sprinting toward the back fence.

The fence was a plank construction, six feet high. Boards gapped here and there, but Richie didn't want to count on there being an opening in the right spot. The kid was younger than him, and taller, lanky. Richie took off around the fence, toward the alley bisecting the block. He had always been broad-shouldered, lean and strong; in high school, coaches had shaken their heads in sad disbelief when they learned how little interest he had in athletics. He had worked out with weights even then, but only because he thought it would make him a better cop. His interests had always been narrowly focused. Lately, he had been slacking off on his running, down from ten miles a week to five or less, some of that at a walk. He'd let his gym membership lapse, too; he said it was for financial reasons, which was partly true, but even the weight bench in his basement was mostly used to dry laundry these days.

Before he reached the alley, he heard a crash. The kid apparently wasn't as athletic as Richie had feared. He had snagged a foot on the fence and come down hard, and when Richie reached him he was still trying to get unsteady legs under him. Richie didn't slow down, but plowed into him at full tilt. The kid went down again, entangling Richie.

They both wound up on the alley's dirt floor, Richie pawing for his flashlight. He scrambled upright and cocked his arm back, ready to use the heavy light as a club, but the kid just sat there, staring at him in the moon's glow, his heart beating so hard Richie could feel it through the cotton T-shirt bunched in his fist.

"You ain't a cop. Since when do security give a fuck who goes in these vacants?"

"Security doesn't," Richie said. "*I* do."

"What for?"

"This is my neighborhood."

"Guess you don't like crowds."

"What I don't like is people breaking into houses that aren't theirs." Richie shined his light onto the kid. He was maybe sixteen. Dark fuzz shaded his cheeks and his hair was cropped close to the scalp. He wore a coat big enough to fit three people his size, baggy jeans, and sneakers that could have served as clown shoes. But he didn't have any visible tats or scars, and his eyes were wide, his face open, almost friendly. Gangstas worked hard to perfect a sort of bored sneer, lips curling down, eyes hooded, or they offered a smirking, phony sincerity. This kid didn't show either of those.

Besides, Richie smelled rank sweat powering through the kid's overdose of body spray. He was scared.

That was good. He wasn't strapped. If he had been he would have shot Richie instead of chucking a crowbar at him. Richie was surprised to find himself somewhat relieved he hadn't.

"What you gonna do?" the kid asked.

"I should cuff you and hold you for the cops."

"Should?"

Richie didn't have the authority to arrest the kid. He could hold him, as he'd threatened, but that would make him late for work. In his three weeks on the job, he had already received two reprimands for tardiness. "If you promise not to break into any more houses I'll let it slide. You don't look like such a bad guy to me."

The kid tilted his chin up. "I bad as shit."

"Yeah, I didn't mean to insult you. Believe it or not, in some cultures that's a compliment."

"This here Detroit."

"Must have slipped my mind." Richie took a little spiral-topped notebook and a pen from his shirt pocket. "What's your name?"

"Why?"

"You want me to get out the cuffs?"

"Wil."

"Will."

"One L."

"What?"

"W-i-l. One L."

"Got it," Richie said. He crossed out the second L he had written. "Last name? Never mind, show me your driver's license."

"You don't trust me?"

"You threw a crowbar at me."

"Can I get that back?"

"You gonna use it to break into houses?"

Wil smiled. "Naw." He fished a wallet from somewhere under his coat and slid his license out. He was seventeen, and his full name was Wilmont Aaron Fowler. Richie copied it down, along with an address on Berkshire, on the east side.

"This your current address?"

"Yeah."

Richie's neighborhood was just south of Detroit's Boston-Edison district, as central as could be. "You came a long way to bust into a vacant. They don't have any closer to home? Give me your digits."

Wil spouted numbers. Richie wrote them down. He tore a sheet from the pad and scribbled on it. "This is me," he said. "Richie Krebbs. Call my cell phone if you need me, not Rampart Security. The receptionist there is a junkyard dog, she'd chew you up and spit out the gristle."

"Why you think I might need you?"

"You never know. Just hang on to it. And stay out of trouble, Wil, or I *will* make sure you go to jail. You feel me?"

Wil smiled. A gold tooth glinted in the flashlight's beam. "I feel you."

Richie got to his feet and helped Wil up. "I hurt you?"

"It's cool."

"Good. Keep away from vacant houses."

Wil nodded, and Richie left him there. He had wasted too much time, was going to be late anyway.

Nothing he could do about it now.

O O O

"Check it," Kevin Roche said. Kevin Roche was a husky black guy wearing a ball cap so tight it must have cut off the flow of blood to his brain. Lettered in gold on the cap's crown was "Security," and there was a three-bar chevron above that, testifying to his rank as a sergeant at Rampart Security. That meant an extra two hundred bucks in his bi-weekly take-home. And he got to drive the truck, until Rampart considered Richie fully trained and able to patrol solo.

Kevin had inclined his head toward a white van parked in front of a two-story home. Lights glowed from two upstairs windows onto an immaculately manicured lawn. Through a bay window on the ground floor came the rectangular, bluish haze of a wide-screen TV.

"That van?" Richie asked.

"Wasn't there last night or the night before, right?"

"I don't remember it, but I might have been blinded by all the Benzes and Lexuses."

"Need to make note of this kind of thing," Kevin said. "Anything that changes."

They were patrolling Palmer Woods, an upper middle class neighborhood, emphasis on the *upper*, in a white pickup truck with a gold stripe along its side and a light bubble on the roof. In the event of trouble, they had their Maglites, a radio, and a digital camera with a zoom lens. Most upscale Detroiters wanted to live beyond Eight Mile Road, so Palmer Woods, just the far side of Seven Mile, off Woodward, was in riskier territory. The people who held out there got to feel like they were bucking the odds, pioneers in the foreign landscape that Detroit had become, and they paid dearly for the protection offered by a private security company.

Kevin was training Richie in the ways of patrol, which Richie found more than a little ironic given that he had been a street cop for six years, whereas Kevin's previous law enforcement experience consisted of nineteen months on the security staff of the Sears at Summit Place Mall. But Kevin had been at Rampart for three years, during which time the company, and Detroit's private security industry as a whole, had enjoyed enormous growth while the rest of the city imploded. He seemed smart and capable, and Richie had tried a few times to talk him into applying to the DPD. But Kevin had no interest in being a real cop, so Richie didn't push it.

The job sucked. Leaving his house to drive to work made Richie's neck ache, sent tendrils of pain into his head. His gut churned, and every minute he spent on duty he had to fight back the impulse to flee, to get into his second-hand Tempo and drive as fast as he could, to head for Maine or Mexico or someplace else where he knew no one, where he wouldn't feel like a failure every time he caught a glimpse of himself in the mirror.

"Let's have a look," Kevin said. He pulled the pickup to the curb behind the van and left the headlights on. They got out of the truck. Kevin went wide to look in the driver's window, while Richie took small windows in the rear doors.

Inside, he saw racks and shelves and a couple scrawny bouquets of flowers. Petals carpeted the floor. "It's a florist's van," he said. "Or somebody has a really green thumb."

"Florist," Kevin agreed. He tapped the van's side. "'Bloomin' Love,' it says."

"Cute."

"Could be a fake. Or stolen."

Richie went around to the passenger side. Just then, a light came on over the house's front door. The door opened and a man stepped out. "Excuse me," he said. He was silhouetted against light from inside, the lamp above him revealing a heavyset guy with a fringe of gray hair. "Help you?"

"Rampart Security, sir," Kevin said. "This your van?"

"Yeah, I own the business. My car's in the shop so I drove a company van home. Doesn't fit in the garage."

"That's fine sir, we're just checking."

"Thanks." The man closed his door, and the overhead light clicked off.

"Answers that," Kevin said. "Let's roll."

Back in the truck, they cruised the community's quiet, winding streets. Kevin played WJLB softly, turning it off any time he called in to headquarters. Another perk of seniority, controlling the radio.

"Do you ever think there's something, I don't know, a little screwy about what we're doing?" Richie asked.

"Screwy how?"

"We haven't really done much tonight. Checked out that guy's van. Took pictures of a car we saw twice, on two different streets."

"Might be casing houses."

"I get that. But shouldn't the police be doing this?"

"Should, maybe. Don't."

"That's because they keep getting their budget cut. They don't have the personnel to keep someone out here when nothing's going on."

"Maybe nothing's going on 'cause we're here."

"Maybe," Richie admitted. "But if the residents here paid what they're shelling out to Rampart as taxes, the PD could assign someone to regular patrols."

"Wouldn't be me," Kevin said.

Not me, either, Richie thought. There's the problem with that scenario.

"You don't want your job," Kevin said, "there's other folks would like it."

"I'm not saying that. It's fine. It just seems strange, is all."

Richie did not, in fact, want the job. But it was work, and for the past thirteen months, since being fired by the PD, the only employment he had been able to find had been a swing shift stint at an Arby's and a broom jockey position at the Fairlane Town Center in Dearborn, where people had looked at him, if they noticed him at all, as if he'd been a curiously colored centipede. He took those jobs because he and Wendy needed the money, same reason he had taken the spot at Rampart. All he had ever wanted was to be a cop, and having failed at that, he was without a goal, as lost in his own life as a traveler without a map.

Having come perilously close to upsetting his supervisor, whose reports to management would determine how long he remained on trainee status, he went for a quick change of subject. "Hey, on my way to work tonight I caught a kid trying to break into a vacant with a crowbar."

"What'd you do?"

Richie told him the story, describing the house, Wil, the abbreviated chase, and Wil's surrender.

"Where'd you say that house was?" Kevin asked when he finished.

Richie had described the location, but he did so again. Kevin, like other lifelong residents of the city, imagined they knew every house.

"It's on the northwest corner of Longfellow and Fourteenth," Richie said. "A couple blocks from my new place."

"No shit?"

"What?"

"You know what house that was, don't you?"

"Is it famous?"

"Ever hear of Angela Morton?"

Richie knew the name. He studied crime like some people did baseball stats, and this one had been big news. "That little girl who was abducted, what, ten years ago or so?"

"Little more, I think."

Richie remembered the broad strokes, if not the fine details. A young girl had been snatched, apparently from her front yard. No ransom demand had ever materialized. Neither had a body. It had been front-page news for a few weeks, the lead story on the evening news, and then it had tapered off. There had never been an arrest. "Was that her place?"

"Northwest corner, right? Big ol' tree in the front?"

"That's right."

"My momma was obsessed with that case. She cut out newspaper clippings, watched everything on the TV. She used to drive me and my sister by that house and shake her head and tell us never to talk to strangers."

"Thirteen years," Richie said.

"Say what?"

"It was thirteen years ago. I can't remember her parents' names, but I do remember that."

"Damn."

"Crime's kind of a hobby of mine. Learning about it, not doing it."

"Good thing."

"Wow." Richie shook his head. "That was the Angela Morton house. I never put that together before. Trippy."

"Was a long time ago," Kevin said.

"Thirteen years."

"Yeah."

"Poor kid."

"You think she's dead?"

"Of course she is. People who take kids like that, without asking for ransom, almost invariably do it for sex. Most of their victims are dead in twenty-four hours. Less than. Just …"

"Just what?"

"Well, Wendy and I are trying to have kids. Makes you wonder. What if the bastard who took Angela Morton still lives in the neighborhood?"

Kevin made a right turn, driving slowly past the big, expensive homes. "Then," he said, "you better figure out who it is. And right quick."

2

The man had studied dolls. He knew Barbies backward and forward, knew the history of Madame Alexanders, and remembered that the first talking doll was Mattel's Chatty Cathy. You pulled a string on Chatty Cathy's back and a phonograph record in her gut played one of eleven phrases. He'd had one once, an original from 1959, but that had been years ago and she had been lost somewhere along the way. Chatty Cathy always looked like a little girl, even though she more than a decade older than he was.

You had to love her for that.

Now there were so many dolls on the shelves it was hard to choose. Interactive dolls that would go to sleep, waking when they were touched. Dolls that made feeding sounds when you stuck a bottle to their lips. Dolls that gurgled and babbled and kissed you back. Dolls based on popular TV characters, and dolls for older girls that took as their models the sluttiest girls in high school.

His inclination was to buy a doll that didn't do anything, the old-fashioned kind that excited the imagination, but he didn't want a doll that would be perceived as boring. He stood with his hands in his pockets, studying the steel shelves, scanning the packaging. He knew what she had to look like: a strawberry blonde, with a spray of freckles across her nose. There weren't many like that.

As he searched, he let his gaze drift every now and then to the little temptress sharing the aisle with him. She had long brown hair falling in waves to the middle of her back, and freckled shoulders. She was squatting to investigate something on a low shelf, and her sundress rode up her plump thighs.

He cleared his throat. "I have to get a doll for my six-year-old niece, and I can't decide," he said. "Which one of these would you want?"

She pointed to the iCarly Chat and Change doll. "iCarly," she said.

"How old are you?"

"Five."

"What grade are you in?"

"Kindergarten," she said. "Next year I'll be in first."

"That's right. My niece is just a little older than you. But not as pretty."

He pulled the iCarly doll from the shelf and looked at it instead of at the girl. Talking to her here was dangerous. Her parents were probably close by. He shouldn't have struck up a conversation, but she had made it so easy, squatting there like she wanted him to say something.

He didn't care for dolls patterned after current celebrities. They weren't timeless. In a couple of years nobody would remember who or what an iCarly was and it would mean nothing. He put it back and took one that did nothing except drink and wet. The coloring was close, and though this was a baby doll, not a seven-year-old, like the angel she would memorialize, she would do.

He would know what she represented.

He always liked to have a new doll for the next would-be angel. And he was feeling it again, that tickle, that electric twinge, telling him that hunting time would soon be upon him.

"She's too old for that doll," the girl said.

"That's okay. There'll be another one who will like it." He hurried out of the doll aisle. As he reached the corner, a woman who had to be the girl's mother almost ran into him. She had the same wavy hair, the same slender shoulders.

He stopped himself from saying anything to her, or bidding the girl good-bye.

At the register, he paid with cash. He would have used a card—nothing wrong with buying a doll, it happened every day—but sometimes store employees liked to pretend they were friendly and interested in their customers. "Have a good day, Mr. Welker," the clerk might say. Or, "Thank you, Charles. Do you go by Charles, or Chuck?"

He hadn't done anything. But just in case, he didn't want the mother to hear that.

The clerk was chatty, like someone had pulled a string in his back. Welker responded with monosyllables and grunts, and eventually the clerk got the idea, closing his big yawp. His acne-riddled face burned red as a stop sign. He handed Welker his change and a crinkling plastic bag containing the doll, and as Welker turned toward the exit, he shot one more glance back toward the doll aisle, hoping for a final glimpse.

3

Eight years earlier, when Richie was twenty-four, a beautiful woman named Wendy Riggs had surprised and delighted him by agreeing to be his wife. Since then, not a day had passed that he didn't give thanks for his good fortune. In that regard, if not in others. Sometimes, though, most often in the dead of night, the hours when painful truths confronted people, he wondered if winning Wendy had used up all his luck, leaving him none to protect his career.

Richie's grandfather had moved from Wheeling, West Virginia to Detroit in 1948, to work for Ford at the Rouge Complex. Richie's father had worked there too, building America, he said, until the day he got in a fight with a foreman. He broke the foreman's nose and came home from work early. He never went back. Eventually he found work at a machine shop, but he was never the same man again. The new job didn't pay as well, and since he refused to let his wife work, the family had to sell their home. They moved from one rental house to another, picking up and leaving whenever the rent was hiked or a landlord complained about the lawn or refused to fix a leaky sink. Booze and gambling ate away at the old man's spirit, turning him bitter and mean.

By contrast, Uncle Keith, Richie's mom's brother, was a Detroit cop, and he seemed to love his work. He was always smiling, quick to laugh. Every time he saw Richie he slipped a five-dollar bill into one of the boy's pockets. He had been killed in the line of duty, back in 1997, and his funeral, unlike Richie's father's, had been a grand affair. Richie grew up idolizing the man, even though in his heart of hearts he feared he was more like his father than his uncle.

Richie wasn't as naturally gregarious as Uncle Keith, but he was smart. He graduated with a degree in criminal justice from the University of Michigan—Dearborn, and set his sights on a career as a detective with the Detroit PD. After making it through an academy, he became a Student Police Officer and then a full-fledged Detroit Police Officer. The night of that promotion, he had Uncle Keith's badge tattooed on his left thigh, bottom up, so he could read the badge number when he looked down.

That was when things started to go wrong. He was one of the few white patrol cops on the mostly black force, and he had difficulty bridging that cultural chasm. He chafed against what seemed to be arbitrary rules and regulations. Richie had learned almost everything there was to know about criminal history and behavior. He had looked upon the job as an intellectual exercise, good guys using their brains to beat the bad guys, and at the patrol level that wasn't even close to reality.

The six years he spent in uniform were the longest of his life. Stress wore away at him, affecting his health and his emotional state. Finally, he mouthed off at a lieutenant who was bullying a rookie— falling short of his old man's attack on the foreman, but not by a lot. The result, though, was the same.

When he was let go, it came as a relief in every way except financial. In the midst of the worst depression in Detroit's history— the city had fared far worse than the country as a whole—and forced to rely on Wendy's salary from the city, they had been at risk of losing their home. After anguished debate, they stopped making their $1,800- a-month payments, to which they had agreed when both were employed, and put that money in the bank. About the time they were finally foreclosed, they bought a bigger, nicer house for nine thousand in cash, in a neighborhood ravaged by vacancies.

He was sitting at the kitchen table when Wendy came in, freshly made up and ready to leave for work. Her brown hair was so dark it looked almost black; it cupped her head, curling forward slightly at her firm jawline. The color set off pale blue eyes and skin she defended ferociously with sunscreen. Her lips were full and pink, her cheeks narrow without being gaunt, her body slender and toned. She was wearing a conservative charcoal suit but with a lilac blouse to add some color, and black leather zip-up boots with two-inch heels.

"You sure you have to go?"

She graced him with a smile. "You like to eat, don't you?"

"Is that a double entendre?"

"Not this time. I couldn't even stick around for a quickie. I have an early meeting."

Richie stood and wrapped his arms around her. Her return hug was strong, and he breathed in her fresh scent. "Mmm."

"I love you, babe. See you tonight."

Then she was gone and he was alone, her slightly musky aroma clinging to him.

Richie worked a midnight-to-eight shift for Rampart. Wendy's hours at the city's Planning and Development office were nine-to-five. As if it weren't hard enough to conceive a child—it had been for them, at any rate—their schedules left them precious little time to try.

He wasn't used to sleeping during the day, but he made a point of being in bed by ten so he could get up when Wendy came home. On this day, he managed a restless three hours, then gave up and rolled out of bed. He made a cup of coffee and sat on the living room couch drinking it, clad only in a white T-shirt and khaki shorts. The very picture of suburban manliness. If Wendy came home and saw him, it could set their baby-making back years.

But he couldn't stop thinking about the Angela Morton case, and the possibility that her abductor—and presumed murderer—lived in the neighborhood. They had picked this house not because of the quality of the schools or the neighbors, but because they could afford to buy it with the cash they had amassed. It was a far better house than they'd have been able to afford on their salaries—even on his police department salary—a couple of years earlier, and although there was some guilt associated with intentionally sticking the bank with their old house, they were able to rationalize that. The bank hadn't been willing to even consider a refinancing proposal. And the house they bought had already been foreclosed, so they weren't ripping off some homeowner in a jam, but buying a house from yet another bank with too many bad debts on its books.

The cardinal rule of real estate was supposed to be location, location, location, but they had settled for price, price, price. There were only five occupied homes on their block, one more than that on the next. The block the Morton house anchored only had a couple. Another three blocks away was Madison Elementary, boarded up and fenced off.

The neighborhood would either come back or it wouldn't. If it didn't, he and Wendy weren't out much. If it did, they'd made the right play.

Richie wondered if he would have been more or less inclined to move there, had he realized that corner house was the Angela Morton house. He couldn't decide.

He did settle on a different decision, however. He finished his coffee, carried the mug into the kitchen, rinsed it and set it in the dishwasher. For nine large, this place had not come with appliances, but they'd brought their own from the old house. He went into the master bathroom to shower and shave, then got dressed.

The April sun was high on that fine Detroit afternoon, the kind of day that made him forget that a month ago he had been shivering, shoveling snow off the walk or getting to work with feet that would stay wet until he got home and took off his shoes and socks. There were once again leaves and blossoms on the trees, birds perching on limbs singing their birdie songs. A teenager rode past on a low-slung bike, flashing a smile full of gold. The scents of car exhaust and diesel were slightly undercut by the earthy aroma of overgrown yards. Parts of Detroit were returning to the land of their own volition, and while this one wasn't on the leading edge of that trend, it wasn't too far behind.

Richie walked the couple of blocks to the Morton house. He couldn't see much that he hadn't noticed the night before. The place occupied a big corner lot with plenty of yard around it. The elm tree looked like it had caught some kind of blight; while the rest of the street was in the process of being swallowed whole by nature, this tree was losing its leaves, and Richie wondered if it would stand on its own for another year. The house was good-sized, three stories, with dormer windows jutting out from a steep, shingled roof. Its red brick walls had faded unevenly, leaving pinks and whites, angry crimsons and deep carmines and giving the house an overall surface coloration that resembled a bad rash. An open porch fronted the street, three stone stairs leading up to it. The door had been painted red once, a long time ago. To the left of the door were three living room windows with boards over them, and three more directly above those, probably in a master bedroom.

Richie walked around the house, through the broken gate. The boarded-up windows back door appeared intact, so perhaps Wil Fowler had kept his word.

The place had stood here for what might have been years—he would have to try to find out if anybody had rented it after Angela's abduction—without being burned down or occupied by squatters. Richie thought about doing exactly what he had told Wil not to, breaking in to see how it looked on the inside. Kevin Roche was right—if Angela Morton's killer was still in the area, he wanted to know it before he and Wendy had kids.

It was broad daylight, though, and the few neighbors had likely noticed him wandering around the place. He was not a cop, had no legal authority. Academic interest would prove a flimsy defense in court. And his abbreviated career on the cops would make him a target in prison.

He chose maturity over curiosity, and walked home. There, at least, he could get online and refresh his memory about the facts of Angela's disappearance.

O O O

Richie checked out some of the true crime websites he frequented, then the archives of the *Free Press*, *The Detroit News*, and a couple of the TV stations. As he had remembered, the case had been big news for a while, slipping into the back pages after weeks went by with no progress.

Each source offered the same basic tale. On a hot July twenty-third, the day after Angela's eleventh birthday, she and her father, Jarod Morton, were at home in their big corner house. She heard the chimes of an ice cream truck rolling up the street, and told him she wanted a Popsicle. He sent her outside to stop the truck while he retrieved his wallet from his bedroom.

By the time he emerged, the truck had moved down the street, and Angela was gone. He caught up with the truck, but she wasn't among the kids gathered around it. He asked the neighbor children. No one had seen her. He was dumfounded—he had only been a couple of minutes behind her. There were other people out on the street. But Angela was missing.

He drove around the neighborhood, screaming her name until he was hoarse, questioning neighbors. No Angela. He went home and telephoned Angela's friends in the area. No one had heard from her.

Jarod's wife, Barbara, came home and did what Jarod should have done immediately: phoned 911. DPD issued a Be On The Lookout. Amber Alerts weren't common in those days, so that wasn't done, but Detroit was a border city, and guards at the Port Huron crossing were notified.

Thirty-six hours after her disappearance, the FBI was called in. They descended upon the Morton house and launched their own investigation.

All of it was for naught. Angela Morton was never seen again. There were few leads, most easily dismissed as cranks, none that went anywhere. Hateful letters were sent to the family. Detroit residents placed flowers and stuffed animals and candles and other memorials outside the house, and as always, the small-hearted and the cruel left other, less pleasant messages.

Richie looked at photographs of the now-familiar house, pictures of Angela Morton, skinny and long-legged, with limp blond hair hanging almost to her waist. She had been a pretty girl who was dressed, presumably by her parents, in drab, ill-fitting clothes that looked like they had come from thrift stores. There was something about her deep green eyes that captivated Richie, a haunted expression, as if by the age of eleven, she had seen more than most people did in a lifetime.

In the few pictures of him that Richie could find, Jarod Morton was a strange-looking man: long-haired, with a nose that almost lunged out of the frame and eyes that slanted away from the nose as if they were afraid. He had meager, pursed lips, and cheeks as baggy as a chipmunk's pouches at the end of winter. He looked impossibly weary. Richie wasn't at all surprised by that, given the circumstances.

Finally, Richie had his fill of it. He found himself fascinated by the case but overwhelmed by a profound sadness. The news accounts were dry, avoiding detailed speculation as to Angela's fate. To Richie, there was no doubt that she had been snatched, probably by someone with a car or van, molested, and killed.

He shut down the computer and went back to bed. It took a while to drift off. When he did, his dreams were chaotic, fraught with anxiety. Images of a young blond girl and a big old house and an ice cream truck with a skeletal driver filled his head. When the driver threw open the window to take orders, a darkness inside the truck threatened to seep out into the world, and though Richie tried to shout a warning, his voice would not come.

4

Evening, detective," the uniformed cop said. "Looking sharp."

"Frank Robey always looks sharp," another uni said. He held a tray of paper coffee cups. "He's a regular fashion plate."

Frank tugged on one of his French cuffs. "Fashion's for people with too much time on their hands," he said. "What I got is style, and that's timeless."

"You're all class, Robey."

"I got class I ain't even used yet." It was a Louis Jordan line, and Frank was a Motown guy. But his musical knowledge was extensive, and a good line was a good line no matter who you stole it from. "Now, where is she?"

"DB's in there. Second floor." The uniformed cop jerked a thumb over his shoulder, indicating the apartment building behind him. The buildings in the brick complex had four units each, two upstairs and two down. The ground floor apartments sported fenced patios, the uppers balconies. Half the windows were dark, but people moved behind them just the same, parting curtains and fingering open blinds.

Frank read the uni's name tag: Keener. "Isn't the victim a woman, Officer Keener?"

"Uh, I think so. That's what I heard."

"Then the appropriate phrasing would be 'she's in there,' wouldn't it? Or perhaps, 'the victim is in there?'"

"Sorry, sir. She's in there."

"That's better. She's a woman who has been murdered, not an object."

"Yes, sir."

Frank walked past Officer Keener and heaved his bulk up the stairs. He was getting too old for this, and he had let his weight get out of hand. Fifty-two. The goal he had set for himself was retirement at fifty-five. He hoped he was in shape to enjoy it. It would suck to have a heart attack kill him and throw off all his plans.

At the door, he could smell her. Blood and death. Each had its own particular odor, blood metallic and death almost sweet. In his experience they were so often intermingled that they seemed like separate but related aspects of the same thing, like the blended aromas of a peanut butter and jelly sandwich.

Walking into the apartment was like passing through a membrane into a different world, an alien one full of horror and violence. Her front window had been smashed with a potted plant, which was sprawled on the floor amid spilled dirt. Frank walked past it, taking a mental picture of the scene for later reference, to accompany the actual photos the crime scene techs would put in the file. The victim was in her own bathroom.

So much blood coated the walls, floor, and ceiling, it seemed impossible that any remained in her body. Someone might have pried open the lid of a five-gallon can of red paint and shaken it. Blood soaked the pages of a hanging calendar, coated the mirror, puddled in the tub, and filmed the outside of the toilet.

Frank was, he admitted to himself, looking at the blood to avoid confronting the body. He closed his eyes for several seconds, took a couple of breaths through his mouth, and opened them again.

She was naked. Posed. On her back, legs spread wide, hands placed right atop left on her abdomen, heavy breasts sagging against her arms. Her head was cocked to the right, eyes and mouth open. Her skin was light, the kind that Frank had sometimes heard called "high yellow" in the early years of his life, and more recently "yellowbone." When it came to racial attitudes, much progress had been made, but the way ahead was still so long and perilous, he didn't know how more forward motion would ever happen. Not his problem, though, not right at this moment. The woman's brutalized body was his immediate concern.

She had a bloody slash across her forehead, dipping down through her brow to the corner of her left eye. Two more split her cheeks, radiating out from the corners of her mouth, exposing teeth and jaws. The wound that Frank guessed had killed her was in her abdomen, an eight-inch gash partially covered by her hands. Intestines glistened in the opening. Her genital area had been stabbed multiple times. Frank didn't try to count. The details would be in the coroner's report, if he could stand to read it.

"Pretty sick, huh?"

"Yeah," Frank said. "Sick as shit." He turned away from the body, faced his sometime partner, Calvin Matthews. Calvin's skin was darker than Frank's, almost the color of a French roast coffee bean. He was a slender man, a detective who bought his suits off the rack, ideally on sale, and it showed. Frank favored expensive fitted suits and high-end shoes, feeling that he functioned better when he looked good.

He and Calvin didn't get along, and the animosity went deeper than different haberdashers. Calvin seemed to resent Frank's age, his experience, his seniority—none of which were within Frank's control, or things he would change if he could. He had decided he didn't much like Calvin on the first night they were partnered, when Frank had caught a call about someone standing on the shoulder of I-94, shooting at the giant Uniroyal tire. Frank had been chuckling as he hung up the phone, and described the situation—better handled by unis than detectives, although they would go check it out—to Calvin. "What do we know about the suspect?" Calvin had asked.

"Not much. He's a got a hard-on for tires, and he's a brother with a nine-mil."

Calvin had pursed his lips like an aquarium fish. "He's African American, you mean?"

"*You* may be African American," Frank said. "He's a brother."

Since then, they had grated on one another, though Frank respected Calvin as a good detective. Still, by mutual agreement, the partners rarely worked together. Lieutenant Jackson knew about the tension, knew they drove separately and ran their investigations the same way. He tolerated it because their individual arrest stats were almost twice as good as when the two had worked as a team.

"Her name's Rosemary Robinson," Calvin said. "Lived here alone. It's a one-bedroom. Neighbors say she worked at Rags and Riches, a women's clothing store in Foxtown. Sales clerk. She's twenty-two. Mother lives in Southfield, father deceased."

"Anybody hear anything?"

"We're still canvassing the complex, but nothing so far. People say she was quiet, kind of stuck up, maybe. Didn't socialize with the other folks here."

"Any of 'em look good for this?"

"They didn't like her much, doesn't mean they would do this to her. I think we're looking for some sort of sexually motivated psycho."

"Way it looks," Frank said. "I hate to think we've got some kind of sexual predator on the loose, but ..."

"I know what you mean." Calvin cast a hand toward the grotesque mess that had been, so recently, a young, vibrant woman. "This ain't good for anybody. The D least of all."

It seemed an odd comment, but Frank knew what he meant. Detroit had been through too much. In many ways, the first decade of the new century had seen the death of two major American cities. New Orleans was working hard at coming back. Detroit, so far, was still suffering its death throes, dying in slow motion.

If Calvin was right—if this turned out to be the work of a serial or spree killer—the publicity could only hurt the city.

"Let me know what the canvass turns up," Frank said. "We'll need to know if she had any enemies. She got a boyfriend?"

"Don't know yet. That's the first thing I thought, but then, that front window."

Frank had already arrived at the same place. "How you see it going down?"

"Guy spots her through the window. Grabs the plant off the walkway outside, pitches it through the glass. She locks herself in the bathroom, quick, not even taking time to grab her phone. He breaks the door down and goes to work."

"So he brought his own knife?"

"Must have. Wouldn't take time to look for one in the kitchen."

Frank had reached a similar conclusion. His first impulse was that she was close to her killer. But if she were, why wouldn't she have let him in? Wouldn't a lover have known he could open the bathroom door by simply pushing a screwdriver into the hole in the knob? Why risk all the noise of smashing a window and shattering a doorjamb?

Maybe the first impulse was still right, though. Frank was happy to listen to theories, but he was not in the habit of announcing his own conclusions until they were ironclad. This one was a long way from that. "I'll check at her work tomorrow, find out who her friends are and what they know. This complex have security cameras?"

"Only in the office."

"Perfect."

He heard vehicles outside and went to the window. A crime scene van had pulled up to the curb. "Techs are here," he announced. "Guess I'll go notify her mother." He jotted the address down from Rosemary Robinson's address book. "Keep me posted."

O   O   O

"No, you're wrong, you're wrong!" Eulalia Robinson sagged against Frank Robey, nearly knocking him down despite his not insignificant size. He wrapped his arms around her, as her back and shoulders heaved with sobs. She balled her hands into fists and flailed against him, crying "No, no, no!" over and over.

Frank didn't blame her, not a bit. She had already lost a husband and two sons, to bullets and heroin. Now her last child was gone, snatched away in a fit of brutality. Making these notifications was the hardest part of the job, by far. The night's bloody crime scene might well return in nightmares, but he would remember this woman's pain during his waking hours, and that was far worse.

As he held her and suffered the pounding of her fists, he reminded himself that as awful it was for him, that didn't come close to how it was for her.

O   O   O

When he left Mrs. Robinson's home, his suit jacket soaked with her tears, Frank felt a familiar darkness clouding the edges of his vision. It came and went on its own schedule, though nights like this were apt to set it off. Trouble was, most days in a police detective's life were similar. He spent his working hours toiling in the cesspool of humanity's worst acts, murders and rapes and arson fires, thefts of property and dignity and life that demonstrated over and over in how little regard some people held others. The darkness had an almost physical presence: a dull throb at the temples combined with a narrowing of his field of view and a nearly claustrophobic tension, as if he were walking down a tunnel that closed in on him with every step.

He got into his unmarked Dodge Charger and drove toward a place that never failed to feed his inner darkness. Probably he should have looked for something that would cheer him up, would lighten the grim load that burdened him at such times, but instead he accepted it, took it on his shoulders and carried it around.

The neighborhood streets darkened his mood all the more. A tree grew through the roof of a house that was decaying back to the land. The burned-out husk of an automobile sat at a curb outside another house, as if someone might come out and try to start it. The sharp tang of smoldering lumber filled the air; that and a blackened pile were all that remained of a home that had been torched in the last day or two. During his lifetime, the country had decided to change from being a producing nation to a consuming one. Problem was, no one had consulted the people who produced, and Detroit had been a center of production. The coast-to-coast economic recession didn't help matters any. Frank cruised the streets slowly, working toward his goal, the one place that would always confirm that it wasn't just Detroiters or Americans who were awful to one another, but people in general. When this mood settled on him he invariably sought this place out, dark drawn to dark.

5

The place didn't really need another doll. Charles Welker knew that. He just liked to bring in new toys from time to time, fresh ones. They reminded him of what he had so briefly possessed, and they brightened the room. They brightened spirits, too. When one of them was afraid—and sometimes they were, sometimes they didn't seem to understand the signals their own bodies threw out there—then a new doll could help her relax.

His work day done, he had retired to the nest. He put the baby doll, still in its packaging, on the low shelf with the others. Better if she could open it herself, then she would know that it was new, purchased just for her. Beside the shelf was a white dresser with pink knobs, fresh new clothes in its drawers. New clothes in the closet, too. Other toys and a few books on more shelves. A big bed, of course, with pink and white bedding and a tall post at each corner.

This was his favorite room in the house. He had been redecorating it for weeks, trying to get it just right. He still plenty of time, almost seven months. Lots of time. It had to be perfect, though.

Because *she* would be.

There had been other would-be angels in the nest, these last few years. But they weren't the *real* angel. They hardly mattered. None had ever been as perfect as the real angel, that first angel.

Soon, though, he would have another real angel.

And he had been waiting a very, very long time for perfection.

6

"My sister called today," Wendy said. Richie had already made dinner, a habit he had picked up when he started working nights. Chicken Maximilian, popovers, and salad greens from one of Detroit's new neighborhood garden plots, planted where once houses had stood. It all waited in the kitchen.

When she came in, he was sitting in the living room, leafing through the latest issue of *Criminology*, a professional journal that he could ill afford but refused to give up. Trying to make his way through an article about new research tied to the Hare Psychopathy Checklist, a topic that he ordinarily would have found compelling, his mind had kept drifting back to Angela Morton's disappearance. He tried on theories like some people did shoes, but they all had major flaws and he discarded each in turn.

"Laurie called?" he asked, too distracted at first to parse her words. "Why?"

"Because she's my sister?" Wendy put her purse down on a table by the door and started flipping through the mail. Bills and more bills; Richie had already decided that other than the magazine, none were envelopes he wanted to open. "That's what siblings do."

"I guess." Richie hadn't had a sibling since he was twelve; he wasn't sure how it worked as adults.

"She wanted to know if we're coming to visit our nephews this summer."

"Is she paying?"

"Not that I'm aware of."

"Then I'd have to say probably not." The problem with having a sister who had married a well-off orthodontist and moved to Florida was that she lost all connection with how the rest of the world lived. "She's always wanting us to go on a cruise or something."

"Because she loves us and never sees us."

"Because she can't comprehend the fact that we can't afford it."

"That too."

Richie forced himself to put his thoughts of Angela Morton into a mental box and close the lid. For the moment, anyway. He kissed Wendy, and as happened often these days, with fertility much on their minds, that kiss led to more.

Later, they ate dinner together, and then Wendy worked in her home office while Richie showered and prepared himself for another night protecting what remained of the city's wealthy. He kissed her again before he left, but she was so involved in her project that she didn't seem to notice that he was taking off an hour earlier than usual.

He knew he shouldn't go inside. Breaking and entering was against the law, whether a home was vacant or occupied. He was slightly less likely to be charged for breaking into an empty, but that would be up to the discretion of the Wayne County Prosecutor's Office.

He wasn't even sure why he wanted to go in, what story he expected the long-vacant house to tell him. But he was fired up with curiosity, and it had been a long time since anything had caught his interest in this way. Since he didn't expect to find much intellectual stimulation on his Rampart shift, he would take it where he could. Parking outside the Morton house, he grabbed his flashlight and went around the back.

Wil Fowler wouldn't have needed his crowbar. The back door was boarded over with a sheet of plywood, but the wood of the jamb was so soft that Richie was able to tug it free. He set it to one side. The door was rotten and warped. He pulled it open and shined his flashlight into a kitchen.

The place stank of mold and rot. Black patches scaled the kitchen walls and congregated on the ceiling. Tiles from the yellow and black linoleum floor had peeled up and separated. A refrigerator stood open, mold furring its interior. Richie was surprised that a wooden kitchen table still stood in the center of the floor, with a single metal chair next to it. The Mortons—or whoever had occupied the house after them, if anyone—must have left in a hurry.

Cobwebs were thick enough in the interior doorway to reflect his flashlight beam back at him. With some trepidation, he picked up the steel chair and used it to tear through the webbing. On the other side was a living room. Leafy green plants grew up through the cushions of a couch. The smell was cloying, making Richie regret his decision to break in. He started toward the middle of the room, then noticed that the floor sagged in the center and had broken through in one spot. His flashlight showed snatches of a basement below. With great care, he backed up to the room's edge and stayed close to the wall as he went through an arched doorway into a high-ceilinged foyer.

A staircase climbed to the next floor. The longer Richie stayed, the less he expected to learn, but he wanted a look at Angela's room. The fact that furniture had been left behind seemed to increase his odds of finding something, although those odds might have been evened out by the age and general condition of everything in the house.

He put a foot on the lowest stair, testing it. During high school, he and three friends, Phillie Garcia and Bart Santiestevan and Bob Waddell, had broken into a house that was reputed to be "haunted." In fact, it was only partially abandoned and poorly maintained. They had gone in through an unlocked back door and found oceans of garbage, walls thick with crud, spider webs as thick as tissue paper. In some rooms the floors were buried under knee-high piles of newspapers. The power was out, but the refrigerator still had food in it, spoiled and stinking. They had climbed the stairs and found what must have been the owner's bedroom, where a nest of rats squirmed on the mattress of an antique brass bed. A stack of *Playboy*s had been scattered, exposed breasts and behinds shown off on glossy paper covered in rat droppings.

On the way back down, Phillie had stepped too hard on a stair and crashed through the wood. His leg shoved in past the knee, and shards tore his jeans, scraping and splintering him. The others worked him free and they hurried from the house, only to find police officers outside aiming flashlights and guns at them. Richie and his friends were taken to the precinct, where a cop explained that the house's owner was a mentally ill man who went off his meds from time to time, and was briefly institutionalized until he regained an even keel. Once, he had caught people breaking in and threatened them with a shotgun. Police had confiscated the weapon, but because of his mental illness he was never jailed. If he had been ruled capable of standing trial, he could have argued that he was only defending his own home. The kids were lucky, the officer told them, that the man was currently back in a halfway house. Parents were called in, but Richie talked fast and convincingly, dropping Uncle Keith's name, and the boys weren't charged with trespassing.

Richie attributed to that incident the beginnings of his interest in the psychology of the criminal mind. That, combined with his uncle's example, cemented his desire to enter the law enforcement profess-sion. The night had been at once frightening and exhilarating, the details remaining vivid in his imagination half a lifetime later.

Especially the sight of Phillie's bloodied leg, after the wooden stair had chewed it up. Richie climbed carefully, with a hand on the banister despite his concern about the filth caking it, to help distribute his weight. And to break his fall, should he punch through the floor.

The landing at the top was carpeted, but the carpet was squishy underfoot. Richie trained his flashlight beam on the ceiling and saw multiple discolored spots where rain had leaked through. The entire upstairs was probably rotting out from under him. He remembered those rats on the bed in the other house and his skin crawled. This had been a mistake, coming in here.

Finish up quick and get out.

He pushed through a door that hung partially open. This room still had furniture in it, too, all of it covered in a thick scrim of webbing. A desk in the corner, an old metal filing cabinet with the drawers opened and emptied, a spill of rust down one side. Richie picked a scrap of paper off the floor and, using it to shield his fingers, pulled open the desk's center drawer. It contained a couple of pencils and about a cup's worth of small, hard mouse turds. How many diseases was he risking by just breathing the air in this place? If this house killed him, he decided, he would come back and haunt it.

He was moving away from the desk when his light scraped across the surface and snagged his attention. With the paper scrap, he wiped away the layers of webbing and dust. Someone had used the desktop as a kind of permanent scratchpad, scrawling lists, dollar amounts, calculations, doodles, and more, until it looked like generations' worth of graffiti on a public wall, one layer of writing covering the one below until most of it was illegible. There was one exception, written on the surface in ballpoint pen, pressing so hard, going over it so many times it was carved into the wood. "141," it said. Just three digits, encircled in similar etched fashion and left clear of further writing. Whatever they meant, they must have been important to somebody—presumably Jarod Morton or his wife, unless someone else had taken the house after them.

Richie dusted the rest of the surface and found the same number written in other places. Sometimes the numbers were surrounded by heavily marked circles.

"One forty-one," Richie mused aloud. "What the hell is that about?"

After one final sweep of the room, he moved back onto the landing. The next room was a master bedroom. He didn't stay long. The bed was still there, king-size, and he didn't want to see what might be hunkered down on that mattress. After that he found a bathroom. A shower curtain had collapsed, rod and all, and the shape of it lying there in the tub made him think for a moment that it had a body under it.

The last room upstairs had to be Angela's. The walls had been painted a pale pink and stenciled with characters from the *Rugrats* cartoon. The little blond girl on that show had been an Angela too, Richie remembered. Angela Morton was probably too old to have been named after her, but he wondered if the cartoon Angela had been a favorite of hers.

Her bed and dresser remained in the room. Both had fallen apart, and chunks of the ceiling had caved in as well. A cool draft blew through from there, raising goose bumps on his neck. Richie checked the window, which had boards nailed up outside, the glass surprisingly intact.

He put one hand down on the dust-caked windowsill and peered out between the boards. Her room faced onto the street. Houses across the way would have been occupied then, probably by other families with kids. That's the kind of neighborhood it was in those days. The infamous white flight had been well under way, but thirteen years ago, there were still some white families in Detroit, and this would have been an area where they might have been comfortable.

Richie felt odd depressions in the wood of the sill. He ran his light across them, careful not to shine it out the gaps between the boards. There were three small holes in a triangular formation, filled in with wood putty or spackle and painted over at some point, and another set on the window frame itself.

On the way out of the room, he noticed a similar arrangement of filled holes in the outer doorjamb, at his eye level. A second set faded into the surface of the door. Like the 141 scratched into the desk, he filed them away in his mind, puzzles to which he would find no answers tonight. For one thing, he needed to get to work. For another, there had been nobody here for years who could explain.

Descending the staircase, the lesson of Phillie Garcia came back to him and he didn't rush. Nearing the bottom, he thought he heard another sound over the creak of his own weight on the old floorboards. A rat, probably, if it hadn't imagined the noise. He had to get away from this place, find a gas station restroom and wash his hands. He couldn't go home without having to explain to Wendy where he'd been, and suddenly the whole thing struck him as foolish.

Fascinating, yes, but foolish just the same.

As he cleared the last stair he heard it again. A soft creak. Was someone else in the house? Adrenaline started pumping. Richie was alert, listening for the faintest noise. Fight or flight reflexes kicking in, he killed his flashlight and gripped it at the base of the handle, ready to use as a club if need be.

He was almost to the kitchen when a big black man swung through the doorway holding a light and a gun.

7

Freeze!" Frank Robey shouted. "Police!"

The intruder netted in his flashlight's beam froze, as commanded. Frank summed him up quickly, the way cops did.

White, lean but fit, light brown hair a little on the shaggy side, striking blue eyes wide with fright. He carried a flashlight of his own, which he held at shoulder height, ready to swing.

"Put that down," Frank ordered.

"I can explain," the man said.

"Save it." Frank ran his own flashlight down and saw that the intruder was wearing uniform pants with a gold stripe down the leg. He had on a light windbreaker, but it was open in front and there was what looked like a badge pinned to the chest. "What are you, uniformed security?"

The man put his flashlight on the floor, lens down, and held his hands out. "Yes, I'm with Rampart. I used to be on the job, patrol out of the Northeastern."

Frank holstered his duty weapon. "What's your name?"

"Richard Krebbs. Richie, I go by Richie."

"Krebs? Like Maynard?"

"Who?"

"Never mind, you're too young. What are you doing in here?"

"That's … uh, hard to explain. Just looking around is the short answer. Satisfying my curiosity. I know it's trespassing, but it's a vacant house, looks like it's been that way for a long time."

"It has," Frank said. "You know its history?"

"Yes. I just moved into the neighborhood recently. I'm, I guess you could say, a bit of a crime buff. When I realized what house it was I had to check it out."

"I saw your flashlight from outside," Frank said. "Looked like you were taking a good long look."

"Like I said, crime buff. My uncle was on the job too, maybe you knew him. Keith Ritts?"

Wow, that name took him back. Keith Ritts was already legendary in the DPD when Frank joined, after a brief career in the FBI. Ritts spent a lifetime in uniform, known and loved by civilians as well as fellow cops. He'd been a hero on numerous occasions—the time he had gone through the ice off Belle Isle to save an infant had made national news, but there had been other instances over the years, as well. His picture still hung on a wall at 1300 Beaulieu. "Ritts was your uncle?"

"Reason I became a cop," Richie Krebbs said.

"You and a lot of people." Frank relaxed. Keith Ritts had done Frank a solid early in his career at the DPD. He introduced Frank to a CI who had helped him crack his first big case. Nothing in it for Ritts; they couldn't even reveal where the tip had come from, in order to keep the informant safe on the streets, he had just done it to put a bad guy behind bars. Maybe this guy was Keith Ritts' nephew and maybe not, but if he knew enough to mention the name then he probably had been a cop himself, as he said. And Rampart Security did a pretty thorough pre-employment screening. Not that security companies didn't sometimes employ flakes and losers, but still. "You shouldn't be in here."

"I know. I was just on my way out."

Frank took a closer look at Richie's face. His blue eyes had an inner luminosity; they seemed to burn with their own glow even when the flashlight wasn't shining directly on them. But they were sad eyes, too, eyes that looked as if they were so accustomed to disappointment they expected it at any moment. "Yeah, maybe I remember seeing you around, time to time. I'm Frank Robey."

Richie stuck a hand out and Frank took it by reflex. "I remember you. Always had a good rep. Pleased to meet you, Frank."

"Likewise, I guess."

"You keep an eye on this place? I wondered if somebody did. Hasn't been vandalized."

"Sometimes," Frank admitted. "I worked the Morton case when I was with the Bureau. I guess it got under my skin."

"Seriously?"

"Yeah."

Burnout was a concern common to every law enforcement professional except the most callous or corrupt, and Frank was no stranger to its symptoms—irritability, sleeplessness, and loss of appetite among them. He had never reached what he considered a dangerous threshold, but he had tiptoed toward it a time or two or twenty. Since his earliest days at the Bureau, he had taken the requisite classes that warned of the dangers—of the fact that as a law enforcement officer, he had to keep his emotions in check on the job. At just the moment when a natural human reaction would be terror or sorrow or rage, he had to be at his calmest, his most controlled. He could spend days or weeks doing work that carried very little emotional freight, say, running an audit of the financial records of a suspected white collar criminal, and then in an instant be called out to a scene like an armed bank robbery in progress, where the chances of shooting or being shot were astronomical. He tried to practice all the recommended safeguards—keeping in touch with friends who weren't cops, having outside hobbies and interests, trying to hold the big picture in his mind, to remember that although cops saw people at their worst, most of the time humanity was better than that.

Still, there were bad times, when all the precautions seemed useless. Times when the emotional turmoil threatened to swamp him, as if he were a small boat on a stormy sea. One of the worst had come early in his career. He had been a young field agent in Detroit when a man, one of life's perennial losers, had finally reached the end of his line. The man had botched a bank hold-up, shot a guard, and then taken his ex-wife and three young daughters hostage in their apartment. Frank had been far from the most senior agent at the scene, but he had been there, had been in the HRT trailer and overheard one of the little girls screaming as her father shot her mother and then started in on her sisters.

The sound of those screams had never left him, nor had the sight of three small bodies, limp and bloody on the floor, after the final shot had sounded and agents stormed in.

That family had been black. When Angela Morton disappeared, there was no apparent connection between the cases. But then Frank saw a short video the Mortons had taken in their backyard, and the instant he heard Angela's voice, it summoned back that doomed little girl's scream. Angela had her hooks deep into his flesh from that moment on, and she never let go.

So "under his skin" was an understatement. He had never been able to let it go. The Bureau had pulled him off it and he had quit the Bureau, joined the DPD so he couldn't be transferred away from Detroit. The Bureau wanted him to move to Denver, but Tiana, his wife, had been sick by then, and he refused to move her away from family and friends. Even then, he had known that was only part of it. Angela Morton was the rest. Every now and then he got his case files out and pored through them, looking for whatever it was he had missed. What everybody had missed. There had to be something. He thought he was drawn back here in search of his darkest core, but there was more to it than that—the place reminded him of why he was a cop.

"I'd love to talk to you about it sometime."

"Yeah, I know, you're a crime buff."

"You think we could? Patrol never really agreed with me, but I've made a study of crime and criminals, criminal psychology, that kind of thing. I'd be glad to buy you a meal and have a conversation."

"I guess." He would lose his enthusiasm once Frank cut him loose. Or so Frank hoped. He took a business card from his jacket pocket, handed it over. "That's me," he said. "Got all my numbers on it."

"I don't have a card," Richie said. "Not like I really need one in this job. But I can write my info down for you."

"That's okay," Frank said. "Just call me and I'll get it from you later. Is that Krebs with one b or two?"

"Two."

"Oh, okay. I think Maynard only had one."

"Who is this guy Maynard?" Richie asked again.

"Maynard G. Krebs. Bob Denver played him. Greatest beatnik in TV history." He chuckled. "The G stands for Walter."

"I think I've heard of him. Some old sitcom—"

"*The Many Loves of Dobie Gillis*. Great show, so far ahead of its time the world still hasn't caught up to it. Like *Green Acres*."

"I guess you're an aficionado."

"You know it."

"*Arrested Development?*"

"Best of the modern era." Now Frank felt better about this guy, and about his decision not to book him on a trespassing charge that would be hard to explain and that no prosecutor would take anywhere near a courthouse. "Let's get out of here," he said. "Did you bring a hammer to put that board up again?"

"There's one in the car." Richie said.

"Get it. And stay out of houses that aren't yours."

"You got it, Frank."

O O O

On the way to work, although it made him ten minutes late again, Richie stopped at a 24-hour store and bought a padlock hasp. Despite his promise to Frank Robey, he had to check one thing. Frank had let him nail the board over the door again, but he had nailed it into the same soft wood.

During his lunch break, which came at an hour when his body had not yet been convinced it should be hungry, he drove back to the Morton house. He made two circuits around the block, to make sure Frank wasn't watching. No sign of him. If he was keeping a close eye, either he was inside another house, or he had some sort of silent alarm set up.

Setting the plywood aside, Richie went back in. He used his light sparingly, just enough to pick his way through the living room and up the stairs. At the doorway to Angela's room, he tucked it under his left arm, pointing toward the jamb, while he fitted the hasp he had bought over the three depressions he had found. The holes in the hasp, where someone would screw it into a doorframe, were a perfect fit. He shut the light off and went back to the windowsill.

This was the tricky part, because if the flashlight's glow could be seen from outside, it would be here. But he had to know. He put the hasp down over the depressions in the sill and it matched those too.

Angela had been locked into her room.

He turned off the light, made his way back down the stairs. On the way, he wondered if Frank knew about the locks. In the living room, he stopped, fished his phone and Frank's card from his pocket, and dialed Frank's mobile number.

"Robey."

"Hey, Frank, it's Richie Krebbs."

"Maynard, right," Frank said. "That didn't take long."

"I wanted to run something past you. Did you know that there were padlock hasps on the outside of Angela's door, and on the window?"

Frank didn't reply for several long moments. Richie was wondering if he had hung up or dropped the call, but then he said, "No, I didn't know that."

"They're filled and painted over. You can see them with a flashlight if you hold it at an angle, and you can barely feel them. In broad daylight you'd probably never notice them. But they're there."

"Doesn't mean there's a connection to the case. Other people lived there before the Mortons."

"Doesn't mean there's not, though. If she was padlocked into her room, that might change the complexion of the case a little, right?"

Another long silence. "It could."

"That's what I thought."

"Are you back in that house, Krebbs?"

"Just for a minute, to confirm my hunch."

"Get out."

"I'm going."

"I mean it. Get out now or I will book your ass."

"I'm on my way," Richie said. "But Frank?"

"What?"

"Maybe we should meet, talk about this. You got breakfast plans?"

"No."

"How about Breakfast House and Grill? On Woodward. Say, eight-fifteen?"

"Sure, if you're buying."

"Of course." There went a day's pay. Detroit's Breakfast House & Grill was no low-budget dining spot, but it was the first place that had come to mind. He didn't want to take the cop to a Big Boy's, not if he was trying to weasel information out of him. Wendy would be pissed, but it would be worth it to pick Frank Robey's brain about the Morton case.

Once he had put away his phone, he realized that Frank was no longer in the neighborhood. Which gave him a little more time in the house. He had seen the upstairs and the ground floor, but he hadn't made it into the basement.

He found the door back in the kitchen, in a corner that had been so socked in with cobwebs he hadn't noticed it at first. Once he swept the webbing away, he jerked it open and flashed his light down the narrow staircase. More webs, a couple with spiders the approximate size of Chihuahua dogs clinging to them. Richie had left his hammer on the kitchen table; he retrieved it, then braved the staircase, swinging the tool ahead of him to clear the webs.

The basement was unfinished, mostly a place for storage, with a furnace and laundry area. Exposed studs and crosspieces were webbed in, and rodents had been here as well, leaving their tiny black calling cards. Random junk littered the floor, bits of broken furniture and other things the Mortons had presumably tossed down over the years, or else all at once when they were getting ready to leave.

Richie took a quick look around and was about to head back up when he saw an odd vertical shadow under the stairs. Shining the light on it, he could see a gap next to one of the studs, extending about four feet up from the floor. He ducked under the staircase and tugged on that stud. It swung toward him on hidden hinges.

Here there was an existing hasp, but it was on the inside of this presumably secret door. Whoever had done all the aftermarket lock installation here had wanted to be able to lock himself *inside* this room.

Through the door, the room opened up to the same eight-foot height as the rest of the basement. It was obvious at a glance what this place was—somebody's fuck pad. The walls were covered with plywood sheets. The room contained a king-size mattress resting on the ground, and that was all. No, not quite all—as Richie played his light about the place he saw D-rings bolted to the floor and walls around the mattress. Whoever the *somebody* was—and he couldn't help believing the house's last known residents, the Mortons, had been responsible—was a bondage fan. With those D-rings, a number of different scenarios would be possible.

A shattered mirror lay on the floor, close to the wall opposite the bed. Richie shined the light on the wall until he found where it had been tacked up, in front of a small, round hole in the plywood. The hole was about five feet from the floor. He could put his palm over the hole and cover most of it. He aimed the light through the hole and saw what looked like another room on the other side, much smaller, but definitely big enough for a person.

On a hunch, he picked up a big shard of the mirror glass and held it to his eye, mirrored side facing away. He could see through it. A two-way mirror, mounted over a hole in the wall in a room like this? That only meant one thing.

It took a few minutes before he found the second hidden door. When he got into the little room on the other side, he found two straight-backed chairs. The space in front of the hole was big enough for a person, or maybe a tripod. On the wall, below the hole, in what appeared to be the same hand as upstairs, was the number 141.

Here, though, it wasn't written in ink. It was written in what Richie hoped was paint. But it was old, brown, and flaking, and he was afraid it was blood.

8

Frank Robey was already at a booth, drinking coffee, when Richie got there. It was the first time he'd really had a look at the man, since back at the Morton house Robey had been shining a flashlight in Richie's face. Frank was a broad-shouldered black man, thick through the chest and middle, but his black pinstriped suit fit well and minimized his size. His jacket was open, and a tiepin bearing Superman's "S" insignia held down a silk tie. His hair, more pepper than salt, was neatly cut in a way that accentuated the square shape of his head. Most cops his age Richie had known would be counting the days to retirement. The more mathematically minded might have converted the days to minutes.

Frank wore gold rings on two fingers, but not on the ring finger of his left hand. A web of fine lines radiated from the outer corners of his eyes, as if he either liked to laugh or squinted a lot. He smiled when he saw Richie, then seemed to remember he was supposed to be angry and closed his mouth. While it was open, Richie noticed a slender gap between his top front teeth. "Maynard," he said.

"Thanks for meeting me, Frank," Richie said as he sat down. "Have you ordered?"

Frank held up his coffee. "Just this. Wanted to make sure you were really coming."

"Wouldn't miss it. How was your night?"

"Shitty."

"Why?"

"I'm a detective in Detroit. No, that ain't fair. I love this city and I love the job. But it doesn't exactly make for pleasant breakfast conversation."

"I can handle it."

"I bet you can. Okay, here it is. Too much of my night was spent in a small room with a homicide victim. She was twenty-two and attractive. She had been stabbed and slashed at least once for every one of those years. Probably more than that, but it'll take a while to count them all. She looked like an early stage in the invention of Swiss cheese."

"Stabbed and slashed where?"

"Face, abdomen, genital area. Unless you mean her location, which was in her bathroom."

"Sorry," Richie said. "That's gotta be rough."

"Her mother thought so."

"Ouch."

"Tell me."

A waiter appeared. He wore a stiff white shirt and a necktie. Between the waiter and Frank, Richie felt decidedly underdressed. Frank ordered stuffed French toast, and Richie decided he'd settle for the apple cinnamon waffle. When the waiter was gone, Richie leaned closer to the table. Each booth was walled off from the others, but he kept his voice low just the same. "So I told you about the padlocks."

"And I told you to stay out of that house."

"I know, Frank. I just had to check my theory."

"Okay, you disobeyed my strict instructions. So elaborate. What do you believe these theoretical padlocks mean?"

"Assuming they were put in by the Mortons, they mean that Angela was essentially a prisoner in her own home."

"She went to school."

"After school. When she was at home. Did she ride the bus, or did her parents drop her off and pick her up?"

Frank looked toward the ceiling. "Dropped her off, picked her up." He had one of those deep voices that made Richie think every word he said might be a recitation from the Old Testament.

"That's what I thought. They didn't give her too much freedom. I bet she didn't go to a lot of sleepovers."

"I don't remember if that question was part of the investigation."

"Maybe it should have been. Not finding fault, just saying. You probably didn't do a complete search of the house, right?"

"We looked around. The parents were there the whole time. The crime scene was the front yard, not inside. And by the time the Bureau got into it, the locals had already turned the house into a command center. There was no point in us doing a top-to-bottom search."

"Of course." Richie didn't want to sound like he blamed Frank for the fact that Angela had never been found. He didn't. He just didn't think the investigators had all the information they needed. "Here's the thing. While I was back in the house, I went into the basement."

Frank narrowed his eyes disapprovingly. That, Richie realized, could also account for the lines there.

"Look, I know how you feel. I was trespassing. You can take me to jail if you want. Just not until after I tell you what I found."

"I decide to take you to jail, Maynard, I do it on my schedule, not yours."

"Understood."

"Yeah, only I believed that you understood me the first time."

"Frank, do you want to hear this, or not?"

"No, but I don't think you're going to stop unless I shoot you, and this joint is far too swanky for that. Besides, you haven't paid the check yet."

"In the basement, under the stairs, there's a hidden door."

"Uh-huh. Harry Potter live there?"

"Behind the door, there's a rape room."

Frank gave him a smile, but it was a frozen one. He wanted to be incredulous but he wasn't certain enough to pull it off. "You sure you ain't confused the Morton house with Saddam Hussein's palace?"

"I can show you."

"I don't budge till I've enjoyed my French toast. After that I'll probably want about sixteen hours of sleep."

The memory of the place still made Richie's gut tighten. "It's a playroom of some kind, and I don't mean for little kids. There was nothing in the room but a mattress on the floor. And a mirror. A two-way mirror. It was on the floor, broken, but when it was hanging up it was in front of a hole in the wall. On the other side of the hole was another room, a little one with a couple of chairs in it."

"A viewing room."

"Yeah, but the hole wasn't big enough for more than one person to watch at a time. I'm thinking it was a video room. Put a camera in front of the hole, up on a tripod."

"Shit is so wrong."

"Got that right. I think it's worse than it looks, though."

"How's that?"

Richie waited quietly while the waiter put their breakfasts down. The food looked delicious. He hoped they would still want it when he was finished talking. "Put the two pieces together. Angela's a prisoner in her own home. Downstairs, someone's shooting home-made porn."

Frank winced. "You know how to ruin a good breakfast."

"I know, I'm sorry. It's just … it changes things, you know?"

"It might."

"Maybe she was never abducted. Maybe she was a runaway."

"At eleven?"

"An abused eleven."

"I suppose it's possible."

"It would explain a lot. Who knows what might have happened to an eleven-year-old runaway in Detroit? Thirteen years ago. She could have wound up on the Cass Corridor or just about anywhere, and you wouldn't have been looking for her there. Not on her own."

Frank shook his head. "We were looking at a stranger abduction. We scoured every inch of the yard, the sidewalk, the neighborhood. Talked to every single neighbor. We did everything we should have done. Except we didn't search the house well enough, apparently. But the locals had the case for a day-and-a-half before they brought Bureau into it."

"Given what the father told you, there wouldn't have been any reason for you to search the house."

"You can't take the father's word in a case like that."

"You shouldn't, no. Trust me, Frank. It would have been almost impossible for you to find this room, under those circumstances. With the parents watching you, wondering why you were snooping around their basement instead of out finding their little girl. Nobody could blame you."

"You found it right away."

"I got lucky. I almost missed it, but I got real lucky."

"Well, I want to take a look. You're right, it could change things."

"Did you ever have any good suspects?"

"There was a guy who confessed. He was a registered sex offender, a real shitbird. But he turned out to be nothing more than an inadequate personality looking for headlines."

"Like those losers who keep confessing to the JonBenét Ramsey killing."

"Exactly like that. Gigantic waste of time and resources. There were never any solid leads, just a lot of tips that didn't go anywhere."

"And never a trace of the girl?"

"Not even a believable sighting. She just vanished."

"You did look at the parents."

"Of course. First thing you do. Her father, Jarod, claimed he had called all her friends' houses, but some of those parents said he never called them. And she didn't have all that many friends to begin with. Couple of families we checked with didn't even know who she was. We debriefed the parents, Jarod and Barbara, separately, like you do, and we asked him about those calls. He said he was confused about who he was calling, since he was so frantic with worry. Said he probably called some places more than once and missed others."

"I can see that," Richie said. He had started eating his waffle, and it was just as good as it looked, good enough to overcome his emotional turmoil. Frank's French toast was already half gone. "Being that worried, with your daughter missing."

"Sure. They both passed polygraphs, no problem. Jarod was a little cool, maybe not as emotional as he could have been. He said he was trying to stay calm for Barbara's sake. She was considerably younger, and she was absolutely insane behind it."

"I bet. How about their jobs, you talk to co-workers?"

Frank looked at the ceiling again. Richie looked, too. It was way up there. "He ran a little portrait studio downtown. No employees, a one-man operation. Barbara was a part-time cashier at a super-market. I interviewed her manager and a couple of the other employees, but she wasn't that close to anyone."

"What about Angela? You said she didn't have many friends. What about babysitters, day care, anything like that?"

"She went to school and she came home. Never was in day care, never had a babysitter that we found."

"Her parents never went out?"

"From what you tell me, they had all their fun in the basement."

"So what happened?"

Frank shrugged and waited while the waiter topped off his coffee and vanished again. Frank spooned a little sugar into it, stirred. "Nothing. The city was all up in arms. Neighbors came out in force. Flyers posted everywhere, thousands of them. Nothing ever turned up, though. Jarod and Barbara moved out of the area, stopped calling the PD. That was strange, usually parents call every day. Multiple times. Sometimes for years. The Mortons just took off after about six months. You saw the place, they didn't even take most of their things. Left forwarding information, but after a month or two they were gone from there too."

"Which might mean something in itself."

"Might."

"Does the number one hundred forty-one mean anything to you?"

"In what context?"

"I don't know. It was scratched several times into a desk upstairs, and written on the wall of the little observation room in the basement in what looked like blood. Like someone was obsessed with it."

Frank considered, then shook his head. "No clue."

"I want to look into the case," Richie said.

Frank gave a mirthless chuckle. "On what authority?"

"I don't have any, Frank. But you do. We could team up on it. Look, everybody walked away from this one. It still eats at you, or you wouldn't watch the house like you do. For most of the past thirteen years nobody's been working it. And yeah, it's probably too late to do anything. But you haven't let go of it, and I'm offering to help out." He didn't want to sound like he was begging, but he wasn't far from it.

"No," Frank said. "I don't think that's a good idea."

"Why not?"

"Why?"

Richie wasn't sure how to answer that. He was drowning in a sea of dark despair. From beyond her own grave, Angela Morton had thrown him a lifeline, if only he could find a way to grasp it. "I don't know, honestly. I don't like my job. I don't much care for my life, you want the truth, except I got lucky in the marriage department. I thought I'd like being a cop, but that didn't work out. This, though— I have a feel for this kind of thing. I know how their minds work. Criminals, I mean. It's like I've spent my life preparing for an occupation—a calling—that doesn't really exist. And then here's this thing, this case, right in front of me. It's got its hooks in me and I want to see it through."

"I can't go to my lieutenant and say some civilian wants to work a cold case with me. Much less one who's already been canned from the force."

"I'm sure not. And the FBI isn't going to reopen it on my say-so. I don't know about you."

Frank shook his head. "We didn't exactly part on the best of terms."

"But if the two of us looked into it on our own time, and our own dime, and turned something up? Something that could get it re-opened … what's the harm?"

Frank forked the last of his French toast into his mouth, chewed and swallowed. "I'll have to think about it," he said.

"Do that." Richie drank some more coffee. It was good coffee, but he was going to have trouble sleeping, he'd had so much of it. "Oh, and in your homicide? There's a boyfriend, guaranteed. He did it."

Frank lowered his fork. "Why?"

"That's not a stranger murder. That's an intimate friend who's pissed off. And, okay, crazy. He's probably got a record of other violent offenses, but nothing this heinous. If you don't get him on this one, though, it won't be his last."

"You sound just like those damn BAU guys at the Bureau. Obnoxious motherfuckers, every last one of them."

Richie couldn't suppress a smile. "I've read every public word those guys have ever written," he said. "Those guys are my heroes."

Frank smiled, too. "Maynard," he said, "you got some strange ideas about heroes."

9

Welker woke up in the nest, on the thick pink carpet, his head aching. He didn't remember having fallen asleep there, but he must have. The door was still closed, the dolls in their places. He had a small, soft, pink blanket under his cheek.

He stood, touched his face. It felt numb, as if his fingers were probing a store mannequin. He recognized the sensation without alarm. It would pass, and then it would return, and the cycle would grow shorter and shorter. It had always been this way, since the beginning.

There had been a kind of electric thrill to that first one. Since she had gone, the others had fallen short in one way or another. Twenty-one of them—counting by the dolls arranged on the shelf—he had sent to be with the angels, when they didn't measure up. They had fussed too much or they had given in too easily, they had bit or kicked. Something, always something. Always some flaw that took away from the buzz he should have felt.

Not that he had regretted a moment of it. He knew that by society's standards, what he did with his angels was frowned upon. That's why he had to keep it secret. That's why the nest was locked and the playroom was in his attic, soundproofed. Society judged. Ignorant people didn't understand the natural way of things.

Soon, though. Seven months, a little less.

Charles took another look at the nest. Everything in its place. Everything an angel would want to see. He went out, down the hall and into the kitchen. He made himself eat a hurried breakfast and take a shower, then dried off, wrapped a bathrobe around himself, and locked the bedroom door. His vault was behind a false panel in the closet. He moved the panel, opened the vault, and took out a large scrapbook in which he had mounted photographs. The scrapbook was one of nine, and between them all, he had hundreds of photos.

He knew what he was doing to himself. The anticipation was getting to him, and he let it, allowing the familiar tingling sensation to flood his thoughts, to heighten his senses. He could feel every imperfection in the rough edges of the scrapbook paper, every thread in the bedspread he sat on while he slowly turned the pages. He smelled his own sweat, the slight citrus scent of the soap he had showered with that morning, a hint of bergamot from the kitchen, his morning tea. When he turned his head and looked out the window, every leaf on the trees outside stood out in stark relief. The sun was so bright it made his head hurt.

He couldn't stay in the house another minute. He put the album back into the vault and closed it up tight. Dressing rapidly, he left his bedroom, locking the door again. He pulled on a light jacket, and went outside. He locked the front door and stood on his walkway for a moment. The sun blasted the ground. He could almost see his lawn withering under its assault.

Knowing that his angel would be here in just a few months was almost too much to bear. Looking at the photos made it that much worse, and that much better, heightening delicious anticipation.

He would go for a drive. So many choices, so many places to hunt. A playground, a park, the mall … He just needed to take the edge off. He didn't want to betray his angel. But he needed to get his emotions in check, and only one thing would do that.

He got in his car, backed out of the driveway, and drove.

10

Frank sat on a big leather chair in his living room, reading glasses on, perusing a *Superman* comic book from 1961. Superman had posed as the white-faced Bizarro Number One in order to catch some criminal Bizarros. Bizarros did everything backward: they said "goodbye" when they meant "hello," they laughed when they were sad. They lived on a square world called Htrae. Frank chuckled while he read. Whatever was going on in his life, comic books—especially Superman comics—could be counted on to take him away from his worries for a while. Some comic fans disparaged Supes as a "big blue Boy Scout," but Frank had no problem with a hero who stood for Truth, Justice, and the American Way, as the old TV show had put it.

He had come home after breakfast with Richie Krebbs and had taken a stinging shower. He couldn't get the water hot enough to wash away the sense that he had failed Angela Morton. The things he had told Richie were true; he had come into a situation already in progress, and if there had been any pressing reason to perform a thorough search of the house, it should already have been done. Nothing in his interactions with Jarod and Barbara Morton had led him to suspect that they were anything other than worried parents.

But he had quit the Bureau to remain in Detroit. His hometown needed him more than Denver did, more than anyplace. At the Bureau, he would have been one more faceless agent, going where he was sent, doing what he was told. But as a detective with the Detroit PD, he could make a difference in the place he had always lived. While he went about his job, he had kept Angela's case in mind, watching for anything that might intersect it, however remotely. He combed through every child abduction file that crossed his desk, every molester apprehended. Thirteen years had slipped by. The girl was certainly dead, or she would have turned up.

His failure wounded him every day. He was a military vet, albeit one who had served between major wars and had never seen combat. He was a widower; Tiana had died seven years ago, after her lingering illness. Viewed over the long term, every human life had its small triumphs as well as tragedies. One had to embrace the ugly along with the beautiful, but when he thought about eleven-year-old Angela, with her golden hair and her harrowed eyes, he could only fix the ugly side in his mind.

The Superman comic helped, for a while. But when it was done and he needed sleep, he wanted to hear a friendly voice. He didn't want Angela's voice, which he had never actually heard except in a brief snippet of home video, to be the last one speaking to him before he rested. He slipped the comic into its Mylar bag, folded the top down and pressed the tape closed. Setting it on the table that stood beside his chair, he picked up the phone and dialed Marcia Alexander, the emergency room nurse he dated.

She answered on the second ring. "Hey, lover."

"What's happenin', lady?" he asked. Sometimes he liked to lower his voice an octave, put a little Barry White into it. Sometimes it worked.

"What's happening is I'm trying to get ready for work. I don't want to be late again."

"You don't think those emergencies will wait?"

"Not hardly."

"I would. I could be bleeding to death but I'd hold it in there, I knew a nurse looked like you was on the way."

"You're a special case," she said. "And I mean that in the mentally ill way."

He had wanted to tell her about Maynard, but that would take too long. "If you're in a hurry I'll let you go, Marcia. Just wanted to hear your voice."

"You've heard it."

"Then my plan worked."

"You're a crazy man, Frank. When I'm gonna see you?"

"Our shifts keep clashing like this, I ain't sure. Next couple days, I hope."

"Me, too. I got to go, Frank. Sweet dreams."

"'Bye, baby." He put the phone down on the little table, next to Superman. The call had helped smooth him out, but there was a tension between them that was new, and it bothered him. He hoped they could work through it or this wouldn't last, and for the first time since Tiana's death, he had found something that he wanted to last.

He left the phone and the comic book and went to bed.

o o o

By one in the afternoon he was awake and dressed again, in a charcoal gray suit with fine red and blue threads, an off-white shirt and a red tie. His shift wouldn't begin for hours, but Rags and Riches was open and he still needed to find out who Rosemary Robinson was dating, if anyone.

Frank was not a great believer in intuitive leaps. He believed that in cop work, the best results were achieved by the accumulation of small details: physical evidence, circumstantial evidence, eyewitness reports, and interrogations. Some called him a plodder, and he had to admit that to a great extent, they were right. But his plodding produced results, and in the end that was what counted. Slow and steady won the race.

Maynard's theory jibed about this case with his gut reaction, and the questions he'd asked about the Morton case indicated that he had an aptitude for detective work, so Frank didn't dismiss it. He parked near Grand River and Library and walked a few doors to the store, which sold both vintage and new. The clothing in the window was colorful, lots of flowing lines and ruffles. The mannequins wearing it all had dark skin, and so did the staff who greeted him. "Something for your wife?" a girl who couldn't have been older than eighteen or taller than five feet asked him.

"Not married," he said. He pulled back his jacket to show her the badge hanging on his belt. "Store manager here?"

The girl didn't blink. "Keandra!" she called. "Po-po here for you!" She tilted her head toward the back of the store. "She in back."

"Thanks," Frank said. "Po-po" wasn't as common in Detroit as in some other cities, but maybe she had picked it up from TV. He made his way between densely packed circular racks holding dresses, blouses, pants, and more. Somebody had worn too much perfume, and it lingered in the air.

At the back of the shop, a woman who was maybe four or five years older than the clerk in front came through a swinging wooden door with a questioning look on her face. "You the manager?" Frank asked.

"That's right."

"Frank Robey," he said, showing the badge again.

"I'm Keandra White." She wore a light blue dress with small flowers on it, gathered at the waist and flared at the hips, with a deep V neckline that displayed impressive cleavage. Her hair was braided and pinned close to her head with a tortoise shell clip. She smelled like jasmine, not the perfume he had walked through up front.

"I'm here to talk about Rosemary Robinson. She work for you?"

"She's one of my best salesgirls. What about her?"

"I'm afraid she was killed last night."

Keandra clutched the nearest rack and bit her lower lip so hard that it would swell up later. "I guess you hadn't heard," Frank said. "I'm sorry."

"No … I hadn't," Keandra said.

"If you'd like to go in back, sit down …"

"No, that's okay. Ain't any customers here anyhow."

"She get along with the folks here? Her coworkers?"

"Mostly. You know, they's always competition between the girls, since they get commissions. But I don't think she got any enemies or like that."

"She have a boyfriend?"

Keandra rolled her eyes. "You ask me, that dude's the one."

"What do you mean?"

"I don't mind a little jealousy, you feel me? A little bit of 'this shit is mine' is kinda sexy. But that boy—he call the store twice a day, when she working, before her break and after, to make sure she still here. If she goes out with some of the girls after work, he gets all up in her business. Mostly she just works and then goes home, or he come through and pick her up and take her out."

"You know his name? Where I can find him?"

"He like to be called AK Dirty, but he ain't no gangsta. His name is Donald. Donald Ayres. He work at a carwash."

"Know which one?"

"I don't know the name of it. On the east side, like Kleen Wash, with a 'K,' something like that."

"Know where he lives?"

"East side somewhere, all I know. When he ain't at her place."

"Got a phone number for him?"

"Yeah, I think. Hold up." She went back through the swinging door. Frank heard rustling from the back. The young girl who had greeted him first spoke to another sales clerk in hushed whispers, glancing his way. He tried to send them a reassuring smile but it wasn't coming.

"Here you go," Keandra said. She banged through the door again with a yellow Post-it in her hand, digits scrawled on it.

Frank traded her a business card for it. "Thank you. You think of anything else that might help, anything at all, get at me, hear?"

"I will," she said. Her eyes were hooded, her mouth a thin line, lips clamped together.

He knew he would never hear from her. With a little luck, it wouldn't matter.

O O O

Frank had seen the Kleen-Wash Keandra mentioned, out on Gratiot, past the airport and near 7 Mile Road. It was on a stretch that had included several car dealerships, both new and used, but many of those were closed, nothing left but wide expanses where weeds split the tarmac and empty showrooms, their big windows dulled with dust and neglect. The carwash somehow remained in business. The building was a long, piss-yellow concrete block rectangle, with shaded areas off to the sides where employees dried and detailed vehicles. Standing at the edge of the roadway was a large triangular monument sign on which the owner posted special deals and various aphorisms that struck his fancy. Today the sign said,

"Honk if U Love Jesus. Text if U Want to Meet Him Sooner."

When Frank rolled up, he saw half a dozen guys lounging around a radio blasting D12. They wore maroon polo shirts, most with baggy jeans. A black Benz sat under a canopy, its owner standing off to one side in a suit that cost as much as any five of Frank's, smoking a cigar and watching two men and a woman towel off his ride.

Frank had called for a patrol car to meet him here, but a quick scan told him he had arrived first. When he pulled into the drive, one of the loungers jumped up, grinned, and tried to wave him into the cleaning lane. Frank shook his head and pulled into a customer parking slot. He got out of the car and hiked back his jacket. "I'm looking for Donald Ayres," he said to the young man who had tried to direct him in. "He here today?"

The guy gave him a quick nod. "Yo, Donnie!" he shouted toward the people wiping down the Benz.

One of the men stopped wiping, glanced at Frank, and dropped his towel. He bolted in the other direction, tearing past the smoking man, who stood with his arms crossed over his chest watching him go.

"You couldn't'a let me get a little closer?" Frank dashed back into his car and cranked the engine. Donald Ayres had already cleared the far end of the lot and was cutting up a residential side street.

Instead of trying to cross Gratiot and go back the way he came, Frank sliced across the lot to an alley behind it and gunned the Charger. When he reached the corner, he caught a glimpse of Ayres dodging into a yard.

Go after him, or circle around the block? Where the hell was the backup? He thumbed the radio mic and barked out his location, declaring that he was in hot pursuit. He settled for going around the block, figuring that Ayres would come out on the other side rather than trying to hole up in somebody's yard. If he went inside a house, that would be a different story—and if he had in fact murdered Rosemary Robinson, which was looking more and more likely, then Frank dearly hoped he would not do so.

Frank swung a hard right, then another at the next corner. When he pulled onto the street, Ayres had just charged out from between two houses. His jeans were roomy, weighted down with chains, and he had to tug them up as he ran. The shoes didn't help either, oversized Yums with no laces. Prison dictated fashion—prisoners couldn't have belts or shoelaces. Kids in the hood thought there was something romantic about the look and emulated it. Ayres might have had some speed if he hadn't been trapped by his own fashion choices.

Frank shoved his foot down on the pedal and the Charger shot forward. Ayres gave him a wide-eyed look and darted for another yard, one with cracked concrete instead of grass, across the street. Before he reached it, a man came out his front door holding a 12-gauge. He pointed it at Ayres and said something Frank couldn't hear. Ayres glanced once at Frank, then came to an abrupt halt.

When Frank pulled into the driveway, the man swung the shotgun toward him. Frank unclipped his badge and held it out the window. "Police!" he called. "It's okay, brother, I got it from here."

"You get that car off my property," the man said as Frank got out.

"I just need to pick up this boy and then—"

"After you move the car." The man was in his sixties, his hair steely gray. He wore a white tank top-style tee that showed corded muscle and a flat belly. Cat was at least sixty. Frank wished he looked that good with his shirt off.

"Sir, I'm a police officer and I'm making an arrest. Please don't interfere."

"Don't listen to him!" Donald Ayres cried. "He just harassin' my ass!"

"Shut up, Donald," Frank said. "Sir, I'd hate to have to arrest you too."

"You could try. I'm sick to death of these punks runnin' wild on my street."

"Don't blame you a bit, sir, and you have every right to defend your home. Pointing a weapon at a police officer is a different matter. If you'll just put the gun aside for a minute, I'll wrap this up and be out of your hair."

The man thought it over for a second, and shifted the shotgun so its barrel aimed toward the sky.

"On the ground, Donnie," Frank said. "I bet you know the position."

Donald Ayres dropped to his knees and lowered his torso onto the concrete. "You straight up buggin', man, I ain't did nothin'," he said. His upper teeth jutted out from his jaw, too far to wrap his lips around. "You gots to cut a nigga some slack here, dog. I—"

Frank cut him off. "Haven't you heard? We got a brother in the White House now."

"Yeah? He ain't done shit for me. What he done for you?"

"You looking at it wrong, Donald. Ain't what he does for you, it's what his example lets you to do for yourself. Listen, it's a new world, and we don't use that word anymore. We got to respect ourselves, we want other folks to respect us." He twisted Ayres's wrists behind his back and snapped cuffs onto them. "I'm gonna check your pockets now, so don't wiggle around."

In Ayres's right front pocket he found a folding knife with a six-inch blade. He gave it a quick look, spotting dry, flaky brown sediment in the groove that the blade slotted into. A little Luminol would confirm the presence of blood, and a few weeks in the crime lab, if it wasn't too backed up, might even prove that blood belonged to Rosemary. Frank didn't object to all modern crime-busting techniques, he simply preferred the old ways.

He hoisted Ayres to his feet. "Come on, Donald," he said. "You're under arrest. I suppose you've heard of Miranda?"

"Don't know the bitch."

"You will."

"Y'all did your job the way you're supposed to," the man on the porch said, "I wouldn't have to keep this here loaded beside my door."

Frank pushed down on Ayres's head and eased him into the Charger's backseat. "I'll tell the mayor how you feel," he said. He moved around to his door, got in, and keyed the ignition. "Maybe he'll have you over to shoot some hoops."

O   O   O

Later, he called the number that Richie Krebbs' phone had left on his. "Maynard," he said when Richie answered.

"Only one man calls me that."

"Wait till I hack your Facebook page and put it on there."

"How do you know I have a Facebook page?"

"I didn't—but now I do. I'm a detective, remember?"

"I guess you're good at it. Anyway, I do have a page, but I don't use it much. You might reach all eleven of my friends, though."

"I am good at it. Damn good. Today I arrested a guy, and he confessed before I even got a chance to book him. I figured I should let you know, because you were right."

"About what?"

"Rosemary Robinson's boyfriend. That's who I busted. He still had the knife on him. I told him the lab would show that his knife had her blood on it, and he broke down."

"Cheating or performance?"

"What?"

"Was she cheating on him, or did she tease him about an erection problem?"

Frank considered the question. The guy knew his stuff, no doubt about that. "He didn't say anything about cheating...."

"Performance, then. Give him time, it'll come out. She laughed at him and he went nuts. Maybe she didn't even laugh. Maybe she tried to be nice, told him it was no big deal. To him, it's a *huge* deal."

"You might be right."

"I was right before."

"Which is why I'm calling you. I thought the same thing all along, but that doesn't make you any less right. Gives me some faith in your judgment."

"Which means?"

"Which means," Frank said with a sigh. Dude was making him spell it out. If he didn't owe Keith Ritts ... but no, it was more than that. It was unfinished business that wouldn't ever let him go. "Which means if you want to tackle the Angela Morton thing together—in my spare time, not on the clock—I'm up for it."

"If Rosemary's boyfriend had been able to say the same thing, she'd be alive today."

An unexpected laugh tore from Frank's lips. He didn't find anything funny about murder, but Maynard displayed a quirky way of looking at the world that amused him. "That mean you're in?"

"Oh, I'm in, Detective Robey. I am so in."

"Okay, then," Frank said. "When do you want to get the party started?"

11

They met at Frank's house. He had a spare bedroom that he used for a home office, and he kept copies of the Morton files there in white cardboard boxes. He carried in a folding chair for Maynard, and added a card table to spread files out on. The walls were empty, and he had tape and thumbtacks in case they wanted to stick anything up on them.

Richie looked around the house when Frank let him in the front door, just as nosy as any cop. "Nice place," he said.

"Thanks. *Architectural Digest* has been beating down my door for years, begging to do a cover story." He and Tiana had bought the place fifteen years ago, and there was nothing special about it except that he could make the payments. It was a good-sized brick house in the Middle Woodward neighborhood, essentially a two-story rectangle. Tiana had a knack for decorating, but after her death he hadn't wanted to be surrounded by the things she had left behind, didn't want to feel like he was living in a dead woman's shadow. So he had undone many of the touches she had brought to the house and replaced them with his own, which tended toward comic book memorabilia. The result was comfortable, for him, but often made visitors look around for a pre-teen boy.

They went upstairs to the office. Frank took a pair of gold-rimmed glasses from a pocket, unfolded them, and put them on. He pulled the files from the cardboard box, fanning them out on the table. Richie jerked a thumb toward steel shelves at the back of the room, filled with long white boxes. "Bring your work home much?" he asked.

"That's not work," Frank said. "Those are comic books."

"Comics? Like Spider-Man and all that?"

"Yeah, I got some Spidey stuff in there. Really more of a DC man, though. Superman, Batman, Justice League, those classic characters. But I have some Marvels, too. Even some of the indy stuff, and Archies."

"Are they worth anything?"

"Some of them might be. That's not why I keep them, though. I just like reading them and having them." He indicated the blank walls. "I used to have a bunch of original comic book art hung up around the house. Neal Adams, Gene Colan, Joe Kubert, Barry Smith, Jim Lee. Hell, I have a Jack Kirby *Captain America* page."

"Is that rare?"

"Classic as it gets."

"Where is it?"

"Took it down, put it in a closet. I learned a lot from comics, about doing the right thing and being strong and brave. After I couldn't find Angela Morton, I figured I had let my heroes down. I still enjoy reading the comics but couldn't bear having those pages up on the walls, staring at me."

"I'd love to see them sometime."

Frank held Richie's gaze for a few moments. He seemed sincere, and although he obviously knew little about comics, that didn't mean he might not appreciate the artistry that went into them. The most unexpected part was that because Richie didn't have an interest in comics, then his request, which didn't seem to have been made from simple politeness, instead indicated an interest in being Frank's friend. Frank had not gone into this looking for a friend—certainly hadn't chased into the Morton house the other night expecting to find one. But if it happened, he didn't think he would be disappointed. He got along with the folks on the job, but it wouldn't hurt to know a guy who wasn't actually a cop. "One of these days," he said after a while. "Right now we got work to do."

"Yeah," Richie agreed, taking the offered chair. "I've been thinking about it non-stop, and the more I do, the fishier it all seems. We've got a girl who's a prisoner in her own home. She's abducted on a day when she was home alone with her father. Mom's off at work, right?"

"Yeah."

"And he's not on the phone to nine-one-one in five seconds. Instead he's calling friends of this girl who apparently doesn't have friends, driving around the neighborhood by himself—none of which can be verified."

"He actually did call a couple of her classmates' homes. We pulled his luds. He made some calls, just not as many as he claimed."

"He also said he was trying not to show emotion because he wanted to stay strong for his wife. But given our new information, a lot of his actions take on a different cast."

"Such as? You sound like you're trying to say something, Maynard, but you ain't said it yet."

"Frank, the guy had an adult playroom in his basement, with a secret viewing room. He kept his daughter locked in her bedroom. I shouldn't have to spell it out. He's a textbook sexual sadist."

Frank shook his head. He didn't want to think about that. As a cop he'd had to deal with plenty of horrible incidents. You couldn't do the job without running headlong into examples of human beings treating each other worse than vermin. "No," he said, sadness rasping his voice. "You don't have to spell it. You think he killed her."

"I think she knew something she wasn't supposed to, or he was afraid she would tell somebody at school about things being done to her. Maybe she *had* told someone. Either way, he decided the only safe thing to do was to get rid of her."

"So we should have been looking for a body the whole time?"

"I'm sure you were looking for a body, at least after the first twenty-four hours or so."

"That was part of the detail, yeah."

"Of course it was." Richie thumbed through some of Frank's files. "And the parents left town what, six months later?"

"About that. After things cooled down."

"Where'd they go?"

Frank rifled through a file until he found it. "They left an address in Indianapolis. Like I said before, after a few months they stopped answering the phone, and anything mailed there came back as undeliverable. I had some Indianapolis cops go by the house, but it was just a rental that was already occupied by another family."

"And nothing after that? No word from them?"

"The Bureau never could track them down. I check with contacts there every couple of years. They haven't really kept up the search, but there has never been any sign of the Mortons. I thought they had accepted the reality that they'd never see Angela again, and didn't want the reminders. God knows after I lost my wife Tiana, there were times I wanted to burn this house to the ground and move on."

Richie waved a hand at the walls surrounding them. "You didn't, though."

"No. I decided I could move on emotionally, and it didn't mean I didn't love her. After a while, it wasn't necessary to stop being reminded of her."

"Because you're sane," Richie said. "And because you didn't murder her." He dumped some photographs from one of the file folders onto the card table. "She looks like a sweet kid. She didn't deserve those parents. She didn't deserve what they did to her."

"Hell, no."

"So we have to find them. Jarod and Barbara Morton got away with murder. So far. It's time we brought them back."

"The finding is gonna be the hard part. If either one was incarcerated anywhere, I'd know about it—my Bureau contacts would see to that. But they haven't turned up anyplace."

Richie fingered a tear sheet from *The Detroit Daily News*. On it was an advertisement for Jarod's photo studio, Little Angels Photography. The ad featured a black-and-white photo of a blond girl who had to be Angela, taken when she was seven or eight. Feathered angel wings swelled from her back. The lighting was soft, from the right and slightly above her, casting shadows on the left side of her face and neck. The shadows were soft, too. Frank had looked at it a thousand times, thought it was nice, painterly. Other pictures were of an older Angela, up until her eleventh birthday.

"There aren't any baby pictures," Richie said.

"Nothing before that angel shot. These are the ones they gave us, and I tore out that newspaper ad when I saw the girl in it was Angela. I didn't ask for baby pictures because I was looking for ones that would help us find her."

"Yeah, you're right. These are the ones the search effort would have needed."

"Right."

"You don't have any idea where they might have gone after Indianapolis?"

Frank picked at his fingernails. "Not a clue."

"We have to find out more about them. Especially Jarod. I don't know that Barbara was even involved in what he did to Angela. She was the one who finally called the police, right?"

"Soon as she got home and found Angela missing."

"Then Jarod's the one we have to focus on. We have to learn whatever we can about him, and about Angela."

"A little late for her."

"It is," Richie admitted. "But what if he and Barbara have had another kid?"

o o o

Miss Genevieve Tait was in her sixties, a thin African-American woman with a nervous air about her. She wore a pink cardigan over a white blouse, a blue skirt that went well past her knees, dark hose and blocky blue shoes. She had a gold necklace with a crucifix on it over the blouse. She looked like she was on her way to teach at a Catholic school, but she had been retired from Madison Elementary, the public school Angela had attended, for a decade. When Richie and Frank knocked on her door, she didn't take the chain lock down until Frank showed his badge and ID and offered to let her call police headquarters to confirm his identity. Then she admitted them into a home that smelled like shampoo and made liberal use of the color pink, as if she redecorated every day to match her sweater.

"Do you remember Angela Morton?" Frank asked after they were settled on her couch. She sat in a straight-backed chair with one hand tucked under her chin. Maybe she was afraid her head would droop in public.

"You don't remember all your kids," she said. "You say you do, you tell them you'll never forget them. Me, I taught fourth and fifth grades for thirty-three years. If I remembered all the children, I wouldn't have room in my head for my own name."

"I'm sure," Frank said. "What about Angela?"

"Mostly what you remember are the exceptionally bright ones, and the troublemakers. You remember the bright ones because if they become a senator one day, or president, then reporters are going to come around asking about them, and how would it look if you had a future president in your class and you couldn't recall them?"

"That would look bad," Richie said.

She let the comment pass. "But you also remember other ones who stand out in one way or another. The ones who are always polite, always cheerful. The ones who excel at something unusual, like the violin. Finally, there are some who are just plain memorable. Not good, not bad, just … just children you can't put out of your mind. Even if you want to. Angela Morton, she was one of those."

"What was memorable about Angela?" Richie asked.

"You would look into her eyes," Miss Tait said, "and you could see she was troubled."

"Troubled how?"

"That's hard to say. Just troubled. Most children her age, they're full of spirit. They can't wait to experience the world. Their curiosity hasn't yet been numbed or deadened. They're optimistic, always thinking that tomorrow things will be even better than today."

"But not Angela?" Frank asked.

She plucked at something invisible on her skirt. "Not at all. She never, that I recall, talked about tomorrow, about the future. She was shy in class, a loner. I had to prod her into taking part in classroom discussion."

"Did she ever talk to you about her home life?"

"Heavens, no. She wouldn't. I didn't press, though. If she had anything she wanted to say, she knew she could say it to me."

"Were there any other teachers she might have been closer to?" Frank asked. "That you remember?"

"She wasn't particularly close to any of us," Miss Tait said. "I suppose Miss Washington. Gladys Washington. She taught music. Angela enjoyed music."

"Is she still in Detroit?" Richie asked.

"I'm afraid not. The district cut funding for her position several years ago. I understand she moved to Chicago. At any rate, she was killed by a housebreaker."

"I'm sorry to hear that."

"That's a dangerous city. She was a fine music teacher, too. A great loss." She looked like she might start weeping about the loss at any moment.

"What about friends?" Frank asked. "We're having a hard time locating anyone who was friends with Angela."

Miss Tait switched hands, moving her left one up under her chin and reaching into her sweater pocket with the right. "She was not blessed with many of those, I'm afraid."

"Can you think of any? Anyone she knew who might still be in town?"

"You might try Tamara Ferris," she said after a moment's reflection. "I believe she still lives in the Detroit area."

"Is that still her name?" Richie asked.

"As far as I know."

"Thanks for your time," he said. He hoped Tamara Ferris could offer more insight than Miss Tait had. And he hoped talking to her didn't make him as nervous.

O   O   O

They found Tamara Ferris in Warren. She was twenty-four, unmarried, working as a bartender at a Chili's. "High class joint," Frank said when they went in.

"Only the best." Richie said. "Just don't ask me to buy you a meal. I'll be paying off that breakfast for the next two years."

"Not a problem," Frank said. "One of us is gainfully employed."

"Good," Richie said. "If we have to slip Ms. Ferris a double sawbuck you get to do it."

"Double sawbuck? You been reading mystery stories?"

"Just trying to catch up, since you've got the edge on practical experience."

Flat-panel TVs mounted on the walls showed various sporting events, none of which attracted much of an audience. The people sitting around the bar were focused on one another, bursts of laughter punctuating the conversational din. Behind the bar, a slender woman held court. She had short, straight hair, dyed black, and was dressed in an equally black tank top underneath a black long-sleeved shirt. Her jewelry—earrings, a necklace, and a single bracelet, was chunky, and unsurprisingly black as well. Richie sensed a theme.

He and Frank made their way to the bar. She glanced over, arched one eyebrow.

"Tamara Ferris?"

"Yeah?"

"I'm Richie Krebbs."

"Richie?" she echoed. "You got ID? I'm not sure you're old enough to be in here."

"You can call him Maynard," Frank said, pushing in behind Richie. He showed his badge. "You can call me Detective Robey."

"I'm a little busy here," she said.

"Break time," Frank said.

"Okay, hang on, let me get someone to cover." She raised a panel on the bar and stepped out, then went into the back for a minute. When she came out she was accompanied by a guy in a tight black T-shirt. He eyed Richie and Frank with suspicion. "Okay," Tamara said. "I hope this doesn't take long, that dude don't know a margarita from his left ear."

"We'll try not to inconvenience the social drinkers of Warren," Frank promised her. "Someplace private?"

"Let's go outside," she suggested. "Okay if I smoke?"

"As long as we're outside," Richie said.

Behind the restaurant, she lit a cigarette and took a long drag. "Mind telling me what's up?"

"It's nothing you've done," Frank said.

"We're looking for information about Angela Morton," Richie added.

Tamara blew out a stream of smoke and shook her head. "I don't know anyone with that name."

"Not now," Richie said. "A long time ago. Fifth grade."

Frank showed her a picture of eleven-year-old Angela. "This help?"

Tamara's eyes widened, though she tried to hide it by looking up and blowing more smoke. "Oh, that one. That *was* a long time ago. I have no idea where she is."

"You heard she was abducted?" Frank asked. "You were still in school with her then."

"Yeah, I heard. Scared me to death. For weeks I could barely sleep, wondering if I'd be next. But like I said, that was a long time ago. Time passed. I got over it." She halted the cigarette inches from her lips. "She hasn't been found, has she?"

"I'm afraid not," Richie said. "We're just trying to get a better sense of what she was like. Back then. We heard you were friends."

"As friendly as Angela got with anybody, I guess. She wasn't allowed to hang out after school. Her parents picked her up and she went right home. In the morning they dropped her off a few minutes before first bell."

"They were pretty strict?"

"You could say that. I had a sleepover party for my birthday that year. I really wanted her to come. But she wouldn't even ask them. She just said they wouldn't allow it."

"That's too bad," Frank said.

"Even during school, she was a little strange. At the end of the day she got very quiet, very withdrawn. Like she didn't want to go home, but she didn't want to stay at school either. That's in retrospect. At the time I didn't analyze it or anything. I guess I was as close to her as anyone was, but even with me, there were whole areas she wouldn't talk about."

"Such as?"

"Such as, if we got to talking about boys, or getting married. She would just clam up, turn red. You could see her going inside herself, sort of. And if we talked about sex …" Tamara gave a sharp laugh. "Yes, even at that age, sometimes we wondered about sex. Curiosity, you know. But not Angela. She would have nothing to do with that."

"Did she have any nicknames?" Richie asked. "Was she an Angie, or Angel? Anything?"

"No, not at all. She was always just Angela. That's what she said sometimes, when she was talking about herself. Just Angela."

"Low self-esteem?"

Tamara nodded. "The lowest."

"Anything else you can tell us about her?"

Tamara wiggled her shoulders. "She was the prettiest girl in class. We all thought that. But not her. She was positive she was ugly. Hideous. She had that great blond hair and those big green eyes. Perfect facial structure. At eleven, I was already jealous of her looks."

"But she didn't see it?" Richie asked.

"Not at all."

"Thanks, Ms. Ferris," he said. "We appreciate your help."

"That's it?"

"Unless you have anything, Frank."

Frank shook his big, square head. "No. Thank you for your help."

"Any time." She dropped the cigarette butt, stepped on it with a boot that added three inches to her height. "I don't mean that."

"Didn't figure you did," Frank said.

O O O

Driving back into Detroit, Frank, behind the wheel, turned to Richie. "That was a wasted trip. Didn't even get that burger."

"Not necessarily wasted," Richie said.

"What? You get something I didn't?"

"I got a picture of a frightened little girl. One who was especially frightened of sex, of romance. She wanted to be ugly and unappealing. She didn't want to talk to her peers about sex because she knew so much more about it, about the reality of it, than they did."

"Because of her father?"

"That's my guess."

"God, I'd like to be in a room alone with him for ten minutes."

"Let's make it happen," Richie said.

"You really think we can find him, after all this time, when the Bureau couldn't?"

"Isn't that what this is about?"

"He's got a thirteen-year head start."

"We just have to go back farther. We have to learn who Jarod Morton was, and then we'll figure out how to find him."

"That sounds like more of that BAU shit. Profiling."

"It's not voodoo, Frank. We understand him, we'll know where he would have gone."

"I don't see it."

"Trust me, then. What we have to do is find out where he came from. Was he born in Detroit?"

"I've read his file enough times to know that," Frank said. "He and Barbara moved here from someplace in Virginia. Reston."

"Then we have to go to Reston."

"Go to Reston? You got a job, don't you? Because I do, and unplanned absences aren't exactly popular with the brass."

"Then plan it. But plan fast. The trail's cold, Frank. The sooner we go, the better."

Frank flipped on his turn signal, shaking his head in dismay. "Virginia. Shit. Probably want me to buy the airplane tickets, too."

"That," Richie said, "would be awesome."

12

Wendy didn't remember the last time she had seen Richie so amped up about anything. Not since he had been fired from the police force. No, earlier than that, because the last couple of years there he had been able to see that it wasn't going well. He had been in constant conflict with his superiors, with his fellow cops. He wasn't cut out for bureaucracy, should have been a carpenter or a chef or something, working on his own, creating things. He was good at that, handy around the house; though he downplayed those accomplishments, saying they were things any guy could do, she knew that wasn't true. She feared he had taken his father's experience too much to heart, that he craved the safety of a steady paycheck, even when he wasn't suited to the job.

He had been like this when they got married, she guessed, and then when he first joined the police. He had a grin on his face that reminded her of high school, when he had been a passing acquaintance who she would never have imagined marrying. He couldn't stay in one place, and when he did his foot was tapping, or his fingers were. He kept running his hand through his brown hair, which was longer than he'd worn it during his cop years but still short enough to meet Rampart Security's more relaxed standards.

She was glad to see it, because she had grown tired of the depressed Richie. He hadn't had anything to look forward to for a long time, anything to get excited about. His passion for this was obvious, and although they could hardly afford the expense, perhaps it was an investment in his mental health they couldn't afford not to make.

"Do you know what it means to me to have someone trust my instincts?" He had lit at the kitchen table for about the third time since he had started telling her about the house he had broken into and the man he had met there. He had called in sick to Rampart and had gone out somewhere with his new cop buddy, Robey. Wendy made dinner, then kept it warming in the oven until he finally got home. They'd only been in the house a few weeks; the kitchen still didn't feel like it was hers. Now food was in front of them, on the table, but they hadn't eaten much. "A working detective. All the times I tried to get them to take me seriously when I was on the job."

"Maybe they didn't take you seriously because you wouldn't sit still," Wendy said.

He rested his hand flat on the tabletop. It wouldn't stay there long. "Wendy, I'm not kidding about this."

"I know, Richard." Almost no one called him that, her included. Except when she was upset with him, or wanted to nail him to the ground. "I get that it's kind of an affirmation for you."

"It's all I've ever wanted, Wen. Just to be listened to. I know I'm good at this kind of thing."

"I understand that. I think you should go for it."

"I appreciate that." He buried his face in his hands, but only for an instant. "They'd fire me, though. Rampart. I can't take vacation time yet."

"I also know the job at Rampart isn't exactly your dream career."

"But it's a paycheck. Not a big one, but more than we've had in a long time."

"Not a big one is right."

"More than my last couple of jobs. At least it's something."

She loved her own job, felt like she was helping Detroit figure out its own future. She saw enough of the financial sinkholes in which people found themselves mired that she didn't want to encourage Richie to walk away from yet another job. They had paid cash for the house, but they still had groceries, utilities, property taxes and all the other expenses that ate away at a family.

She didn't want to see him sink any deeper into depression, though. If he did this and it worked out, maybe that would spur him to try the cops again. Another city, or maybe a different law enforcement organization. And if it didn't work, then maybe he would finally be able to let that dream go. "It's a crap job, Richie. Watching the houses of the rich to make sure the poor don't rob them? That's what the police should be doing."

He hung his head, shaking it slowly. "But they're not, are they? Someone else has to, and it might as well be me."

It killed her to see him looking so sad. "I know how much you hate it."

"Do you? I can't stand to go to work at night. I sit there in the truck for my whole shift wishing I was anywhere else in the world."

"I'm not blind. That's why I'm saying this. You've got a chance to help find a son-of-a-bitch who murdered his own daughter? You've got to take it."

He stared at her, the gratitude on his face as real as a five-year-old's on Christmas morning. "You sure about that, Wen? This all happened so long ago. We have real problems here, now. We need two incomes, and I don't want to lose another job."

"You're overeducated and overqualified anyway," Wendy argued. "If you're lucky enough to lose it, you'll get another one."

Richie took up his fork and jabbed at the overdone chicken breast on his plate. "I'm not so sure about that. Jobs are scarce everywhere these days, especially in Detroit. There are plenty of unemployed cops around. I have a lot of competition."

"Richie, don't think I'm not scared about losing the income. I know we need the money, and I know losing that income could put a strain on our marriage."

"Right," Richie said.

"But this is about something bigger. Too big to just walk away from. Someone abducted, maybe killed a little girl and got away with it. You might be in a position to do something about it. Isn't finding out worth sacrificing a shitty job? Maybe cutting some corners around the house for a while?"

"You really mean it?"

Wendy held back a sigh. They had done nothing but cut corners since he had lost his police job, which hadn't paid that well to begin with. They had never earned much money, and she tried to tell herself it wasn't important to her. If it was, she could have found a corporate job instead of working for a city deep in deficit spending. "Thirteen years is a long time, Richie. Do you honestly think you can do something? If she's even still alive, it's a little late to save her."

"Whoever did it wouldn't have stopped with her, Wendy. This kind doesn't just stop. We think it was her own father. If he's still alive and physically able, he might have had more kids, who he's abusing or murdering. Thirteen years isn't that long for him. He could still be in his thirties, with decades of abuse ahead of him. And next to that rape room, there was another room, for observation or filming. There might be other people around who were part of the whole thing."

She picked up her own fork, held it poised over her plate, but didn't go any further with it. What she was about to say surprised her. She was pleased, she discovered, that she was still able to surprise herself. "Then you don't really have a choice, do you? If you thought there was something you could do but you didn't do it, then you wouldn't be the guy I married."

Richie was far from perfect. Even while she was granting her permission, her blessing, he wanted more, wanted it to seem like her idea. He was manipulating her, to an extent.

Or was she manipulating him, to get back the cheerful Richie that she loved?

She wasn't perfect either. Sometimes she drank too much, she owned more shoes than were strictly necessary, and if she were to be brutally honest, she didn't really like dogs or cats, or understand people who did. She had a sarcastic streak that edged into meanness if she didn't keep a handle on it, and sometimes she chose not to. Perhaps worst of all, though she seldom admitted it to herself and had never said anything to Richie, there were times when she wished she weren't married. It was nothing to do with him, just her. She valued her independence, her privacy. She liked to be able to arrange her life to suit herself, without taking someone else's needs into account.

But she did love him, so she kept that uncomfortable truth to herself. Anyway, he hadn't played the card that she couldn't resist but also wouldn't be able to forgive, and that bought him some points. They had been trying to have a baby for ten months now. Once they succeeded, if anyone molested her child, she wouldn't rest until she had hunted him down and killed him. Richie could have brought that up and she would have caved instantly, then spent the rest of her life resenting him for it.

"All right," he said at last. "I guess I'll do it."

"I really think you should."

"If you're sure …"

"*Richard.*" She let her anger show in her tone. She had given him what he wanted. If he kept pushing, she might start to regret it. He would use up what remained of their minimal savings on this quest, possibly even plow thorough credit and put them deeper in debt.

She couldn't stop him, though, and the strain that trying to would put on their marriage could be disastrous, too. The combination of financial issues and infertility problems had been hard on them. They didn't need one more thing coming between them, not now.

She just hoped he really could solve this case. And that he could do it in a hurry. Nothing would be better than that, for both of them.

She picked up her chicken with her fingers and tore into it. She was, she discovered with surprise, famished.

O O O

The lights of Windsor, Ontario sparkled on the black surface of the Detroit River. From this vantage point, the Canadian city looked like an enchanted wonderland, albeit one dominated by a Caesar's casino. Marcia Alexander figured that from the other side, Detroit probably looked about the same. Distance diminished a city's flaws.

Frank had called her at work and made plans to pick her up. They'd had a couple of drinks at the Lake Lounge bar—well, she had, he was driving and had stuck to tonic water and lime—and now they were walking through Chene Park and back up to the towering Ren Cen, where they'd parked. One of their first dates had been to Chene Park, for a summer concert by The Commodores. Since then it had been a sure thing, a place they could go to rekindle their feelings for each other, complex though they might be. They walked hand in hand in the cool night air, the river breeze enveloping them in diesel fumes and the slightly fishy tang of the water. She listened to his story and tried to put out of her mind the next-to-last patient of her twelve-hour shift, an alcoholic with esophageal varices who had left her scrubs covered with mucus.

"You know how much this case has haunted me," Frank was saying. He walked with his head down, gaze on the cobblestones, not even looking at the river view. "Thirteen years. I never thought I'd get another shot at it."

"But now you got one," Marcia said. A boat cut down the river, its wake faceting the reflected lights.

"Now I do, all because this stupid ex-patrol officer didn't listen to me and trespassed. I can't tell Lieutenant Jackson that. So I got to pretend I got this lead in another way."

"You're lying to Jackson?"

"More like not telling him everything. Because I can't just let it go again. Not now. Anyway, I didn't mean that, about him being stupid. Maynard. He's a smart guy. I feel stupid we didn't find it first."

"You weren't the lead on the case." She hadn't been with him then, but he had talked about it so often she felt like she had watched the entire thing unfold.

"No. I did what I was told. But I should have found it. Somebody should have."

Sometimes she wondered how he had ever found the strength to become police. As an ER nurse, she had known plenty of cops, and Frank was too nice by half. He was softhearted, occasionally soft-headed. Maybe men built women up in their minds, perceived them as better than they were. Women didn't have that problem. She saw Frank's weaknesses and frailties as clearly as he did, if not more so. Their professions showed them both, on a daily basis, horrors that most people never imagined. A person had to be able to take them in and then send them away again, not dwell on them. Frank had seen terrible things, but this one event, this little girl's disappearance, he had never successfully packed up and sent off. Sometimes he had nightmares that left him sweating and trembling. He never said, but she'd heard him shout out a few times, and she was convinced the nightmares were about the Morton girl.

"But using up your vacation time, Frank? We were going to go away together."

"It's Virginia, not Antarctica or someplace," he said. "It's a couple of days. I've got enough stored up, we'll still be able to go to New Orleans."

"You say that now. What happens if it's someplace else after Virginia? And then after that?"

"I'll still have enough time for us, Marcia. Don't worry about that."

"I'm not sure how I'm supposed to not worry."

"Because I say so."

"You'll excuse me for not accepting that as a guarantee."

He stopped, faced her and took her other hand. "I know things haven't always worked out like we talked about. But this … this is something I got to do, babe."

Marcia was nine years younger than Frank, but that still meant she was past forty. The years might have meant something different to a woman than to a man, but she had not wanted to be single at forty, and certainly not at forty-five. She wanted to get married. Frank said he did, too, only not yet. He wasn't even able to discuss when he might become ready. Although Marcia was a patient woman—another survival skill an ER nurse needed—she couldn't wait forever.

But he was a good man, and often a kind one. He claimed that he couldn't let the girl's case go, and she believed the truth was that he couldn't let any of them go; that he took the horrors inside himself and held them there. She wasn't sure if that was brave or dangerous, but the fact that he kept going in spite of it made her hopeful. She had wanted children once, giving up that dream as the years passed and she watched other people's children become sick or injured or die. Still, she wanted someone to lie beside her at night, to hold her and stroke her cheek when she was ill, to laugh with her, to look at her with love as her breasts sagged and her hips grew and her pace slowed and her hair grayed. Frank was older, the years would show on him first, but she was ready to watch him age and thought she could do so with a measure of generosity and grace.

First, though, he had to let her.

"You have to do it, then you'll do it. But if you fuck up my trip to New Orleans, you'll regret it, mister."

"I won't. I promise."

"You better not." She gave him a stern look, then thought better of it. He was a grown man. He wasn't looking for her permission to go to Virginia, just her understanding. "You do what you need to, Frank."

"I mean to."

"That's good. Right now, though, I need you to take me home."

"Mine or yours?"

"Either." She didn't care where they went. She just wanted some loving before her next twelve-hour shift began. And if he was leaving town, they didn't have time to waste.

Maybe she wasn't as patient as she had always thought.

13

Welker was running.

His attempt had been awkward, amateurish, driven by desperation. A little girl, alone on a kindergarten playground after the rest of the class had gone inside. She was on the far side of an iron fence, ginger-haired, supple, and gorgeously pouty. He knew he didn't have much time; any moment her teacher would do a head count, realize one girl had been left outside, crouching by the fence, plucking the petals from a spring flower—a weed, really, though she wouldn't know the difference.

He had been cruising past the kindergarten, watching the others disappear through the door single file, and hadn't seen her until it was too late to stop. Instead, he turned at the corner, left the car at the curb and hurried back on foot. Until he had her in sight again he was afraid she might have noticed that the rest of the class was gone. But she was still there, the flower in her hand not much more than a green stalk. Not a teacher in sight. Could they really have forgotten her?

He had to work out his patter in a hurry, but he had plenty of experience with that. "Hi there," he said before he even reached her. "Do you like flowers? I have an amazing garden, but I need some help with it. I hurt my back, it's hard for me to bend down and pluck the weeds or cut pretty flowers for my mother."

She looked up, let the stalk drop from her fingers. "I don't know you."

"No, you're right, what a smart girl. I'm Bill. What's your name?"

Her precious, perfect lips were parting to answer him when the school door banged open. "Chelsea!" a teacher called. She wasn't much more than a kid herself, a few years out of high school. Heavy, with a dull face. "Chelsea, who is that?"

"It's okay, Chelsea and I were just talking about flowers," Welker said. He started back toward his car.

"No, wait," the teacher said. "Who are you?"

"Nothing, no one."

She spun around and spoke to someone inside. Welker was sure he heard the word "police." Then she started toward him at a jog.

He broke into a sprint. Forget about not looking suspicious— the last thing he wanted was for her to take down his license plate number. He shouldn't have even tried to approach someone, not out in the open like this: broad daylight, no cover. He should have planned better.

By the time he rounded the corner and yanked his door open, he was panting, sweat gluing his shirt to his sides and back. The teacher had pushed through a squeaky gate; her clunky shoes were loud on the sidewalk. Welker dropped into the seat, fumbled his key into the ignition, and twisted it. The engine caught and he jammed his foot on the accelerator. The car lunged forward. A pick-up truck honked; he had cut it off. In the rearview, a young guy flipped him the bird. He didn't care—the teacher had made the corner, but the truck blocked her view.

After he made a couple of turns, away from the angry pickup truck driver, away from the school, he realized he was shaking. He pulled to the curb again, in front of a well-maintained apartment building, three stories, stucco-sided. He had to get it together. He was so close to having her in his life again, he couldn't blow it. At the same time, the tension, the anxiety, was very nearly unbearable. One decent experience would see him through the next few months. Just one. She had to be out there somewhere, looking for the same thing, looking for him, even if she didn't know that exactly.

He drew away from the curb, carefully this time. At war with himself.

Thoughts roared through his head, a dizzying, deafening mental express train, windows blinking past like a movie projected at the wrong speed, each with a young girl's face staring at him. Leave it alone, he thought, stay safe. Just one, he thought. Just one time.

He thought: it really won't be long, now. Not so long. Not compared to how long you've already waited.

14

During his most recent period of unemployment, Richie had spent an inordinate amount of time watching reality TV. On one home improvement show—ironic, he had thought, that he saw it inside a house in the early stages of foreclosure—he had seen a home-decorating tip that struck him as so utterly ridiculous he had laughed out loud, then called Wendy at work and told her. The "expert" on the tube said that all-white interiors had become fashionable, but that since bookshelves didn't fit that color scheme, one should turn them around so the spines were at the backs of the shelves and the blank page ends faced out.

Annette Morton didn't quite subscribe to the all-white theory of interior design, but she wasn't far from it. The overwhelming use of white in her home was tempered by lots of gold and a handful of pinks. She had apparently solved the books conundrum by simply not owning any. To be fair, bookshelves might have crowded out some of the angels with which she surrounded herself—angel sculptures, angel paintings, angel pillows, even an angel tapestry on one wall. Richie couldn't remember the last time he'd seen a real tapestry outside of a museum.

Her daughter Janine had met them at the door of Annette's Reston townhouse, attached to a row of four other nearly identical houses, wood-sided and painted in shades of brown and tan. Similar rows were staggered around the cul-de-sac. A golf course engulfed the neighborhood like a hungry snake hoarding prey too large for a single meal. Two days had passed since Richie and Frank had agreed to make the trip, days in which Frank had arranged some time off and Richie had been informed that his job would be forfeit if he took time off before six months of employment. He accepted that news with equal parts relief and dread.

Janine was in her late forties, tall and angular, with short reddish-brown hair. She looked like a person to whom a smile would constitute a sort of neuromuscular treason, necessitating a swift and surgical response. Her eyes were crescent-shaped with the outer ends pointing down, and her nose jutted out abruptly below the brow, then broke almost straight toward thin lips. The skin over its bridge was so tight it was paper-white. The eyes and nose were family traits; for an instant Richie thought he was looking at a photograph of Jarod Morton come to life.

Frank showed his badge and ID. Even for the flight down, he had worn a suit and tie, with a silk pocket square and French cuffs. By contrast, on the airplane Richie had worn a reproduction of a Mitch Ryder tour T-shirt from the year of his birth that Wendy had given him, and a pair of faded jeans. He still had on the jeans but had consented to putting on a long-sleeved shirt and a corduroy sport coat, the nicest one he owned. "I'm Frank Robey, with the Detroit Police Department," Frank said. "I called Mrs. Morton a couple days ago, and she agreed to see us."

"She's expecting you. I'm Janine Morton, her daughter." She turned away from the men at the door. "Mom, those police from Detroit are here!"

"Well, don't make them stand outside," another female voice said. It sounded considerably older than Janine's, with a little bit of a quaver to it, and just the slightest hint of a Southern accent. "Come in, gentlemen, please."

In case they hadn't heard for themselves, Janine conveyed the gist of the message with a raised eyebrow and an open palm directing them toward a staircase. "Just down half a flight."

Richie started noticing the angels in the entryway, where there was a small wrought-iron table, painted gold, with a marble top. On the marble sat a statue of three cherubic angels, all chubby cheeks and rounded bellies, dimpled thighs and fluffy, feathered wings. Paintings of angels graced the staircase.

Annette Morton waited in a sunken living room with a cloud of plush white carpet, high ceilings, and massive windows looking onto a grassy field. At the field's far edge were more townhouses just like this one. Richie figured they were probably short on angels over there, since this house certainly met or exceeded the neighborhood quota. At a quick glance, he counted sixteen in the living room alone.

She sat near the windows in a solid chair, upholstered in an eggshell-white fabric. The chair had to be solid because she couldn't have weighed less than two hundred and fifty pounds, and possibly more. Her skin was relatively unlined, except around the eyes and lips, and she might have been anywhere from her mid-sixties to late seventies. Her hair was pure white. She seemed to have no aroma, and the house didn't smell of anything except a hint of recently spritzed pine-scented air freshener. "Have a seat, gentlemen," she said with a gracious smile. "I hope you don't mind if I don't stand, it's just so hard these days to get up and down."

"That's quite all right, ma'am," Frank said. "We'll try not to take up too much of your time. I'm Detective Frank Robey, and this is May—Richard Krebbs, my associate. He's a private investigator." Both men sat on chairs slipcovered in white cloth.

"It's an honor to have you in my home," Annette said. "I didn't realize when we spoke on the phone that you were a Negro, Mr. Robey. I can usually tell."

"Mother!" Janine said sharply from the doorway.

"I'm sorry, Mr. Robey. Sometimes I forget how times have changed. We mustn't use such outdated terminology, must we? I apologize deeply."

"I'm sorry, too," Janine said. "Mother isn't prejudiced, none of us are. She just speaks what's on her mind."

"That's all right," Frank said.

"I meant no offense, Janine, these men understand that. You needn't apologize on my behalf." The words were spoken with an edge, as if Annette was used to doling out verbal discipline.

"Sorry, mother." Janine mumbled.

"Hadn't you some errands to run, Janine?"

"I really don't have—"

"I'm certain you told me that you did."

Janine had been dismissed, and she knew it. "I … well, yes, I suppose I could pick up those prescriptions. For me and Jenny."

"That's a lovely idea. We'll be fine here. Would you gentlemen like anything to drink before she goes?"

"No, ma'am," Richie said.

"Thank you, Mrs. Morton," Frank added. "We don't want to be a bother."

Janine was hovering in the doorway, as if she didn't want to leave her mother alone with the two strangers. But when Annette twitched her fingers, Janine excused herself and climbed the stairs. A minute later Richie heard the jingle of keys, and then the front door closed. Hurried footsteps sounded on the sidewalk outside.

"Now we can speak freely," Annette said. "She's a good girl, but she's somewhat overprotective."

"Freely is good," Richie said.

"On the phone, Mr. Robey, you said you wanted to talk about Jarod."

"That's right. I was one of the FBI agents who investigated when his daughter was abducted. I'm with the Detroit Police Department now, and I'm still trying to get to the bottom of that."

"That was a very sad time, very sad indeed. I hope you haven't made the trip down here for nothing, though. I'm afraid Jarod is no longer with us."

"By that you mean—" Frank began.

"I mean he's dead. Shuffled off this mortal coil. Isn't that how the poets say it?" She waggled her fingers at the room, where one's gaze couldn't flit without landing on an angel. "I believe in angels, gentlemen, I always have. And that's what Jarod is now, an angel. He's sitting on a cloud, strumming a harp. Sometimes I'm certain he looks in on me, at night while I'm sleeping. When I wake up I can just feel a presence, you understand? I know it's him."

"When did he die, ma'am?" Frank asked.

"Oh, I haven't the faintest. He was never one to keep up with his mother. Not like his sisters, that one."

"Would anyone know? His father?"

"My husband died when Jarod was only seven, I'm afraid. We already had Janine and Jennifer, and then Jarod came along several years later. My husband's health was poor by that time, but he had a few years with us before Jarod had to become the man of the family."

Richie glanced around at the room. The place was frilly, girlish. Jarod might have been the man of the family, but there was no indication in this room that a male had ever lived here. "Was that in this house, Mrs. Morton?" he asked.

"Yes, we've been here since the early 1970s. Mr. Morton used to work for the Department of Agriculture, and in those days it was an easy trip into Washington. Plus when he needed to travel, Dulles Airport is right close by."

"Yes," Richie said. "Did Jarod have his own room?"

"Well, of course he did. He still does, for that matter. I've hardly touched it since he left. I just couldn't bear to."

"May we see it?"

"I'm not sure I understand what purpose that would serve."

"I'm not either, ma'am," Richie said. "Maybe none. We're just trying to understand the family better. Jarod, his wife Barbara, and their daughter. Sometimes to get to know a man, it helps to get a glimpse at the boy he was before."

"Well, if you all think it's important, help yourself. I hope you don't mind if I don't show you up. I can still make the stairs a few times a day, but I try not to overtask myself."

"If you just tell us which room, Mrs. Morton, that'll be fine," Frank said.

"Top of the stairs, second door on the right," she told them. "The door is closed, but it's never locked."

"We'll be right back."

"I'll be awaiting your return," she said.

Frank gave Richie a look as they climbed the stairs, the half-flight back to the entry level and then up another flight, with a landing midway, to the top floor. There were five doors off the upper landing, one of which was open and obviously led into a master suite. Behind the middle door, also ajar, was a full bath. Frank opened the door to Jarod's room and they went in, shutting it softly behind them.

"She's a piece of work," Richie said quietly.

"Yeah she is. Definitely queen of the coop—you see the way she booted her daughter out the door?"

Richie nodded. "And this is supposed to be a boy's room?"

It hardly qualified. There were even angels in here, sculpted cherubs mounted on the wall. The bedding was white, as were the walls and dresser. There was a plain wooden desk and a bookcase with a few odds and ends on it: a small tourist's reproduction of the Statue of Liberty, a store-bought trophy with the legend "World's Greatest Son" stamped on the base, a Bugs Bunny mug filled with pens and pencils.

"I would have gone nuts if I grew up here," Richie said.

"You and me both." Frank opened the closet doors. Semi-opaque plastic bags hung inside, like cocoons full of unseasonal attire. "No wonder he got out when he could."

"I don't think we're going to learn much more here," Richie said.

Frank gestured toward the door. "You're the boy wonder."

"Hardly, but thanks." Richie opened the door and stepped out. At the top of the stairs was a statue on an ornate wooden stand. It was an angel, a young girl angel with her hands clasped together and wings arching up from her back. Dust had settled into her crevices, and when Richie picked her up, the table was slightly discolored where she had stood. "This thing might have been here for thirty years," he said. "Heavy, too."

"Don't break anything. She'll know."

"Definitely." Richie put the statue back down, centering the base over the off-color spot. Only when he stepped away from it did he realize that the angel's pose reminded him of the photo of young Angela Morton from the ad for her father's portrait studio.

Back downstairs, Annette Morton had turned in her seat to observe the landscape beyond her windows. When the men returned, she slowly swiveled toward them. "Did that satisfy your curiosity?" she asked.

"It might have helped," Frank said. "Thank you."

"It's my pleasure. I don't get all too many visitors these days."

"Does Janine live here with you?"

"She lives close by. Her sister Jennifer does too, with her husband and child."

"Was Angela your first grandchild, Mrs. Morton?" Richie asked.

"She was, yes. And I don't mind telling you, she came as a bit of a surprise."

"In what way?"

"Well, I had met Barbara, of course. Jarod's wife. She was quite a bit younger than Jarod when they met. She moved in with him when she was sixteen, I believe. He was twenty-three. I'm afraid none of us saw much of them for the next while. Then one day he up and told me that he was moving to Detroit with his bride and their new child. Imagine my shock."

"They didn't tell you that they'd had a daughter?"

"You'd have thought their marriage was a state secret in the first place. One day they're living in this awful apartment in Herndon, the next he tells me he's gotten hitched, on the day of her eighteenth birthday. Of course, as soon as I heard about the wedding I made sure there was an announcement in the local paper. You'd have thought I had committed some sort of crime. We were all, I guess you'd say, banished from his life after that. The next I spoke to him, they were racing off to another state with a granddaughter I didn't know I had. One who, given the arithmetic, was conceived before her parents were married. I gather that's why it was all so secretive. And why they wanted to get out of town, so when the child started school, her classmates wouldn't know she'd been conceived out of wedlock. They wouldn't hear of a baby announcement."

"Do you have a copy of that wedding announcement?" Frank asked.

She waved toward a wooden cabinet with a marble top. Sculpted angels frolicked on it. "Inside there I have a kind of scrapbook," she said. "Help yourself, if you would."

Richie went to the cabinet. An old-fashioned key rested in the lock. He turned it and opened the door. Inside were a cloth-covered scrapbook and some accordion files holding letters, cards, and other papers. He lifted the scrapbook out. "This one, Mrs. Morton?"

"That's right, in there. Toward the back."

Richie flipped through the pages. There were family photos showing life before Jarod, then some of the family with the new baby. Her husband had been tall and rail-thin, and he possessed the familiar Morton eyes and nose. In later pictures, he looked like he had already died and just hadn't fallen down yet. Finally Richie came across a yellowed newspaper clipping announcing the wedding of Barbara Alderdyce of Centreville to Reston's Jarod Morton. It was brief and to the point.

"You didn't know Barbara Alderdyce well?" he asked.

"As I said, I had met her a few times, but I expect I could have walked right past her without recognizing her. She was young and she looked cheap to me, but what does a mother know?"

"So they moved to Detroit," Frank pressed. "And they had Angela. Or the other way around. Did you ever see the baby?"

"I went there once, the girls and I. To meet my granddaughter. Jarod acted as if it were the biggest imposition one could imagine, and Barbara wasn't much better. We stayed a few days, and never were invited back."

"Then, thirteen years ago, Angela disappeared."

"A terrible thing, just terrible."

"And Jarod and Barbara moved to Indiana. Indianapolis."

"That sounds right."

"But they didn't stay there long. About six months?"

"I suppose it was about that."

"And where did they go from there?"

"I don't recall offhand. They moved around some, I suppose."

"Did Jarod stay in contact with you?"

"He loved his mother."

"I'm sure he did, ma'am. But did he keep in touch while he and Barbara were moving around?"

Annette sighed and cast her gaze toward the thick white carpeting. "He used to send cards, on my birthday and Christmas. After Detroit, he missed some birthdays, sometimes missed years altogether. Finally he didn't even write a return address on the envelopes, but I always knew they were from him. I keep them in the files, there."

Richie removed one of the accordion folders from the cabinet. "Yes, in there," she said.

He thumbed through old report cards and letters from other relatives and found a stack of greeting cards in their envelopes. They had been rubber-banded together but the rubber had broken and stuck to the sides of the outer envelopes. "This is them?"

"That looks right," she said.

He flipped through the envelopes, sometimes stopping to pull out the card inside. Some were signed "Love, Jarod and Barb," some simply "Jarod." Later he stopped writing his name, and just put a "J" or left the inside blank altogether. Most of the cards depicted angels. At least he knew what his mother liked.

Richie scanned the postmarks, looking at cities and dates. "I see envelopes from Omaha, Nebraska and Tucson, Arizona," he said. "The most recent ones are Tucson, but they're six, seven years old."

"I told you, he's passed," Annette said. "He would send cards if he were able."

"I'm sure he would, Mrs. Morton," Frank said.

Richie put the envelopes back into the folder and returned to the scrapbook. He turned pages until he found class pictures of Jarod, a thin boy with a weak chin and what appeared to be watery brown eyes. Jarod's earlobes, he noted, were attached to his head instead of separate from it. He didn't remember that from the newspaper photos of Jarod from Detroit, but the older Jarod had grown his hair long enough to cover his ears. Richie looked further but couldn't find any pictures in which Jarod's hands were visible—even in his baby pictures he was wearing mittens. "Mrs. Morton, I don't see any pictures showing your son's hands or bare feet. Do you mind if I ask, were his fingers webbed at all? Or was his middle toe longer than his big toe? Anything odd physically about him that you remember?"

Annette's mouth gaped open until she realized it and clamped it shut. "Why, he was a beautiful child, as you can plainly see."

"I don't mean to imply that he's not. He's quite handsome in these pictures."

"Yes, he was. I ... I'm sure I don't know why it matters, but yes, in fact he did seem to have a bit of, I suppose you'd call it extra skin, between his fingers. More than some people do, at any rate."

"I see. Thank you so much for your time, Mrs. Morton." He pushed the scrapbook back into place in the cabinet, closed the door and locked it. "We appreciate it a great deal."

"If it helps you find whoever took my granddaughter, it's worth it," she said. "I never knew the child well, but that doesn't mean she was ever anything less than precious to me."

Frank was staring at Richie in surprise. Richie cocked his head in the general direction of the front door, and Frank gave him a subtle nod. "We think it'll help, ma'am," he said. "Like my partner said, thank you so much."

"I won't see you out," she said. "But I'd appreciate you locking the doorknob as you go. The world is so full of evil, isn't it?"

15

In that uncertain state where dreams mesh with reality, each impacting the other, Welker saw a field of young ladies. Some of them he had known, but others were strangers. A stranger, he'd heard, is just a friend you haven't met yet. Letting his gaze roam across the field, he hoped that was true.

The girls wore shorts and T-shirts, summer dresses, tights and sweaters and puffy down coats. They were white, most of them, but their hair colors and styles spanned every variation imaginable. They met his eyes, licked their lips, and traced small fingers down their necks, along the lines of their slender shoulders, where their wings grew.

Welker woke up then, opened his eyes, saw the time in glowing red numbers on his digital bedside clock. The numbers seemed to vibrate. He closed his eyes, rubbed them, and opened them again. The field of girls was gone; their absence left a cold place in the bed, though they had never been there at all. There was no field, he knew.

Nothing worth having was that easy to take.

He pushed back the covers and got to his feet. He was not sleeping well these days, and had needed a nap, though he couldn't make it a long one. Hunting was no good after dark; the objects of his desire were daylight creatures. He still had not firmly committed himself to the hunt, this time, still told himself he would wait for his true angel.

But that, he realized, was self-delusion. The more he thought about her, the harder the need gripped him. He felt like he was trapped in a tunnel, and the end, through which the only illumination leaked through, was drawing closed. The end he had entered had already shut tight behind him. Even the walls were narrowing—he could touch both sides with his extended fingertips, though earlier he would have had to walk from one to the other.

He knew of only one key to unlock the tunnel, to open the trap.

He needed to hunt, to step up the pace.

He had been confining himself to the city, but he had to spread his net more widely. There were plenty of small towns, out in the country. People there were not so fearful. They didn't lock their doors at night, they let children ride bikes or play in the yard. The population was smaller, of course, more far-flung, and that could be a disadvantage. So he would mix up his efforts, trawl in the city and the rural communities, thereby increasing his chances of finding just the right would-be angel.

He would stop pretending he could control his desire, and give in. His desire would control him.

After all, it had always been strongest, hadn't it? As far back as he could remember. Why try to delude himself?

His decision made, he felt better already.

16

The sun was sinking behind lush Virginia greenery by the time they checked into a room at the Hampton Inn in Sterling, a few minutes from Dulles Airport. Frank drove the rented car—that, the flights, and the hotel put on one of his credit cards—singing along softly with Smokey Robinson, Sly Stone, and Archie Bell and the Drells on Sirius XM's Soul Town station.

When they got into the room and dumped their suitcases on the floor, he turned to Richie. "The hell was that? Does he got webbed fingers? What does that tell us?"

Richie sat on one of the beds. The room was comfortable, indistinguishable from other such rooms across the country, which Frank supposed was a comfort to business travelers. Richie blinked those big blue eyes a couple of times and pressed his earlobes into the side of his head. "I don't know if you remember, or if you ever noticed because his hair was long," he said. "But his earlobes grew straight into his head, they weren't set apart from it like most people's. The fingers and toes were kind of a long shot, but sometimes they go along with the lobes."

"Go along how?"

"They're all fairly common indicators of a genetic disorder in the primal brain. They're not necessarily predictors of behavior, but they're relatively common traits among multiple murderers. When I saw the earlobes I had to check on the others, because the more traits someone presents, the more likely they are to indicate brain dysfunction."

"You are shitting me, Maynard. You got to be."

"I'm not. Like I said, you can't see someone's earlobes and just lock him up. There are a lot more factors than that in the development of a killer. But if you see all those physical traits together, then you might want to take a close look at that guy."

Frank broke into a smile. "I knew there was a reason I brought you along. You *are* the boy wonder."

"Not really," Richie said. He was wearing a smile of his own, though, and Frank recognized gratitude in it. "I told you I paid attention to everything the FBI profilers write."

"I guess someone has to. It's all mumbo-jumbo to me." Richie was still sitting on the bed nearest the window, so Frank headed for the bathroom. "When I was at the Bureau I always thought that shit was nonsense, some kind of black magic juju. Sometimes I liked having a good crime lab at my back, but that profiler shit got my goat. Far as I'm concerned, the only way you solve a crime is through old-fashioned legwork. Asking the questions, getting the answers, figuring out what to ask next."

"It's easier if you can narrow the field a little," Richie said. "That's all profiling does. Narrows the field."

Frank gave him a contemplative look. "Maybe. I'm gonna drain the snake," he said. "Then I saw a Logan's Roadhouse close by looked like it had my name on it. That okay with you?"

"Sure," Richie said. "I guess the one here won't have people in a mural wearing Pistons jerseys, will it?"

"It does, I'll double the tip."

O   O   O

Frank was paying the check—tipping fifteen percent, no Pistons jerseys in evidence—when his cell phone rang. He slipped it from his pocket. A local number. "Robey," he said.

"Detective Robey?" It was a woman's voice, one he didn't recognize. "My name is Jenny DeVries. Jenny *Morton* DeVries. I'm Virginia Morton's daughter."

"The one who wasn't at the house today." He signed the credit card receipt and took his copy, tucking it in his wallet along with the card.

"That's right."

"What can I do for you, Ms. Morton?" Frank ticked his head toward the door, and Richie followed him out.

"I got your number off a business card at Mom's. I was hoping I could talk to you for a few minutes. It's about my brother."

"We're at Logan's Roadhouse in Sterling," he said. "We could meet you here, or someplace else that's more convenient for you."

"I … wouldn't want to go anyplace around my home," she said. "Are you staying near the restaurant?"

"We're at the Hampton Inn, right across the street from the restaurant." He gave her the room number.

"I'll be over as soon as I can," she said.

"We'll be there."

He explained the unexpected appointment to Richie as they walked across McClellan, which dead-ended at the hotel. Beyond that was State Route 7. Frank was sure he would be hearing the highway traffic all night. He didn't mind, though—he had lived in the city his whole life; quiet nights unnerved him.

Back in the room, Richie pulled a fistful of peanuts from his jacket pocket and dropped them onto the desk. "I love those places where you can throw the peanut shells on the floor," he said. "I know it's a big national chain but there's something down-home about it."

"You, Maynard, are a Class-A sucker," Frank said.

"That just might be true. But I have free peanuts."

"You do at that. Toss me a couple of them things."

They ate peanuts and chatted for a while, then Frank read a couple of *Superman* comics while Richie watched *Marley & Me* on HBO. Frank was glad for the break from thinking about poor Angela Morton and her strange-eared, web-fingered father. When he opened the door at Jenny Morton DeVries' knock, it all came rushing back too fast.

She was maybe forty-three or forty-four, not as tall as Janine and a few pounds heavier, looking somewhat like a cross between her sister and her mother but without the more extreme aspects of either. Her hair was longer, auburn and curling up at the shoulders. But the family eyes and nose were in evidence, the eyes pink at the edges as if she had been crying. Frank caught himself trying in vain for a glimpse of her earlobes. "I'm Frank Robey," he said, offering his hand. She took it with a firm grasp. Her fingers seemed appropriately webbed, but no more.

"I'm Jenny. Jenny Morton DeVries."

"Come on in. That's my partner, Richard Krebbs." It was still hard to call him Richard, but at least he hadn't started to say Maynard this time. He wondered if Maynard had noticed the promotion from associate to partner.

Richie wheeled out the desk chair for her and perched on the end of his bed. "Thanks for meeting us here," he said. "If you have any information about Jarod—"

"I don't know how much I can tell you about him that you haven't already heard," she said. "I'm just so worried about him, and if you find anything out—"

"Hold up," Frank said. "You're worried about him?"

She sat in the chair Richie provided and turned so her gaze landed somewhere between the two men. "I sort of feel like a turncoat here, talking to you."

"It's okay," Frank said. "We're just trying to find out what happened to your niece, Angela. We're digging into your brother's history a little, trying to understand the family better."

"I get that, I guess." She started to stand up again. "Maybe I should go. I shouldn't have come here."

"Jenny—" Richie began.

"Look, Ms. Morton," Frank interjected. "You called me. You came here. You obviously have something you want to talk about. I know it's difficult, but sit down, take a deep breath and let's get through this."

She sat again. "I know. You're right, I'm sorry."

Frank kept pushing, but gently. "What do you mean, you're worried about him? Your mother told us he's dead."

"You might have noticed she lives in her own little reality," Jenny said. "She would rather believe he's with the angels than that he's alive but just not in touch with her."

"And that's what you believe? That he's alive?"

"I don't know, really. I think so. I think Janine is in touch with him sometimes, but she won't ever tell me or Mother for sure."

"Really?" Richie asked.

"Ours has never exactly been a very average family, Mr. Krebbs."

"I'm getting that idea."

"If he's out there, I want him found. I want to know that he's okay. If he's in trouble, I want to help him. I'm the middle child, closest to him in age, and it hurts to think he's talking to Janine but not to me. Is that selfish?"

"Not at all, Ms. DeVries," Frank said. He was well aware that he modulated his speech according to his audience. He didn't think it was necessarily a racial thing. He had known plenty of white cops who had one speech pattern on the job, a completely different one when off duty. On the other hand, he had known more black folks who had a voice they used only with whites than white people with a black voice. "It makes perfect sense to me."

"What do you mean about your family's peculiarities, Jenny?" Richie asked. Frank let him take the lead. "Tell us about that."

Jenny chewed on her lip and twisted a lock of hair around her finger. The swivel chair rocked from side to side. "Our … our father was—well, he was fine with us girls. Good to us, generous and loving. But with Jarod …"

"How was he with Jarod?"

"He knew he didn't have long to live, I guess. I didn't understand that then, I'm only four years older than Jarod. But in retrospect, I think that's what it was. He knew he was dying. Before he did, he wanted to make a man out of his only son."

"Which meant what?"

"Toughening him up, I guess. Sometimes he … God, I feel like such a bitch for even saying this. Sometimes he hit Jarod. Beat him. He was doing it for Jarod's own good, because he knew he would have to be the man of the family."

"Your mother used that same phrase," Frank said.

"She understood that's what Dad was doing. When he hit Jarod. Sometimes Dad would leave the house—I think he was embarrassed when he realized what he had done—and Mother would cuddle Jarod."

"Not surprising," Frank said. "Considering what he had been through."

"And the cuddling," Jenny continued, as if Frank hadn't spoken. "Sometimes it was in her room. In her bed. I mean, nothing bad, you know. But I think it might have been confusing to Jarod, just the same."

"That's possible." Richie said.

"Anyway, maybe that's why he won't talk to her anymore. Because somehow he blames her for what happened back then, with Dad. And maybe he blames me too, because I knew about it and didn't make it stop."

She finished and brought her feet up onto the chair, wrapping her arms around her legs. "I never meant to hurt him in any way. If you find him, can you tell him that?"

"We will," Richie promised.

"If he's alive, and if we find him," Frank added.

"That's all I want. For him to know I only ever wanted the best for him."

"Can I ask you a couple more questions?" Richie said. "Since you were close to him. They're personal and they might seem rude, but they might be important."

Her voice came from someplace far away. "Go ahead."

"Do you know if Jarod was cruel to animals, as a boy? Torturing neighbors' pets, pulling the wings off flies, anything like that?"

She nodded her head, still refusing to look at either man. "He did. I caught him once with the Worthingtons' cat, they were our neighbors. He was holding it down and jabbing a pin in it, over and over. It was yowling and writhing but he kept at it. He was mortified when I caught him. He told me it was the only time he had ever done anything like that, that he just wanted to see what it would do."

"And you never witnessed any other incidents?"

"No."

"And did he wet the bed that you know of?"

"Yes. That I know for sure. Mother was working, when we were young, and I used to have to get him up and ready for school. I had to change his sheets and launder his pajamas when I got home. Off and on until he was about ten, I think." The last three words were hard to understand, because she took in a set of deep, hitching breaths as she spoke them. Once she had powered through the words, sobs took over. Her shoulders spasmed and she bucked forward, pressing her hands against her face. Frank went into the bathroom for tissues, which were encased under the counter. He managed to wrench the box free of its holder and carry it back into the bedroom.

Richie was crouched beside Jenny Morton. He said something soft and presumably soothing, which Frank couldn't hear over her weeping. He touched her leg and her shoulder and she leaned even more, almost falling from the chair into his arms. Richie's gaze met Frank's for an instant, surprise registering on his face, but then he turned it so Jenny could rest her head on his shoulder. The whole thing looked awkward; her weight pushed Richie back so that he was against the edge of the bed, the two of them interlocked and writhing on the floor like wrestlers, or lovers.

Frank sat on the bed, tissue box in hand, and waited. After a couple of minutes she disentangled herself from Richie and accepted some tissues. She took her seat again, blew her nose, dabbed at her eyes. "I'm sorry," she said. "I told myself not to fall apart, and look at me."

"Families are complicated," Frank said.

"I suppose that's always true. Mine certainly is."

"I think it's universal," Richie added.

Once again, Jenny pushed off the chair's arms and rose unsteadily to her feet. "I really should go," she said. "My husband will be wondering what's happened to me."

"Thanks for coming," Richie said. "I think it'll help."

"If we need any more information, can we contact you?" Frank asked as he stepped aside to let her move toward the door.

"I'd rather you didn't. I suppose as long as you're very discreet, it would be okay. I try to keep my son from hearing much about his lost cousin, so I didn't tell the family I was coming to see you."

"Understood," Frank said. "I won't be in touch unless it's absolutely necessary, and I'll be discreet if I am."

"That's fine," she said. She shook his hand, then sniffled and left the room.

17

When she was gone, Frank turned to Richie. "What the fuck, Maynard?"

"What?"

"You two rolling on the floor, I thought I was gonna have to get myself another room."

"I was just comforting her. You've never comforted a grieving woman?"

Frank remembered holding Rosemary Robinson's mother in his arms, just a few days ago. That had been different, though. He hadn't found her remotely attractive. But Maynard's hands had been pressed against her back, his face lost in her hair, and the whole tenor of the moment seemed sexually charged.

"Course I have. Not on the floor, though. Not like that."

"I didn't expect her to bowl me over, Frank. It just happened. It's nothing."

"You want Wendy to see you doing *nothing* like that?"

"She'd understand."

"I hope so." Frank carried the tissue box back into the bathroom and gave himself a minute. In the instant that Richie's eyes had met his while he cradled Jenny Morton in his arms, he recognized something in the other man, something that maybe he should have seen sooner if he was half the detective he made himself out to be.

There was a dark center to Richie Krebbs. He was drawn to places like the Morton house and people like, well, like Frank himself, and like Jenny Morton, who had a hole inside her that could never be filled. He wanted to investigate crimes because that brought him nearer to an understanding of the blackness in some human hearts; it fed his beliefs about human nature and convinced him that his worst fears about it were well founded.

Frank recognized it in Richie because looking at him in that moment had been like looking into a mirror.

He sat outside the Morton house when he was depressed for the same half-formed reasons, because when he took the sadness and hurt of the world into himself, he craved confirmation of the world's ills. He had never quite figured out the why of that, but thought it might be because facing the terrors that dwelled inside the hearts of others made him feel that at least it wasn't only him, that he was not alone in the darkness but had more than enough company there.

He believed the ability to confront the evil in himself and others was what made him an effective criminal investigator. Now he believed that it was what had drawn him and Richie together. He couldn't say that out loud, though. If they talked about it, if they admitted that the basis on which this unconventional partnership was formed was their common understanding of the world's evil, they wouldn't be able to face each other.

Frank ran hot water into the sink, soaked a washcloth, and rubbed it over his face. After drying it with a towel, he stepped back into the bedroom. "So, did all that add anything to your psychobabble profile?"

"Yeah," Richie said. He was still standing beside the bed, unsure of what to do with his hands. Finally he picked at a hangnail, and that seemed to satisfy him. "It confirmed a theory I had, anyway. I know you don't think much of this whole profiling thing."

"I'm just old-fashioned. Don't completely trust computers, either, for that matter. Or smart phones. I don't want my phone to know how to do anything but make a phone call, and sometimes I don't even want that. I'm just not sure about trying to make this guy into a psycho killer or something. All we know so far is he had a room we think was a rape room in his house and he might have killed his daughter. Emphasis on *might*."

"I'm not trying to make him into anything he's not," Richie said. "I'm just trying to understand him."

Frank plopped into the desk chair Jenny had vacated. "Whatever. What's your theory?"

"I think Virginia Morton let her whole 'man of the house' idea get out of hand."

"In what way?"

"In the way that when she cuddled him in bed, she did a lot more than cuddle."

Frank couldn't keep himself from making a face. "Eww."

"I know, man. It all fits, though. Something twisted him like a pretzel, sexually speaking. His sexual focus was redirected away from women his own age and toward little girls. Those things I asked about, cruelty to animals and bed-wetting, they're often predictors of sexual sadism. I don't think he directed that sadism at adult women, but at his daughter. Then something happened—she got too old, she was going to tell, something—and he killed her."

"Makes me want to puke, to think I shook that man's hand."

"You couldn't have known. Guys like this, they fit in. They function in society. He was a worried father, and you had no reason to think otherwise. He passed a polygraph, right?"

"Breezed through it."

"That's how diseased these guys are. He barely knows what he's doing is wrong. He understands that society doesn't tolerate it, so he has to keep it hidden. But he thinks that's society's problem, not his."

"I had him here right now, I'd put a cap in him."

"We have to find him, that's all."

"You got any more ideas on how to do that, I'm all ears."

"She said she thinks Janine is in touch with him. Can we get access to her phone records?"

"No wonder they booted your ass off the job. We don't have nearly enough for a warrant. We'd be laughed out of a judge's chambers with this case."

"Okay, let me think about it for a while. There's got to be a way."

"Think all you want. While you are, think about this. I introduced you as a private investigator, back there. But you're not. A P.I. has to be licensed. You're strictly freelancing here, Maynard, and if you get caught messing around in people's lives, it could be bad for you. I couldn't protect you then."

"Thanks for the vote of confidence, Frank. Don't worry, I know the risks. But I also know you couldn't do it without me."

"You think?"

"I know."

Frank smiled, and that brought a grin to Richie's face. "What?" Richie asked.

"You might be right," Frank said. "I probably couldn't. But I was picturing you in prison just now, and it was kinda funny."

"Thanks," Richie said. "I'll do the same for you."

O   O   O

Richie called Wendy and gave her a bare-bones description of his day. She didn't want to know the details of the case, and he was happy to oblige, because he preferred that she be protected from knowing the full depths of human behavior. Frank eyed him over the top of his comic book when Richie mentioned the sister who visited their hotel room. Again, Richie skimped on details, causing Frank to give a *hmph* and go back to his reading.

When Richie was done and checking e-mail on a laptop he'd brought, Frank pulled out his own phone and called Marcia. His conversation didn't go as well as Richie's had, and there were times that Richie winced, wishing he wasn't even in the room.

Finally, with the room quiet once again, Richie called Wil Fowler's number. He just wanted to check in with the kid, make sure he was staying out of trouble, and that he knew Richie really would keep up with him like he promised. The phone just rang. No answer, no voicemail. Richie gave up after fifteen rings. The night was getting late anyway, and the day had been a long one. Richie went into the bathroom to brush his teeth. In the mirror, his eyes looked vacant, like the windows of that "haunted house" from his youth.

Was he fooling himself with this whole adventure? Frank was right, not only did he have no legal authority to pursue what was really a criminal matter, but his lack of authority could in itself be a crime if he crossed the wrong line. He had lost a job—one he didn't like, to be sure, but a job nonetheless. Frank had been covering expenses, but so far it had only been a day. He couldn't expect the man to keep that up. If this dragged on, he would have to pitch in, and he plain didn't have the money.

He didn't think he could walk away from it now, though. The job had already been sacrificed. More important, though, was the fact that they had made progress—limited, true, but real nonetheless—in understanding Jarod Morton. The more Richie knew about him, the more he believed Morton was a dangerous man who needed to be found.

He took a long, hard look in the mirror, then flipped off the light.

O O O

Marcia had five minutes of break left after she hung up. She had gone to the cafeteria and bought a cup of tea, which she carried outside to drink while some of her friends smoked their cigarettes. As long as she had been a nurse, she had never quite been able to get over how many medical professionals still smoked. She thought it was insane, but there were many, many ways to die—most quicker than lung cancer—so perhaps smokers were just playing the odds, figuring a bullet or a heart attack or someone running a stop sign would get them before their lungs filled with soot.

Now she sat on a bench watching smoke waft up into the cones of light overhead and then disappear, and she thought about Frank. Worried about him. She hadn't seen him this engaged in his work in some time. He had always been a good cop, but these last few years he had become a little detached from the job. She had taken that as a good sign, a healthy change as he drew nearer retirement. With this case, though, he was back in it up to his eyeballs. This thirteen-year fixation he had with a missing girl was unsettling. And the fact that he had been drawn back into it by someone who wasn't even a real law enforcement officer concerned her. She didn't know if pursuing the case would get Frank in trouble, but if he didn't have Lt. Jackson's permission, it might.

Besides, it took Frank's head places she didn't want it to go. She had given up on the idea of having her own kids, but had always held onto a faint hope that she could marry someone with children, or adopt. Frank was adamant that he didn't want to be responsible for kids, didn't want to bring any into what he described as the "American decline." Detroit students had some of the lowest test scores in the country, he was fond of reminding her. She had thought maybe she could bring him around, but as long as his mind was focused on this missing child, that seemed unlikely.

So should she look elsewhere? She was smart, educated, had a good job, and wasn't hard on the eyes. How difficult could it be?

The wail of an ambulance ripping the night knocked such considerations from her head. She downed the last of the tea, crushed the cup, trashed it and went inside to get ready for whatever came next.

18

Frank beat Richie into the bathroom in the morning, but after a few minutes he came out again. "You want to use it before I shower, go ahead," he said. "And you might want to put on the radio or something, because I sing in the shower. Good and loud, too. Loud, anyhow."

"Thanks for the warning," Richie said. He went into the bathroom, where Frank had lined up a series of pills on the counter. "Jesus!" Richie called before he closed the door. "What are you, a pharmacist?"

"What?"

"All these pills!"

Frank came to the door, stepped inside, and fingered each pill in turn. "That's for my cholesterol," he said. "That's for allergies. Two Advil, for general aches and pains. Maybe I should take three, I'm gonna spend another day with you. That's an iron supplement, that's Vitamin C, and that"—he kept his finger on the last one, a blobby orange thing—"that's a Flintstone. Barney Rubble, to be precise."

"Maybe next time your mommy can let you pick the vitamins all by yourself," Richie said. "Now get the hell out of here, and close the door."

o o o

Without a warrant, Fairfax County officials wouldn't let Richie and Frank peruse the county's birth records. A local librarian proved more helpful, however, showing them how to use the library's historical newspaper index to search for birth announcements. They looked at *The Reston Times* and *The Fairfax Times* there, then went to other individual newspaper archives from throughout the county. Richie sat in front of a monitor dredging up internet records while Frank perched on a stool, grumbling and scanning ancient microfiche. The microfiche reader had a fine layer of dust on it and after about forty minutes, Frank launched into a sneezing fit.

Richie had allowed his attention to be diverted by a story about the murder of a teenage girl in Reston in the early 1970s, the first murder in that "new town's" history. He sensed, rather than felt, Frank's presence behind him. "There a baby girl in that story?"

"Not as young as we're looking for," Richie admitted. He closed the window and turned the swivel chair, glad Frank had drawn the stool straw. "I'm getting nowhere."

"I already got nowhere, on technology that was antique during the Civil War. I had to relight the candle three times."

"Candle?"

"I'm fucking with you, Maynard."

"I knew that." He had been pretty sure, anyway, but the last time he'd used a microfiche reader had been seventh grade, and honestly, his mind had been fixated on the way Cathy Hill had looked in her knee socks and plaid skirt.

"So what now?"

"We assume that Jarod Morton was lying somewhere along the line, to somebody."

Richie dragged his sneaker across the patterned carpet, making a mark. The library wasn't as quiet as he had expected. Libraries rarely were, he had learned, but even knowing that he never adjusted his expectations. Which said more about him, he guessed, than about libraries. "That's no surprise," he said. "But why? To who? His mom?"

"I don't know that. I just know he's a liar."

"Maybe somebody got the date wrong along the way. I've looked at every birth announcement within a year of where we thought it was, but maybe we need to cast a wider net."

Frank tapped the top of the monitor. "You got the wheel," he said. "I'll be in one of those comfortable chairs reading a magazine."

○ ○ ○

True to his word, Frank was semi-sprawled in a big chair with a copy of *The Atlantic* in his hands. He held it carefully, not curling the covers or breaking the spine. Intent on his reading, he didn't look up until Richie spoke his name. Then he carefully closed the magazine with one thick finger holding his place. "You look like death on toast, Maynard. What's up?"

Richie sat beside him. Frank put the magazine down on a table and straightened up, composing his face into a serious mask. "I think I found something," Richie said.

"Some mention of Angela?"

"Not precisely."

"What, then?"

"I found another story. A lot of stories, actually. About a little girl, six years old, named Kayley Ann Carrington."

"Never heard of her."

"She disappeared from her home in Herndon in 1995."

"Ninety-five? That's when the Mortons moved to Detroit."

"That's right. That's not all, either. The way she disappeared? She heard an ice cream truck and ran outside. Her mother grabbed a wallet and followed a minute or two later, but by the time she got out there, the girl was gone. It was the day after Kayley's birthday."

Richie watched Frank's face while he described what he had read. He had a feeling his own had gone through similar changes in front of the computer. First the man's jaw went slack, his eyes hooded, his mouth gaping open. The furrows that ran from beside his nose to the corners of his mouth deepened and the ones carving his forehead developed kinks.

"Tell me you made that up," he said when Richie finished. "Tell me this is your idea of a joke. I'll kick your ass, but then I'll get down on my knees and thank you."

"I would if I could."

"Oh my God."

"You should see the pictures."

"No."

"It's her, Frank. Kayley Ann Carrington is Angela Morton."

"But …"

"You can look at the screen, it's still up."

"Maynard, you have any idea what you're saying?"

Richie stared at the carpeting. He had given up making simple lines, now he was drawing circles and figure eights and triangles. He didn't see any of it; all he saw were pictures of a little blond girl with green eyes, an infectious smile, and the slightest overbite. "I'm saying Jarod Morton snatched Kayley and took her to Detroit, claiming that she was his daughter Angela. I'm saying he had something to do with Angela's disappearance. Maybe he was delusional enough to think Barbara would go along with it. Then when she came home and found Angela gone, he came up with the first story he could think of—the same trick he had used to get her in the first place."

"And it explains why his mother didn't know she had a grandchild until Jarod and Barbara were moving away," Frank added. "They took the girl. God knows what they told her, but in Detroit she had a new name."

"But then she disappeared again."

"Jarod again, obviously. Which means—"

Frank picked up where Richie didn't want to go. "It means she's dead, I expect."

"Probably Barbara knew how they got her, at least in the broad strokes."

"She damn sure knew she didn't give birth to her. Still, hard to believe a woman would go along with something like that. A mother."

"See, people think women are somehow immune to these heinous acts. Truth is, women can get as deeply into … heinosity, as men do. That's not a word, but you know what I mean."

"I guess."

"Katherine Mary Knight in Australia killed her husband, cooked his flesh, and tried to serve him to her stepchildren. Karla Homolka tried to make up for the fact that she wasn't a virgin when she met Paul Bernardo by drugging her little sister and letting him deflower her. Then when the sister died before he could do it, Karla found him another teenage virgin who looked a lot like her. Women can be every bit as awful as men. It's not as common, but it's not unheard of."

"Maybe Barbara was one of those, then. Maybe she was the one who wanted a daughter in the first place. But then Jarod killed the girl and hid the body somewhere. He didn't tell Barbara he was going to. She flipped out. She thought she had a daughter for life, and then she was gone. She made such a fuss...."

"She made such a fuss that she almost blew the whole thing. He didn't want a real investigation, but she demanded one."

"Good thing for him the bureau screwed up, isn't it?"

Frank turned on him, one massive paw clenched into a fist, an expression of pure rage twisting his face. He held it for a long minute, a sculpture carved by an artist with a grudge against the world. Then the muscles of his face all let go at once, and Richie didn't think he had ever seen a person look more sad.

"We fucked up," Frank said. "We didn't look closely enough at the right guy. We let Jarod and Barbara Morton kill that girl and disappear. You don't think he'd just stop, do you?"

"He won't stop, Frank. Pedophiles in general almost never lose the urge. Those who start to kill are even worse. Westley Allan Dodd admitted to having molested around two hundred and fifty kids by the time he was caught, which only happened after he murdered three boys and tried to snatch another. The Justice Department says most child molesters average almost four hundred victims. Pedro Alonso Lopez claimed to have killed more than three hundred and fifty young girls in South America, and he was able to show authorities a lot of dump sites to back up his story. People like them don't just stop."

Frank eyed Richie with an expression of distaste resting uneasily on his face. "You carry all that shit around in your head all the time?"

"Everybody needs a hobby."

"Man, you are one sick fuck."

"Not as sick as Jarod Morton. Who knows how many he's hurt since Detroit? He might have another victim in his house right now."

19

Charles Welker was at the mall when his phone rang. He kept it muted; only the insistent vibration in his pocket alerted him to the call, and he ignored that. A ringing phone might call attention to him. So might reaching into his pocket. He kept his hands visible. Non-threatening: that was the impression he wanted to create. He could be anyone. Nobody looking at him would have a reason to think twice.

When hunting one's own kind, one had to blend in.

But the hunting was poor, so he left the department store. So few parents shopped for their little ones at the big department stores anymore. They went to Target or Kmart, the more upscale ones to Gap Kids. Once department store children's sections had been rich territory, but no longer. He still tried them, out of habit, even though it had been years since one had borne fruit.

On the escalator, he tugged an earbud free and draped it over his shoulder, Bach leaking from the plastic nub. Slipping his phone from his pocket, he called into voicemail and listened to his message. He frowned, pressed a button to replay it.

He didn't like it, not one bit.

Welker had a plan. It had been in place for a very long time. The schedule was set, had been set, and now, now it looked as if he would have to speed things up. He hated to do that, but if it had to be, it had to be. Better to change the timetable than to lose everything. It meant sending a message, though. That was complicated.

Everything was so complicated.

A quartet of teenage girls strolled past, giggling, clutching plastic shopping bags. They dressed like whores, jeans so tight they were like nothing at all, breasts hanging out of their blouses. Welker looked at them and felt only contempt. They were already used up, their innocence and beauty long since spent. It was no coincidence that the great painters of history had always used children, naked children—angels—to symbolize beauty, to represent healthy sexuality.

Goosing the schedule, he hated that. Loved and hated it at once, loving the opportunity but fearful of changing something so long established. Already tension roiled his gut, tightened his shoulders, his neck, his jaw.

There was an arcade on the far side of the walkway. Arcades were popular hunting grounds. Fertile. He had discovered that on his own, and then he had learned, via the Internet, that others felt the same. The Web wasn't safe anymore, but back in the day it had been wide open. People had talked about anything, shared notes and photographs, met people who loved the way they did. Even met the occasional angel. A beautiful time, more innocent than today.

Arcades could be dangerous, though, because so many hunted there. Employees were trained in how to interfere with the free expression of human love. Police watched them closely. Welker stood outside, observing for several minutes before going in. He didn't see anyone who looked like an undercover cop. Two employees wore cheap red vests and nametags, and they were more involved with their own flirtation than in watching their customers. He went in, watched some boys playing shooting games, and an older couple, college maybe, laughing over a snowmobile race game. The place was noisy, raucous, and stank of body spray and adolescent sweat.

A girl played Whack-a-Mole, giggling hysterically each time she swung the oversized mallet. She was gorgeous, with dark ringlets and a sheen of perspiration lending a glow to her face. She wore a Winnie the Pooh T-shirt and yellow tights, baggy at the knees. Finding a doll that matched her would be a breeze.

When her game was done, she collected two yellow tickets from the slot. "You did good," Welker said.

"I know."

"You're strong."

"I whacked a lot of moles!"

"I saw that. What's your name?"

She looked at him, really noticing him for the first time. Her eyes were frank, appraising him clearly. "I'm not supposed to talk to people I don't know."

"I'm Perry." He gave her his biggest smile. "See, now you know me."

"I need to find my brother."

"He's just over there." Welker nodded toward a part of the arcade she couldn't see, behind a big sit-down game. He had no idea who her brother was, much less where. "How old are you?"

This was a question she was more comfortable with, and her answer was confident, even proud. "Five-and-a-half. I'm almost six."

"You're getting big," Welker said. Big, but too young for him. Just barely, but enough. "You should find your brother."

"Okay." She spun away from him and dashed off. He watched her go, a tiny pang of regret, of loss, snatching at his heart. Too young, though. He had standards.

Some things were just wrong.

He left the arcade, returning to the relative quiet and bright spaciousness of the mall.

The food court, maybe.

The tension from his phone call hadn't left him. He needed something to ease it.

Someone to love.

He needed an angel, and he needed her soon.

20

The apartment was on the eleventh floor of a high-rise building overlooking Lake Anne, in the oldest part of Reston. It wasn't large, but with the French door open and a springtime breeze wafting in off the balcony, it was airy and pleasant. Below, the sun glinted off the lake in crisp daggers of light. A sailboat cut between them bearing a young, tanned couple over the water.

Reston, from what Frank had read, was in many ways almost the anti-Detroit. That beautiful lake out the windows was man-made, and every inch of the city had been planned out before the first spadeful of earth was turned. Intended as an upper middle class bedroom community for D.C., when the nation's economic focus shifted from making things to moving information, Reston and the communities around it had experienced a digital gold rush. The flush years here were the bust years for the Motor City.

"When I retired, I sold my house in Centreville and got this place," Carl Mueller said. He was a beefy man, red-faced, with his shirtsleeves rolled up to expose hairy, ruddy forearms. His hands were large, the right one almost swallowing up the beer bottle he held although it was only three in the afternoon. "It's close to everything. I can walk to the store, to church. I can fish right downstairs. I got everything I need right here. Centreville was nice, but it's a rural community, y'know. Everything spread out, got to drive anywhere you go."

"It's a beautiful place," Frank said, a little surprised to find himself back in Reston so soon after the visit to Annette Morton. "I'm only a couple years away myself. Looking at this, at you, makes me wish it was tomorrow."

"Don't get me wrong, there's times I miss the job." Carl laughed. Northern Virginia was a pretty cosmopolitan place these days, full of federal employees and high-tech types, engineers, venture capitalists and so on. But here and there a thick Southern accent reminded Frank that the state had been the cradle of the Confederacy, once upon a time. "Not often, y'know, but now and again, sure. Sometimes I find myself thinkin' about it, the action, the excitement. But it's a young man's game, never knowin' what'll happen when you go through a door." He tipped the bottom of the bottle toward Richie. "You were on the job, too?"

"Patrol," Richie said. "Never made detective, and I decided it wasn't really for me."

"Takes a certain kind, for damn sure."

"Guess I wasn't that kind."

Carl took a seat, kicking back in a big leather recliner facing the balcony. There was a telescope on it. Frank wondered if it was for watching stars, or watching the people who lived on the other side of the lake. He didn't like to think that way about a brother in blue, but he got that vibe from the retired cop. "So you want to talk about Kayley Ann Carrington," Carl said.

"We stopped in at the Centreville PD and they told us you were lead on the case," Richie said. He turned his back to the view. Frank sat on a couch, legs apart, hands clasped and dangling between his knees.

"Bet your ass."

"Do you remember the details?" Frank asked.

"Some cases you don't forget. A year, five years, ten, don't matter. It's like it was yesterday. I could write out the same report today that I did at the time."

"I know the feeling," Frank said. He suspected that Carl Mueller was haunted by Kayley Ann Carrington, the way he was by … well, by the same girl, as it turned out.

Same girl, different disappearance.

"Every detective's got a few, I guess. So yeah, I remember her. What do you want to know?"

"We've read the news coverage," Richie said. "We know what was reported, but the Centreville cops wouldn't let us see the file. Fairfax County wouldn't even talk to us about it. Frank's got no jurisdiction here, no official standing. We hoped you could paint us a more detailed picture."

Carl drained off the last of his beer, set the bottle down on a table beside his chair, and got up. "Anybody want one?"

"No, thanks," Frank said.

"Your loss." Carl opened his refrigerator. Glass clinked, then the door shut and he returned to the recliner. He took a deep breath, swallowed some beer, and rubbed the back of his neck with his empty hand. "Kayley had just turned six, the day before. She had a party with some friends from kindergarten. In September she woulda gone into first grade. They played games, they ate cake and ice cream. Her favorite present was a backpack she was fixin' to use for school. Big girl school, she called it.

"Then the next day she heard the Good Humor truck and she ran outside to get herself a popsicle. This was a little country town, like I said, and ice cream trucks didn't go there every day like they do here in Reston, some other places. Her momma wasn't ready for it, she had to fumble for her wallet, fetch it outta her purse.

"Well, when she got outside, there's no Kayley. Ice cream truck's down the block, kids gathered around it. She asked after her daughter but no one saw her. No one saw another vehicle, but who woulda noticed something, everyone focused on the ice cream man? Kayley was gone. Just gone."

"You checked out the parents?"

"Of course. You got to look at the parents. Automatic, y'know. But they were clean as two whistles. Nothin' in their past, no suspicious behavior. They were distraught, of course, beside themselves. I still hear from 'em sometimes, wantin' to know if there's been any news."

"Were there any other suspects?" Richie asked. "Anybody who looked good for it?"

Carl cranked his head back, tipped the bottle. His lips were thick, rubbery, the bottle's rim disappeared between them. When he pulled it away, he stifled a belch with the back of his hand. "Nada," he said. "There was no one. Nobody saw anything, like I said. Nobody heard anything. We waited for a ransom demand, but nothing ever came. No clues, no tips—I take that back, plenty of tips but they was all worthless, time wasters, a lotta nothin'. I been a cop for a lot of years, I know there's always somethin', always a lead of some kind, just so long as you can find it. But here, there was nothin'. Like she went outta that front door and fell down an invisible well." He closed his eyes tightly. "Sometimes I still see her picture, when I'm tryin' to sleep. Every cop has cases he couldn't solve, that's part of the deal. But this one? Well, it wears on me, I don't mind sayin'. It wears on me."

"I hear you," Frank said. "Let me ask you something else." He showed Carl a photograph of Jarod Morton. "This guy look familiar?"

Carl studied it, chewing on his lower lip. "Yeah. Got a name?"

"Morton. Jarod Morton."

"Where from?"

"Here," Richie said. "He grew up in Reston."

"I didn't know many Reston kids, except the ones I went to school with. When I grew up, we all went to Herndon High. That was somethin', I tell you, all these Reston hippies in with the farm kids like me and the other hicks from the small towns, the blacks. A real meltin' pot, and sometimes it didn't melt together so good."

"He's younger than you," Richie said. "You wouldn't have gone to school with him."

"I'm just sayin'. Thing is, he looks familiar." He took the picture from Frank, examined it from different angles. "Morton. Yeah, I remember him."

"From what?" Frank asked.

"I don't think he was livin' in Reston then," Carl said. "Herndon. At least that's where his shop was." His voice gained confidence as his memory sharpened.

"Shop?"

"Portrait studio."

"Why do you remember that?"

"Those days, Herndon hadn't exploded like it has now. Or it was just. It was the early days of the tech boom, and it caught everybody by surprise. But because we'd all been small towns until then, all us cops had gone to school together, we paid attention to what each other was up to. We talked. Someone like this joker turned up, word spread fast."

"He did something?" Frank asked. "What was it?"

"He touched a kid. A little girl, in his studio. The girl complained, her parents freaked out, reported it. He said he was just trying to move her, posing her, you know, and his hand mighta slipped. In the end, the parents didn't press charges and it never went to trial. But you can bet cops talked about him, spread his name around. You know, watch out for this guy, that kinda thing."

"Professional courtesy," Frank said.

"Exactly."

"This was before Kayley's disappearance?" Richie was intense, leaning toward the retired cop like he was conducting an interrogation of a hostile suspect. "This thing with Morton touching the girl?"

"I think … yeah, it woulda been way before that."

"Did you look at Morton, then? When Kayley was abducted?"

"I think that's why I remember him. I talked to my buddy in Herndon, guy who had told me about him. But like I said, the parents hadn't wanted to prosecute, the little girl said it maybe happened like he claimed. Morton wasn't a convicted sex offender or anything, he was just a guy who had been accused, and then had the accusation withdrawn. There wasn't no reason to poke around in his business, any deeper than a quick glance. I talked to a couple of other guys, sex offenders, you know, but they all checked out."

"Morton and his wife moved to Detroit almost immediately after Kayley's abduction, did you know that?" Richie asked, the words pouring from him in an agitated tumble. "When they got to Detroit, they had a little girl. They called her Angela. Do you want to see her picture, Mr. Mueller?"

Frank saw Carl Mueller turn defensive. He put his feet on the floor, drawing his knees together. He hunched forward a little, lowering his shoulders, bringing his arms in front of his face. His eyes narrowed and the smile he wore sat coldly on his lips, not coming anywhere near his eyes.

Until this moment, Frank had not completely trusted Richie's motivation. He had thought that maybe the younger man looked at the Morton case as an intellectual exercise, or a way to prove something—to Frank? To his wife? Maybe just to himself. To prove that he could cut it as a detective.

Watching him, though, Frank was convinced. Richie genuinely cared about Angela Morton. At this instant, she was the most important person in the world. Frank felt a weight lift from his shoulders, as if now he could truly share his burden.

"Now look here," Carl said. "I didn't have any reason to suspect Morton. I said I talked to the guy in Herndon, guy who knew Morton. I didn't know him, only knew the story I'd heard. I had frantic parents on my hands, a missin' little girl out there somewhere. Course I looked in every direction, but some directions were more promisin' than others."

"Angela Morton was Kayley Ann Carrington," Richie said. Frank tried to signal him, to warn him to back off, but Richie was zeroed in on Carl. "If you had moved fast enough against Morton, you could have saved her."

Carl's head swiveled toward Frank, as if seeking an ally. "You couldn't have known," Frank said. "There wasn't enough to point you toward Morton. Were there any other incidents, abductions or molestations of young girls around that time that you can recall?"

Carl relaxed a little, his deep chest filling with air, his right fist unclenching. "There was something over in Falls Church. I had a couple of talks with cops over there about it, but it didn't go anywhere. A little girl who was picked up by a guy in a car. He drove her a couple of blocks then let her out, never touched her." He looked at the picture of Morton that he still held between the thumb and index finger of his left hand. "Guy could have been Morton, I guess, way she described him. If I'm rememberin' right, you know. It was a long time ago. No way to know for sure."

"Yeah," Richie said. "There are so many guys like that around—"

This time Frank cut him off with a slashing motion of his hand. "One more name for you, Mr. Mueller, and we'll get out of your hair, leave you to your pleasant retirement."

Carl looked somewhat shell-shocked, but he nodded his head.

"The name Barbara Alderdyce? That mean anything to you?"

"You're askin' about ancient history here. I don't have my files, you know. Haven't looked at some of those in a decade. More than."

"I'm just asking if it rings any bells."

"Yeah." He handed the photograph back to Frank, scooped up the beer bottle like it was a life vest and he a drowning man. "Yeah, it rings a bell, all right. I locked up her old man, Kent Alderdyce. He tied Barbara and her sister to chairs, made them watch while he worked over his wife, their mother, so bad she spent three weeks in the hospital. Her jaw was wired shut, y'know, she ate soup through a straw. I'll never forget Kent Alderdyce. I'm pretty sure one of the daughters was Barbara. Not a common name in these parts, Alderdyce."

"There were two daughters?" Richie asked. "That's what you said, she had a sister?"

"I think the other girl's name was Claire."

"Does she still live in the area?"

"She killed herself. Hanged herself in her garage, right after Barbara got married."

"What about the father?"

"Oh, Kent's still around. His wife divorced him after that hospital trip, left the area, but he didn't go anywhere."

"You remember where he lives?"

"I can get you the address." He got out of his chair again, took a phone from the kitchen counter. "That's easy, only take a minute."

21

When Kent Alderdyce had been arrested all those years ago, his house would have been out in the country. It still looked like a small rural home, sagging under the weight of years, its peeling paint long since bled of any color, but the greater Washington metropolitan area had surrounded it and appeared to be closing in fast. Afternoon traffic was thick, delaying Frank and Richie's arrival until the sun was going down.

"You scared Mueller," Frank said as he parked outside the house. "You get a little intense."

"That's a problem? Guy was a cop. He could have saved Angela—Kayley, whatever her name is. Could have avoided all this, allowed her to have a regular childhood, but he didn't go after the one guy he knew in the area who liked to grab little girls."

"He said he interviewed other sex offenders. He didn't have enough to go on with Morton."

"It's a good thing self-justification is a renewable resource, because he's using more than his share. I can't believe you're excusing him."

"I'm just explaining. I know how he feels. Maynard, I kick myself every day for failing that girl. The way I can live with myself is that I did what I could. I'm sure he feels the same way."

"So if you make a mistake, it's okay as long as you tried."

"Human beings make mistakes. We do what we can. Trying is all we got."

"Sorry, Frank. You want me to go easier on Alderdyce?"

"I want you to remember that you're not a cop. Here, I'm not either. Alderdyce cooperates, we can talk to him. He tells us to go fuck ourselves, we put on condoms and walk out the door."

"That's a fetching image."

"Just let me take the lead."

"You're the boss."

"Remember that." He got out of the car and walked to the front door. Maynard was unhappy about being dressed down, but Frank didn't want him stepping outside the lines and maybe setting them both up for a harassment beef.

He climbed three concrete steps and was reaching for the doorbell when the door squealed open. "Y'all cops or tax collectors?"

Frank chuckled and showed his badge to a man in his sixties, with steel-gray hair cut as short as a wire brush and a lean, angular face. A hawk's face, predatory. Some men started pumping iron in the gym or the joint and never stopped. This man was one of those. There would be a weight bench in the back yard or the basement. No, probably in a bedroom vacated by one of the daughters, that would make more sense. Get the girls out of the house and take over their space for his own narcissistic pursuits. Free weights, too, not some pussy Bowflex deal. His pecs bulged against a grease-stained white tee, biceps stretching the sleeve openings, forearms corded and taut. He had tattoos on both arms, some of them jailhouse but others more elaborate and colorful.

"Kent Alderdyce?"

"Could be."

"I'm Frank Robey, a detective with the Detroit police department. My associate, Mr. Krebbs, is investigating in a private capacity."

"Detroit, you say?"

"That's right. You don't have to talk to us, but we'd appreciate a few minutes of your time. We're not trying to jam you up behind anything, sir, we're just trying to locate your daughter Barbara."

"Y'all're lookin' for Barbie?"

"Yes, sir."

"Come on in." He moved away from the door, making room for them to enter a small, cluttered combination living and dining room.

"Callie," he said. "Couple cops here looking for Barbie."

A slender woman emerged from the kitchen, wiping her hands with a dishtowel. She barely came to her husband's shoulder, and she was at least twenty years his junior, far too young to be Barbara's mother. "Welcome to our home," she said. Her smile looked as genuine as plastic pearls.

"Thank you, ma'am," Frank said. "We'll be out of your hair in no time."

"If you can find Barbara, you stay as long as you'd like." She glanced toward the floor, then shook the towel in the direction of the kitchen. "I'll—excuse me."

She hurried back to where she'd come from. There was no door between the kitchen and the front room. Frank couldn't see her, but he heard her clattering around in the kitchen.

"Have you heard anything from Barbara?" Richie asked.

"Not in years. I was hopin' maybe y'all had somethin' new to go on."

"After she left here, she moved to Detroit, right?"

"How would I know? My first wife, Alyson, she took Barbara and Claire and walked out on me. I tried to get in touch with 'em, but she did everything she could to turn the girls against me. It worked, too."

"That was after you put her in the hospital, right?" Richie asked. "And went to jail?"

"That was nothin'. A domestic dispute, that's all. Got blowed way out of proportion. She'd been lookin' for an excuse, anything, to dump me, and that was all it took."

"Well, we weren't there so we can't say," Frank said. It turned his stomach to be civil to a man like this, a man who had bound his own daughters and forced them to witness the systematic beating of their mother. Kent could kick them out with a word, though. They had to play him carefully. "So you haven't heard from her since she moved away? Were you at her wedding?"

"Heard about it. People talk, right? But I wasn't invited. I expect Alyson was."

"Gentlemen?" Callie came out of the kitchen again, carrying a tin tray with cans of beer, glasses, and an iced tea pitcher crowded together on it. She handled it like an experienced waitress, but there was a tentativeness to her voice, the slightest quaking in her hands. "Would you like something to drink? Kent likes some sweet tea this time of day, but we've also got juice, beer, milk and water."

Frank looked to Alderdyce for a cue, but the man didn't even glance at his wife. "You know what I want," he said.

"Oh, of course, I'm so sorry." She set the tray down on the dining table and poured tea into a glass, ice cubes tumbling from the pitcher. "Here's your sweet tea, darling."

He took the glass from her and downed a big drink, swallowing loudly. "Y'all want anything?" he asked, his lips glistening.

"No," Frank said. "Thank you, we're fine."

"Well, I wish I could tell you somethin' useful. But I just don't know what to say."

Callie took the tray back into the kitchen. She moved back and forth quickly and quietly. Walking on eggshells, as if to speak too loudly or move too suddenly might attract her husband's wrath.

Frank found himself despising the man. He had reason, if only theoretical; his reaction was more in response to what he had heard about Kent Alderdyce than to anything he had witnessed. Alderdyce was physical, he was blunt, and he was far from diplomatic. He frightened his young wife. All that added up to a man that Frank wouldn't want to hang out with, but it didn't really merit his instant, visceral distaste.

Still, his temper was flaring, and it wouldn't take much for Alderdyce to set him off. Frank was a physical man as well, not unfamiliar with violence or unskilled at dealing it out. He didn't like that in himself and he tried to tamp it down when he could. But he didn't think it wise to try to deny it.

And Kent Alderdyce was bringing it out. Frank breathed heavily, sweat trickling down his ribs. He had to get away from the man before he took a swing.

"Excuse me, Mrs. Alderdyce?" he said suddenly. He went into the kitchen without giving Kent a chance to react. He heard the man complain, but Callie was already closing the refrigerator and regarding him curiously.

"Yes?"

He spoke rapidly, keeping his voice low. "Ma'am, I'm a police officer. I've seen a lot of women in difficult situations."

"I'm afraid I don't—"

"I'm telling you, I've seen women whose husbands batter them. I know the signs. I see the way you act around your husband, like if you blinked wrong he'd come at you."

"No, you're wrong, I'm sorry, but there's nothing like that—"

"You know why he went to prison, right? Why he lost his wife and daughters? You know Claire committed suicide when she knew Barbara was away from here for good?"

Callie's right hand went to her mouth. Her nails were immaculate, polished and long. Her makeup had been applied carefully, too, and Frank thought maybe there was some shading on her left cheek, underneath the foundation. "I don't …"

"Just go, ma'am. As fast as you can. Get to a shelter, leave the state, take a new identity. He isn't going to change. And if you don't get away from him, sooner or later he's liable to kill you."

O O O

Richie moved between Kent Alderdyce and the kitchen door. The powerfully built man took a step toward him, leading with chin and chest.

"When Henry Lee Lucas and Charles Manson went to school for the first time—first day of first grade—their mothers dressed them in girls' clothes," Richie told him. "Both of them. You know who they are, right? Serial killer and cult leader?"

"Heard of 'em, I guess. What's it to me?"

"I'm just saying, maybe you're lucky you had girls. Maybe if you had appreciated them more you'd still have them."

"I still don't—"

"I don't mean anything by it. Just an observation, that's all. How a kid is brought up has an impact on the rest of that person's life. Some folks never have a chance, their parents are so wretched. I'm just making a comment."

In fact, what he was doing was trying to talk loudly enough to drown out what Frank was saying to Callie in the other room. Frank's voice rumbled like thunder from a distant storm, and Richie didn't think Kent would like what Frank was saying.

Richie had learned much about crime and criminals, but when he had been on the job, he rarely had a chance to use that acquired knowledge. As a result, the moments he had enjoyed the most, the ones he still recalled with pleasure, were those occasions that got his adrenaline pumping. Running down a drug dealer, through streets and alleyways. Getting into a fight with a pimp armed with a knife— a real brawl that ended with both of them bruised and bloody, the pimp in cuffs. The one time he'd fired his weapon, at a guy cranked up on some stupefying drug cocktail that had convinced him he was immortal and left him so paranoid that he reacted to the arrival of a police car by unloading a shotgun at it. Richie's three shots had missed anything vital, but his partner had put one squarely in the man's chest.

Now, up in Kent's face, he felt the same adrenaline surge that had wired him up on those occasions. He wouldn't mind a bit if Kent swung on him. In a fight, the big man could certainly kick his ass. But Richie would enjoy every second of it.

"You need to get out of my way," Alderdyce said. His fists were clenched, his muscles tensed. This was it. Bring it, big guy, Richie thought, going up on the balls of his feet, ready to move in any direction. Let's mix it up.

"We're leaving," Frank said from behind him. His deep voice was startling. He tapped Richie on the back, and swept past him. "Thanks for your cooperation, Mr. Alderdyce."

"What did you say to her?"

"That's none of your concern, sir. I just think you ought to know that there'll be people keeping an eye on you. And on her. Just bear that in mind."

"Listen here, y'all can't come into my house with your high-toned, fancy-talkin' bullshit and—"

"It's impressive, isn't it?" Richie interrupted. "He dresses himself, too. And him a black man. Hardly seems possible."

"I believe we're done here," Frank said. "Good evening, Mr. Alderdyce."

Frank covered the room in a few quick strides. Richie followed. No fight after all. Still, his heart raced and his blood was on fire. He felt alive in a way he hadn't in months.

Frank slid in behind the wheel and Richie took his usual passenger seat. "Call Carl Mueller," Frank said.

"Why?"

"I want him to have some of his law enforcement buddies watching Alderdyce. I told the wife to get out, but she wouldn't go, not right away. I could be wrong, but I wouldn't be surprised to see him go after her tonight. I want someone to be close by so they can move in when he gets violent. Guy gets on my damn nerves, and that's a fact."

22

While Frank showered the next morning, Richie used his cell to call Wendy. He had checked in last night, but only briefly, the Kent Alderdyce visit weighing on him. In the morning, they exchanged glancing pleasantries for a couple of minutes, the sort that a man didn't mind speaking when there was another man in the next room. When she abruptly switched topics, he knew she had something significant to say.

"So, I had lunch with Marcia yesterday. We had a nice chat."

"Oh, really? What did you two talk about?"

"We talked about you."

"Me?"

"Both of you. You and Frank."

"Surely you could have found something more interesting—"

"It is, after all, the men in our lives that Marcia and I have in common," Wendy interrupted. She had a tendency to do that.

"I suppose that's true."

"Of course it is."

"What about us?"

"About the ways in which you're alike, and how you're different."

"Such as?"

"I told her about how you're a romantic. You bring home flowers, you perform little gestures that are essentially meaningless, but very pleasant just the same."

"Okay …"

"Frank's not that way."

"I wouldn't expect him to be." The shower had ended, and the toilet flushed. He tried to block it, to concentrate on what Wendy was saying.

"Well, apparently he's in love with Marcia. Marcia's sure she's in love with him. But he's somewhat commitment-shy, let's say. He tells her he loves her but he won't take any of the steps that might lead to a deeper, more permanent and profound relationship."

"He's a cop, remember," Richie reminded her. Frank came out of the bathroom, a towel wrapped around his substantial waist, and started digging in his suitcase for his clothes. "It's hard for cops to put that aside at the end of the day."

Frank raised an eyebrow at this. He was still rifling his luggage, but he was listening.

"What else?" Richie asked.

"I told her there are … issues that we're dealing with. That things are not always perfect in paradise."

"You told her that?"

"You think I should have lied to her?"

"Maybe by omission. A little bit, anyway."

"I didn't tell her everything. Just that things were great, but they could always be better."

Richie knew what she meant. The stresses over money, over his job, over his moods, his depression. Their disagreements over whether or not to have children. The stresses always seemed to revolve around him. She was the rock, he the uncertain tide. But he let it go; this wasn't the time to get into a conversation like that.

"She described him as solid and dependable," Wendy said. "Admirable traits, if not necessarily sexy."

"Anyway," Richie said, unwilling to respond out loud to that.

"Anyway, I'm just saying. She could stand for him to be more like you in some ways. And I could probably stand for you to be a little more like him. But not a lot. I love the way you are."

"Thanks," Richie said, feeling a little awkward. "I love you, too."

"We talked about other things too. The hospital, the city. But I won't bore you with the details."

"Thanks," Richie said again.

"You should get some breakfast," Wendy said.

"I'm planning on it."

"Have a good day, my love."

"You too."

Frank finished dressing as Richie put away the phone. "What was all that?"

"You don't want to know."

"Oh, I do. You have no idea how much."

"They had lunch yesterday. Wendy and Marcia."

"They did?"

"They did. And talked about us."

"What else is there? Probably had to fan themselves afterward. Getting each other all hot and bothered thinking about our animal natures."

"I'm not sure it went like that."

"That's how it's going in my head," Frank said. "You can play it any way you want in yours."

"You about ready for breakfast?" Richie asked. "I'm starving. I've never known a man who took so long in the shower."

"I'm trying to put off calling Lieutenant Jackson back."

Richie had forgotten that. Frank's phone had gone off early that morning, and Frank had let voicemail take it. But while he listened to the message, a shadow seemed to pass across his face. "Bad news?" Richie had asked.

"Jackson," Frank said, naming his boss. "I'm supposed to call him back. Which ain't good."

"You going to get it over with?"

"I'll wait," Frank said.

"Okay. While you wait, I'm taking a shower."

Now they'd both showered, and Frank still hadn't called the lieutenant. "Let's get breakfast," he said.

"Before you make your call?"

"I don't want to spoil my appetite."

"Well, mine's about to turn my stomach inside out and start eating itself, so I'm ready."

"Let's go," Frank said. "And let's leave our phones in the room."

○ ○ ○

After breakfast, Richie sprawled on his bed wearing jeans and a long-sleeved black tee, facedown, his legs kicked up at the knees, reading one of Frank's comics. He looked like a high school kid. He was jabbering about something, but Frank was on the horn with Lt. Jackson and trying his damnedest to block out Richie's commentary.

When the call was over, he closed his phone and sank into the desk chair. They'd done everything Frank could think of to delay returning the lieutenant's call, short of running over his phone with the rental car.

"Something?"

"Talking to the Lieut."

"So this Superman, he's squeaky clean, isn't he? Anybody else had his powers, he'd be sneaking peeks through dresses, apartment walls, right? If I was him and I came up against some lowlife meth cooker, I'd punch him so hard his head would go into orbit."

"I have to go home," Frank said.

"Home where?"

"Where you think? How many homes I got, like I'm Donald Trump or some shit? Home Detroit."

"Why? It's not like you're not working."

"This trip's on me, you know that. Jackson says I've got cases piling up, hot ones, not thirteen-year-old cold cases. They need me there."

"Well, the department's stretched pretty thin, I guess."

"It is that."

"So, when?"

"Today. Now. I gotta get to the airport, see if I can't grab a flight. He wants me at the precinct before the end of the day."

Richie sat up, closed the comic, and tossed it on a pile of them at the edge of the bed. "So that's it, Frank? We're done? After what we found out about Kayley Ann Carrington, we just walk away?"

"Don't be putting words in my mouth, Maynard. I said *I* have to go. Don't mean you do."

"You think I should keep on it?"

"Maybe I suffered an ear injury somewhere. I could have sworn I just heard you talking about how much progress we've made."

"We found out who Angela Morton really was. That doesn't get us any closer to knowing what happened to her."

Frank ticked off his points on the fingers and thumb of his left hand. "We know who she was. We know Jarod Morton took her. We know when Angela disappeared, the story he told was a straight-ahead description of how he did it the first time. That means he was responsible for that disappearance too. He made his own stolen daughter vanish."

Richie fell backward on the bed. The stack of comics shook, and a couple of them slid off onto the floor. "Pick those up," Frank demanded.

"Sorry." Richie straightened, bent forward, and picked up the comics.

"Superman is a straight arrow," Frank said. "He doesn't kill, doesn't break the law, doesn't take the easy way out. He does what's right, what's decent. He's an alien, here on Earth through an accident of fate, but he loves his adopted world and his adopted country as much as any native American. He teaches about honesty, about decency, about ethical living."

"He's not exactly the life of the party, is he?"

"He might be a little humor-challenged sometimes, but he's no Batman. Now that dude is one sour-ass motherfucker."

"I'd accept help from either of them on this case. I get that Morton's still out there, maybe. Still a threat. But I don't quite see where to go from here. I've never worked a case like this."

"You go to Tucson. That's the last place we know he was, so that's where we start. Anyway, I'm not saying I won't help you, Maynard. I'm just gonna have to do it from Detroit is all. I'll be a phone call away."

"Keep your battery charged."

"We need to get to the airport, man. You can put your Tucson ticket on my credit card."

"Dude, I'm putting *everything* on your card."

O O O

Driving to Dulles, Richie was uncharacteristically quiet, his jaw twitching from time to time, fingers clenching on the wheel, then loosening again. Frank fiddled with the radio, tired of satellite and wanting something local, knowing there had to be some Washington soul stations with a strong enough signal to find from here. He found one and cranked the volume when he recognized Marvin's "Inner City Blues."

"Makes you want to holler sometimes, and throw up both your hands," he said.

"What's that?" Richie asked. Frank didn't know if he was asking what the song was, or what made him want to holler.

"It's Marvin Gaye," Frank said. Tackle the simpler question first. The other would take longer to explain than they had. "The Prince of Soul."

"That's good?"

"Just because you're young and white don't mean you shouldn't be educated about some of the best music in the world, Maynard. What do you listen to?"

Richie shrugged. "Whatever Wendy has on, I guess. Or whatever's on WCSX."

"You got to surround yourself with beauty, man. With life's finer things. Keeps a man grounded."

"Didn't Marvin Gaye shoot his father?"

Frank shook his head sadly. Maynard wasn't stupid, he was narrowly focused. That was just like him—the only thing he remembered about Marvin was the murder. "Other way around. Marvin Gay senior shot Marvin. He said Marvin beat him up first. It was bad all around, no question. Those were two men who would have been better off they'd had a grandma around."

"A grandma?"

Frank watched the trees blur alongside the car. "Black men— those who do well in the world—have a lot of respect for their grandmothers. They show us what's right and wrong, point us down the proper path. Don't put up with any shit, you know?"

"Mothers can't do that?"

"They can. But sometimes it takes a certain amount of experience to gain the appropriate wisdom. And it's always easier to stay smart when it ain't your own kid in trouble, but your kid's kid. Of course, a lot of grandmothers wind up raising their grandkids anyway."

"What about your mom?" Richie asked. "You going to make her a grandmother one of these days?"

Frank chuckled. "Don't let's get carried away, son," he said. "I believe that train has left the station. At my age, being a father would kill me dead. You're young, though, you could still have kids."

"Wendy wants them," Richie said. "But there's no Mama Krebbs to be a grandmother."

"Sorry to hear that," Frank told him. "I got both my parents still, and enough close family to field my own football team."

"Must be strange," Richie said. "Not strange, different. My folks are both gone, my brother, too."

"Yeah," Frank said. He was quiet for a minute. "My pops, though, he ain't well. Heart problems. Sinking fast, really, what Mama says."

Richie's hands were tight on the wheel, his knuckles white. "Sorry to hear that, man."

"Thanks."

"The fucked-up thing about life is that sooner or later you've got to say goodbye to everyone you ever loved. You leave them behind or they leave you, doesn't matter which. That good-bye day is gonna come around."

"Sure enough is."

"You build a room for 'em in your heart, and then one day that room's empty, and it never gets filled again."

"Can we talk about something else? How about them Pistons?"

"Yeah, sorry," Richie said. "Wendy says I have a morbid streak. If she knew the half of it, she'd have me committed."

"She don't, maybe I will."

"Speaking of kids, you remember that one I told you about, Wil Fowler?" Richie asked as he followed airport signs toward the rental car return.

"One L Wil," Frank said. "The punk you caught bustin' into the Morton house."

"That's right."

"What about him?"

"You think you could check in on him, after you get back? I want to make sure he's keeping out of trouble."

"Seems like he goes looking for it. Wasn't for trouble you never would've met him."

"I don't think he's a bad kid. I know he was trying to break in. But that house had been empty for so long, it's not like he was trying to steal anything."

"He was after something. Maybe his problem is that he's too dumb to know a recent empty from an old one." Frank figured the kid for a dope fiend of some kind. He'd fooled Maynard, but maybe that wasn't hard to do. Fowler was like ten thousand other kids in Detroit, kids who'd been seduced by dope and would do whatever they could to get money to buy it. He had seen the Morton house, not a bad looking house despite its age, and guessed there was something there worth having. Copper wiring, plumbing fixtures, anything that could be sold. Scrappers did it all the time.

Frank didn't have much patience for that kind. He worked to help people, to keep the streets safe, and the people who took part in the drug trade, users and sellers alike, were flushing their own lives away. They wrecked their lives while pumping money into cartels that bought American guns and used them to kill anyone who got in their way. In northern Mexico, bodies were stacking up like firewood in the fall, and it was spilling over into the American border region. Last thing he wanted to do was to babysit some junkie who had made a good impression on Richie Krebbs.

But Richie kept looking over at him. He wouldn't let it go. And it didn't have to cost Frank much effort or time. "I'll look in on him," he promised. "Okay?"

"That'd be great. Just let me know."

"I will."

"Thanks."

"You'll be good, Maynard. Go to Tucson, find that asshole Morton."

Richie pulled into a long line of rental returns and killed the engine. "Don't worry about me, Frank. I'll track him down."

"I'm not worried. You stay on your toes, that's all. I'll talk to you whenever I can."

They hauled their bags from the trunk while a young, lanky white guy in a uniform jacket and a ball cap inspected the car. "Here we go," Richie said. "Let's get to the terminal and buy us some full-price, last minute airline tickets."

"Fuck it," Frank said. "Who needs to retire, anyway? I'll just work until I drop."

23

Richie had never been west of the Mississippi. He knew it was more of a cliché than an actual dividing line: splitting the country, but falling a good distance east of its midpoint. Still, he watched out the airplane's window as the continent unspooled, its flat center sliding past, with the steep wall of the Rockies holding it in. As they traveled south he saw what looked like bare earth, and lots of it; only when the plane dropped closer to land could he make out patches of green dotting it.

At the Tucson airport, he followed signs up a ramp and out of the building, into air that felt superheated and oven-dry compared to the Michigan springtime or even-more-humid Virginia. The heat seemed to suck the moisture from his pores. He would have to pick up some bottled water or risk desiccation.

He thought he had strayed into an alien landscape. Tall, fat saguaro cacti, the kind seen in just about every Western movie ever made, stood in swaths of dun-colored gravel. Other plants, spiked things that might have emerged from the imagination of Dr. Seuss, comprised the rest of the visible landscaping.

A breezeway led into another enclosed space containing the auto rental company counters. He went to the Budget desk and showed his ID. In a short while, he had a rented Nissan—which he hoped none of his Motor City friends saw him driving—and he was headed toward a strip of low-rent motels alongside I-10.

The truth was, he didn't have too many friends to worry about. Being fired from the job had broken him, as surely as if someone had cut the cord to an electrical appliance. He'd let his personal relationships go to hell, with the possible exception of his marriage; had stopped calling people, stopped attending social functions, stopped feeling like he had anything to offer in conversation. He'd stayed at home with his books and journals, poring over the lives and crimes of serial killers, arsonists, rapists, and pedophiles, learning what he could about how they worked and what drove them. He couldn't say if he would ever have a chance to apply his esoteric knowledge, but he had given some consideration to writing a book about the subject, if he could come up with new and different insights.

Now, though, he had been granted another chance. He had a new friend in Frank, and a new opportunity to put his knowledge to work in a way that could help someone. Among the disturbing facts clogging his brain was that even after prison or therapy—or both— devoted pedophiles almost always returned to their old ways.

If Jarod Morton yet lived, he was still abusing young girls.

They had to find him.

But he couldn't just waltz into the Tucson police headquarters and ask if Morton was in town. Even with Frank along, the Virginia police had barely tolerated them. Cops had routines, procedures for sharing information, but they took time and the pulling of strings. He and Frank hadn't followed those. Richie didn't have any legal status at all, and could count on no cooperation from the locals. He was on his own in this strange new world.

Once inside his room at the Lazy 8 Motel, next door to a steak joint called the Silver Saddle, air conditioner rumbling beneath the window, he took the phone book from a nightstand drawer and flipped through it. He didn't expect to find Jarod Morton listed; in this respect, at least, Tucson lived up to his expectation.

That token gesture completed, he fired up his laptop and navigated to the archives of *The Daily Star*, Tucson's daily newspaper. He typed Morton's name into the search box, and again came up empty. Next he typed the words "missing girl," and watched the wheel spin while the website considered his request. This search turned up a disturbing number of stories. Richie had to pay a small fee for an archive account, but then he spent the next several hours reading about missing girls, from as young as eleven months to as old as eighteen years. They had been abducted by relatives, by strangers, by caretakers. They had run away. Some had never been found, and no clues seemed to exist as to their whereabouts. One had turned up in a small village in the interior of Mexico, four years after her disappearance. Another was found in Pasadena, Texas, working at a brothel frequented by oil field roughnecks.

Many, though, were found dead.

Richie took out a small notebook and started making notes on the cases that shared at least superficial similarities. He was looking for victims in the age range that Morton seemed to like, looking for blondes, looking especially for any cases in which a girl disappeared from her own home while she was there with her father, and the mother was absent. Not that Morton would necessarily pull the same stunt again, but he might, since it had worked at least once.

There were so many missing kids in the news; too many. Richie had told Frank about Westley Alan Dodd. He knew the stories of Danielle Van Dam and Samantha Bree Runnion and Amber Hagerman. He'd heard about Catholic priests with abuse allegations numbering into the hundreds. Those were just the cases that dominated the news, but from the looks of things, if every victimized kid made headlines, there wouldn't be any room left for other stories.

He went to missingkids.com, the website of the National Center for Missing & Exploited Children, and spent some time reading the stories and statistics there. When he finished he was drenched in cold sweat, as if someone had emptied a pitcher of ice water down his back. He shut off the room's air conditioner and took a warm shower.

Wendy wanted kids, and he thought he had too. But how did you bring beautiful, innocent creatures into a world where predators waited like wolves with slavering jaws eyeing plump little rabbits? How could you protect them from dangers you couldn't see, could barely comprehend?

Probably you couldn't. Richie knew more about the dangers lurking out there than most people ever would. Sometimes Wendy told him he knew too much about the awful things that could happen, and not enough about the good. But so many people who became victims never saw it coming because they didn't know the possibilities. Richie would not be one of those. He wanted to protect everyone, but that was a burden he was not strong enough to carry. Not even Frank's hero Superman could do that.

At any rate, they had stopped using birth control. They hadn't had any luck yet. And if having a kid was expensive, he had learned, it was nothing compared to the cost of fertility treatments, should they be required, even with the decent medical insurance Wendy got from her city job.

When he returned to the desk, slightly revived by the shower, Richie had a lot of notes but nothing concrete. He had found no positive indication that Morton had ever lived in Tucson, much less preyed upon the local population. On the other hand, there was plenty of evidence that somebody had, or more likely, many somebodies over the years.

Before he shut down the machine, he did one more thing. In his word processing program, he designed some business cards. He would be visiting people, potential witnesses, even people who had known Morton, if he could find any. He put his name and cell phone number on the cards, and at the bottom typed "Private Investigator." He studied that for a few minutes, unsure, then deleted those words. Frank had introduced him that way, and he could probably get away with saying it. But putting it in print was dangerous. In Michigan it wasn't particularly hard to get a PI's license; on the basis of his years with the PD and his short time with Rampart, he would qualify, and would just need to have Detroit's chief of police sign off on it.

For now, though, he would have to imply that he was a PI, taking great pains to let people know he wasn't a cop. Satisfied, he found a shop that could print the cards for him, then closed the laptop and stretched out on top of the bed for a quick nap.

o o o

"I've heard people say that too much of anything is not good for you, baby," Frank began, keeping his voice in its lowest register. "But I'm not—"

"Oh no you don't," Marcia interrupted. "Don't you go gettin' all Barry White on me. Not now."

"I'm just saying I missed you, baby." She had picked him up at the airport and was driving him home. He had been hoping for some loving when they got there, but it seemed the conversation was taking a different turn.

"You missed me, you should've stayed here. Or you should be here when you *are* in town."

"I try to be, Marcia. You know the job's irregular, keeps me working strange hours."

"Like mine don't? I make time for you, Frank. You don't do me the same courtesy." Her hands were tight on the wheel and she kept her gaze dead ahead, not even sparing him a glance. That told him she was serious—if she was only ranking on him, she'd let him know it.

"You know I love you, babe."

"If I do know it, it ain't because you done anything lately to show me."

"I tell you all the time—"

"And now you're not even listening! I said *show* me, not tell me. There's a difference."

Woman lived in scrubs, but she could pull it off like not many he had known. She had enough in back, and up front too, swelling those baggy clothes in the best places and letting them hide any imperfections. Way she was sitting, so far away from him that if she shoved over any more she'd have to reach in through the window to steer the car, Frank didn't guess she was going to let him see any of those imperfections in person, at least not before some serious apologizing happened. "I know that, Marcia."

"Then act like it. I'm not asking for a marriage proposal, just a little effort, a little commitment to the relationship. That's a scary word, commitment, ain't it? But that's what I want, and instead you're running all over the country with your new buddy, chasing after a case that ain't even yours." She took in a deep, hitching breath. "I had to watch a young man die last night with three bullets in his chest. I don't want the same to happen to you, goddamnit."

She turned a corner and they were on his block. Her eyes glistened. "How's that old bastard McNabb?" she asked, pointing to a house four down from Frank's. Frank always used the three words together when discussing his neighbor, and Marcia had picked up the habit. "He still as rude as ever?"

"Meanest man ever walked the Earth," Frank replied. "Saw him shoot a puppy last week."

"Really?" Now she looked at him, her eyes wide and damp.

"No. But it wouldn't surprise me a bit if he did."

"God damn, you are a terrible person. Maybe I should date old bastard McNabb 'stead of you. Probably make me a happy woman."

"You could try it," Frank said. "Have to get past the alligators in his moat first."

Marcia pulled into Frank's driveway and cut the engine. "Am I getting out?" she asked.

"I'd like it if you did."

"You might try making me feel like you mean that, Frank."

"Come inside," he said, "and I'll do what I can. For about an hour … then I got to get to work. Lieutenant is expecting me today."

"An hour, huh? I guess I can try to finish that fast, long as you do your best work."

Frank opened the car door and got out, stretching his cramped muscles before getting his bag from Marcia's trunk. He had skated, this time.

Didn't mean it would last, though.

24

Welker sat in his car, fingers tapping lightly on the steering wheel, beating out a rhythm nobody else could hope to hear. It was there in the pulse of his blood through his veins, in the hammering of his heart, the screech of adrenaline coursing through him. A sweet sad symphony of love and longing.

He wanted to start the engine, back out of the parking space, and race home. He wanted to resist his urges. They were normal, natural, as much a part of him—of every human being—as fingers or toes. But that didn't mean they didn't cause him pain, pain that came from knowing that some people misunderstood, didn't believe he only meant the best for his angels.

He could no more deny his feelings than he could deny his heartbeat, or his breathing. He had tried too many times, failing always. When he felt like this—every nerve cell in his body tingling, the world outside the limits of his body somehow off, as if his senses had been knocked a quarter of the way out of whack, floating through life—there was only one way to make it all real again. He had work piling up; he'd been unavailable to his clients for days. He knew he should go home and tend to that, forget about the hunt.

But he also knew he couldn't. He was too far out there, in the zone, a hunter with the scent of his prey tickling his nostrils.

And there she was.

She played in a sandbox, mounding sand up into shapes that her mind probably imagined were romantic castles. The angel's mother sat on a bench, earbuds shoved into her nodding head, reading a fat hardcover novel with romantic echoes of its own, Welker had heard, and meant for much younger readers. For teenagers. The angel's mother had married badly, and now she sought the love she had never felt in the pages of a book. That's not where you find it, he wanted to tell her. You need a man, a real man, to show it to you.

You should have found one before you got to be too old. The mother must have been in her mid-twenties; the angel, six-and-a-half or seven. Just right. Welker was jittery, as if he had electrodes attached to the soles of his feet, his testicles, his eyeballs. The angel was clad in rainbows and she had wings, thickly feathered and bursting from her back, and a golden glow around her that diminished only slightly as it rose heavenward. She wasn't perfect—there was only one perfect angel—but she was close. She would do, for now.

The situation was ideal, because there were dense bushes near the sandbox, on the far side from where the whore mother sat, all pendulous udders and thick thighs packed like sausage meat into a denim casing, worrying at a fingernail with her teeth as she read. He eased from the car, shutting the door softly, double-checking to make sure it was unlocked. That could be the trickiest moment, getting the angel into the chariot. He glanced at the mother again, to make sure she remained buried in her story, and hurried around to the far side of the bushes. One more check of the mother, and he started softly calling "Perry! Perry, where are you?"

On hands and knees, he pushed through the bushes, close to the sandbox, wearing a worried smile and enough leaves on his head to make him look harmless, slightly goofy. "Oh, hello," he said.

The angel looked at him, expressionless. Her eyes were big and green. She didn't say anything.

"Have you seen Perry?" he asked. His voice was just above a whisper. The mother didn't look up.

"Who's Perry?"

"He's just a pup," Welker said. He held his hand about six inches off the ground. "Just a little bitty guy, black and white, with big floppy ears." The oldest game in town, and it still worked.

"I haven't seen a puppy."

"He got out, and he came this way. Now I can't find him."

"My mom can help you look."

"No! I mean, she's reading her book, she wouldn't have seen anything."

"I haven't either."

"If he's run into the street, been hit by a car or something, my son will be so sad. He loves that puppy."

"How old is your son?"

"He's six."

"I'm seven."

"You're a big girl. And smart, I can tell. Can you help me look for Perry?"

"I don't know."

"What's your name?"

"Missy. Missy Trimble."

"That's a beautiful name, Missy. Mine is James. Jim. My son is Jim, too, Jim junior. It's nice to meet you, Missy. Thanks for chatting with me, but I have to go look for Perry now."

Welker backed out of the bushes and stood on the other side, calling out, "Perry, where are you?" so quietly that the mother wouldn't hear over whatever garbage she was blasting from her MP3 player.

On his third call, Missy Trimble came around the bushes. "I can help," she said. "For a minute."

"I'm sure a minute is all we'll need, darling," Welker said. "A minute will be just right."

25

Frank answered his phone with a dry chuckle.

"What are you laughing at?" Richie asked.

"Your ringtone."

"What ringtone?" Frank's standard ringtone was Marvin Gaye's "What's Goin' On." Richie had heard it dozens of times since he'd met the detective.

"I was gonna give you 'Bumpy's Lament,' Frank said. "From the *Shaft* soundtrack. But then I decided that should go to a brother, and I had this feeling you needed a Gil Scott-Heron tune. I thought about 'We Almost Lost Detroit,' but the verdict ain't in on that yet."

"So what did you assign to me?"

"Heh." Frank's usual laugh was that single sound, rising up from someplace deep in his chest. If he had ever strung two of them together, Richie hadn't heard it yet. "You got 'Whitey on the Moon.'"

"Nice," Richie said. "So did you want to know why I called, or did you just want to crack yourself up?"

"That sounds good. Cracking myself up. I just got to my desk half an hour ago and I'm already swamped. Good thing you didn't call me an hour before that."

"I don't want to know."

"No," Frank said. "You really do."

"What does that mean?"

"Means that while I've been here dealing with paperwork a mile high on my desk and Lieutenant Roland Jackson busting my balls, I also took a few minutes to check into your friend Wil Fowler. Maybe he's not the good a kid you think he is."

"What do you mean?" Richie asked again.

"I mean, he was arrested this afternoon."

Richie wanted to believe he'd misunderstood Frank's words. His left hand clenched into a tight fist. "For what?"

"He was picked up with a bunch of rare coins that were taken from a home in Hamtramck that was burglarized on Thursday."

"He stole the coins?"

"He was in possession of stolen property. He's admitted to nothing, way I hear it. But when you met him, he was on his way to break into a house, right? Maybe that's his thing."

"That house was vacant," Richie said.

"Did he know that? Sometimes a dark house looks like a dark house."

"You've seen the Morton place. You know how it looks."

"Yeah, I guess. I'm just saying, how much you really know about this kid? Not much, right?"

"No, not much. It was more a sense of him that I got. That he wasn't really bad. Maybe just troubled."

"Or maybe he really is bad, and your perp radar is on the blink."

"Anything's possible, I guess." He hated to admit to the possibility that Frank was right, but he couldn't deny it. He had been a failure as a cop. He had all the book smarts anybody could ask for, but there were no fields he knew of in which book smarts equated to practical experience. Maybe he was just a lousy judge of criminal personalities. "He seemed anxious, scared. Curious, not criminal. But I could have misread him."

"Could be you did."

"Stay on top of it, Frank. If you can, I mean. I know you're busy."

"I will."

"Thanks."

"Your turn, Maynard. Got anything for me?"

Richie told him what he had learned, which wasn't much. Nothing conclusive. Frank listened patiently. "Okay," he said when Richie was done. "I got an idea for you."

"What? I'm open to anything."

"Find some old phone books, from back to when we know Morton was in Tucson, based on the postmarks on his mother's mail. Work forward, see can you find out where he lived when. Maybe he's still in touch with a neighbor."

Richie didn't have any better ideas, and he had a few hours of daylight left. "I'll give it a shot."

"You find anything, let me know right away."

"I will."

"Okay, brother. Be cool." Frank hung up the phone. Richie sat on the edge of his motel room bed, wondering if he would ever be more than an amateur, with more promise than results. The worst part was that there might well be innocent children relying on his efforts, kids who would be victimized if he didn't figure out where Jarod Morton was.

He saw paralysis creeping his way. In order to dodge it, he had to stay on the move, keep working. He might not be any better at this investigating thing than he had been at patrol, but he was determined to keep trying. If in the end he proved to be an absolute failure, so be it, but he didn't want to be able to say he hadn't given it his best.

O   O   O

Richie drove the Nissan to the Pima County Library's main branch on Stone. There a helpful reference librarian found telephone directories going back eight years. She left him at a table with the books, and he flipped through the white pages first, looking for Jarod Morton's name. It didn't appear, and neither did Barbara's.

The building was modern and functional, and most of the people making use of it seemed to be in good spirits. Richie watched them from his table for a few minutes, floppy phone books in a pile before him, then had another idea. He took the top one from the stack, the most recent, and opened the yellow pages.

In Detroit, Morton had owned a photography studio. It might have been easier for him to change his name than to change the way he earned his keep. Richie went to the photography listings, but nothing struck him as likely. He closed that book and took the next one from the stack.

When he had gone back five years, he found it.

The business was called Family Photos Portrait Studio. It was on the west side of town, at Oracle and Orange Grove, wherever that was. Although the business name was vague, the photo in the eighth-page ad clinched it.

The picture showed a beaming little blond girl, arms folded over her chest, her head lying sideways on her arms. From behind her back rose a pair of white, feathery wings. It wasn't the same photo Morton had used for his business in Michigan, but the pose was unmistakably similar. And while the girl wasn't Kayley, she was of the same type.

His hands trembling with anticipation, Richie went into the older phone books and found identical ads for two more years, then nothing again.

He was stacking them up again when he had yet another inspiration. He returned to the current phone book, and paged through the photography studio listings again. The ad wasn't there; no ad like it appeared. But one listing with no photograph and precious few details, just a single-line listing, was called Little Angels Portrait Studio. He should have spotted it the first time through.

He jotted down the address and phone number, made a photocopy of the Family Photos ad with the angel, and returned the books to the reference librarian. She was in her early fifties, he guessed, lean, with laugh lines bracketing her eyes, long brown hair streaked with silver that she wore loose down her back, and a smell that reminded Richie of a pool hall in Dearborn. After a moment he realized that if you took away the beer, the predominant aroma was talcum powder.

She looked at him as if wondering if she should call security. "Sorry," he said. "My mind was wandering, there."

"I gathered. It looked as if it had gone to Outer Mongolia."

"Basically." He set the phone book on her desk and showed her the address. "Do you know where this is?"

She studied the paper briefly, and gave a brisk nod. "That's in the Park Place mall," she said. "Do you know it?"

"I'm a stranger here, just got in today."

"All right, then. Let me write down some directions for you. You have a vehicle?"

"Yes."

"Good. It's not particularly close."

She tore a piece of paper from a steno pad and wrote for a minute or so, then handed it over. "Make sure you can read my chicken-scratch."

It looked like a penmanship textbook to Richie. "Yeah, no problem."

"Is there anything else I can do for you?"

He was tempted to ask if she had kids, and if so, did she know what kind of predator lurked in her city. Instead he gave her the most authentic smile he could muster. "Thanks for your help."

"It's why I'm here."

He thanked her again and hurried back to the rental, which had grown almost unbearably hot sitting out in the open. He cranked the air and put the directions on the passenger seat. She had him cutting down to Broadway on Campbell, and then following Broadway for several miles. Traffic wasn't too bad, just starting to pick up a little as the afternoon rush hour grew near.

The mall appeared on his right, sooner than he expected. He pulled into a crowded parking lot and found a space way in the back, then hiked toward the Food Court entrance. Inside, he found a directory sign and located the studio, not far away, toward the Sears anchoring the mall's eastern end.

The photo studio had framed pictures in the front window, big ones with dark backgrounds. Most of the photos were of families, but a couple showed little girls, one of them wearing the angel wings and an expression that was shooting for beatific and landed somewhere between mischievous and smug. There were no black-and-whites in evidence, and none of them looked much like the work of Morton's that Richie had seen. But that angel bit was a giveaway.

He moved toward the door. Inside was a man wearing a pale denim shirt with the sleeves rolled back, and jeans. He had curly reddish hair, wire-rimmed glasses, and a growth on his chin somewhere between a soul patch and a goatee. He was posing a little girl, maybe three years old, on an elevated platform, bolstering her up with big pillows to make sure she didn't fall over. A young couple watched from a nearby bench. The family looked Hispanic; the little girl wore a ruffled pink dress with small black polka dots, two pink bows in her straight black hair.

Richie didn't like the way the guy was fussing over her, touching her, even with her parents right there. But he had seen pictures of Jarod Morton, and this guy wasn't him.

He waited until the man was done and the family had left, the parents telling their daughter how beautiful she was, how proud they were. Richie had hung around outside, trying not to be overly conspicuous, and he hadn't seen anything happen that would have been considered inappropriate. The parents hadn't taken their eyes off her the whole time. When the young family was gone, Richie went in. The photographer was shoving his big pillows into a built-in bench. He was bent over when he spotted Richie. "Can I help you?" he asked, straightening up.

"I'm looking for Jared Morton."

The guy looked blank. "I'm sorry, I don't know who that is."

"He's a photographer. He used to work here in town." Richie showed him the photo from the ad. "He used to do this angel shtick, like you do."

"A lot of portrait photographers do that."

"Seemed like kind of a specialty of his."

"You need a gimmick to compete these days. When I got into the game, there was a talent barrier—you needed to understand lighting and exposure, know your way around a darkroom. If you had to send your film to a lab for processing and printing, your overhead was just gone. But now everything's digital. Press a button and shoot, fix any mistakes on the computer, press another button and print. And if you screw up, you talk the client into taking prints on a pebbled canvas surface, which hides a lot of flaws. With so many people jumping into the business, you've got to have something special that sets you apart. Some do boudoir stuff, some do costumes. There used to be a guy in town who did that angel bit with the kids, but he retired, I guess, or moved away. Something. Anyway, when I saw that he was gone, I started doing it. People seem to like it. Everyone thinks their kids are little angels, when they're really young, anyway."

Richie asked a few more questions, but the answers were unhelpful. If this man knew Morton, he was a convincing enough actor to disguise the fact. Richie wanted to leave him with some kind of warning, but he didn't know if the man had done anything wrong. Sure, he'd been touching that girl, but he was a photographer, and she too young to take a lot of direction. He had to put her in the right poses. Richie couldn't let his righteous fury toward the world's Jarod Mortons manifest itself in a distrust of all portrait photographers.

Richie had one more idea, but he'd have to hurry. It was getting late in the day. City business records should show who had owned the Little Angels Portrait Studio until four years ago. He rushed to his rental and raced back toward downtown, blinking into the sun's brutal glare as a headache started to fester behind his temples.

Traffic was heavier now. He hit the doors of City Hall at just shy of a full sprint.

When he got to the City Clerk's office, it was empty except for a round-faced man with tiny eyes, blinking furiously behind thick glasses. He was handling papers, trying with increasing agitation to paperclip thick stacks of forms, dropping the rejects in or near a black plastic receptacle, and then feeding certain stacks into a large stapler on the desk and hammering it with a pudgy fist. Richie found the whole process oddly fascinating, but the clock was running. "Excuse me."

The man looked up, blinking faster than ever. "We close in five minutes."

"What I want shouldn't take any longer than that."

The man gave an exasperated sigh. "What is it?"

Richie briefly outlined his mission. "All right," the man said. "But you're not making me late for happy hour."

You get me what I need, and there'll be a lot of kids happy for more than an hour, Richie thought. He didn't say it. Instead, he let the man do his job, and in seven minutes he left bearing a home address for someone named Jerrod Mannheim, the owner-of-record of the defunct Little Angels Photography Studio.

O O O

The house was a tiny pink stucco box, faux Santa Fe style, with a bad case of mange. Gray patches showed through where pink stucco had worn away; in other spots it had been patched with white. Stalactites of rust streaked down from the roof. Richie's gut clenched when he saw a Big Wheel in the yard and a pint-sized basketball hoop in the driveway.

He stepped to the front door and pushed a button that appeared to have no effect whatsoever. Before he could knock, though, a ferocious yapping sounded from inside; a better signal and alarm system than any electronic one. A moment later, the front door swung open, enveloping Richie in a fragrant cloud of smoke from Mexican cuisine.

A stout Latino in a white T-shirt and brown dress pants stood in front of him with a napkin in his hand and a thin film of sweat in his forehead. "Yes?" he said. "Something?"

"Excuse me," Richie said. "I was looking for someone who I guess used to live here. His name was Jerrod Mannheim. I have some photographs of him and his wife."

He showed the man his photos. The man studied them carefully and asked, in heavily accented English, "Why you want him?"

Richie had considered the question in advance. Not knowing if he might be talking to people who were friends of Morton, or enemies, he had come up with a neutral response. "He might be owed some money. Won't really know if it's him until I find him."

"He doesn't look familiar. What did you say his name was?"

"Jerrod Mannheim."

"I don't know no Jerrod Mannheim,"

"He used to live at this address."

"We've been here what, Karina, two years? Two and a half?"

"*Sí*," a female voice answered from behind him. Richie couldn't see much of the house or the other speaker.

"So you don't have any forwarding information for the previous resident? You don't know where he moved to?"

"No, we're renting this place. Someone else rented it before us. Karina's cousin."

"Who's the owner?"

"I don't know. We send our rent checks to Tempe, to a property management company."

Richie could have Frank try to pull some strings, see if he could get the management company to cough up what they had on Jerrod Mannheim, if, in fact, they had owned it when he lived here. But without a warrant, it seemed unlikely they'd find anything very helpful, and the company would no doubt drag its metaphorical heels. "Thank you," he said. "Oh, one more question. When you moved in, did you notice if any of the windows or inside doors had hasps on them? For a padlock?"

The man stared at Richie, as if he had taken complete leave of his senses. "No."

"Great. Sorry to have disturbed your dinner. Smells great."

"It's no problem," the man said, wiping his forehead with the napkin. "I hope you find that dude you're looking for."

Having seemingly exhausted his other options, Richie walked from house to house in the gathering dusk, canvassing the neighbors, showing his pictures of the Mortons, trying to find anyone who knew or remembered them. He was surprised to see the sun going down so early. Back home it was still light until almost eight-thirty these days. Here, it was not even seven and that famous desert sun was already making a dive for California. Glancing down a side street, he saw what looked like a scrawny, pale dog, then realized it had to be a coyote. No roadrunner in sight, though.

Twenty minutes later, he did see a roadrunner, but it was moseying along the side of the road, not running at all. It was hunched forward, tail back, resembling nothing so much as Groucho Marx in his bent-over strut, coattails flipped behind him. So he had seen a roadrunner and a coyote in the space of a half hour, although neither had rocket skates or dynamite. Thinking about cartoons made him wonder what Frank was up to. Instead of checking in, he kept knocking on doors.

Most of the neighbors were Hispanic, most having dinner, not all of them as welcoming as the man at the first house had been. Nobody actually called him a nosy *gringo*, but he could sense the sentiment behind some of the glares he collected.

At a small brick house painted a shade of green that made him think of serious illness, Richie stood at the top of three concrete steps, talking to one of the few Anglo women he had encountered in the neighborhood. She was hugely pregnant, and seemed nervous.

"No," she said in response to the photograph. "I've lived here for seven years, I don't remember ever seeing him."

From inside the house came heavy footsteps. She shot a worried look at the door. "Okay," Richie said. "Thank you." Before he could step down, the door opened and a male voice thundered from within.

"Who the hell you got out here?"

"It's—it's nothing," she stammered.

"I was just asking her some questions about one of your former neighbors," Richie explained.

"You a cop?" He moved into the light so Richie could see him: a lean, angular face, with just enough of a brush of light-colored hair to square off the top of his head and enough beard to do the same below, sloping shoulders, muscles bunched against the sleeves of his T-shirt. The expression on his face implied that he thought the woman had better things to do than talk to strangers.

"I'm not a cop, but I'm assisting the police on a criminal investigation." He didn't specify which police.

"If you're not a cop, what are you doing here bothering people's wives?"

"Like I said, just asking some questions."

The man glared at his wife. Richie suspected he had Alderdyce disease. "My dinner's getting cold."

"I told you to go ahead and start."

"It's not on the *table* yet."

Richie had never really been clear on what "hackles" were, but he thought his were being raised. This guy came across like he was spoiling for a fight, and Richie didn't want to disappoint. At the same time, he was here for something more important. He flashed the photo of Morton at the guy. "Do you remember him? He used to live down the street, maybe four years ago. Went by the name Jerrod Mannheim?"

The man didn't even look at it. He was intent on Richie's face, as if watching for hints of weakness. "Never seen him."

"All right, then," Richie said. "Thanks for your help, both of you. Sorry to have disturbed your dinner."

"Next time you think about doing that, don't do it," the guy said.

"Don't worry," Richie said. "There won't be a next time." He deliberately turned his back on the couple and went down the stairs, walking toward the street. He half-expected to hear pounding footfalls behind him, or to feel a meaty paw on his collar. Neither happened, and he moved on to the next house with an adrenaline tingle in his hands and arms and a tightness at his midsection.

Two houses later, another white woman opened her door. She was probably in her late fifties, but carried herself with a weary air that suggested a more advanced age. Her hair was white, her face lined, and the way she wrung her hands made Richie wonder if there was a drop of moisture left in them. She invited Richie into a foyer filled with photos of herself with what must have been a husband and a pair of kids, from infancy through graduations and weddings. Richie showed her his pictures. The place smelled like a church Richie had been in once, and he realized that she had at least a dozen candles burning in the living room.

"I'm sure I remember him," she said, tapping on Jarod's picture. She pointed in the direction of the tiny stucco house. "He lived over there, in that pink one."

"That's right," Richie said. He tried to keep excitement out of his voice, but this was the first person yet who admitted to recalling Morton at all.

"My Murdoch, he was a plumber, and he used to keep his van parked in front of the house. Good advertising, he always said. He had his slogan on it. 'Got leakin' pipes? Call Deacon Sipes!'"

"He was a deacon?" Richie asked.

"He was a deacon in our church, and he liked the way the slogan rhymed. One night that man you're asking about—he wasn't a regular customer or anything—he came over to the house, knocked on the door. He said that he'd had some kind of plumbing problem, a pipe burst, I think it was. Water …"

"So it was an emergency," Richie said.

"That's right. Murdoch went over. He stayed a couple of hours, then came back, said the man had paid him on the spot. No problems about the charge or the extra for after-hours."

"What else do you remember about the man?" Richie asked, trying to guide the conversation back toward Morton.

"Nothing, really. I never really knew him."

"What about his wife?" Richie tapped on a picture of Barbara.

"Oh, no, he was definitely a bachelor. Murdoch said it was a man's house, sloppy the way men are. There was no woman living there."

"You're sure?"

"Positive."

"And kids didn't visit him or anything?"

"If they did, I never saw them."

"Is Murdoch here? Maybe he remembers something."

"No, I'm afraid I lost Murdoch. It's three years ago now. That darn van, too. It rolled over, on the interstate. They tell me he didn't suffer, but I'm not sure I believe that."

"I'm very sorry for your loss," Richie said.

"Thank you."

"And that's all you can remember about the man? You wouldn't know where he moved after he left here?"

"Oh, no, I wouldn't know anything about that."

Richie made a move toward the door. "Would you like a cup of tea?" she asked. "It'd be no bother."

"I should keep going," Richie said. "I appreciate the invitation, and the information. Thank you so much."

"If you're sure …"

"Yes, I really have to go." Richie got a hand on the doorknob before he was trapped into an extended visit. She was lonely, and he'd been polite, and maybe that was all it took sometimes.

Outside, he reflected on what she had said. She had been utterly convinced that Morton had been a bachelor, which Richie found interesting. If her memory was correct, and she seemed pretty clear on it, then Morton had lost Barbara somewhere along the way. Maybe she got tired of him molesting children, maybe she figured out what happened with Angela. Either way, she was out of the picture. It didn't mean he hadn't hooked up with some other woman in the intervening years, but pedophiles tended to have a hard time establishing lasting adult relationships. Chances were, Richie was looking for a single man instead of a couple.

It also gave him two directions to look in, though. He wanted to find Jarod Morton, but if he could find Barbara, she might be able to help him do that.

The one thing he was sure about was that Morton hadn't stopped taking little girls. He might have learned to cover his tracks better, but if he was alive, he was still at it. Of that, Richie was absolutely convinced.

26

There was much about her job that Katharine Dunning hated. Some aspects she loved, though, and in the end those outweighed the hate, or she wouldn't have kept at it. She didn't mind being called at home, in the middle of dinner or a good dream, because that meant she was important to the community, valued. She liked tracking down a runaway or citing a speeder or catching a housebreaker. Busting meth dealers was an outright thrill. She loved walking through downtown Waterton—what little there was of downtown Waterton—and having the locals call out, "Hey, Sheriff Kate!"

What she hated was when there was a child in trouble, one she couldn't help. And she hated what she was doing now, which was driving out into the country to pay a visit to a registered pedophile who lived on his family's farm. Bobby Ray Livesay had been keeping out of trouble, or so he claimed, but all in all, he was one human being she'd have preferred to shoot dead rather than talk to with a civil tongue. And she didn't consider herself a violent person.

Then again, she doubted that exterminators thought of themselves as violent when they eliminated vermin and other pests.

Stanislaus County's countryside was gorgeous, no two ways about that. It was largely flat, but infinitely varied—cultivated land, wild, raw country, affluent farms and then places like the Livesay spread, that looked like one of the bigger farms had upchucked its unneeded leftovers onto a weedy patch of nowhere. Whatever its faults, though, Kate preferred the country to Modesto, and Modesto to any city larger than Modesto. Once in a great while circumstances forced her into San Francisco. Five minutes after she got there, she was late getting out.

She lived in the country herself, albeit not as far out as Bobby Ray. Just her and King, now. King was a German Shepherd police dog, too old to work but excellent company just the same. She hadn't dated since her husband Roger had died wearing his badge. Not that she hadn't had offers; she was a handsome woman, trim, with rust-colored hair that some thought she kept too short, but it was easy to deal with that way, and clear blue eyes that stopped people short. Sex and romance had simply stopped being part of her life, and she was fine with that. Guys like Bobby Ray reminded her of just how much horribleness crept into the world under those guises anyway, and she thought them best left on the back burner. Way, way back.

The sky was a blue so vibrant the mind could barely conceive of it, with a sun that would, in another month or so, raise the valley temperatures from scorching to spontaneous combustion. For the moment, spring reigned, making the trees billow with greenery. The fields wore a plush carpet of wildflowers everywhere there weren't crops. Flanking the road, California poppies waved their brilliant orange petals like pennants as she drove past.

When she turned onto the Livesay property, she thought there should be some kind of outer manifestation, a dark cloud across the sun, a sudden downpour. Something. But the sky's forceful cheerfulness remained, contrasting the chill that swept through Kate's bones. If that girl was here …

The girl's name was Missy Trimble. She was six. She had been taken from a park in Modesto, pretty much from directly under the gaze of her mother, who was young and not terribly bright and seemed to think that once she had suffered through pregnancy and labor, all the hard stuff should have been finished. She hadn't even been able to provide investigators with a picture of Missy, until she remembered that a Facebook friend had posted photos of her own daughter's fifth birthday party, which Missy had attended.

Now every cop in Stanislaus County was looking for Missy. Beyond that, really. An Amber Alert had been issued, which meant that private citizens and law enforcement alike would be on the lookout, up and down the coast, at the Mexican border, and on every road heading east into Nevada.

Fortunately, on her turf Kate only had the one registered sex offender to check on. Bobby Ray had been caught exposing himself to a nine-year-old boy in a public men's room, on the upper level of the Vintage Faire Mall in Modesto. After his arrest, his home was searched—he'd been living in a Modesto apartment at the time— and child pornography was found on his personal computer. He had served a stint in prison, then moved back to the family farm. Since then, so far as Kate knew, he had stayed out of trouble.

Abducting a little girl didn't seem like his style. But she wasn't about to operate on that assumption, not without checking him out. The long driveway up to the broken-down old farmhouse was a rutted dirt trail, with weeds growing up in the center strip. By the time she came to a stop in front of a porch that looked like a stiff wind could tear it off and blow it into the next county, there were three people standing on it.

The Livesays looked like they have lived together for so long their features had melted together. The parents were essentially shapeless, blobs that started out thick and got thicker. They had short, stumpy legs, no necks, and faces that seemed to have been put together with Mr. Potato Head parts stuck into putty. Kate didn't care to make casual judgments about people, but she believed they were both accidents of nature, mistakes who never should have been brought to term. Given that, it was astonishing and yet inevitable that they had found each other and produced their own accident. She doubted that Bobby Ray had been raised with any kind of moral center at all, and probably not much in the way of cultural or other education either. Standing there on the porch they looked like a set of Russian nesting dolls, Bobby Ray the outer shell, then his father, and his mother on the inside. Father and son both wore blue-and-white plaid shirts and blue jeans, while the mother had paired her jeans with a yellow blouse that had faint blue checks.

"What bring you way out here, Sheriff?" the elder Livesay asked when Kate emerged from the cruiser.

"I bet it's me. It's me, isn't it?"

"It is you, Bobby Ray."

"Jeezus peezus! You folks just don't leave a guy alone, do you?"

"His mistake was a long time ago, Sheriff Kate," his mother said. "Why you got to come around stirrin' things up?" Kate had known the woman's name once, and the father's too, but she had forgotten both. All she remembered was Bobby Ray.

"His 'mistake' was a felony, ma'am, and he's a registered sex offender."

"He ain't done nothing lately!"

"That'll be for me to decide."

"Sheriff …"

"Bobby Ray, I want to talk to you alone, without your parents. You got someplace we can go?"

"What's wrong with right here?"

The next words from Kate's mouth brought an involuntary shudder. "I think your room would be better, Bobby Ray."

"You got a warrant, Sheriff?" Mr. Livesay demanded.

"I could get one if I needed it, but I don't."

"It's okay, Sheriff," Bobby Ray said. "We can go to my room."

Kate felt like she was about to enter a malaria ward, but she steeled herself and climbed the four creaky stairs to the rickety porch. Ignoring angry glares from his parents, she followed him into the house.

After the relatively fresh air outside, the interior smelled like the place where they kept the garbage. A sour odor assaulted Kate's nostrils, and she opened her mouth, breathing through it, fighting a sudden wave of nausea. Every now and then she took another big whiff, just in case she caught the unique scent of death. She was hoping not to, but if it was here, she had to know.

The place reminded Kate of some thrift shops and low-end antique stores she'd been in, where faint trails cut through furniture laden with things, *stuff*, bric-a-brac with no particular meaning to anyone, even people as odd as the Livesays. Little of it was whole, and none of it matched anything else or related to anything that she could see—not a particular interest or hobby or collection. The only spot that looked like it got any real use was the couch facing the television. She wondered how three people as out of shape and apparently unmotivated as the Livesays could run a farm at a profit. She supposed government assistance was involved. *Your tax dollars at work,* she thought. *Maybe there's something to those tea parties after all.*

Bobby Ray carved through it like the old hand he was. Kate followed as rapidly as she dared, fearing she would jostle something and bury herself in a landslide. When they got into his room, he sat on the bed. She closed the door and looked around. There was a desk with a computer on it, but the desk chair held a stack of magazines a foot high, leaving her nowhere to sit unless she was willing to touch them. Which she wasn't.

"Bobby Ray, are you sure this is the best way to live?" She felt a little like a social worker, but she had long since learned that a rural sheriff was an officer of the law last, and social worker, priest/confessor, occasional banker, and career consultant first. "I'm not sure it's that healthy for you."

"I do okay here, Sheriff," Bobby Ray said. "I have to help my parents out on the farm. They're getting old."

"You're no kid anymore, Bobby Ray." In fact, he was thirty-six. His hair was thinning, fading toward silver at the temples. His face was still relatively unlined, the way heavy people's could stay longer than hers had. What had struck Kate about him on the few occasions they'd met were his fingers, as thick as if someone had sewn Vienna sausages together to make hands. "Living in a room at your parents' house. It just doesn't seem right."

"Jeezus peezus, Sheriff, what do you want from me?"

She decided to let it rest, to move on to the truly pressing business. "The reason I'm here, Bobby Ray, is this. There's a little girl missing, from Modesto. Her name is Missy. Do you know anything about that?"

Bobby rubbed his eyes, as if awakening from a deep sleep. "Sheriff, I don't … I only did that that one time, and that was a boy. Girls don't …"

"Just tell me if she's here."

"Of course she's not here," he said. "I just said, I don't like girls. I mean, not that way. And I've been good, honest, I haven't touched anybody or anything. Anyways, where would I keep a girl?"

Kate looked around the room, which was only slightly less congested than the rest of the house. It was an excellent question. "What would I find if I looked on your computer, Bobby Ray?"

He rocked forward and back on the edge of the bed. "Oh, you don't have to do that, Sheriff! Do you? Ahh, jeezus peezus!"

"Wrong answer." The computer was on, a screen saver bouncing colored rays across the monitor. Kate touched the space bar and MySpace came up on the screen. "What are you doing on MySpace?"

"I have friends," Bobby Ray said. "I have thirty-one friends. I talk to them on there."

She touched a couple more keys, bringing up the computer's search window, and typed in ".jpg." When she clicked "enter" the computer processed for a moment and listed hundreds of files, most of them number strings with that suffix. She opened a few at random. Bobby Ray was rocking harder, his breath coming loud and fast.

The images were all of pornography. Men and women, men alone, most of it men with men. She was confronted by more penises in the few moments she clicked through the open windows than she had seen in her entire life, sex organs of every shape and color and description, white and black, hairy and shaved, most of them erect. But she didn't see any children, which came as a great relief.

"Sheriff," Bobby Ray muttered. He had wrapped his arms around his thick torso and was rocking so hard she was afraid he would break the creaking bed. "Come on! That's not illegal, is it?"

"I'd have to check the terms of your release, but I don't think so," she said.

"I told you, I don't know anything about that girl. I don't go to Modesto anyways. I stay here, and I have pictures, that's all."

"I could keep looking on here and I won't find any kids?"

"Cross my heart." Bobby Ray performed the motion as he spoke. "You won't find a single kid."

"All right." She closed the windows she had opened, glad to make all those naked male bodies go away.

"You won't tell my folks, will you? About the pictures?"

"That's between you and them, Bobby Ray. You don't want to let them know, you don't have to tell them. I won't say anything."

"Oh, okay, thanks. Thank you, Sheriff."

"And you don't know anything about this missing girl? You haven't heard about anybody who might have her, might know something?"

"Like I said, I'm not interested in girls."

"I think that's been made abundantly clear. I don't care who you like, Bobby Ray, as long as it's adults and nobody's getting hurt, okay?"

"Okay."

"You stay out of trouble, now."

"I will, Sheriff, cross my heart."

Kate left him sitting on his bed, in a room that looked like it still belonged to a boy. His parents were in the front room, father sitting on the couch that faced the TV, mother standing in the kitchen doorway. "Everything okay, Sheriff?" Bobby Ray's father asked.

"Looks that way. I'm sorry for the intrusion."

"He knows if he got up to any trouble, I'd whop him one."

"I don't think that'll be necessary, thanks." She let herself out the front door, sucking in fresh air as soon as she was able. Poor Bobby Ray, she thought. He never even had a chance.

27

She was in the nest now. Missy Trimble, she said her name was. Just like that, Missy, then a momentary gap, then Trimble, as if she rarely spoke one of them without the other.

Welker had locked her in, from the outside. He'd told her that if she needed him, if she had to use the bathroom or anything like that, she could pound on the door and he would hear her, let her out. She was an agreeable girl, although she had fussed and cried at first. Once he had pointed out that nobody could hear her she had calmed down. Now she was taking the whole thing almost as an adventure. She regarded with some amusement the baby doll he gave her, and she asked after her mother with some regularity. All in all, though, she was better behaved than most girls on their first night in a strange man's home.

Of course, so far he hadn't laid a hand on her, beyond what was necessary to muscle her into the car and to keep her quiet while they drove away. She might well do some screaming later on.

He had left her in the nest so she could have some time to herself, to reach an acceptance of the new reality in which she found herself. He needed time alone as well, to get online and see if his message had been received. If he could just make a simple phone call, or a visit …

But no, they had set up their communication procedures for a reason. If he went to prison, he would never see his angel again. He had to stay safe. Changing the schedule was bad enough, but speaking directly, or even sending an e-mail—those were things that could be intercepted, used as evidence in court. The communication method they had come up with was virtually foolproof, and their messages would be taken as purely innocent by anyone who happened across them.

It worked, and he was comfortable with it. He was frustrated because it could be so slow, and he didn't know how much time he had. Events needed to race along at a speedy clip. He drummed his fingers on the keyboard as he waited for the computer to come to life, listening for Missy, just in case.

When he was done here, he would have to go back in, to see just how comfortable she had been able to make herself. He wanted his guests to be comfortable. He was a good host that way, really he was.

He always took good care of his angels.

28

Richie was back in the motel room after dinner, exhausted, wrung out, his headache full-blown. A couple of times, out in the neighborhood, he'd thought about quitting altogether. The idea skated across the surface of his mind, and he shoved it away quickly. He wasn't about to give up. He doubted that he could. Although it was late, Detroit time, he called Frank. The cop answered almost immediately.

"We have to go back farther," Richie said.

"Farther?"

"Into his past. He was like a ghost, here. Nobody knew him, nobody saw him. I mean, we could try to subpoena records from the property management company that rents his house, see if they have a forwarding address. But that'll take forever, and they'll fight it. We can run ads looking for people who visited the portrait studio, or even who suspected that he touched their kids. If I had any official standing here, I could see if the cops had any complaints about him. But it doesn't look like anybody knew him, or knows where he is now."

"There are a lot of dead ends in police work," Frank said.

"I'm not calling this one a dead end yet," Richie countered. "Somewhere in his past, he split up with Barbara. Something happened between them, and we have to find out what that was.

When he was with Barbara, chances are more people knew them. Someone might still be in touch with her. And she might know better than anyone else how to find him. Where were they before Tucson? Omaha?"

"Yeah, that sounds right."

"I guess I'm going to Omaha." He hated to ask the next question, but after hesitating for a few uncomfortable seconds, Frank apparently figured it out and decided to cut him a break.

"I'll buy your ticket, Maynard."

"Thanks, Frank."

"Just tell me when you're going."

"Soon as I can. First thing in the morning, I guess."

"I'll take care of it. I'll call you back with the details."

"This is just so awful," Richie said. "All these kids in Tucson who disappeared during the time he was here. No way to tell if he's behind any of it, but I have this terrible feeling."

"I know what you mean. It's bad." He said it in understated tones, but Richie knew how he really felt. The fact that Frank had never been able to find Angela Morton still grated on him. What made it infinitely worse was knowing that his failure might have had equally tragic consequences for other children.

"I feel like I reached down into a sewer, to pick up something floating on the top, and I fell in," Richie said. "Now a whirlpool's dragging me deeper and deeper. And my reaction to it is scaring me."

"I know what you mean. You don't have to do this, you know. Nobody's paying you, nobody expects anything from you."

Richie ignored the comment. He'd already been over that, and decided to keep going. "You deal with this kind of thing all the time," Richie said. "How do you cope? Well, I guess I know how you do, you've got your comic books."

"You might want to give it a try sometime. I was just reading one. Here, you got a few minutes?"

"I'm not going anywhere. I'm beat, but I don't think I'll be able to sleep any time soon."

"All right," Frank said. "Hold on." He put down the phone, and Richie heard rustling. Then Frank breathed heavily and was back. "Okay, *Action Comics*, 1967. Cover's early Neal Adams, one of the best artists ever. Even then you could tell the guy had the chops. On the cover you've got Lex Luthor in the foreground. He's that bald dude."

"Yeah, I know who he is. I saw the movie. That was Gene Hackman, right?"

"Uhh, okay, we'll go with that," Frank said. "Never paid much attention to those movies, after the first one. Anyhow, we've got Lex Luthor, wearing this dorky purple suit, and cackling like the supervillain that he is. He's saying, 'Which one are you going to rescue, Superman? You can't save both!' And then in a thought balloon under that, he's thinking, 'And whichever one you save will kill you!'"

"He's a real son-of-a-bitch, isn't he?"

"He is that. Anyway, in the background there's Lois Lane, falling off a building, and Jimmy Olsen dangling from a rope over a pool full of hungry sharks."

"Isn't Superman fast enough to save them both?"

"Ordinarily, yes. But they're entirely enclosed in huge green kryptonite cages. And what Superman doesn't know yet is that both have more green K jammed in their pockets. If he could get through the cages, he'd just be exposing himself when he reached them."

"Wow, that guy's really a dick."

"Damn straight. Okay, here we go. Page one, panel one. It's an establishing shot of Metropolis, with *The Daily Planet* building in the foreground. Coming out of the building is a word balloon, with big loud letters, saying, 'Great Caesar's Ghost!' Next panel, we're inside Perry White's office at the *Planet*. Clark Kent, Lois Lane, and Jimmy Olsen are there, facing White, who's furious, waving a newspaper at them, pounding his other fist on his desk. On the newspaper you can just make out the name *Gazette*, and a headline about a jewel heist. 'I pay you people to be reporters!' White says. 'Why did the *Gazette* scoop us on this jewel heist?'

"'Jeepers, Chief, I don't know,' Jimmy says. 'I was covering that trouble on the waterfront,' Lois says. And in the next panel, Clark says, 'And I was at that City Council meeting that almost turned into a riot.'

"One more panel is closer on Clark, who has a little smile on his face. 'Not even Superman can be everywhere at once, right?' he says."

"Isn't it a little stupid for him to bring up Superman?" Richie asked. "Doesn't he try to keep his identity a secret?"

"Yeah, but everybody knows he idolizes Superman," Frank told him. "And they're supposed to be friends. He didn't mention Superman a couple times in every conversation, people would get suspicious."

"Okay, sorry for the interruption. Go on."

"Next page," Frank said. "Top panel. Perry's pointing toward his office door. 'If I wanted excuses, I'd write 'em myself,' he says. 'Now get out there and find me some news!' Next panel, they're in the hallway, outside. In case we couldn't tell that, there's a caption that says, 'In the hallway, cub reporter Jimmy Olsen makes a sheepish admission.' Jimmy says, 'Well, I guess it'll be up to you two to get the goods on those jewel thieves. I've got a flower show to cover.' Clark says, 'Don't worry, Jimmy, you'll get your big break one of these days.' In the next panel, Clark stops short with a puzzled look on his face. 'Lois, I think I left my pen in my office. I'd better go back and get it.' 'All right, Clark,' Lois says. 'See you later."

"In the next panel, Lois is walking away, with a determined look. Her thought balloon says, 'Thank goodness! I'm going to get to the bottom of this jewel caper, and it'll be so much easier without Clark getting in my way.' Next panel, Clark ducks into a supply closet. 'I couldn't let Lois and Jimmy know,' he's thinking. Next panel, he's pulling his shirt and tie aside and you can see the Superman costume underneath, with that big red S. 'But with my super-hearing, I overheard another jewel robbery, taking place right now.' In the next panel, Superman's flying out a window of the *Planet* building, thinking, 'I must put a stop to it. It just may be connected to that heist last night.'"

Richie had closed his eyes. He was lying on the motel bed, trying hard to envision the gaudy, four-color world Frank described. He didn't make a habit of reading comic books, but he had seen them, read a couple of Frank's the other night in the hotel—Superman's blue-black hair, his costume of blue, red and yellow. Jimmy Olsen had red hair and was probably wearing a bow tie and a plaid jacket. Lois would be some sort of mid-sixties fashion diva. Frank kept reading, and Richie settled into a pleasant half-dream, letting the story unfold like some mental movie. The jewel robberies were, it turned out, a sham to lure in Superman's well-known friends Lois and Jimmy. Once Luthor had them trapped, he knew he could count on Superman coming to the rescue. He thought he had the perfect setup, in which Superman could only rescue one friend, but at the price of watching the other one die. And in the process, of course, he would become weak enough for Luthor to finish off in a slow and painful fashion—Luthor's ultimate revenge.

Only it didn't quite work out that way. Lois had been pushed from a building and Jimmy was being lowered into the pool of sharks. Since Superman couldn't physically reach either one, he relied on other powers. He used his super-breath to create a cushion under Lois, lowering her to the ground as gently as if he had carried her there. Then he used his freeze breath to freeze the shark tank water, thereby immobilizing the sharks. When the rope lowered Jimmy, he was cold and uncomfortable, but not hurt. In the meantime, Superman used his heat vision to melt the concrete beneath Luthor's feet, and then a puff of freezing breath to harden it again, trapping Luthor. Once Superman had the various crises dealt with, he took Luthor into custody and sent him into someplace called the Phantom Zone.

By the time Frank was done, the cares of the day had been, if not washed away, then at least subject to a decent rinsing. Richie let his yawns overtake him. His eyelids heavy, he thanked Frank for the dramatic reading and wished him goodnight. Sleep, somewhat unexpectedly, looked like a possibility after all.

O O O

Wil Fowler hadn't been arraigned yet. Frank had interceded, resulting in Wil spending the night in a holding cell instead of being booked. Frank had him taken to an interview room, and when he got into the precinct that morning, he watched the kid for a few minutes through the two-way mirror. Wil looked tired but wired—not too different from how Frank felt, after his late night phone call from Richie. Wil probably hadn't slept much. He had bags under his eyes big enough to hold a week's groceries, and he was picking at his fingernails like he wanted to play a tune on them. Maynard was right, the kid didn't look gangsta. But he was a thief just the same.

When Frank went into the room, Wil glared at him with a look they must have taught in kindergarten to kids who grew up on the streets, narrow-eyed, jaw set. "Wil Fowler, my name is Frank Robey. I'm a friend of Richie Krebbs."

"Who dat?" Wil didn't sound particularly interested.

"He caught you breaking into a house, and didn't turn you in because he thought you seemed like a decent kid. You remember him?"

"I guess."

The interview room had horrid yellow walls and a floor so ugly some linoleum manufacturer must have made the tiles by accident, then paid someone to haul them away. The wood laminate table had been scarred by a thousand cigarettes. Tobacco smoke, a vaguely pine-scented disinfectant, and sweat were the predominant odors, as they were in most similar rooms Frank had experienced. He thought the building could burn to the ground, but those smells would remain. "He remembers you. Asked me to look in on you."

"He wanted to do me any favors, how come I spent the night in a cage?"

"You ought to count your blessings, son. On the real. You could've been booked and spent the night in the city jail. You'd be begging for that holding cell in no time. You were kept in holding as a favor to me."

"Aiight," Wil said, "what about it?"

"What about it is, I want to know is Richie right, or is he wrong? I want to know what kind of judge of character he is. You some kind of bad-ass motherfucker?"

"Bad-ass enough."

"I'm not convinced," Frank said. "You jack those coins they busted you with?"

"I ain't thieved nothin'. I told the cops, I found 'em."

"Yeah, everybody finds three thousand dollars' worth of rare coins."

"My lucky day."

Frank sat across the table from him. Wil studied him with that same dismissive gaze. "You don't look very lucky, from where I'm sitting," Frank said. "Looks like maybe it was your unlucky day."

"Whatevs."

"Son, I'm trying to help you out here, but you got to go a little ways to meet me. Start with the truth. Why were you returning stolen coins to their owner?"

"Say what?"

"Just answer the question."

"Who says I was?"

Frank was silent, waiting.

"Aiight," Wil said after another minute of unspoken attitude. "Like I said, I found 'em. Thought I'd give 'em back to the dude they belong to."

"You knew they were valuable."

"I didn't know what they was worth. Bunch of old coins. Couldn't use 'em in a pop machine, didn't mean shit to me." He was quiet for another moment, but his expression had changed. He looked at Frank with something approaching curiosity. "How you know that? That I was takin' 'em back?"

"Since we're talking straight now," Frank said, "it was an educated guess. You were walking down the street in Hamtramck, headed in the direction of the house they were stolen from. No fences in that neighborhood that I know of. Couldn't figure where else you might be taking them. But I didn't know for sure until you confirmed it just now."

"Shit," Wil said.

"Look, Wil, you don't got to be a tough guy with me. You don't got to prove anything. If Richie's right about you, that you're a decent kid, mixed up in God knows what, there's still time to get yourself extricated from it, dig? But that starts and ends with you being straight with me. I'm the only friend you got in the world right now."

"Then I guess you're right, dog, I was just born unlucky."

○ ○ ○

On his own authority, Frank had Wil released. He believed the kid's story, to a point—not that he found the coins, since that wouldn't explain how he knew who their owner was, but that for reasons he wouldn't or couldn't explain, he was on his way to return them. A squad car had rolled up the street and Wil tried to duck discreetly into an alley. His furtive motion attracted the officers in the car, and they caught up to him, asking to be shown what he was carrying. When he displayed the coins and couldn't explain them, he was taken into custody.

Frank explained that he wasn't out of trouble yet—he might still be charged with possession of stolen property, even though the theft itself couldn't be hung on him. Wil kept up his detached demeanor, but there was a moment at which Frank thought the kid wanted to thank him, maybe even had the slightest glimmer of moisture in his big, vulnerable eyes. Whatever Richie had seen in him, Frank got a taste of; some sort of inner fire, a flawed exterior that nearly hid a stronger core. Wil was mixed up in something; that much was certain. Maybe he wanted out, but whatever it was, he would keep it to himself, carve his own path, instead of breaking down under interrogation.

Calvin Matthews strolled up as Frank watched Wil leave the precinct. Actually, Calvin didn't so much stroll as strut, reminding Frank of a starling combing a supermarket parking lot for scraps of food.

"You let the kid go?"

"He didn't take the coins."

"He had them, though."

"That's right. And he was taking them back to the owner."

"He tell you that?"

"I deduced it. Sometimes that's what detectives do, Calvin. We make deductions."

"I read Sherlock Holmes too, Robey. I prefer Walter Mosley to Conan Doyle, but that's just me."

"Didn't take Holmesian abilities, man. Just talked to the cat."

"And you bought his story."

"That's right."

"I'm gonna make a note on my calendar, so next time we see him in here with stolen property I'll remember how many days it was since you cut him loose."

Frank didn't want to trade jabs all day. He shook his head and started toward his desk. "Glad you learned how to use a calendar," he tossed over his shoulder. Calvin shot something back at him, but Frank couldn't hear it. Just as well.

He had plenty of work to do, and there was no telling when Richie might call again.

O   O   O

Frank headed for his desk, and the stack of paperwork waiting for him there. He thought that during times of budget crisis, it made sense to keep cops out on the street as much as possible. But a bean-counter somewhere had convinced the brass that the cost of paperwork inefficiency was too high to be borne. Making detectives sit inside typing out form after form would somehow result in cost savings for the city. Frank didn't follow the logic, but he did what he was told.

He had just sat down when his cell phone vibrated in his pocket. He pulled it out. His sister Yolanda. "Yeah?"

"Frank?" Her voice had a quaver in it. She didn't sound like the confident sister he knew, who would boss around a five-star general if he crossed her path.

"What is it?"

"It's Pops."

"What?"

"You gotta get to the hospital, Frankie."

"What happened?"

"They're still not sure. He was having trouble breathing, and he collapsed. It's not good."

"I'm on my way." He was pulling the phone from his ear when he stopped himself. "Wait, what hospital?"

"Wayne County Receiving."

The one Marcia worked at. That was good. She would take care of him. "I'm on my way."

O   O   O

Marcia intercepted him in the parking lot as he tried to pick out the shortest route from his car to the hospital entrance. She put one hand on his arm and the other on his shoulder. "It's bad, Frank," she said. "But he's hanging in there."

"What happened?"

"They're still running tests, but they think maybe it's acute respiratory distress syndrome. ARDS."

"What's that?"

"It's a usually sudden and severe lung disorder," she explained. "The lungs fail to work properly, which means they're not pushing oxygen into the blood, or removing carbon dioxide."

"What's it come from?"

"It's often associated with some other disease, or shock, or a severe infection. In your dad's case they don't know yet."

"They fucking well better find out." Frank knew his anger was misplaced—he had no reason to direct it toward Marcia. But she was there, and he wasn't thinking clearly, was simply reacting. They started toward the door. "I'm sorry, babe, I didn't mean that. What's gonna happen to him?"

"They don't know. It's often fatal, though. He's in a coma now. He might come out of it in a day, a week. Maybe never. You got to prepare yourself for whatever comes."

"Thanks, Marcia," he said reflexively. *Prepare yourself* sounded like good advice, but Frank had no idea how to follow it. He'd just been talking to Maynard about the fact that he still had his family. How did you flip a switch that changed you from someone who had both parents and all your siblings to someone who didn't? He wasn't sure how to make that adjustment, or if he would ever figure it out.

Then again, he might not need to. She said he might come out of it in a day or two. Should he put himself through the agony of trying to let someone go who wasn't really leaving?

His knees felt like plastic pop bottles that had sat in the sun too long; floppy and full of semi-congealed liquid. He didn't want to collapse on the way into the hospital, so he forced himself to take step after step, keeping up with Marcia, trying to present a bold front to the people they passed. Sweat rivered down his sides, soaked his collar.

Marcia led him to a private room on the third floor. His mother sat in a chair in one corner, wearing a blue dress and her usual canary yellow cardigan. Yolanda was there, and their sister Claire, too; the two of them standing together against a wall. His mother usually carried more tissues on her person than a Kleenex salesman, and if the snowy mountain range growing around her feet was any indication, today was no different. She looked up when Frank entered, her eyes red and bleary, nose chapped. She sniffled twice, let out a long wail, and launched herself from the seat and into Frank's arms.

"Oh, God," she said. Sidney Bechet's "Blue Horizon" drifted softly from a CD player near Pops's bed. One of the old man's favorites. "Oh, God, oh my dear God in heaven."

"Momma," Yolanda said. "Momma, calm down."

"It's all right," Frank said.

"No it's not. Don't do no good to be out of control."

"She's just grieving."

"The time for grieving is not yet. Might come, but not yet."

"She's upset," Frank said.

"We're all upset. She don't have to deal with it by getting snot all over that nice suit."

"It's okay." He wrapped his arms around his mother, held her until the shuddering sobs quieted. "Can somebody please tell me what happened?"

He eased his mother back into her chair, where she manifested another tissue from someplace. She kept them up her sleeves, in pockets, sometimes tucked into holes in the hems that she seemed to have burrowed there for just that purpose. "He was … he was in the kitchen," she said. "I was fixin' some supper, and he come in and said he was thirsty, needed a drink. He looked bad. I told him to sit, got him a glass of water. He started to pull the chair out and then he just fell over. Knocked the chair down and scared me half to death. I dropped the glass, it shattered on the floor. The whole thing's just a mess."

"Don't worry about the glass, Momma. It's not important. How we paying for this private room?"

"Don't think about that yet, Frank," Marcia said from the doorway. "He's got the Medicare, and I can pull some strings."

"All right." Frank gulped in a deep breath and went to the side of the bed. Pops had always been a man of substance, heavier than Frank, but he carried it well. He possessed that special grace one expected to see in athletes. He had been one, in his younger days. Never pro, but good just the same. Football, baseball. Not tall enough for basketball, to his eternal regret. He'd been a musician, too, a horn player, which Frank thought made it especially ironic that he had been brought low by a respiratory ailment.

Then he'd worked in the Detroit salt mine, had a career down there scraping salt off the walls and bringing it up. Salt for the Midwest, salt for the East. Salt for everybody. He was proud of it. It was hard work, grueling. But people need salt, he always said. No matter what else comes and goes, folks always need salt. That's job security.

And it was. He had spent decades down there, beneath the city. That might have contributed to his condition too, Frank thought.

He had never been rich, but he'd been solidly middle class. He had raised up three kids, put all three through college, and wanted them to have the advantages he never did.

Frank had never noticed how much he had shrunk with age. A broad smile and a hearty laugh could disguise a lot. But he looked small in the bed, light, as if a stiff wind could toss him across the room. His face was gaunt and gray. His hands looked feeble, like he could barely hold a thought. His eyes were closed, and he had a mask over his nose and mouth, tubes going in and out to breathe for him. With all that, his chest rose only slightly underneath the sheets, in time with a hissing sound. Frank thought it would drive him nuts if he had to stay in here for long. So would the odor, a kind of bubble-gum-flavored disinfectant smell.

They'd told him it wasn't good, and he had to agree. It didn't look good. He picked up his father's right hand, squeezed it. But there was no return squeeze. That was a first, in Frank's experience, and it brought tears to his eyes, a lump to his throat that he couldn't swallow down. Maybe this was it. The end of something; the end of being a man's son.

Frank laid the hand back down gently, blinking back tears that wouldn't cooperate but instead slid down his cheeks, as hot as molten rock.

30

While Richie had never been in Tucson before, at least he had known people who had been there. En route to Omaha, by way of Las Vegas, he couldn't think of a single person who had ever told him they'd visited Nebraska. He was sure people did so, and quite possibly he had encountered them from time to time. But none had seen fit to mention it to him.

From the air, the landscape looked more Midwestern than Western, as though it had been painted on a huge canvas rather than sculpted in relief. The landing was smooth, the taxi short, and he was out of the airport and in another rented car, this one on his own credit card, the additional hit to it weighing heavily on his mind. There would come a time of reckoning, when the bills arrived and Wendy flipped out. Frank had offered to pay for it all, and Richie might yet have to take him up on that.

The city was bigger and busier than he had expected. The older buildings reminded him of Detroit, lots of brick and fading paint, but there were also new skyscrapers that defied his expectation of a sleepy little meatpacking town. He got a room at the Satellite Motel, just because he liked the pictures he had seen online of its octagonal shape.

Once he'd settled in, he booted up his laptop and started searching the *Omaha World-Herald* archives. Almost immediately, he found four stories about girls who had disappeared during the time he believed Jarod Morton had lived here. All had been white, three blondes and a brunette, ranging in age from seven to eleven. The fact that they had vanished was almost all they had in common. They had lived in different neighborhoods, gone to different schools, come from families of different income levels. One had been taken from a school bus stop, one from home, one from a theater, and one from a park. Although the public got involved in each case, raising reward money, forming search parties and the like, none had ever been found.

Having determined the grim reality, he duplicated the steps that had been at least partially successful in Tucson. A trip to the library turned up old phone books, which confirmed that Morton hadn't lived here under that name or under the Mannheim one, but that a photo studio using the exact same angel-style portrait, a place called Angelic You Portraits, had been located in midtown during the years in question.

He went to the City Clerk's office in Omaha's City Offices Building on Farnham Street, and learned that the registered owner of Angelic You had been someone calling himself Gerald Miller. So between Detroit and Omaha, Morton had changed his name, and then again between Omaha and Tucson. How many other times had he done the same?

Richie drove to the largely upper middle class neighborhood of Elkhorn, which had been a separate city when Morton had lived here but had since been consumed by a growing Omaha. He found the address, a house that looked as if it had always been on the less prosperous end of Elkhorn's demographics. It was brick, a single-story ranch, with a garage and another addition that looked like they had been added on years after the fact, by someone who wasn't all that skilled a builder. The yard was lush, but needed mowing.

Richie was sitting in his rental looking at it when a sage-colored Ford Escape pulled into the driveway. A harried-looking but trim blond woman emerged, in business wear and conservative pumps. She brushed hair off her face and opened the back door, and two little girls who looked like smaller mirror images of her bounded out, scrambling toward the house while carrying on what seemed to be continuous sibling warfare. Richie watched her take in a deep breath, straighten her spine, and march across the yard. A single mother, he guessed, with two exhausting handfuls to deal with in addition to a high-stress job. He was already sure Jarod Morton didn't live here anymore, although the kids looked like they might be his type.

He almost hated to disturb her, but on the other hand, he was getting kind of used to being a nuisance.

He was out of the car while she was still unlocking her front door. By the time she was inside and beginning to close it, he was hustling toward her. "Excuse me," he said. "I'm sorry to bother you, I can see you've got a lot going on. I was just wondering if I could ask you about your house."

She appraised him for a long moment. Her eyes were set far apart, her mouth was wide, her jaw firm. He had a feeling that steady gaze was a tool she employed often. "What about it? You want to buy it? Because if you have fifty bucks in cash we can probably reach a deal."

"I'm not in the market, thanks." He handed her one of his new business cards. "Actually, I'm looking for information on what I believe is a former resident, a man named Gerald Miller."

"I've never heard of him," she said. "I bought the house three years ago from a widow, an elderly woman who was moving into a nursing home. I got a good deal on it, I thought. She didn't tell me about the leaks or the infestations. Or the screwy wiring."

"You don't know who owned it before her?"

"No. She didn't live here very long, I don't think. The first year or so, I occasionally got mail for a previous resident, but I don't remember what the name was."

Another dead end, then. Once again, he could track down records, but that might take a while. And since Morton's forwarding address had expired—if he had ever declared one—what good would it do? "Did you live in the neighborhood before?" he asked.

"No, I lived in Deer Park. This is farther from work, but it's cheaper. With those two little terrors growing up, cheaper is good."

"Do you know if any of your neighbors were living here six or seven years ago? People who might remember who lived here then?"

"People around here don't seem to move much," she said. "Honestly, I haven't really made a lot of friends. There are neighbors I say 'Hi' to, you know, but that's about it. Most of them have been around a while, though, so you could always ask. What's this about, anyway?"

Richie thought about her living here with those two girls, who would have been just Morton's thing, and he couldn't bring himself to be specific. "I'm looking for someone," he said. "Someone who lived here then. Nothing more than that."

"Okay," she said, seemingly satisfied with his obvious dodge. "Listen, I have to go rustle up some grub and make sure they don't cut each other's hair again."

"You do that." He shook her hand, pleased at the firmness of her touch. "And thanks for your time."

O O O

Richie spent a second afternoon knocking on doors and asking questions about Jarod Morton, trying to convince people that he wasn't selling anything. He passed out business cards and pretended he was a private investigator without actually saying so. He dropped the word "police" when he had to. He was treading a fine line, but hoped he wasn't making a big enough nuisance of himself that anyone would report him.

There were a few empty houses on these blocks, but not many, nothing like Detroit. As the first woman had said, the neighborhood seemed stable. People remembered Morton and his wife; not in great detail, but a glint of recognition came into their eyes when they saw the pictures, and Richie got the occasional "hmm, yeah" response he'd been looking for.

At the sixth house he visited, three down from the Mortons', and across the street, he finally got a little more.

A woman answered the door. She was in her mid-forties, with dark brown hair, bangs cutting straight across just above her eyebrows, tied back in a short ponytail he could see from time to time as she turned her head. She had broken one of her front teeth along the way, and it sometimes snagged her lower lip in a way Richie found charming. She had an air of faded ex-cheerleader about her, and sure enough, behind her in the living room was a glass-fronted case with trophies inside it. She gave him an inquisitive look through a bug-spattered screen. "Yeah?"

"I was wondering if I could ask you a couple of questions," Richie said. "I'm not selling anything, don't worry. Here's my card."

She pushed the screen open enough to snag the card from his fingers, glanced at it, flipping it over to see if there was anything on the back. "About what?"

"A former neighbor. Gerald Miller." He pointed out the house. "He lived right there, with his wife, seven years ago." Richie flashed a photo.

"Oh, yeah, I remember them. Did you want to come in for a minute?"

"I don't want to impose," Richie said. "This is fine. What do you remember?"

She chewed on her lip. "Him I didn't know that well. But Barbara … I thought maybe Barbara and I could be friends. I mean, I tried. I reached out, you know? I had her over for coffee a few times. She was around my age, and she seemed nice enough."

"Did something happen?"

"She was just a hard woman to get to know, I guess. Very private?" Sometimes her voice rose at the end of a sentence, making it sound like a question. Richie found himself nodding along, responding to questions he wasn't sure she was asking. "More than private. I mean, I'm not one to pry, but she never wanted to talk about herself or her husband."

"Do you remember anything about her personal life?"

"Oh, a couple of times I thought she was going to open up, and then it was like she caught herself? She pulled back right away. I mean, she'd chat about the weather, the neighbors, whatever, but not herself. It was like she had this dividing line between what was safe and what wasn't. With most people, I guess it's like politics and religion, at the beginning? But with Barbara it was always … I don't know, I guess her marriage, her family, what went on behind closed doors."

"And you never got any hints about what that was?"

"No, not at all. She was a pro when it came to steering a conversation. For all I know, there could have been orgies every night, or they might have slept in separate bedrooms at opposite ends of the house. Usually you get a sense of that kind of thing from people, but not with her. She was too closed off."

"Then what happened? They moved away?"

"No, that's the weird thing. That may be why I remember Barbara so well. One day I realized I hadn't seen her around for a week or so. I started paying attention, watching for her, and I still didn't see her. I went over to the house and rang the doorbell. *He* came to the door. It was one of the only times I ever had a conversation with him. I asked for Barbara and he said she was visiting family back home. I asked where home was, you know, very casual. He said she was in North Carolina. I asked a few more questions, but he kind of blew me off. He wasn't exactly rude, but he was short, like he had something better to do than stand there talking to me? He wasn't telling me anything anyway."

She gnawed on her lower lip a little more, exposing that snaggletooth, her eyes darting this way and that. "He made you uncomfortable," Richie speculated.

"Yeah. Very much. I couldn't even put my finger on what it was. It was just this … vibe, I got from him? It wasn't how he looked, although I wouldn't call him a good-looking man. It was more … something about him was just kind of creepy. The way he talked, the way he stood there."

"How was that?"

She demonstrated as she described his posture. "Kind of … compressed, I guess you'd say? His shoulders forward, holding onto his own hands, twisting them. It's like he was nervous and that was making me nervous. Like he was coiled, was ready to spring. I've known a lot of athletes. He was no athlete, but there was that kind of contained energy you sometimes see before a game. Am I making sense?"

"Sure," Richie said. "I get it. What happened then?"

"Well, I never saw Barbara again. He said she was visiting family, but he didn't say when she'd be back. I had the impression that maybe something had happened, they'd separated or something and she'd gone home to her folks. Of course, I had no way of knowing. He wasn't going to tell me anything, and I had no way to reach her. I did call the police once."

"You did?"

"When she didn't come back? I was worried. She had never told me there was anything wrong in the marriage. Of course, like I said, she just didn't talk about that. But a woman picks up on signals. I called, they went over. I don't know what he told them, but after that, I could feel him shooting me the evil eye whenever he walked out of his house. Another few months went by, and he moved away. I was relieved. I didn't think I could stand having him for a neighbor for any length of time, by himself."

"And that's the last you heard of him or Barbara?"

"Until today. I mean, the neighbors talked a little, at first? But that faded fast. Nobody had any answers. I was the one who knew Barbara the best, and that wasn't very well."

"So you can't think of any neighbors who would know where he went after he moved away?"

"No. Definitely not. Like I said, she disappeared and then he did. I don't know if he followed her to North Carolina or what."

"All right," Richie said. "I really appreciate the information. If you can think of anything else, anything at all, you've got my number on the card."

"I will," she said. "I hope it was helpful."

"I think it was. Thank you again."

Richie knocked on a few more doors, but the woman had been right. Although people remembered the Mortons from the neighborhood, no one remembered them better than she did. In fact, when he asked, she was pointed out as the only one who was friends with them. "Friends" seemed like a stretch, but Richie didn't argue the point.

31

Sheriff Kate had the lights flashing and the siren blaring, and still the farm truck in front of her trundled down the road as if it were the only vehicle on wheels. She leaned on the horn, and if anything, it moved farther into the center. She briefly considered shooting it.

After what seemed like an hour, the driver caught a clue and swerved right, almost plowing into an oak tree growing beside the road. Kate roared past, not even slowing to memorize his face in case she ever saw him again.

She'd had a call twenty minutes earlier. The Teeters, a farming couple she knew, had found a little girl walking alone on a quiet country road. She had been scared, and they had taken her home, then called the sheriff's office. The fact that she might be Missy Trimble had sprung to mind immediately, and Kate realized, just a moment later, that it didn't matter if she was or not—any little girl out by herself could fall prey to whatever fate Missy had, and she wanted to get to the bottom of it.

When she reached the turnoff into the farm, she was going so fast she nearly barreled right past. She stomped on the brakes, and the Yukon skidded and slid and generally made a commotion, but it came to a halt. Kate backed up, pointed it down the gravel drive, and approached the house at a more commonsensical speed.

The Teeters met her at the door. Lance Teeter was pure farmer, lean as a fence post and seemingly tall enough to have to duck under a barn door. His face wouldn't have looked out of place on currency, or Mount Rushmore. Kate understood the appeal of tall men, she thought, especially to short women, which Pamela Teeter was, just as tiny and round as he was long and angular. You could feel safe if your man could hold up the sky.

"Where is she?" Kate asked, dispensing with politeness.

"She's at the table, having some cake," Pamela said. Her hair was a pleasant silver color, contradicting the youthful appearance of her smooth face and hands. "That girl can eat."

"She's probably starved," Lance said.

"Take me to her."

Lance and Pamela parted like the two sides of a double door, and Kate passed between them. "On your left," Pamela said.

Kate turned. The kitchen was open, off the dining room. A thin girl with a cascade of dark blond hair sat licking chocolate crumbs from a fork. She wore the sleeveless summer dress with arching rainbows on it that had been described in the reports and shown incessantly on the local news. Her eyes were deep-set, and Kate knew who she was instantly. She had studied the pictures nonstop. "Missy?"

The girl dropped the fork onto her plate with a clang that echoed through the small kitchen. "Yes?"

"You are Missy Trimble, right?"

"Yes. I mean, yes ma'am."

"Are you all right?"

Missy rubbed her stomach and looked at the cake on the counter, with a big wedge cut out of it. "I think I ate too much."

Kate considered sitting at the table, but settled for crouching on the floor beside it, a little lower than Missy. "I mean, from being taken. Do you know who took you away from your mom?"

"Oh. That was a man."

"Do you know who? Or where he had you?"

"No. I mean, at his house, I guess."

"Did he hurt you?" The Teeters hovered at the door. Kate drove them away with a stern glance. "Did he touch you any place private, Missy?"

"I don't think so."

"Do you know what I mean?"

"I don't know. Maybe."

Kate had trained for this sort of thing, but she trained for a lot of things. This wasn't one that came up often, fortunately, but she wished she had a defter hand at it.

"Can you describe the man who took you?"

"He was old, I guess."

"How old? Old like me?"

"Maybe not that. I don't know."

"Older than your mom?"

"I think so."

"Was he a white man, or what?"

"Yes, white."

"Did he have white hair?"

Missy stared at the ceiling as if she could see him there. "No, it was brown, I guess."

"Heavy? Tall, short? Is there anything you can tell me about him? He can't hurt you now."

"He never did hurt me." She looked almost indignant at the prospect.

"But you were afraid, weren't you?"

"At first I was."

"Only at first?"

"Could I have some milk?"

"Of course, honey. I'll get you some." Kate was glad for the chance to stand up and stretch. She hadn't expected to be squatting for so long. She found a glass in a cupboard and some one-percent in the refrigerator. "Here you go," she said, and this time she did sit.

Missy drank, then set the glass down on the table with a thud. The ghost of a milk mustache graced her upper lip. "So, he didn't touch you?" Kate asked. "What did he do?"

"Talked to me. Or tried to. Some grown-ups aren't very good at talking to kids."

"That's true," Kate said. "Anything else?"

"He stared. A lot."

"Did that make you feel uncomfortable?"

"Duh! He was staring at me."

"Did he make you ... undress?"

"No. I mean, I did at bedtime."

"Was he there?"

"No. He had this room, like a little girl's room, that I slept in. There were some nightgowns in it, and I found one that fit me. He gave me a new doll, a baby doll, even though I'm way too old for that. He had stuffies, books and toys and things, and lots of dolls. He told me their names."

"Whose names?

"The dolls. He said each doll was a special little girl. He said they were Jenny and Susie and Rachel and ... I don't remember the others. Is that okay?"

"Sure, honey," Kate said. "What else *do* you remember?"

"I started reading a book about witches that was pretty good, but then I fell asleep."

"And he didn't come into your room during the night?"

"No. I guess in the morning he came in and woke me up, when breakfast was ready. He made eggs and toast and sausages and, and ... what's that orange melon?"

"Cantaloupe?"

"Yeah! I like cantaloupe. And a big glass of orange juice." She smiled at the memory. "He made a pretty good breakfast."

Kate gave her a second to relish what seemed like a decent memory. The guy was a son-of-a-bitch, whether or not he molested Missy, but scaring her with the truth of her close call wouldn't do her any favors. "Then what?'

"Then we drove around for a while, and then he let me out."

"Were you relieved?"

"Some I guess. But also scared. I was all alone and didn't know how to get home."

"But then the Teeters came along."

"That's right, and they were nice. Especially Mrs. Teeter. She makes a good cake."

"Looks like it," Kate said. "All right, Missy, I'll tell you what. I'm going to call the police in Modesto, because they've been looking for you, and your mom has been looking everywhere for you. Pretty much the whole city has. You've been on TV a lot since you were taken."

Missy blushed for the first time. "Me? On TV?"

"That's right. You're kind of a star."

"No, I'm not."

"Missy, when you get home there are going to be at least a dozen reporters shouting questions at you, shoving microphones in your face, waving cameras. We'll try to hold them back, but it might be bad, do you understand?"

"I guess so. Like Hannah Montana or something."

"Something like that. And you don't have to talk to them. You don't have to say anything at all."

"Okay."

"In fact, it would be better if you didn't. If you don't cooperate, they'll eventually go away and leave you and your mom alone."

"Okay."

"I'm going to drive you down to Modesto, okay? I don't want you to worry about a thing."

"All right."

"You're safe with me."

"I know. I've just never ridden in the back of a police car. I heard on TV you can't get out."

"That's right, you can't. But I'll tell you what. Because I like you, you can ride up in the front with me. How would that be?"

"That," Missy said, "sounds like fun."

"We'll try," Kate said. "It'll be a long drive, but we'll have as much fun as we can."

32

There had been times, some not so long ago, when this one would have been fine. At least for a while. But not now, not when the real angel was so close. This one's wings had been but nubs, not the luminous, spreading beauties of the true angel. She had been imperfect, flawed in too many ways, and when one was close enough to taste perfection, it became hard to settle for less.

In months and years gone by, she would have done. Welker had tried, oh how he had tried, to make do with what was available. He sought and he sought. But none were just right.

In moments of lucidity, he knew that the way he loved went against the standards of society, what people considered decent. They were misguided, but that didn't mean he didn't feel the hate venting off them, like steam through a city manhole.

Even the woman he so rarely thought about anymore, the one he called The Other when she crossed his mind at all, had turned against him in the end. Oh, she had been happy at first, and he supposed he had been as well. She was young, and he was still confused, searching, trying to discover what he wanted and needed in life. She had wanted to be rescued from her family's home, and she had been delighted to be presented with the young angel.

But that delight hadn't lasted. As he became more aware of his own tastes, he told her the angel would have to go one day. She had agreed. The Other knew her place, at first, and being agreeable was her role. But she had never forgotten, never moved on. She became less tolerant of his attempts to find a new angel. Eventually, she started to laugh at him, speaking dismissively of him and to him, calling him crazy, and worse.

She was the one who was damaged, the one who couldn't see the wings sprouting from their backs, the glow around the likeliest ones, heaven's finger touching individual lives. She couldn't see it and she questioned his sanity when he said he did.

She'd had to go. That fact became abundantly clear. He hadn't liked doing it—not in the moment, at least. In retrospect, though, there was a certain liberation in it. He didn't think of The Other often, but when he did, that's how he liked to remember her.

In his times of clarity, he recognized his own pattern for what it was. When he finished with one, he was sated, for a while. He set his urges aside, focused on other things, trying to keep his mind busy, to ignore the need that grew steadily, day by day. During those times, he paid closer attention to his work, to the images and papers that earned his keep. After a while, he would start to notice them more, the angels and the would-be angels. They were in the streets, the playgrounds. They were on television. They filed through school doors. They were quite literally everywhere he looked. Their long-lashed eyes cast glances that would once have been described as come-hither looks, and that's how he saw them. They wore tights, or snug-fitting jeans, or dresses that showed soft shoulders and lanky legs.

Little by little, the urges took him over, moving from background to foreground, until concentrating on other tasks became next to impossible. Visions of angels swam before his eyes constantly. He became hyper-aware, then, the touch of a cup of tea burning his hand or a sip from a cool drink making his teeth ache with the chill. The fabric of his everyday clothing chafed his skin. Colors became more vibrant, strident even, forcing him to wear dark glasses, even indoors, even at night, just to mute their assault.

That was when he hunted, when the fever was upon him and he could think of nothing but the whisper of soft young skin, the warmth, the angelic glow that would encompass him. Lucidity was gone then, worries about societal condemnation gone, his mind focused on only one thing.

He would reach that stage again soon. He had not possessed the imperfect angel, but had let her go, let her return to earth with her grubby wings unclipped. Unsatiated, the urge would rise again quickly. It would be this way for a while, he knew. Reason and obsession battling for supremacy, obsession winning, most of the time, until he had her. Until he had the true angel back in his arms.

He bustled around the shop, doing nothing useful, checking his computer frequently, rearranging stacks of paper, trying to plan a day's work but knowing at the same time that the plan would come to nothing, that he couldn't sit still, couldn't spend more than a minute or two on any given task. It was too close, *she* was too close. The blindness was already stealing upon him again.

It would not be long. Circumstances had interceded to move up the event, and he was glad now that they had. The waiting was awful. But the closer the day came, the harder the waiting got. He'd thought that the last one, Missy, could take the edge off, but she couldn't. He might try again, someone else.

Yes, he almost certainly would have to try again. He could feel it already, surging up inside of him like a rising tide, blood coursing, hot and insistent, through his veins. He would have to try again, and it would have to be soon.

33

It was late afternoon when Richie was finished. Instead of going back to his room, he headed for the midtown neighborhood where Morton's photo studio had been, hoping some of his fellow merchants might remember him. The effort was wasted; shopkeepers wanted someone in their stores who meant to spend money, which left Richie out. When he showed Morton's picture, all he received in return were blank looks. After a while, he went into a nearby independent coffee shop called CupZ to make use of their free Wi-Fi.

The only customer was a man sitting at a table, reading a newspaper. Dressed in a pinstriped gray suit, he looked like he had stopped in on his way home from work. He took off a few minutes after Richie got a big mug of coffee and booted up his laptop. The loud rustle and snap as the man folded his newspaper, putting sharp creases in its edges, surprised Richie, and he realized it wasn't a sound he heard much anymore. Most people got their news from TV or the Internet. Not just news, but sports scores, even classified ads. Craigslist had taken over that business, he thought. He and Wendy had scored a couch off it just last year.

He remembered an early conversation he'd had with Frank. Frank was talking about his love of comic books, showing him the boxes he had stacked up in his den. "Can't you read those online?" Richie had asked.

Frank looked horrified. "Sure, you *can*. But *should* you? Hell, no. Comic-style stories created just for online viewing, that's different. Not something I'm interested in, but that's its own thing, and I got no problem with it. But that's not comic *books*. The pleasure of a comic book isn't just the story, it's the whole experience. When you're a kid, you're in the drugstore, maybe, while your mother's picking up a prescription. You come across a wire spin-rack full of colorful, illustrated adventures about larger-than-life heroes. That ushers you into a whole new world that somehow you know is not shared by everybody. It's special and just a little bit secret. Forbidden. Your teachers think it's a waste of time, money, and brain cells. It's like somebody invited you into the coolest club there is. You buy one and you take it home, read it in your room at night, turning those thin sheets of paper.

"See, a comic story isn't just the picture in the panel, and the words in the panel on top of the picture. That's part of it, but there's also how the panels are laid out, how they connect to each other, what happens between the panels. What happens at the top of the page versus the bottom of the page. If there's going to be a surprise, it's going to come when you turn the page. You don't get these things, not the same way, not online. You gotta have that tactile experience, turning the pages yourself, with your own fingers.

"Anyway, you get to be older, a teenager, comics are mostly available in comic book shops. Those aren't hip places to be seen, necessarily, but you go there anyhow. Maybe not with your home-boys, or just the one or two who understand. You pick up your comics, but you don't take 'em to school or tell everybody you know about 'em, like when you were younger. They're your thing, something to share only with special people.

"You get older still, you're an adult, going to a comic shop. You know that ain't right, you're supposed to be above all that. But that thrill of discovery from when you were a kid is magnified. The comic shop holds worlds upon worlds, more imagination and wonder than most people ever experience. Ask your neighbor what he's reading, it's the same book four other people on the bus are also reading, that new bestseller by that cat who wrote all those other bestsellers. But not you. You're being taken on a different trip. And again, you can share it with friends, but the real moment, the true moment, is when you're sitting in that chair holding that flimsy thirty-two-page book in your hands, watching the story unfold. That, Maynard, is what it's about, and you don't do that shit online."

Once the man was gone, there was nobody in the place but Richie and the barista, an attractive woman of about twenty-five or twenty-six, Richie guessed. She had a fresh face, with pronounced cheekbones and frizzy red hair. Her eyes were light brown, flecked with gold, and reminded Richie of beach sand in shallow water catching light on a sunny summer day. She was tall and voluptuous, stretching her CupZ polo shirt almost to the breaking point. The arms extending from its sleeves were nicely toned and lightly freckled; on her left wrist she wore a variety of bracelets: metal, wood, and plastic all clacking together as she worked.

The air was redolent with the usual coffee shop smells. Richie's own woody dark roast, cinnamon and nutmeg from the condiment stand behind him, the general warm embrace of the barista's world. But when she passed by, dropping off his mug, straightening tables, the barista brought with her a slightly autumnal, fruity scent that evoked, for Richie, a memory of one brilliant fall day when he and Wendy strolled hand-in-hand through an orchard in Macomb County, sometimes laughing out loud, sometimes engulfed in a comfortable silence.

At one point he was deeply involved in an online search when she interrupted him. "Work or pleasure?"

He looked up, caught her eye. "Excuse me?"

She nodded toward the laptop.

"Oh. That's work." He didn't want to go into any detail, certainly didn't want her to see the sorts of things he was using her wireless service to look up.

"I can turn the music down if it's bothering you."

He had barely noticed it. U2, singing about a street with no name. "No, it's fine. Thank you."

"All right. Give me a shout if you need anything."

"I will, thanks."

Driving over from Elkhorn, a thought had been taking root in Richie's mind. He didn't like it, but he figured it had to be checked out. Barbara going back home to Virginia might have been reasonable; there had probably been enormous stresses in the marriage ever since Angela's disappearance. But if she had gone home to Virginia, why hadn't he just said so? Why make up North Carolina? Yes, they had changed their names—although, interestingly, she had stuck with Barbara for a first name even though he kept changing his—but he had to know some random neighbor woman couldn't easily trace a Barbara Miller who didn't exist to a specific place in a state the size of Virginia. Why go that extra mile and make up a lie? All of it made Richie think Barbara had never gone home at all.

Online at the coffee shop, he checked the local obituaries, going back to when the Mortons had lived in Omaha. He doubted there would be one for Barbara—he thought the cheerleader would have noticed that. But it was the first, most obvious thing to look at, so he did. When that proved as fruitless as he expected, he looked for reports of unidentified female bodies who might have matched Barbara physically. That, too, was a blank.

He felt a hand on his shoulder and started. "I'm sorry," the barista said. She had a good smile, the kind that drew others to it, and she shared it liberally. "I just wanted to see if you needed a warm-up."

She didn't seem to be looking at his screen, or give any indication that she had been. "That would be great," Richie said, closing the laptop a little as he reached for his mug. He held it out and she took her hand off his shoulder. It seemed like she had left it there a long time; he still felt its warmth as she tossed him a casual smile. She held a stainless-steel pot, and she steadied the mug with her free hand, fingers touching Richie's, as she poured.

Richie glanced at the screen. It was on a news story, no photos. She would have had to read the text to know what he was looking at. She finished filling his mug and released it. "There you go."

"Thanks."

"I live to serve."

Works for me, he thought, watching her behind as she returned to the counter. She really was attractive, in an overstated, larger-than-life kind of way. When she was gone, he focused again on his search, widening it.

O   O   O

He'd been at it for a little over an hour, and two more refills, before he found anything. The place was filling up, and he was starting to feel bad about taking a table for so long when he came across a story about a female corpse found buried near a creek bed outside Council Bluffs, Iowa, across the state line from Omaha. The woman had been stabbed three times in the heart, then decapitated, her hands cut off. As far as Richie could tell, she had never been identified.

If it was Barbara's body, it meant Jarod had been clever enough to know that burying it there would cause jurisdictional confusion, making him harder to find and connect to the murder.

From what Richie could tell, given the bare-bones description in the news reports, it could have been Barbara. The age was close, anyway, as were the approximate height and weight. Beyond that, and short of a DNA match, there wasn't much way to tell, considering the condition of the remains.

Getting away with murder was a cliché that had come about because it was supposed to be rare and difficult. The truth, Richie knew, was often very different. From O. J. Simpson to Ted Bundy, people skated on murders all the time. Prosecutors took to court only the cases that were slam dunks, leaving behind other bodies, other families, other loved ones who would awaken every morning for the rest of their lives never quite certain that the killer had been found, that justice had been done. Robert Hansen probably killed at least twenty-one women, hunting them like animals in the Alaskan wilderness, but was convicted on just four counts. In some cases, like that of John Brennan Crutchley—the so-called Vampire Rapist—no murders were ever pinned on people suspected of dozens.

Even cutting off head and hands wasn't a guaranteed walk. Joel Rifkin chopped up some of his victims, hid the parts in separate barrels, and tossed them in the East River, and he still went down. But that, and burying the victim across state lines—they were good moves if you wanted to stay out of prison. They made things a lot harder for the cops. Obviously, Morton had put some thought into disposing of his potentially problematic spouse.

When Richie had read everything he could find online about the woman, he shut down the laptop and closed it. His hands were trembling, and he couldn't tell if it was from the stories or all the coffee. When he set his empty mug on the counter, he shoved a five-dollar bill he couldn't afford into the tip jar. "Thanks for your help," he said. "Sorry I used up so much real estate all afternoon."

"Oh, not a problem," she said. "You come back again."

"Maybe I'll do that."

O O O

Since he didn't know how thick the walls at the Satellite Motel were, Richie called Frank from inside his car. He got voicemail on Frank's cell, and someone at the precinct who promised to take a message. Richie didn't leave one. He couldn't tell anyone but Frank about this. He called the cell phone back. Voicemail again. "Frank," he said. "Give me a call as soon as you can. There's something we have to talk about. Jarod Morton is not only a pedophile, I think he's definitely a murderer. I think he killed Barbara—and maybe Angela, too. You need to see if you can find any reports within two hundred miles in every direction of a girl's body found with no head or hands. You heard me right. As soon as you can." He didn't know what else to say, so he left it at that.

34

Wil Fowler's mother, Carlotta Gray, lived in a small house, not much more than a cottage, on Berkshire near Frankfort. The yard was well kept, but the low stone wall supporting an iron-spiked fence separating yard from sidewalk was covered in graffiti, and when he looked closely, Frank saw a bullet hole in the wall above a living room window. The house had seen its troubles, and he was willing to bet its residents had known their share as well.

He had torn himself away from his father's bedside, mostly at Yolanda's urging. "You're doing no good here," she'd insisted. "He wakes up, we'll let you know. He don't, you're worth more out on the street catchin' bad guys."

He didn't know how much of that he would get done today, but he figured he could go by Wil Fowler's place, see what he could learn about the kid. Wil wasn't home when he arrived, but when he flashed his badge Carlotta let him in.

"Why my boy locked up all night?" she demanded. She was short, not quite reaching Frank's shoulder, but she was wiry and animated, and he got the feeling that crossing her would be a mistake. "You do that?"

"Ma'am, I'm the only reason he's out."

"What you mean?"

"I mean, he was in possession of stolen property, Mrs. Gray. He could have been booked and arraigned and you'd be fetching a lawyer right now, trying to raise bail money."

"That boy ain't boosted nothin'!"

"I didn't say he did. I said he had stolen goods in his possession, which he did."

"What was they?"

"A valuable coin collection that had been stolen recently."

"I never seen it."

"I wouldn't imagine he'd show it to you."

The house smelled of fish, probably what she'd had for dinner. It was clean, but close and dark, and Carlotta's taste in home decor seemed to run toward religious representations of a particularly grim nature. The crucified Jesus painting above her plaid cloth sofa had dark skin and blood streaming from multiple wounds. "He wouldn't dare."

"There you go."

She sat down on the sofa and wove her fingers together. Her expression was slightly less anguished than Jesus's, but not a lot. "He ain't had all the right things."

"Like what?" Frank asked. "What's he missing?"

"His daddy was gone before he was born. He got a stepdaddy, raised him up with me, but he in prison now."

"What's his name?"

"Clinton. Clinton Gray. We married nine years now."

"What were the charges?"

"Oh, he a stupid man. Got hisself a gun, tried to hold up some stores with a friend even stupider than him. He come home with fifty-seven dollars and change, thinkin' he the shit. Next day Clinton go out again, get caught in about fifteen seconds. Next thing, he in for five to seven, leavin' me and Wil here alone."

"I'm sorry to hear that, ma'am."

"So I don't want that boy catchin' no heat."

"That's more or less up to him. I don't want him in trouble, either, which is why I cut him loose."

She met his gaze and held it for a long moment. "I appreciate that, I truly do. Sometimes trouble find somebody, whether he lookin' for it or not."

"I suppose that's true."

"That's how Wil be. He don't look for it, but it look for him just the same."

"I feel you," Frank said.

"I got to deal with his stepdaddy bein' in prison. That's hard on a family, you know?"

"I know."

"Visitin', tryin' to run a house, don't leave a lot of time to deal with a headstrong boy."

"Yes, ma'am."

"I don't want nothin' to happen to that boy."

"I'm sure not."

"Clinton, he a good man mostly. Stupid sometimes is all. Tryin' to provide."

"Yes, ma'am."

"Only time Wil keep clear of trouble is when he sit in his room drawin' them pictures."

Frank was surprised. He had stereotyped the kid as much as anybody else might have, and artwork had not entered into his image of Wil Fowler. "He draws?"

"Can't hardly stop him."

"Can I see his work?"

Carlotta narrowed her eyes at Frank, as if he had just asked permission to torch her house. "Suppose it won't do no harm. You already think he's a thief. How much worse is a thief who draws?"

"There's nothing shameful about being an artist, ma'am. Some folks make a good living at it."

"Easy for you to say, you got a job. You makin' somethin' of yourself."

He didn't want to spend his day fighting a pointless battle. "I'd like to see his pictures, if I could."

"All right." She took him to Wil's room, which was clean, though furnished with a kind of boot camp simplicity. He didn't have a drawing board, but he had an old carving board propped up on a desk, piles of books behind it holding it at an angle and a couple of nails driven into the desktop keeping it from slipping. There was a sheet of illustration board taped to it, with a street scene lightly sketched out in pencil. Nearby was a stack of other sheets.

Frank thumbed through them. Most were Detroit street scenes like the one on the board. Some depicted places Frank recognized: an abandoned building in midtown with all its windows gone and "PAIDAWAY!" painted in giant letters near the top, the anti-Semitic Father Coughlin's vaguely phallic Shrine of the Little Flower, the Majestic Theatre on Woodard, a store on Michigan Ave. called Everything For Dollar. The scenes had been drawn with an almost Impressionistic approach, suggesting real life rather than mimicking it, but the figures inhabiting those places came straight out of Wil's world. They were mostly black folks, standing on street corners, playing strike-out in front of a square painted on a wall, throwing dice, holding bottles in paper bags, kids playing in a street while parents watched from stoops. He had worked them into the scenes with a realism that was almost photographic. Not only was the kid talented, but his combination of ultrarealistic humans set against a suggested cityscape was unique, in Frank's experience.

"He's very good."

"You say so. You clownin' me, or you want to buy one?"

Actually, Frank did. But he wouldn't, not without Wil there to sell it to him. He wanted to make sure it was something Wil didn't mind parting with, and that he got the money. Most poor kids Frank had known who tried to use legal means of bettering their position in life chose hoops or rap. Those dreams rarely panned out, but the example of a single Eminem could spur thousands, white and black, to try. Frank thought a dream that never came true could be devastating, but in the long run he would rather live in a world where people had dreams, even if they didn't materialize, than one in which hope didn't exist at all. As long as there was hope, there was possibility. So he would take the Eminem wannabes, the would-be Lebrons, and be glad that, for a while, at least, people wanted something bad enough to make an effort.

Anyway, a couple of kids he'd met had done all right for themselves. He couldn't think of any he'd encountered who had chosen art for that purpose, and he wasn't sure that was Wil's intention. But he expected Wil could pull it off if he wanted to. "I will sometime. From Wil."

"Yeah, what I thought." Carlotta walked out of the room, leaving Frank no choice but to follow. He would rather have spent more time with the artwork and less with Carlotta.

Back in the living room, she paced and launched into a diatribe about Clinton Gray's troubles. Frank felt an overwhelming urge to flee. She wasn't telling him anything about Wil, not intentionally, at least. Instead, she sounded more concerned about her husband than about the possibility that Wil might be following his path.

He excused himself as soon as he was able, letting himself out into a cool evening breeze. Outside, he felt like he could breathe again. Loud hip-hop blared from down the block, and he let the music wash over him for a few moments, then got into his car and cranked up some Al Green.

O O O

He had the police radio on, and after one song he turned down the Reverend Al enough to hear the steady, crackling hum of conversation. He wasn't ready to go home yet, but he didn't want to go back to the hospital, to the depressing sight of his unconscious father, kept breathing by machines. Instead, he cruised the streets of his beloved city. When Al Green ended he put on a CD by Martha and the Vandellas, *Heat Wave*. His father had played alto saxophone on two of the album's tracks, back in his musician days, before he decided that gigging wasn't steady enough work to pay the bills.

When he heard a report of a domestic disturbance a few blocks from his location, Frank shut off Martha and said he'd respond. A domestic disturbance could be a scary thing. You never knew how people would react to having a cop show up and interfere in their private lives.

But he was nearby, and it would take his mind off his own issues. He rolled up to a house. Most of the streetlamps on the block were out, but the home in question was blazing with light. Two figures were silhouetted against a sheer white curtain, facing each other. Frank could read the tension from the street.

He glanced at the house next door, where faces were faintly visible in the moonlight shining on a front window. Probably the ones who had called in the complaint. He nodded at them once and strode toward the brightly lit house. The people inside were screaming at each other, so loud and frantic that he couldn't make out their words. The tone was bad enough, though, each shouted syllable dripping with contempt.

Frank pounded his fist on the door and announced himself. A momentary lag in the scream-fest followed, but it didn't last. He tried the doorknob, announcing himself again. "Detroit police!" he cried. "I'm coming in!"

He found them in the kitchen. A cheap dining table had been upended, a checkbook and a stack of bills strewn all over the floor. Not hard to see what this fight was about. He faced a white man, backed up against the sink, who looked to be in his mid-thirties, gaunt, unshaven, with tattoos on both arms. He wore a plain blue T-shirt with a small hole at the gut and sweat stains under the arms.

"Tell this bitch to chill," he said when Frank entered.

The woman was skinny, with a dark complexion and black hair. Her backside might have been a boy's, her arms little more than bone and muscle. Her hands were held in front of her, out of Frank's view. She glanced over her shoulder at him, her eyes huge and dark. "Fuck off," she said.

Frank suspected that the five beer bottles and the half-empty White Wolf bottle had something to do with the extremity of the situation. The rounded, yeasty scent of the Miller seemed to buttress the sharp-edged tang of vodka. "Ma'am, I'm a police officer. I'm going to need you both to calm down and talk to me."

"You're gonna have to cuff her, man. She's fuckin' nuts!"

"Both of you, take a step back from this. It hasn't gone too far yet."

"Dude, it's way too far," the man cried.

The woman made a slow, casual pirouette, and Frank's gaze locked on the gun in her right hand, a small, blued, semi-automatic pistol. He almost felt the adrenaline kick up a notch. He held out his left hand toward her, wishing he had already filled his right.

"Ma'am, you've got to give me that."

"She got it from the bedroom closet," the man said. "I keep it in a box there, you know, just in case. I never thought she'd pull it on me."

"This fucker can't hold a job. He spends money on booze and dope and hookers, and I'm fucking sick of it."

"We can talk about all that," Frank said. "But please, give me the weapon before somebody gets hurt."

"That's pretty much the point of a gun, isn't it? To hurt someone?"

"We can work this out, ma'am. Really." Frank took a careful step toward her, gliding, trying to keep his body language unthreatening. He was a dozen feet away, ten feet. Eight.

"I think I already figured out the best way to work it out," she said. She spun away from Frank. He lunged, but the gun boomed an instant before he reached her. He threw his arms around her, driving her to the ground, pinning the gun. She writhed and wriggled but he got a grip on her arm, tugged it free and twisted. He felt her tendons and bones rotating, hoped she would give up before he snapped her wrist. Finally, tearing off a curse, she released the weapon. As soon as it clunked to the floor, he snatched it up, then shifted off her, transferring it to his left hand and drawing his duty weapon with his right.

"Okay," Frank said, "let's all settle down, now."

Then Frank looked at the man. He held a hand over his mouth, but it couldn't contain the blood that spilled from above it, between upper lip and nose. There was a word for that spot but Frank couldn't remember what it was.

Blood splashed down the man's shirt, onto his shoes, the floor. His eyes were already going glassy.

Frank dropped the little gun into his pocket, whipped out his cell, pushed 911.

It would be too late for the man. Frank had been too late before he even reached the house.

Palms against the littered floor, the woman awkwardly pushed herself to hands and knees, wincing. Frank hoped he hadn't broken any ribs when he'd landed on her. Then again, he couldn't say she didn't deserve a little pain.

She reached for the kitchen cabinet and drew herself upright, then saw her husband, sinking while she rose. She let out a pained cry and fixed Frank with a ferocious glare. "Look what you've *done!*" she said. "Look what you've done!"

Frank had known a cop who'd ventured into a domestic dispute in which a man was threatening his wife with a hunting knife: six-inch blade, serrated back edge, a truly wicked weapon. The cop got between them, backed close to the woman to shield her in case the husband made a play. While his back was turned, she picked up a heavy crystal vase and brained him with it.

Frank had visited his friend in the hospital, where his head had been shaved and stitched. The cop had never gone back to the job after that; his short-term memory had turned to shit.

Even a couple engaged in a vicious fight could reunite against the hapless officer stuck in the middle. He hoped this woman wouldn't go that far, and he desperately hoped she wouldn't try to pin her act on him. He'd snatched the gun to keep it away from her, but without gloving up; his prints had almost certainly obscured some of hers. He had to get a crime scene unit out here in a hurry to run GSR tests on them both, and even at that he might have been close enough to her to test positive. He needed another detective here to take their statements.

Two hours passed before Frank could leave, the time filled with flashing lights and sirens, angry looks and recriminations. Dark humor passed between cops and paramedics, outside the hearing of neighbors and onlookers. Frank would have yet more paperwork to do, but that wasn't what bothered him the most. What bothered him was the job, the fucking job. He thought about it as he leaned against the car, eating a Milky Way from his glove box. The adrenaline rush had used up all the sugar in his blood, leaving him shaky. The candy bar helped settle him down.

The fucking, son-of-a-bitching job.

As a boy, Frank had seen his father as something elemental, like the salt he brought up from beneath the city. A man of granite. It took a hard man to do that work. Frank could never hack it down there. But then, his father had seemed a little like Superman. Frank couldn't blow a horn well enough to make it onto a Motown record, could never carry a football for thirty yards with three guys literally hanging off him.

In spite of his other interests, Pops always made time for his kids. Frank remembered the time Pops took him and Yolanda—Claire hadn't been born yet—to the Grand Freedom March, down Woodward Avenue. That had been the twenty-third of June, 1963. Frank had been a small boy, and he didn't remember much about the speechmaking, but he recalled lots of adults. Somewhere between knee and hip height on most grown-ups, he'd been intimidated by the size of the crowd. He clung to his father's hand, and to Yolanda's, so they wouldn't be separated. "You ever see so many black folk all in one place?" his father had asked. "All so happy to be here. It's a beautiful thing." Pops had been right, they were glad. The size of the crowd was overwhelming, frightening, but the mood was joyful. He remembered seeing smiles, hearing laughter and cheery shouts. Grown men hugged one another and slapped palms, and women in tears cried out "Hallelujah!" and "Amen!" and even at his age, Frank had understood that those were not tears of sorrow.

He had read the day's most significant speech later, had seen film of it, and had come to understand that his father had skipped work that day because he knew that it would be something he would want his children to experience. The Reverend Dr. Martin Luther King had appeared at the Grand Freedom March, and he had delivered words that would send chills through Frank's system every time he encountered them, for all the rest of his days. "I have a dream," King had declared, in a precursor to a slightly altered speech he would deliver in Washington later that summer. He had gone on to elaborate on his dream. He had ended his speech with a roaring, "Free at last! Free at last! Thank God Almighty, we are free at last!" and the crowd had gone berserk, screaming and clapping and howling so much that young Frank had thrown his hands over his ears and started sniffling.

Yolanda, older and wiser, had made him uncover his ears. "You want to remember this, Frankie," she had said. "You want to remember all of it!"

Later years had scraped away some of the sheen his father wore. Adolescence tended to do that. Frank had learned to question the old man's seeming perfection. But then more years passed, and Frank had come to realize the sacrifices Pops had made for his family, the effort he had put in, the granite constitution that kept him at it, and admired him all over again. Superman was Frank's fictional hero, but Pops was his real-life one.

Pops gave up on music, gave up on athletics, traded his dreams for a steady gig, a regular paycheck, honest work he could be proud of, down under the ground in the salt mine. Frank's life had been spent in law enforcement, the Bureau and the DPD, trying to do work that made a difference, that helped people. And how did people repay that help? They faced off, they shot each other, and they blamed you.

He had grown up in one country, but now he lived in another, and he hadn't moved. The America he saw in his memory, his father's America, was a place in which people took responsibility for themselves and their actions. They sucked up their troubles and did what was right, or they tried to. That had changed. Now it was a matter of doing what was easy, what was convenient, what seemed to feel good in the moment. Was this progress? He didn't think so. He didn't know what to call it, but he didn't like it.

He keyed the ignition. Martha and the Vandellas slipped from the speakers, smooth as glass, and he felt like a man out of his time, born too late, a man who had never quite found a place where he truly fit.

35

The idea came to Welker while he was on the phone with a client. He'd been leafing through some photographs, old ones, when the phone rang. He picked it up on the second ring. "Charles Welker."

He had worn the name for about a year and a half. It had not quite become second nature yet, the way the others had. He wanted it to be as comfortable as an old shirt, and he wasn't there yet. In part, that was because this one was so different from his usual choices, so alien to his ears. He would get there, but now, thanks to his sister's phone call, the schedule had been moved up and he wouldn't make it on time. That was only one of the reasons he was upset by the alteration.

The client who had called was a woman, a semi-regular, a brunette in her thirties, a young executive type, a go-getter, childless, and with plenty of cash to throw around. He listened to what she wanted, and he was scrolling down a price list, looking for what to quote her, when the idea struck him with almost physical weight.

He needed to take the edge off. He couldn't function in this in-between state, knowing his angel was so close and yet without access to her. At the same time, he knew that none of the others, those would-be angels out there, were quite right. Missy Trimble had proved that. He was saving himself now, saving himself for the real thing. He needed a substitute, but not one that made him think of his angel. One different enough not to suffer by comparison, but who would still satisfy his immediate need.

He finished with the phone call, closed up shop, and got ready for the hunt.

He put on a short-sleeved white shirt, a narrow black tie with red and gold diagonal stripes, pleated khaki pants, white socks and black loafers. He ran his fingers through thinning hair, sending tufts of it spiking this way and that. He eyed himself in a mirror. All he needed was a pocket protector to look like a nerdy engineer or programmer type, out after work. That would do. He wanted to appear unassuming, even harmless. He thought he had pulled it off.

Welker drove a silver Camry, a car that could get lost in the parking lot of any mall in America. He unlocked it, got in, and headed off on his quest.

There were websites where a person could find out in what part of any given city hookers plied their trade. He spent a lot of time online, even more in these last few days, and he had checked those sites from time to time, more out of curiosity than anything else. He lived near that part of town, drove through it at least weekly. They strutted up and down South Ninth Street, and sometimes the side streets, sliding in and out of car doors. More would be out as the hour grew later—like mushrooms, they sprouted in the dark—but dusk had come and the night was rapidly thickening. There would be some out already. Enough. And the harmless engineer he posed as would be afraid to enter that neighborhood after it was fully dark.

He drove the eight blocks to South Ninth, hung a left, pulled into the right lane and cruised the boulevard, five miles below the speed limit, scoping the shadowed doorways and alleys, craning his neck to see around every corner. On his second circuit, he saw two of them, as if they had manifested there after he'd passed by. He couldn't bear the thought of touching either of them, with their ponderous breasts and pillowy rears stuffed into too-tight shorts. One tried to flag him down, making an awkward gesture with her fingers, like a spastic pianist. He ignored her and kept going. It was good that she had noticed him, though. He supposed they talked to each other, imagined a sort of whore's grapevine. Others would hear about the harmless nerd looking for a date.

He made a right off Ninth at Needham, found a station and put gas in the Camry, then headed back for another circuit. Both of the earlier ones had vanished, but more had taken their place. He supposed they were like a hydra: cut off one head, three more grew in its place. A couple of the newcomers were less than hideous, at least from a distance. He feared what a closer inspection might reveal: makeup spackled on over pitted cheeks, teeth missing from meth-rotted gums, blown-out veins in the arms and cottage cheese on the thighs. If it weren't so necessary, he would turn around and go home right now. But he knew he wouldn't sleep; unless he found relief, he would keep trying would-be angel after would-be angel, and that would be more dangerous by far. The last thing he dared do when she was so close was to attract law enforcement's attention.

He hung a left, cruised down Seventh, then cut back over and up Ninth. Again, new ones had arrived. He saw gold shorts, canyons of cleavage, ridiculous plastic heels, every color of hair dye they sold at the dollar stores.

Then he saw *her*.

She was—well, he couldn't say attractive, but petite, anyway, no more than five feet tall, and slender, with a figure that didn't call attention to itself. She wore a pink blouse and a pleated, plaid skirt, knee socks and little black shoes. He supposed she was trying for a schoolgirl look, and given her build, she was nearly able to pull it off. Her hair was ink black, cropped close to her head. Over her shoulder she had slung a small, black, patent leather purse on a gold chain, in which to keep her cash and her condoms, maybe a knife or a little gun. Welker felt a stirring he had not expected. She would do, she would definitely do.

He slowed, caught her eye, pulled around the corner on M and came to a stop. During his circuits on the strip he had seen several police cars, but none were in evidence at the moment. She hurried toward his Camry. He waited until she was almost there, then reached over and unlocked the passenger door. She pulled it open and slid inside in a smooth, practiced motion.

Once seated, she put a hand on his thigh. "Hi," she said. "You looking for a date?"

"I could be."

"I just got out of school. Teacher made me stay late, to punish me. I guess I was a bad girl."

"That's the best kind, isn't it?" Welker asked.

She laughed as if it was the funniest line she'd heard in weeks, and gave his thigh another sharp-nailed squeeze. "You're not a cop, are you?"

"I'm not," he told her. "Are you?"

She unbuttoned her blouse enough to reach inside and pinch one dark nipple between two fingers, making sure he could see. "I'm definitely not a cop. I need to make sure you're not." She slid the hand up his thigh, cupped his genitals, squeezed.

"Okay. Whatever you need to do. I'm not really experienced at this."

"Just unzip and show it to me," she said.

"I guess I could do that."

Welker checked the mirrors, the rear windows, and did what she said. She gave an admiring coo as artificial as her hair color. "What are you in the mood for, big boy? I know a place we can park. It's not far away, it's dark, and nobody'll see us."

"I don't want to do it in the car," he said. "I'm too anxious. Anyway, I don't live far away, we can go to my house. My wife and daughter are out of town."

It was her turn to glance out the windows, as if the suggestion had made her nervous. "You sure? Forty bucks, best head of your life, you'll be on your way before you know it."

"I'm just not comfortable with that," he countered. "Plus I'd like to spend a little more time. How about a hundred and twenty at my place?"

She scraped her nails up and down his leg. "You *are* a bad boy."

He took that as assent and started the engine.

On the way over, she made moronic conversation, talking about the weather, politics, and some contemporary musician she admired, as if Welker could possibly be interested in anything she had to say. He nodded and agreed, so she would think he was paying attention, but his mind was racing ahead, to what would happen when they got home. The drive, so short earlier, seemed interminable. She kept dragging her nails up and down his thigh on the way. Presumably some men found that sort of thing erotic, but to him it had all the sex appeal of doing the same to a blackboard.

There was something about her he found stimulating, though. He'd been half hard when he unzipped for her, and he remained that way for most of the drive, to some extent buying into her costume and her size. But her frank sexuality, the knowledge that it was the one and only thing she had to offer, turned him off as much as the persona turned him on, so that was a wash. Still, if she hadn't been so vapid, if she had just shut up and let him glimpse her from the corner of his eye as she sat demurely in the passenger seat—better yet, if she had cringed in fear—it would have worked a whole lot better.

In the end, that wouldn't matter. This whole encounter was only in part about sex.

He pulled into his driveway, reached up and touched a button on the remote clipped to his visor. The garage door opened with a low growl, and he drove in. "This is a nice house," she said.

"It's okay."

"I like it."

"Wait till you see the inside."

She clawed his crotch again. "You sure you want to go in? We could play right here, pretend we were out in the street. It's naughty."

The garage door closed. He removed her hand from his groin. "No," he said. "Inside. I've got a comfortable bed. You'll enjoy it."

"I can't wait." With a little more effort, she'd have sounded half-convincing.

She waited in her seat while he got out, walked around, and opened her door. That was a good touch, he liked that. She held out her hand and he took it, helping her from the car. He held it through the door and into the laundry area inside.

"This *is* a nice place," she said.

He knew it was nothing special, working class at best. But for all he knew, she lived in a shared studio apartment, or a hovel crawling with vermin. Money had never meant much to Welker, and a good thing, because he'd never had much of it. He was focused on other pursuits, and interested only in money to the extent that it could help him follow his passion. "Come on," he said.

"Okay, but, you said one-twenty, baby. I have to see it."

He pulled his billfold from his back pocket, opened it and withdrew the bills. "Here it is," he said, handing them over. She disappeared the money into her purse with a close-up magician's skill and gave him a big smile. In the harsh overhead light he saw that she was older than he'd thought, with creases at the corners of her eyes, her lips wrinkled like a crone's, barely disguised by a thick coating of lipstick. Her nose was bulbous at the end and had a scar where perhaps someone had torn a stud or ring from it.

"Down this hall," he said. "The bedroom's that open door on the right."

She started toward it. "Usually I date in cars or cheap motels," she said. "This is kind of new for me."

Welker followed close behind her. "Believe me," he said, slowing just enough to grab the hammer he'd left on a shelf above the washing machine. "This is new for both of us."

36

The hospital cafeteria was about as cheerful as an unemployment office at Christmas. Half-hearted attempts had been made to lighten the mood—flowers painted on the walls, nurses in scrubs with Scooby Doo or Minnie Mouse on them, but for the most part it was linoleum tile and plastic tabletops and fluorescent lighting; exhausted residents sitting alone, eating like zombies; clutches of nurses, family members of patients picking at their food, their thoughts a million miles or three floors away; the clashing odors of disinfectant and coffee that had sat on the burners too long.

Frank had met Marcia for dinner after he finally extricated himself from the shooting scene and then visited briefly with his family. She hadn't wanted to leave the building, so they steeled themselves and went to the cafeteria. They filled their trays and carried them to an empty table, drew out steel chairs, and sat. The pants of Marcia's scrubs were pink, the top a colorful floral pattern. Every time Frank saw it he thought he had been in a house that had wallpaper in the same design. He had been in a lot of houses, though. Most had a dead body in them.

Frank dug into his meal, but stopped after a few bites of chicken-fried steak. "You'd think hospitals would serve healthier food."

Marcia waved a hand over her tray. Fresh fruit, yogurt, salad, dinner roll, no butter. "I think it's mostly a matter of what you put on your tray."

He forked another bite of his steak. "So what do you think the prognosis really is?" he asked. He put the tasteless steak in his mouth, chewed and swallowed while she considered the question. "I'm sure the doctors are telling you more than they're telling us."

"They'd like to see more improvement. But it's early yet."

"What do they want to see?"

"They want to see more oxygen in his blood. They want to see him breathing on his own. They want to see him wake up."

"I'd like to see that too. You better not be the first nurse there when he does, though. He might grab your ass, just because he's glad to be alive."

Marcia forced a dry chuckle. "He ain't that kind."

"I know. He grabs any ass, it'll be Momma's."

"*You* could grab my ass once in a while," Marcia said.

"I should, huh? I'm sorry, babe. It's been—"

She cut him off with a wave of her fork. "I know, Frank. It's that damn case. And this thing with your Pops on top of it? It's dragging you down."

"It is that. Every time I feel like maybe we're making some progress, we move two steps forward and slide back half a mile. Like Maynard says, this motherfucker's a ghost."

"He wasn't, you'd have caught him the first time."

"First time, we didn't know it was him we were after. Now we have no idea if he's dead or alive."

Frank had listened to Richie's phone message, while he was waiting to be cut loose from the shooting investigation, but he hadn't returned the call. Maynard didn't know about Pops yet, and that was a conversation Frank wasn't anxious to have. Anyway, the news was too awful, and Frank needed to be in the right place to hear the details. He didn't know where that place was, but he hadn't been there yet.

"Thing is, Frank," Marcia said, "I know this case is bad. And I know this stuff with your father is worse. But you know, life happens, shit rains down. And in your chosen profession, if it's not this bad case, it'll be the next bad case, or the one after that. That thing you told me about, the woman who shot her husband ... there's always someone killing someone, hurting someone, taking advantage."

"Why I do it," Frank reminded her.

"I know that. It's just … it takes a toll. Not just on you. What it does to you takes a toll on me."

"I'm sorry, babe, I never meant to—"

"I know that, too." She put a strawberry in her mouth, looked at him as she chewed it, her tongue flicking out to catch the juice that threatened to escape. She wasn't the daintiest eater, but Frank never minded watching her. "You're a good man, Frank. Maybe the best I've ever known. That's why this is so hard."

Frank didn't like the sound of that, but he kept quiet.

"Here it is," she went on. "You haven't ever asked me, but I would like to marry you, Frank Robey. I mean that. Only you ain't ready to marry. You're barely ready to function in polite society, and you sure as hell ain't ready to be a husband. I need to know I'm not in this alone. That I'm not the only one making an emotional investment. We have to be partners or it just ain't happening. I don't know if you ever will be ready for that, but if you are, leave a light on or something, so a person knows it. Until then, well, I guess I won't be as available as I have been. I'm sorry, Frank. I love you, but I got to look after myself."

Between the job and his Pops, Frank already felt like someone had yanked his guts out, tied them to the axle of a garbage truck, and dragged them all over Detroit. This on top of it, though, this was a harder blow. This was A-Rod taking advantage of the situation to pull his heart from his chest and do some batting practice with it. At the same time, he couldn't fault her reasoning. He'd been shitty company, he knew that. "I hear you, babe," he said. "I'm sorry, truly. Sorry I've been the way I've been."

"That's two of us."

"I'll try to pull it together. And I'll do like you say, I'll put a light on." He looked at the remains of his chicken-fried steak. He wouldn't be eating any more, not tonight. He scooted his chair back. "I guess I'd better—"

"Yeah, that'd be best. I'll look in on the family."

"Thanks." He put a hand on her shoulder, kissed her on the cheek. She tensed in his grip, and he turned away, started toward the door.

Hospital cafeterias. Fuck, he hated those places.

O   O   O

Frank needed a sympathetic ear, and he owed Maynard a call anyway. Instead of going up to his father's room he went out into the parking lot, sat in his car, and dialed Richie's number.

"Frank," Richie said when he answered. "What's up?"

"Ahh, I just had a conversation with Marcia I've been dreading."

"What?"

"Well, she didn't quite break up with me. But I guess you could say she gave me the ultimatum. Get my shit together or let her move on."

"Ouch. What are you gonna do?"

"I knew that, I'd have done it a long time ago. Best I can do is the best I can do, right?"

"Makes sense."

"And it's not just that. My Pops is in the hospital."

"What happened?"

"Some lung thing. ARDS, they call it. He's in bad shape, in a coma."

"Oh, man, Frank, I'm sorry."

"Yeah, me too. He's a tough old bastard, I think he'll pull through. It's hard on Momma and the girls is all. Anyway, I got your message earlier, sorry I didn't call you back. Let's just say it's been a day."

"I figured you'd call when you could."

"So, you think he really killed Angela?"

"I always did. I think he's a murderer," Richie replied. "I don't know for sure if he killed her. But I'm pretty certain he killed Barbara. Thing is, the trail's gone icy. I don't know where to go from here."

"Sometimes you got to think like an astrophysicist," Frank said.

"I'm not even sure I can spell that. What does that mean?"

"It means, astrophysicists determine the existence of unseen celestial bodies by observing the effects they have on those objects around them. You don't see the person you're looking for, you look for the effect he has on his surroundings."

"I'm not following you."

"I'm not sure it's a good analogy," Frank said. "What I'm saying is you deduce the presence of an object you can't see by the otherwise inexplicable behavior of the objects you can see. If you're looking for a guy, you know to some extent what his patterns and habits are, you find the effects of those patterns and habits and the guy will turn up."

"Isn't that what we've been doing? Looking for the photo studio ads, for other disappeared children?"

"That's the basic idea," Frank agreed. "We've done Tucson and Omaha, because those are the places we know from the postmarks that he lived. It's time to spread a wider net."

"Now you're really mixing your metaphors," Richie said. "I'm pretty sure astrophysicists don't use nets."

"Yeah, I got to work on this one. Still, you get the idea, right?"

"I guess. Oh, and hey, I had this other notion that's been poking at me. I think maybe it's time to say it out loud."

"What's that?"

"Well, I saw this guy reading a newspaper in a coffee shop today, and I thought about how you just don't see that much anymore. Actual paper newspapers, I mean. People with laptops, sure, that's what I was doing. But this guy had the old-fashioned kind. And then I was thinking about classified ads, and Craigslist, and during the afternoon this was all kind of pinging around my brain."

"You think you might be able to enunciate it sometime tonight?"

"It's this one hundred and forty-one thing. We still don't know what that means."

"If anything."

"Right. If anything. And then the other piece was, I remembered talking to you about comics, and how you didn't like the online ones. How you share that hobby with people who understand it, but not with everyone. How you keep it private from most people."

"Yeah?"

"And then I thought, people like Morton, pedophiles, they're the same way. They long to share their experiences with people like them."

"I guess."

"They do. There are always pedophile chat rooms turning up, and people getting busted because they trade photos or movies online. And I thought, well, Morton's a professional photographer. We saw that room with the camera hole. What are the chances that he *didn't* share pictures with somebody? I mean, maybe they were all taken just for his own amusement. But maybe not, right?"

"I guess."

"So what you should do, if you can, is maybe tap some of your old FBI buddies, see if there've been photos that have turned up that look like they might be his work."

"How do we tell that?" Frank asked.

"Couple of ways. See if Kayley can be recognized in any of them. And look for that angel wing thing he likes so much. Any kids wearing angel wings would be a good indication. And if the background can be made out, maybe they can look for that specific room."

Frank thought about the task and shuddered. "Yeah, I guess that makes sense. I hate to ask anybody to look at that shit."

"I know," Richie said. "Anyway, I put that all together with this other thing I've been thinking about, the classifieds and Craigslist. Wendy and I got a couch off there, people trade stuff on there all the time."

"But kiddie porn?" Frank asked.

"No, I don't think so. Not that directly. But I was thinking about swapping stuff, and communicating over distances, and it hit me. What if one forty-one is really one *for* one? F-o-r. Not the number. A *trade*."

"I'm listening."

Richie took a deep breath. Frank could tell he didn't want to speak what had been on his mind, but he didn't know yet if it was because it was a stupid thought, or one that was too heinous to verbalize.

It turned out to be the latter.

"We think Morton likes girls of a certain age. He took Kayley when she was what? Six?"

"That's right."

"And she disappeared when she was eleven. That's about the time a girl's body starts to change. Puberty's coming. She's going to start having periods, start to grow breasts and hips. She's not that small child anymore."

"That's true," Frank said. "Happens earlier all the time, but as a general rule, yeah." He still wasn't quite sure where Maynard was going with this.

"But there are other pedophiles out there who like that age. What if he arranged a trade with somebody? One for one? You get my eleven-year-old, I get your six-year-old."

"Oh, God," Frank said. "Oh, shit."

"I'm just saying."

"No, I hear you. It's as good an explanation of one-for-one as any other we've thought of."

"It explains how she could vanish so completely in two minutes. Nobody snatched her, and he didn't kill her. She was right there until he handed her off."

"I can believe that as far as it goes," Frank said. "But what about the flip side? We know he and Barbara didn't have a younger girl. We were there every day for weeks, months, and so were the local cops, the media. No way they could have hidden that."

"They knew the spotlight would be on for a while. Maybe it was a trade that wouldn't happen until after they left Detroit, disappeared from the radar. Maybe the deal was, you get Kayley now, and I get the other girl at some point in the future."

"You are one sick motherfucker," Frank said.

"Hey, I'm not—well, okay, I guess I'm the one who thought of it now. But not originally."

"If your theory's right," Frank added.

"If it's right. I don't see anything that doesn't fit, though. I mean, he practically carved one-four-one in that desk. It was obviously on his mind a lot, and it excited him. It fits what we know about Kayley's disappearance, what we know about his tastes."

"You're right," Frank said. "I hate to say it, but I think you might be onto something. If it's true, then Kayley might still be alive."

"I thought of that. And one other thing."

"What's that?"

"If it's true? If he traded her for a younger model, and it worked? And as far as he's concerned, it did, it's thirteen years later and he hasn't been caught. He might still be doing it."

"Fuck me."

"Yeah."

"And how do we think he arranged this trade?"

"Thirteen years ago, I don't think there was a Craigslist. But there were pedophile bulletin boards and chat rooms."

"True."

"So in addition to looking for pictures that might be his, we should be looking for communication that might be his, in all those places."

"I guess so," Frank said. "I'll see what I can do on that end."

"And there are still newspapers, too."

"What's that mean?"

"There are still papers in every city. Big dailies, alternative weeklies, pennysavers, and everything in between. Most of them still take classified ads. So we need to look through those. I guess that's part of thinking like an astrophysicist. We need to see if he's affecting the world by posting ads someplace. We need to be monitoring chat rooms, and watching online classifieds."

"That's what I'm talking about, Maynard," Frank said. He felt a touch of pride, as if the kid had been a student of his, or he a mentor. "You are one sick fuck, but you got a head on you."

37

In the end, he couldn't bring himself to touch her.

Her name, it turned out, was Audrey Stone. According to her driver's license she was twenty-six, older than he had feared. And those years had been hard ones. He had thought that once she was nothing but meat, he would be able to enjoy her in the way he wanted, to take the edge off his raging desires. He had stood right behind her until she walked through the bedroom door and clawed at the wall for the light switch. Her feet had found the plastic sheeting he'd thrown on the floor.

She started to ask about it, and he brought the hammer around, cutting her question short. It took three swings. The first, as she was turning toward him, caught her a glancing blow on the side of her skull, just in front of her temple. She went down, kicking and clawing and mewling. Pathetic. He swung twice more, crushing bone and driving through brain, spattering it all over his arm. She was silent after that.

Welker made himself undress her there on the plastic, which collected the fluids leaking from her. She was dirty; she had soiled herself as she died. He couldn't tell when she had showered last. He left her naked on the plastic, her schoolgirl clothes beside her. He got out some of his photos, his special ones. He found that he was aroused by the whole thing, as long as he didn't have to touch her.

Looking at his pictures, it didn't take long to bring himself off. He sprayed her with his own fluids, payback for those she had got on him, but then, thinking better of it, he wiped his semen up with her pink blouse. He would burn that in the fireplace later.

Although it had not worked out just the way he'd planned, it eased his tension somewhat. He had found physical release, and that was important. He still had a problem—he had to dispose of her—and he still had a need, but that need wasn't as pressing as it had been. He had been granted the clarity to realize what he should do with her.

He looked at her, her small breasts, her neatly trimmed pubic thatch—still too overgrown for him but fine for some, he supposed—and he understood the purpose she'd been meant to serve all along was not as a substitute, but as a symbolic offering to the angel he would soon possess. He had to examine her a little more closely, so he put on rubber gloves, turned her this way and that, and soon the configuration made itself clear.

He owned several scalpels. Though he was no surgeon, they were not particularly hard to come by, and he had previous experience with them. When he dealt with The Other, he didn't have scalpels, just kitchen knives and a wood saw, and he'd had to make do. Since that occasion, though, he had acquired actual surgical scalpels, and practiced when he could.

He pressed the blade to her flesh, trying to make a smooth, even cut. It was more difficult than he'd hoped. The scalpel was sharp, but her skin gave under his weight and threw his line off. Trying to correct his error feathered the line more than he had hoped. His next cut was hesitant, and when it snagged, he pushed too far down and struck bone. Still, he got through it.

His first slash crossed perpendicular to her spine, just above her shoulder blades. By the end of it, he was more confident, his cut smoother, flesh parting beneath his blade like water before a rudder. The second cut, down the spine, started at the first cut and was about nine inches long. That was difficult, too, her vertebrae bulging and making a straight, even cut difficult. His last one was parallel to the first but not quite as long, at the bottom of the second cut, making a T shape with an exaggerated foot.

The cutting done, Welker shoved his fingers beneath the right flap, at the spine, and pulled. He discovered he needed to do more cutting, to slice through tissue and veins and tendons still joined to the skin. All told, it took nearly forty minutes before he was satisfied with his work. By then, he was used to the smell.

He took a minute, poured a glass of water, sat and looked at his handiwork. Then, refreshed, he rolled up the plastic, pondering upon where best to display his prize.

38

Richie wondered if there was a class people attended, or a book they read, to ensure that neighborhood bars were the same everywhere. They were small, squared-off buildings of brick or block with painted walls and windows—if any—showcasing beer company signs, no light allowed to leak through to the interior. Doorways were blocked by strips of fabric or rubber in service of the same cause. Interiors were dim, with worn stools ranked by a wooden bar, some tables, and a few booths along a wall. There might have been regional differences of which Richie was unaware, but for the most part it seemed that if someone woke up in one of those places, he could be in Omaha or Tucson or Detroit or Dallas, and never know the difference until he stepped outside to get his bearings.

It had probably always been that way. He imagined ancient working-class Vikings swilling mead in a concrete building with a Budweiser sign buzzing on a wall by the pool table, and the stink of urine in the alley out back.

He had happened into such a place in midtown, a place called Jerry's Tavern, three doors down from where Jarod Morton's photo studio had been, hoping he could find someone who had known Morton. Besides, the neon outside had promised bar and grill, and although he'd had plenty of coffee, he had skipped lunch, and he was famished.

He sat at a booth by himself, nursing a glass of beer and eating a hamburger, medium rare and piled high. The booth's cushions were red vinyl with a latticework of black burn scars. His table had an ashtray on it, along with salt and pepper and sugar and Keno slips, to go along with the game that ran on monitors scattered throughout. The table was real wood, equally scarred. The wall was coated with a layer of grime that might have dated back to the Nixon presidency. The music was loud enough to set his teeth on edge, vibrating his beer inside its container: Foreigner, AC/DC, Aerosmith, Van Halen.

A barmaid had brought cocktail napkins and a mismatched knife and fork along with his burger and fries. The joint grew more crowded and noisier as Richie's meal progressed. Most people entered alone, but occasionally two or three came in together, even a few women after a time. Some greeted the burly, ruddy-faced bartender with seeming familiarity; others either didn't know him, or pretended not to. Those sat alone, like Richie, keeping company with their drinks and whatever broken parts drove them into such a dive.

Although Richie was not an *habitué* of such places, he found that it suited his mood. The search for Kayley Ann Carrington—he refused to think of her now as Angela Morton, that was only a name Jarod had given her, and anything that man had provided was tainted beyond redemption—had depressed him more than he'd expected. Depression spiraled, eating its own tail, and coming here, having a drink or three, would certainly not lift him out of it. At the moment, however, being lifted wasn't his goal. Rising above it all seemed too Herculean a task to even consider. Wallowing in it felt more appropriate. This depress-sion and the one that had gripped him earlier were different, though. His seeming lack of career options, his uncertainty about the path his life was supposed to take, had seemed insurmountable, a few days ago. Now those thoughts had been shunted aside, and the black gulf inside him had more to do with the evil acts of others than with anything that came from within.

He was just finishing his burger, dabbing at his mouth with some of those tiny, stiff napkins, when he saw the barista from CupZ walking across the room in his direction. The restrooms were beyond him, so he guessed that's where she was going. She carried a bottle of beer, and she made a half-pirouette around a barmaid carrying a tray of drinks for a table of blue-collar types, then she came straight toward Richie.

"Hey," she said as she approached. Her smile added wattage to the underlit room. She put her beer down on his table. She was still wearing her work clothes. She spoke loudly but easily, accustomed to making herself heard over the music. "I'm surprised to see you here. This is strictly a neighborhood joint."

"That's really why I came in."

"You are *not* a local."

"You know everybody in Omaha?"

"No, but I don't get the feeling you're from around here."

"I'm not, actually," Richie admitted. "I'm from Detroit."

"You're a long way from home."

"Yeah."

"You mind?" She ticked her head toward the opposite bench.

"Feel free," he said.

She slid onto the bench, her knees brushing his under the narrow table. "Sorry."

"No problem."

"You mind if I ask what you're doing in Omaha? Before, at CupZ, you said it was business."

"It is."

"What kind?"

Richie decided that hiding his real mission from her would be counterproductive. He hadn't shown her the pictures of the Mortons earlier, but if she knew as many people in Omaha as she claimed, she might be worth asking. He briefly considered telling the truth about Morton, but when he opened his mouth, the familiar lie slipped out. "This guy might be owed some money."

Her mouth dropped open, her green eyes going wide. "Get out! No shit? Are you some kind of detective?"

"Some kind," Richie said. "The private kind."

"Cool. I've met plenty of cops, but I don't think I've ever met a private dick. That's what you're called, right?"

"I think private investigator is a little more standard, these days."

"Whatever, I like mine. So what is it, a big inheritance?"

He felt he could trust her, but he had been telling the other story for days, and he thought it remained good enough. "I'm not at liberty to say. And I don't really know yet if it's the right guy, until I find him."

"And he lives around here?"

"He lived here for a while, and worked in this neighborhood," Richie said. "We're not sure where he is now." He reached into his pocket and pulled out his pictures of Jarod and Barbara and a copy of the photo studio ad with the angel picture, all fraying at the edges from the heavy use over the past few days. "Any of these look familiar to you?"

While she studied them, Richie studied her: strong fingers handling the photos, those vivid golden-brown eyes moving slightly. "I've never seen them," she said. "Maybe Jerry knows them." She waved the pictures toward the bartender. "Or Bob, the guy at the end of the bar. I think he's been glued to that stool since 1977. If these people are from this neighborhood, they'll know 'em."

Before Richie could respond, she struck off toward the bar. She was comfortable here, obviously a regular. He figured it couldn't hurt to let her do some of his legwork. If her legs were anything like the rest of her, they were up to the task.

"Hey, Davolina!" she called as she neared the bar. The old man at the bar's end swiveled toward her. She put a hand on his shoulder and leaned into him, her breasts pressing against his back as she showed him the pictures. He appeared to enjoy the attention.

He looked at the pictures, shook his head, and beckoned the bartender. Jerry wiped his hands on a dishtowel before accepting the photos. He gave them a quick glance, then looked over toward Richie, shook his head, and dropped them on the bar. Another guy, a blue-collar, working-class type in jeans, a denim work shirt, and work boots, reached over from his stool and clawed the pictures toward him. Although his back faced Richie, the tension gripping him was obvious. He said something Richie couldn't hear. Jerry the bartender jerked his head toward Richie.

"No, Jim, wait!" the barista said, but the guy was already stalking toward Richie, ignoring her words and squeezing the pictures in his fist. He looked furious.

Richie offered a hesitant smile. "Hey," he said.

The man threw the pictures onto the table. "You know this fuck?"

"Not personally," Richie said.

"Because if this prick is a friend of yours, then you're a piece of shit too."

"I don't know him," Richie repeated. "I'm looking for him."

"To give him some money, I hear. For what, to get in on some of his action? He got somebody's kid for you?" He turned around and raised his voice, announcing to the bar, "Hey, this perv hangs out with that guy molested my stepdaughter!"

"Listen," Richie said, "you've got it all wrong." His voice was lost in the blaring rock and the swell of chatter from the other patrons. Tables emptied, and Richie was suddenly hemmed in by a wall of men, some younger than him and some older, most with hard faces. A few, like Jim, were strong and solid. "Look," Richie appealed again. "I'm working with the police."

"You're no cop," one guy said.

"I didn't say—"

"Why don't you just get out of here while you can."

"Fine," Richie said. He started to reach for his wallet, to leave money on the table, but someone grabbed his arm before he could get to it, as if afraid he was going for a weapon. "I'm just trying to leave!" Richie said, wrenching his arm free. Someone else shoved him from behind, and it was on.

It was fine with him. He'd been expecting a fight for a while. Now it had come, and the odds were impossible, but the adrenaline surging through him, spiking from the wrenching of his arm and the shove, left him no alternatives. It was a fight-or-flight response, and flight was not an option. Fury rose in Richie like a flood.

He'd never fought so many people at once, but he suspected most of them would hang back, letting the others do the hard work. One of those who would fight was the one called Jim. Richie sympathized, but he couldn't let his concern for the man's stepdaughter hold him back. Jim was bursting with pent-up rage. That rage was directed at Richie, and he had to be taken out fast.

Richie tried one last time to calm things down, but it was a feint. There was no calming at this point. "Listen here," he said. "I am not what you think—" He stopped mid-sentence, took a step toward Jim, landing on his left foot, and continued bringing his right leg forward. Instead of stepping down, he gave a snap kick that caught Jim just below the knee. He didn't break bone, which he'd been hoping to do, figuring that might bring a quick end to things. Jim cried out as his leg buckled beneath him.

Richie's sudden escalation had taken everyone by surprise, but it would only buy him seconds. He followed up with an elbow to the temple of the man closest to him. That man was in his late forties, graying hair, a ponderous gut. At this point, anyone could land a hurting blow, or scoop a bottle off a table and do worse.

The man fell onto a booth bench, and Richie thought he saw daylight, a hole he might slip through. He started for it. But the gap closed, trapping him.

An awkwardly thrown fist hit Richie in the clavicle, staggering him. Another, from behind, smashed into his kidneys. That one really hurt. Richie jerked forward, running into someone else's fist. It caught him in the solar plexus, knocking the wind from him. He could barely see; a scrim of black and red seemed to have settled over his eyes. He kicked and he hit, targets everywhere around him. He was doing some damage. He bloodied one man's nose, caught another in the groin. That one crashed to the floor, knocking over a table on his way down.

The advantage of the terrible odds was that it was easy to find a target. The disadvantage was that it was easy for them to find him. Richie took a hard shot to the jaw, snapping his head around and sending pain lancing through his neck. More to the torso, big fists pummeling him. He folded in on himself, arms up to try to block the worst of it, but unable in that position to do more. The others surged toward him. He was blinded, deafened, by the punishment.

Then he was on the floor, lying in shattered glass and spilled booze, somebody operating a jackhammer against his ribs—or maybe just a steel-toed work boot—by the time the barista pushed through the mob. She was talking, he could tell that. Over the ringing in his ears, the roar of blood and voices, he thought he heard her explaining that he really was working with the police, looking for Morton, not a friend of his. At least the music had been turned off.

At any rate, the kicking stopped and the men moved away. She knelt beside him, touched him gingerly. "Are you ... should I call an ambulance?"

Richie ran his tongue across his teeth, wondering if he'd lost any—yes, one, an upper, way in back on the right, he probed the gap with his tongue and tried to smile. "You should see the other guy."

"Dude, you *are* the other guy."

Richie tried to shift into a position from which he could get to his knees, and maybe eventually to his feet. He made it almost three whole inches before pain shot through every part of him and he abandoned the effort. He rolled back the same three inches he'd gained and let out a long groan. He felt like the pavement of Michigan Avenue after the St. Patrick's Day parade.

"You're hurt," the barista said.

"I don't even know your name," Richie managed.

"What?"

"You're like, all Florence Nightingale here. Is your name Florence?"

She laughed. "You're not only hurt, you're delusional."

Richie stared at her.

"Okay," she said, "it's Olive."

"No, really."

"What? Who can understand parents? Shit they pull." She prodded at his chest. "Let me call an ambulance."

"It's just … a flesh wound," Richie said. She didn't laugh. "It's just pain."

"Pain sucks."

"Yeah," Richie agreed. "It does." He tried to take a mental inventory. "Nothing broken," he reported.

"You could have internal bleeding. A concussion."

"I could. I don't think so, though."

"We should get you to a hospital."

"I don't want to spend the night in some waiting room," he argued. He didn't bother to mention that he wasn't sure if he could afford it, and didn't know how Wendy's insurance company would react to him checking into a hospital in a faraway city because he'd been in a bar brawl. "I just need some time."

"You think you can walk?"

"Walk, shit, I can't even breathe."

"How about if I help you?"

"Okay." It would hurt, but he was willing to try. If he couldn't get his feet under him, he really did need an ambulance.

He tried rolling again. This time she caught him, helped turn him, and he was able to get his hands underneath him. Remarkably, his palms weren't particularly painful, especially compared to the rest of him. He pressed them against the floor, in a slick puddle of what was probably his own blood mixed with a healthy serving of spirits, and with Olive lifting, he got his knees under him. Olive kept prompting and pulling, and less than an hour later, he was on his feet.

He was unsteady, but with Olive's strong arm wrapped around him, under his arms, he found he could remain upright. She still smelled good, he discovered. She must have put on more of whatever she wore, because Richie's nose was packed with clotted blood and snot, and he could smell her just the same. He almost told her she was an angel of mercy, but that whole angel thing had taken on a different connotation lately, so he left it alone.

"I'm up," he said. "Now what?"

"My place isn't far away. We can walk it. If you can walk."

"If you're helping."

"I'm helping. Come on."

The man named Jim sat at a table with a couple of buddies, holding a bar rag full of ice to his face. He gave Richie the dick-eye. Richie returned the favor. There would be no post-brawl reconciliations here, no easy forgiveness. That was okay. Richie didn't need the guy to like him, as long as he wasn't kicking him.

39

A pair of beefy local cops showed up. They acted relieved when Richie told them he didn't want to press charges. They spoke briefly with Jim, but Jerry and Olive insisted that Richie was the victim, and Richie informed them that even if they did file charges, he wouldn't be around for any trial. The cops talked to Jim about the Morton angle, then reported to Richie and Olive that Jim had only suspected the photographer he knew as Gerald Miller. He'd never had any proof, and by the time the niece revealed what had happened to her, Miller had already closed his shop and disappeared from the area. Finally, the cops left, after promising Jerry they'd be back for a nightcap when their shift ended.

When Richie and Olive got outside, the cool air was like daggers probing his tender points, which were pretty much all of his points. He tried to focus on moving his legs with some degree of coordination, knowing that to fall on his face on the sidewalk would only hurt even more.

As they walked he realized, to his chagrin, that he'd been actively seeking a fight for days. This whole Jarod Morton thing had been building inside him like a kettle on a stove, bubbling up, looking for release. The guy in the airport he'd wanted to clock, that husband in Tucson, even Kent Alderdyce, back in Virginia. He had been half hoping—maybe three-quarters—that someone would take a swing at him. Nobody had, until tonight. Just his bad luck that it was ten guys, or eight, or however many, and not one easy one, some little guy who lived in his mom's basement and didn't get out much.

Olive's place really was only a couple of blocks away, considerably less than the hundred miles it seemed. She supported him the whole way, and he liked the proximity, the substance and weight and warmth of her body pressed against his, and the smell of her, and her occasional attempts at conversation. He thought the walk was actually doing him good, helping to work out some of the kinks.

"We're almost there," he said. "See that doorway, next to the dry cleaner's?"

"No," Richie said. His vision was still a little blurry, his left eye swollen almost shut. "I'll take your word for it, though."

"That's it. Then when we get there, there are just, I don't know, twelve or fourteen steps. I guess I never counted."

"Oh my god, there are *steps*? You're trying to kill me."

"You've managed so far. You'll be fine."

"A minute ago you wanted me to go to the hospital."

"And you said no. I thought you were okay."

"Do I look okay?"

"If you're going to turn into a pussy, I'll leave you here on the sidewalk."

"I'll be fine," Richie said. "It's just … stairs."

"All right, no more complaining."

"Yes, ma'am."

When they reached the door, she leaned him against a rough stone wall while she fumbled with her keys. She got the door open, helped him through, and leaned him against an inside wall while she locked it behind them. She was right, there were stairs. "Stairway to heaven," he said.

"What?"

"It just looks a little like Mount Everest."

"I said no more—"

"I know. I'm not complaining, just commenting."

"Come on, it's not that bad." She looped that arm around him again, and they took the stairs one at a time. She had underestimated, but there were no more than thirty or forty of them. At the top they were in a dimly lit hallway with three doors. She opened one of them.

"Home sweet home," she said. "Come on in."

Like he had a choice, except for rolling back down. "Thanks. You wouldn't happen to have a gurney? Or an operating theater?"

"You said you didn't need a hospital!"

"I know. I don't. I might need some painkillers. Never mind, scratch the 'might.'"

"Painkillers I got."

"Bring 'em on and keep 'em coming."

To say Olive's furnishings were Spartan might have been over-stating the point, but not by much. She sat Richie down on the world's most comfortable futon. There was a low table in front of it, and she told him he could put his feet up if he wanted. That would have required raising them more than three inches, so he passed. She had a couple of jammed bookcases—the only thing that wasn't minimalist, an overflowing collection of paperbacks—a small kitchenette with a couple of stools tucked under a breakfast counter, a single door that led to what Richie figured was a bathroom. The sole attempt at decor was a huge painting on canvas, maybe eight feet square, leaning against the wall opposite the futon. It was mostly abstract, but as he stared at it, Richie thought he saw birds in flight, shapes that could have been trees bending in the wind, part of a flowing river or pond. It was good, somehow calming and evocative of the outdoors, without actually depicting anything specific. He figured if you had one picture that big and that good, you probably didn't need any more.

"You have a lot of books!" he called.

"Hey, I work in a coffee shop and hang out in a dive bar. That doesn't mean I'm not smart. You meet some of the most interesting people in dive bars. Case in point."

Richie didn't know if she was the case in point, or he was, but guessed it didn't much matter. She was smart, he had already figured that out. And in a way he liked, not showy, kind of an entry-level intellectual. She was no college professor, but maybe she could have been.

She came back a minute later, bearing what must have been half the contents of a bathroom cabinet. He recognized gauze and tape and bandages, hydrogen peroxide, various bottles of pills, other things he wasn't as sure about. If it would help, he was willing to try.

She shook half a dozen pills into one hand, went into the kitchen, and came back with a plastic tumbler of water. "Take these."

He took them. The water tasted great. It was like he'd never had water before.

"Let's get that shirt off," she said.

"Like that's not going to kill me."

"You are *such* a baby." She leaned close and unbuttoned it, then drew him forward, sliding the shirt off him, pulling the sleeves over his hands. "That wasn't so bad."

"I guess," he said. Actually, it had been pretty bad.

She went to work, picking at him here, cutting with a straight razor there. She dabbed and bandaged and poked, poured peroxide into cuts. Her touch was gentle but sure, although when she pressed on the bulge under his eye he almost screamed. He managed to hold it in. "Sorry," she said. "That one's nasty."

"I must be gorgeous."

"You only started out okay, so don't worry about that."

"Thanks. Are you a trained nurse?"

"Officially, no. But when you hang out in this neighborhood long enough, you get used to patching people up. Fights are kind of a tradition at Jerry's." She peeled back his gums. "You lose any teeth?"

"One. In back."

"I think you got lucky. Not much I can do about a lost tooth."

"Lucky's not exactly the word I'd use, but you're probably right."

A few minutes later, she knelt in front of him and reached for his belt. "What now?" he asked.

"Don't worry, I'm not going to blow you," she said. "If your chest, back and arms are that bad, I'm guessing your legs and hips are pretty messed up too."

"Yeah, I think they are."

"Then let's see." She unbuckled the belt, whipped it out through the loops and tossed it behind her. "I love doing that."

"Under other circumstances, it'd be erotic."

"Hey, when I do it, it's always erotic. Not my fault you're in no position to respond."

She had him unzipped, and he had to lift his butt off the futon so she could work his pants and underwear off. Having those removed might have been the most excruciating experience of his life. She'd been right; his thighs in particular were a mass of bruises and cuts. He wondered how many colors he would be by morning.

Olive made a disgusted face, but traced her fingers over the tattoo of his Uncle Keith's badge. "Nice tat. But you are a mess."

He guessed he wouldn't get that blowjob after all. He hadn't thought about it until she mentioned it, but then it sounded good. Therapeutic.

She started in on this set of wounds. This time he could see more of what she was doing, at least when she worked on his front, but he didn't want to watch. Instead, he looked at Olive. "I think you're good at this," he said. "Nursing, I mean."

"You'd be surprised how often I hear that line from guys just trying to get at my boobs."

"No," Richie said. "I wouldn't be. That wasn't how I meant it, but you know, they're certainly worth making a try for."

"I grew 'em myself," she said, distracted. "In my spare time."

"That's something else you're good at."

"You know, if you don't have any internal bleeding, which I don't think you do, you really did get lucky. You're gonna be in pain for somewhere between a few days and the rest of your life, but I don't think there's any long-term injury. Bruises, cuts, scrapes. Could have been a whole lot worse."

"It's hard to have exactly that perspective, from my angle," Richie said. "But I think you're right. There were so many guys trying to hit and kick me that they got in each other's way, so none of them could do that good a job of it. When I was a cop, I saw victims who had been beaten by just one person. Put them in the hospital for months, sometimes. A couple of cases had serious long-term repercussions. Partial deafness, blindness, loss of motor function. You're right, I should count my blessings. And I should be thankful that you were there to make it stop when you did."

"You can thank me any time."

"I put a five in your tip jar!"

"Yeah, I saw. I appreciated it."

"I appreciate everything you've done for me. You didn't have to bring me home, didn't have to take my clothes off and tend to my wounds. That can't be pleasant."

"It's not a bad body. I mean, as male bodies go."

"You prefer female bodies?"

"I like mine."

"That's two of us. I guess, if you see you in the mirror every day, the rest of the world sort of pales by comparison."

"It's not like I'm that conceited," Olive said. "I'm just teasing you."

"Well, I'm serious," Richie said. "You make a guy proud to be a mammal."

"I can't tell if you're delirious or funny."

"Let's go with funny, if we have a choice."

She turned his wedding ring on his finger. "Your wife have a good body?"

"My favorite."

"That's good."

He figured the mention of his wife, the touching of the ring, were acts meant to defuse any growing sexual tension between the naked guy and the hot girl taking care of him.

Maybe it worked for a minute, but it didn't last long. She was dabbing something on a cut on his thigh. "Nobody kicked you in the nuts?"

"I got someone else there," Richie said. "But no one got me."

"You are lucky. And they're not unattractive, as those things go."

"They're not nature's most beautiful creation," Richie admitted.

"No, they're not. I tend to like cocks better when they're standing up."

"Well, good luck with that. Not sure I'll be in that condition any time in the next few months."

"I guess it's a good thing you're not home with your wife tonight."

"Yeah, good thing."

She checked a few more spots, and then she had done what she could. He was either treated and bandaged, or left to bruise and ache. "There you go," she said. "That's that."

"Thank you, Olive."

"No problem."

The ibuprofen he had swallowed were starting to take effect in a minimal way, rounding off the edges of his pain. "I really appreciate it. I guess I should get dressed again."

"What's your hurry?"

"It's just—"

"No, you've issued a challenge, now."

"What challenge?"

"You don't think I can get you hard."

"Olive, that's not—"

"No, I'm serious."

Richie wanted to stop her. Part of him did, anyway. She was the one who had reminded him about Wendy, after all. At the same time, they'd been flirting off and on since they'd met, and it had become considerably more pronounced once he was naked. He couldn't deny that he found her incredibly attractive. Just looking at her made him think about sex, in a way that nothing else had in a long time. And it wasn't like he'd be putting his marriage in jeopardy. He wouldn't be seeing her again after tonight, doubted he would ever be back in Omaha.

It was wrong, he understood that. But he had been so immersed in the horrors of Jarod Morton's life that turning away a simple human interaction with a decent person seemed even more wrong. Dangerous. He thought he needed this, needed to be connected to the human race again, not to think that everyone he encountered was hiding terrible secrets.

She knelt before him, grabbed the hem of her CupZ polo shirt, peeled it up and tossed it aside. "You like that," she said.

"I do."

She kicked her sneakers off, then unfastened her jeans and slid them down, returned to a kneeling position. Her panties were light blue cotton, matching the bra. Nothing someone would wear in a flagrant attempt to be sexy, but on her sexy just came with the territory. "You like that, too."

"You can tell?" He was afraid to look down.

"I can tell." She reached behind her back, in that exceptionally fluid way only women could ever master, unclipped the bra, shrugged free of it. "You definitely like that."

"I definitely do."

She leaned against him, breasts pressing against his legs, and took him in her mouth. She was warm and wet and she applied herself in an expert fashion, and he felt himself responding to her, the pain of that response shooting through him as sore muscles tensed, and as quickly he forgot the pain and gave himself over to the responding.

After a few minutes she stopped, reached back into her stash of medical supplies, and found a foil packet. As she tore it open, Richie said, "You are prepared."

"My first time was with an Eagle Scout," she said. "I've never forgotten the lesson."

She had won the challenge. She rolled the condom onto him and joined him on the futon. She kissed him deeply, her tongue finding his, careful not to put pressure on the most damaged parts of him. His hands wandered freely, tracing the line of her waist and hip, cupping her smooth, downy ass, locating the wet heat at her center. Then she shifted again, her back to him now, straddling him and lowering herself onto him. He could barely move, but she took care of that too, bucking against him and pulling away, finding a steady rhythm that worked for them both.

When they were done, she sank onto the futon beside him, stroking his thigh, his ribs. "You're a pretty decent lay for a half-dead man."

"You're excellent yourself," Richie said.

"I know. But I'm not starting from a handicapped position."

"This is true."

They were quiet for a few minutes, enjoying each other's physical presence, the smell of sex heavy in the room. Richie yawned.

"What, you're going to fall asleep on me now?"

"No, it's just been a very long day. With an unexpectedly pleasant finish."

"You mean, you didn't know this afternoon in the coffee shop that we were gonna do it?"

"I had no idea. Did you?"

"I didn't know I'd see you again later. But I thought it seemed like a good idea."

"I guess you were right. If we could have skipped the beating and gone straight to this part, that would have been okay, too."

"That would have taken away the excuse," she said. "I like it better when there's an excuse." She pushed herself off the futon, picked his clothing up from the floor, and tossed them over. "But it's time to go now. I like to sleep alone."

Abrupt, Richie thought. But her home, her rules. Slowly, the pain making itself known again, he began to tug on his clothes.

40

Welker drove through the night, both hands on the wheel, observing posted speed limits. Once, he passed a police car parked off the side of the road. When he was out of sight, he flashed his lights at oncoming cars, warning them of the cop's presence. He wanted to do nothing to attract attention to himself, but if he could make a cop's life a little more difficult, that was just dandy.

His bundle was small enough to fit into the trunk, even with its plastic sheeting. At first, he had cruised the city streets, but there were too many people around, despite the late hour. He needed time to himself, to arrange things just the way he wanted. He was still developing the ideal scenario in his mind.

After a while, he found himself out in the country once again, on those quiet farm roads, passing through small, sleepy towns. In one of those, he passed an elementary school, its playground hunkering back in the darkness behind a chain link fence.

He had found the right spot.

There were houses around, but they were dark as well. Working people lived there, young families; early to bed, early to rise. Once he was on the playground he would be invisible. And although it would still be a while before he could tell his angel what he had done, he thought she would know. The symbolism would be so powerful that she would sense it. She would understand that Welker was expressing his love for her.

He parked on the school's darkest side, opened the trunk, removed the plastic-wrapped bundle and carried it to the fence. The gate wasn't even locked. He was able to support the bundle in one hand and work it open. He put the bundle down inside the gate, looked at what the playground had to offer. A slide, a swingset, a climbing structure, a sandbox, some little rocking horses mounted on thick springs.

Welker found himself drawn to the swing set. Three swings with flat plastic seats of red or blue. Perfect. He dragged the bundle over, unrolled the plastic. The smell was intense now. It didn't disturb him, but he noticed it. The sheet was slick with her fluids, as was her skin. He wished he had a hose to wash her off, but he couldn't see one, figured a school groundskeeper probably wouldn't leave one out overnight.

He took the two outer swings and threw them over the upper bar, wrapping them around a few times, so their seats hung about four feet above the ground. He stood her up and put her arm between the chains of the swing on the right, twisted it around her until it held. She was lopsided, but he did the same on the left, and then she was suspended, toes barely grazing the ground, as if she was just taking flight.

The next step was harder. He had to go back to his car, to the small toolbox he kept in the trunk. He managed to work the middle swing off its chains, then looped those chains around the bar several time, each time moving the chain out farther, so that they hung outside the chains of the other swings, higher than the seats. These chains ended in hooks, which he'd had to pry apart to get the seat off. That worked fine. The hooks weren't sharp, but with a hammer and screwdriver he made holes in the flaps of skin he'd cut, about an inch in from the upper corner. He inserted the hooks through those holes.

When he was done, he felt himself becoming aroused again. A school full of young temptresses, with a playground that carried a unique message into the universe. He couldn't stop to satisfy himself though, not here. He'd spent too much time already. He didn't take a picture, though he had a camera in the car. And he wouldn't need to memorialize this one with a doll, since she had never been an angel until just now. Anyway, there would be pictures on the Internet, possibly within hours, certainly before another night had passed. And the picture in his mind's eye would never fade.

41

Without Olive to lean on, Richie's hike back to his car was harder than the walk over had been. He drove straight back to the Satellite Motel, hoping he wasn't seeping onto the rental car seats. When he got into the room, he spent some time examining Olive's handiwork in a mirror. She had done a better job on him than he could have done by himself, but he was still a fright.

Worse than that, he was done. He had exhausted every avenue. He was a walking bruise—nobody would open up to him now, even if he could think of anyone to talk to. He had sought Jarod Morton, or Kayley Ann Carrington, or both, and all he had found was an ugly version of himself.

He would wait until morning to tell Frank his decision to quit. The man would be unhappy, and he didn't want to deal with that. Anyway, Richie wanted to talk about his evening, and Frank wouldn't be thrilled about that either. One disappointment at a time.

Richie filled a motel glass with tap water, swallowed more painkillers and a couple of sleeping pills, made himself as comfortable as he could on the bed, and then dialed Frank's number.

"I did something stupid," he said when Frank answered.

"Am I supposed to be surprised? Does it have to do with the case?"

"No," Richie replied. "No, it's almost totally unconnected to the case."

"Almost? So what, I look like Doctor Phil to you?"

"I just need a friend I can talk to, I think."

Frank heaved a heavy sigh. Richie regretted making the call, but he had gone this far, and Frank wouldn't let him walk it back. "Okay, Maynard, what is it? And remember, I bill by the hour."

Richie took a sip of water and told him everything. The coffee shop, the bar brawl—during which Frank couldn't help chuckling—and finally the encounter at Olive's apartment.

"Jesus, Maynard," Frank said when Richie was done. "What are you, seventeen?"

"I know," Richie said. "I told you it was stupid."

"Yeah, but that's understating it. You need to throw some modifiers in there. Monumentally stupid, maybe. Outstandingly stupid. Stupid beyond reason. That kind of thing. You're a married man, and you're working on an unsanctioned criminal investigation, for which, need I remind you, I'm paying the bills out of my own pocket. You got responsibilities, man."

"You're not telling me anything I don't know, Frank. Just in case you were wondering."

"I wasn't. It's just, if you know that, then what are you calling me for? You want me to tell you it's all right? I can't do that. It's not."

"I know it, Frank. I screwed up, okay? I fucked a girl. She was sexy, she was willing, and it happened. Is that so bad?"

"In and of itself, it's a beautiful thing. What can make it bad is why you did it, and what your understanding with your wife is, and whether it's affecting the things that really matter in your life. Question isn't did it damage you to do it, question is, would it have damaged you if you didn't? If you said, 'thanks, ma'am, you're very attractive, but I don't think so.' You think you could do that?"

"I don't know, Frank. Maybe not. Everything is upside down right now. I told you, this case has been getting to me. I don't think I have enough Superman in my life to pull me through it."

"Well, why didn't you say so, son? That's easily fixed. I happen to have a fine issue right here. A *Superman* issue from 1972, with an amazing Nick Cardy cover. Well, that's redundant. Let's just say it's a beauty. Superman's kneeling on the floor, scooping up tiny buildings and shards of glass, sand running through his arms. The bottle city of Kandor has been smashed to bits on the ground of the Fortress of Solitude. A look of utter anguish twists his face."

"What's Kandor?" Richie asked.

"It's a city from Krypton, his home planet."

"And he keeps it in a bottle? Why doesn't he move in?"

"It's—never mind, Maynard. You'll get it when you hear the story."

"Okay."

Richie heard the rustling of paper, but then it stopped. Another sound, maybe Frank settling into his chair. "You know why I like these classic Superman stories, Maynard? I mean, as opposed to more contemporary ones?"

"Because you're old?"

Frank chuckled. "That's only part of it. Here's the thing. Even as late as the early 1970s, Superman still had a spirit that harked back to his earlier days. He was created during a time of hope and optimism, when American possibilities seemed unbridled. The more modern stories, they arise out of a civilization that's sinking, where nihilism seems the only rational response, where anarchy won't take hold because it wouldn't bother."

Richie had never heard Frank talking like that. It took him by surprise, and frankly sort of unnerved him. "Tell me how you really feel, big guy."

"Listen, man, what's left to be anarchic about when the entire society is collapsing around our feet? Trying to run on oil we don't have and can't afford to buy, to replace creativity and a spirit of brotherhood with more and more material things that mean nothing. Superman was an icon of optimism, a hero who was all about the belief that one person could change the world, one man could make a difference. Maybe that was never true, but the best Superman stories came about because people believed it might be."

"That's pretty bleak, Frank. You're not exactly cheering me up here. Is it really all that bad, you think?"

"Open your eyes, son. We live in a great country, but it has the potential to be so much greater if we could only learn from history, learn from our mistakes. You weren't around in the 1970s, you didn't see the air pollution, the water pollution. We got the Environmental

Protection Agency out of it, we got the Clean Air Act, Clean Water Act. So we cleaned stuff up. But we knew then we had to get off oil. We done that yet, you think?"

"Not exactly," Richie admitted.

"You want to talk about race?"

Richie didn't, but Frank was on a roll, and it would be hard to stop him. "Sure."

"We've been dealing with race issues as long as there's been an America. We thought we were making progress in the fifties and sixties. The Civil Rights Act. Then here comes Hurricane Katrina, and guess what? All those black folks left to fend for themselves in a drowning city. Ride out the storm in a Superdome that was falling apart around them. You think Detroit would be in the state it's in if it was a predominantly white city? We elect a black president, and next thing you know there's people in the streets carrying pictures of him looking like an African witch doctor, or Hitler, or the fucking Joker. An insult to the president *and* to the memory of Bob Kane."

"Who is…?"

"Cat who created Batman and the Joker."

"We're a long way from healed, I guess."

"No shit. Then we had oil washing up onto the shores of the Gulf, we're breaking the crust of the earth, oil flowing nonstop. Did we learn our lessons from the seventies? If we had would we still be doing this deep drilling shit out there? Oh, they know how to drill, they learned that lesson. They just didn't learn how to make it stop, how to make it safe. You can't make it safe, you shouldn't be doing it in the first place. Back when the Exxon Valdez spill happened, people said we got to get off oil. Jimmy Carter put on a sweater and turned down the thermostat and said we got to get off oil. What'd we do? Burn more oil. Drill, baby, drill.

"We don't learn from our mistakes, Maynard, we don't grow. We don't grow, we don't get better. We don't get better, we stay fucked up. They say only love can break your heart, man, but it don't have to be the love of a woman or a man. It can be the love of a brother, the love of a country, the love of an idea. That idea lets you down, well, your heart gets broke just the same. When you see so much heinous, inhuman shit, it makes you cynical. There's two ways you can respond. You can turn everything in toward yourself, figure everybody else is out after theirs, I'm gonna be after mine, like the rest of y'all. Or you can think, by myself I may not make much of a difference, but if I can affect my own little sphere of influence and other people do the same, then maybe working individually but collectively we can move things forward in some small way."

"And that's what you do," Richie said.

"That's what I *try* to do."

"Seems to me you do a pretty good job of it."

"Seems to me you're looking for a way to do the same. Maybe you ain't thought it through in the same way, and you're still struggling with it, but you're reaching the same conclusion."

Richie hadn't seen it happening, but somehow Frank had turned his diatribe back around onto Richie's situation. And although he hadn't expected it, Frank's assessment made him feel better about himself. Yes, he had done something he shouldn't have. He and Wendy had an understanding, they'd spoken vows, and he had tried to honor them. Then he had gone out of town for a few days, and wound up breaking those vows with the first sexy woman who offered herself.

Everybody made mistakes. His had been a big one, but maybe it didn't mean he was a complete waste.

Frank, in his own twisted way, had pointed that out to him.

Richie just hoped he could live up to the man's confidence.

O   O   O

They talked a while longer, and then the pills kicked in. Richie said goodnight and fell into a deep sleep, troubled by vivid dreams. In one, he saw a young girl walking down a dark street. She was barefoot, and a breeze tugged at her nightgown. He realized there were more children. Most of them girls, but boys too. They all walked down the same street, all wearing nightclothes. They had left behind their beds, their rooms. He didn't know where they were going, but they passed him (he became aware of himself at last, standing on a sidewalk, children streaming by him like a creek flowing around a log) and kept going. He didn't turn but suddenly faced the other way, and he saw where the children were headed: toward a busy highway.

Richie heard the roar of trucks, but they raced by so fast he couldn't see them, could only make out blurs.

The children neared the highway, and Richie fought back rising panic. He tried to grab them but his hands swished right through. When he tried to scream, the wind from the barreling trucks whisked away his words.

Some of the children reached the highway and kept going. He lost sight of them in the blurry dark. He tried to dash out into the road, to warn them away, but wind from the trucks battered him, forced him back. He couldn't follow, couldn't go where they went, and couldn't make them hear. There were hundreds now, thousands, all those children. All those empty beds in empty rooms. He screamed and screamed until his throat was raw, but he couldn't hear his own voice.

Richie woke up with tears stinging his eyes, his throat ragged and dry, the covers twisted around him. His wounds hurt all over again, and some were seeping through their bandages. He forced himself from the bed, tried through the pain and weariness to redress the injuries. When he was done, he got back in bed, but this time sleep was slow in coming.

42

Worries were like river rocks, polished smooth from constant handling, sometimes fitting so well in the palm of the hand it seemed they belonged there, yet with a surprising weight. Stack one on top of another and they could crush the chest, make breathing impossible, and make the heart struggle for every beat.

Frank wished he could talk to Tiana about Marcia. It sounded strange, a man talking to his late wife about a current love. But Tiana would get it. More than that, she had always been smarter than he when it came to understanding people, figuring out the bonds that drew them together and the walls that separated them. He had constructed too many walls, it seemed. He didn't know why he had, he only knew they needed to be toppled.

Reading Superman to Maynard last night, after that long, disturbing phone call, had helped Frank get to sleep, but not to stay asleep. Instead, he had spent most of the night awake, worrying about his father, about Marcia. Of course, about Jarod Morton and the missing child, too. He felt bad that Maynard was taking on the bulk of the case, and when he woke up, he determined to do something about that.

When he reached his desk, he made some calls to the few Bureau contacts who would still talk to him. He convinced one to make an effort to look into the child porn angle, searching databases for pictures of children wearing angel wings. It would be hard for anyone not intimately involved with the case to recognize Morton's work, but Frank hoped the angel fetish was rare enough that his friend would be able to turn up a finite number of examples.

Driving into the precinct, he had discovered Wil Fowler in the forefront of his thoughts. That surprised him, but he knew himself well enough not to ignore it. If Wil was lurking around in his mind, there was a reason for it.

He didn't believe Wil was a thief. But Clinton Gray certainly was. Maybe there was a connection, maybe Wil had been doing something for his stepfather when he was caught with the coins. Frank made a snap decision, and when he was finished on the phone, he left the stack of case folders piled on his desk, went to his car, and made the drive up I-94 to the Macomb Correctional Facility in New Haven.

The road took Frank through some of Michigan's priciest real estate, neighborhoods that had held their value while the rest of the state collapsed. There were glimpses of Lake St. Clair off to the east, and stretches of bucolic countryside: trees with big white bell-shaped flowers, quiet rivers gleaming like hammered copper in the morning sun, red barns perched on rolling green hills. It didn't take long to leave Detroit behind, but Frank's cares were more persistent; they didn't end at the city limits.

He had intended to question Clinton Gray, but he changed his mind en route. He would start with something more basic, and instead of visiting the man, and probably having to listen to lies about the miscarriage of justice that had put him in Macomb, he would begin by checking Gray's visitation records. He wanted to see who was coming out here, who was talking to Gray.

Like a lot of police, Frank didn't especially like visiting prisons. Surrendering his weapon before entering a place where so many people hated his guts always seemed like a bad idea. But he didn't have any choice, and he understood the policy, even if he didn't like it. Cons knew when a cop was in the house. Word traveled like wildfire behind prison walls.

As it turned out, Clinton Gray didn't have a lot of friends, at least not ones willing to visit him in prison. Carlotta came often, Wil once in a great while. On very rare occasions, they visited together. The only other name that turned up with any regularity was that of Otis

Parrott. Frank traced down the dates with his finger and discovered that Otis Parrott's name almost always appeared right before Carlotta's. A day separated the visits, two or three at the outside.

Frank wondered if there was a connection, if Wil was doing favors not for his stepfather, who he seldom saw, but at his mother's urging, on his stepfather's behalf. And if so, what this Parrott character had to do with them. He would have to do more checking, but it was something—more than he had known before the trip. He thought again about arranging an interview with Gray, but decided he would rather not alert the man—and through him, Otis Parrott and Carlotta and whoever else—that he had been here. Anyway, if he didn't get back to work soon, the lieutenant would have his ass on a platter.

O   O   O

Richie was sure there were people who liked Omaha. It had seemed nice enough to him, in the beginning. But now it seemed like a giant mongrel dog that had chewed him up and defecated him out in a doorway. He was done with it, with everything, ready to get out, but he hurt too much to sit on an airplane. He extended his stay at the Satellite for another night, and decided to spend the day indoors, doing online research. He had plenty to keep him occupied. Maybe he had exhausted most of the possible directions to search, but not quite all of them.

He started with Craigslist, which at least covered a finite number of cities; albeit within those cities there were enough categories to make him feel like he was searching not just for a needle in a haystack, but for a single needle in all the haystacks in America. He was looking for anything with the word "angel" in it, and the site's search function helped speed things up a little. But soon he realized that Morton and his friends could have used some kind of code, in which case "angel" might not show up at all.

So he visually scanned every page on every site. He learned far more than he wanted to about people's private lives and personal proclivities, the prices they would pay for used cars and furniture, things they would give away, things they wanted. Broken toasters. Why would somebody want broken toasters? Who knew?

Time passed. Wary of frightening children, he ventured out, picked up breakfast at a fast food drive-through and brought it back to the room. He picked up where he had left off. He looked at Craigslist until his eyes were bleeding. He found nothing.

His other idea was newspaper classifieds, but there were hundreds and hundreds, if not thousands, of newspapers around the country. Most seemed to have a website, and most of those included classified ads. Richie needed to narrow his search. Then he thought, why not start where it started? Detroit. At least, that's where the one-for-one trade had come about, if his theory was correct.

He went to the site of *The Detroit Free Press*, as good a beginning point as any. The *Freep* linked to a separate site, which had a section called "Bulletin Board." Richie started there. He found something almost right away, under the heading "re: Cherubim." It was, of course, the first thing he clicked on. "It's got to be now," the post said. "Time's up." He didn't find anything else in the current listings, but when he scrolled down the page, the ads got older, and he found the beginning of the thread on a page from several days before.

The post was headlined "Cherubim." All the post said was, "I need the winged cherub earlier than foreseen. Sooner the better."

A reply headed "Re: Cherubim," posted only hours later, said, "Should be no problem."

Was that it? Was that all there was to it? Richie looked again at the posting date. It was the day that he and Frank had been in Virginia, talking to Morton's mother and sisters. Jenny Morton had thought her sister Janine was still in touch with Jarod. She'd promised to call if she found anything out, and they hadn't heard from her. But Janine might not have trusted Jenny. Had she reached out to Jarod, told him that cops from Detroit were asking about him, trying to discover his current whereabouts? Had that somehow precipitated a sudden urge to hurry things along? What things, Richie wasn't sure, but from the ads it sounded as if another one-for-one swap might be in the works. He copied the contents of those ads, and the URLs. He'd have to have Frank try to learn the ISPs of those who had posted them.

Maybe the people posting did so because they knew police could seize their phone records. If they were careful enough, they might have posted the ads through an anonymizer service, to protect their ISPs. Still, he had to check.

He called Frank, but there was no answer. He left an urgent message, and started searching the other Detroit papers to see if there was anything else pertinent. He kept at it because he had to, because no one else knew Morton the way he did. No one would be as likely to recognize his patterns, his mark.

43

As much as someone with her responsibilities could be, Kate was a creature of habit. She liked it that way; liked to wake up at six, take a hot shower, and drink her first cup of tea while she prepared breakfast and her second while she ate it. Interruptions knocked her whole day sideways, leaving her off-kilter until she was able to get back on schedule.

This morning, her routine had been interrupted in a big way.

The call hadn't even come from dispatch, but directly from Donnie Ortega, a sergeant in her department who was on the verge of being busted down a rank or two, if not losing his job altogether, due to general incompetence and a major attitude problem. He hadn't been a bad patrolman but he was unsuited to higher rank, and he was a mistake she would have to correct soon.

When she heard his voice on the phone at five twenty-two, she assumed he was calling to complain about something. As she struggled up from the fog of sleep, she tried to prepare a scathing retort—something that would scald the skin from whichever ear he had by the phone. But he kept trying to talk, his voice catching, and Kate recognized genuine anguish when she heard it. Even in Donnie.

"Just tell me what's going on," she said finally, after his fifth stammering attempt.

"I *can't*. You've just got to come down here."

He told her he was at Marshall Elementary, over in Oakwood. Kate didn't like the sound of that. She told him she'd be there as soon as she could and hung up. She skipped the shower and breakfast, hoping she could swing back home after Donnie's emergency. She pulled on her uniform, yanked a brush through her short hair and headed out the door, running on nerves instead of caffeine. The sky was still leaden, though a shimmering silver band in the east hinted at the sun that would soon crest the Sierra Nevada range dividing her valley from the rest of the country.

Traffic was light, and she made good time. When she reached Marshall Elementary, the parking lot and bus entry were both gated off, so she pulled up to the curb. She climbed down from the Tahoe and crossed an expanse of lawn, still damp from the morning's dew. Donnie stood beside the school with a small clutch of what Kate assumed were locals. One woman knelt in the wet grass, weeping into her hands. Kate approached with the uneasy tread of a barefoot woman at a rattlesnake ranch.

"Donnie, tell me what the hell we're doing here."

He hadn't heard her coming, despite the jangle of the gear hanging off her duty belt. He jumped like a kid in a haunted house at the county fair, when a spook lunges out of the dark. "Jesus!" he said. "Sorry, sheriff, you startled me."

"I didn't mean to," Kate said. "But again, why are we here?"

He pressed his lips together until they went white, and tried to swallow a lump that might have been the size of a soccer ball. Instead of speaking, he jerked a thumb over his shoulder, pointing toward something she couldn't see around the school's corner. She saw the flash of a camera from that direction. "Get whoever that is the hell out of there!" she cried. Donnie looked stricken, and she realized how much he didn't want to go back there. "Never mind, I'll do it. You stay here with these people."

Kate went around the corner and saw the school's playground behind a heavy eight-foot steel fence. She could make out playground equipment. The gate gapped, and a man with a camera slipped through it as she approached, casting anxious glances her way. She let him leave without comment and strode toward the gate, curious. She hoped whatever had upset Donnie was minor enough that she could use his lack of professionalism as an excuse to can his ass.

It wasn't.

She saw it when she passed through the gate. She stopped dead, looked away as if it might change what she had seen, then looked again. It hadn't changed, though. If anything, it was worse because the sun had just cleared the distant peaks and a ray of golden light sliced through the morning gray like a spotlight's beam.

What it illuminated was the ghastliest thing she had ever seen. And as a long-time cop, she had seen a double handful of awful.

A naked woman hung suspended from children's swings, her pale flesh smeared in blood or shit or both. The blood on her body was the only trace Kate saw, so the woman had been killed somewhere else and brought here. She was small, with dark hair—Asian, Kate thought at first, but no, her features were Caucasian. Her skull was caved in on the right side, exposing stained white shards and pinkish-gray meat.

As bad as that was, it was not the worst.

The body had not only been hung from the swings, but it had been posed, and although it took a moment for Kate to recognize the statement being made, the morning sunlight splashing upon it offered the clarity of a painting. One rife with religious symbolism.

Whoever had put the woman on the swings had cut two flaps of skin from her back and hooked those onto shorter chains, giving them the appearance of wings. Her dangling toes barely scraped the ground. The whole display, Kate understood, was meant to suggest an angel in flight.

Kate believed that most people were basically decent, and the few who weren't were the exceptions. It was law enforcement's task to keep those exceptions from harming the peaceful majority. Some cops felt the other way, believing that anyone could do anything to anybody at any time, and only the fear of retribution kept people in line. Kate had never subscribed to that theory, and doubted she could do her job if she had.

But a sight like this made her rethink her beliefs. Maybe the whole race should be erased from the planet. A plague, a flood, something Biblical in nature and impact would work. In a pinch, nuclear winter. Fast would be good, although slow and painful might be more deserved.

She didn't know what the pose meant, but there it was. Now she understood how Donnie felt, why he hadn't been able to describe it to her in words. She felt her stomach lurch, took a few quick steps toward the fence, and hunched over, gagging up stinging bile. She spat it onto the ground, hoping she was far enough away that she wasn't contaminating the crime scene. The whole playground—hell, the whole school—was a crime scene, though, and she already knew this was something beyond her department's capability. They'd have to call for investigators from Modesto, maybe the FBI. She was more pissed than ever that Donnie hadn't managed to secure the scene—if the press got wind of this, it would go national. Now she was sorry she hadn't handcuffed that guy with the camera. This was the kind of sick shit that would turn them on, would sell newspapers and lead the TV newscasts. And in the middle of it all would be Sheriff Kate, the country widow, hopelessly out of her depths.

The idea made her want to retire on the spot, let it be someone else's problem. She wouldn't, though. If Kate had been a quitter, she'd have been long since gone.

And thoughts of retirement were rapidly pushed from her mind by another impulse. She wanted to be the one who found the fucker who could do this to a fellow human being. She believed in justice, in the law, in doing things the right way, so she wouldn't put a bullet in him unless he gave her no choice. She would let him go to court, stand trial with a defense attorney at his side. She would just have to make sure she had enough to hang him before that happened, because once she slapped bracelets on his diseased self, she didn't intend to let him live another instant of his life as a free man.

44

Frank sat in his car outside Wil Fowler's house. He didn't want to go to the door, because if Wil and his mother were both home, there would be no way short of a court order—or handcuffs— that he'd be able to talk to Wil alone. He figured if he lived with Carlotta Gray, he wouldn't spend any more time in the house than he had to, and he counted on Wil feeling the same way.

He had been there for twenty minutes when Wil came out the door. Wil heard something from inside and ducked back in, then emerged again. This time he made it three steps from the door before he stopped and went back. He was inside for two more minutes, then burst through the door, hurrying, no doubt afraid his mother would summon him once more. His head snapped up once—Frank thought he could hear Carlotta's screech from the car—but Wil kept going, pretending he was already out of range. Frank didn't blame him a bit.

Frank waited until Wil was in front of the house next door, then thumbed down his window and called him. Wil gave him a look that made Frank think he was just as unwanted an intrusion as Carlotta was. "Yeah?"

"Come here."

"What?" Wil showed a marked lack of enthusiasm, but he obeyed.

Frank gestured toward the passenger seat. "Get in."

"I have to?"

"You're not under arrest, if that's what you mean."

"Okay." Wil shuffled around the car, opened the door and planted himself. "S'up?"

"I want to talk to you about Otis Parrott."

"Who?"

"Otis Parrott. He's a friend of your stepdad's."

"Never heard of him."

"Don't bullshit me, son, it's not appealing."

Wil showed him a blank face, making his ignorance look almost real. "Look, it doesn't matter what you say about him," Frank said. "Mostly I want to warn you. I know he knows your stepfather, and probably your mother. I figure he knows you too. I did some digging around about him and I found out he's a pedophile. He used to work at a school near that house my friend Richie caught you trying to break into, did you know that? Madison Elementary. He was a janitor, around every day, when kids were there."

Wil shrugged. So far, that was what Frank had seen from him the most, that languorous, liquid shoulder movement indicating his utter disinterest in virtually everything.

"All I'm saying is, keep away from him. I've already got my eye on you, and it's going to be on him too. You're in enough trouble as it is, so don't make it worse."

"Aiight."

"Your mother showed me your art, Wil. Those pieces are really tight."

"Yeah, okay."

"I mean it. I don't do it myself, but I appreciate art. You've got real talent, you could go places."

"Aiight."

"Don't think I'm shitting you, son, because I'm not."

Wil shrugged again, and Frank let it go. "Cool," he said. "Get out. Do whatever you were gonna do. Just remember what I said."

Wil opened the car door and slid out without another word. Frank wondered why he was going out of his way to help a kid who seemed determined not to help himself. Wil's art, he guessed. Anyway, police work was rarely about making a dent in the big picture. It had more to do with affecting one person at a time. If he could make a difference in Wil's life, that would be a contribution.

When he'd been Wil's age, he had been the same way, suspicious of authority, resentful of adults who believed they knew more than he did. He watched the kid saunter away, as if he didn't have a care. Frank hoped that was true, that whatever his stepfather and mother and Otis Parrott were up to didn't rub off on him.

He doubted that was the case. But if he hadn't been able to hope, he wouldn't have been able to go on. So he held tight to his desire, and wished it upon the boy.

o O o

A light spring rain fingertapped against the windows. Wendy realized her own fingers were moving along with it, drumming on the desk and the papers she had spread there. Maps, surveys, zoning charts, letters, petitions, all the things she would need to figure out which Detroit neighborhoods should be eliminated and which should stay. It was a responsibility she hadn't asked for, but at the same time she would rather be involved in the process than not. She had brought lunch in, a Caesar salad, but most of it sat, lukewarm and wilted, on a far corner of the desk.

The phone startled her, breaking her concentration. She made a mark with a yellow highlighter, to keep her place, and caught the phone on its third ring.

Richie. They did the pointless stuff first, the "how are you" and "I miss you." Then Wendy started probing, trying to find out the truth behind the casual evasions. Richie said he was fine, but he didn't sound fine.

"Is Frank still in Detroit?"

"Yeah. Just me out here on the road."

"That must be lonely."

Richie hesitated before answering. "It is."

"What?"

"Nothing. I'm lonely. It's a motel room. The motel's octagonal, but that's only interesting for so long."

"Come home, then."

"I will as soon as I can. Probably tomorrow. I'm just not quite there yet."

"Okay." She had noted the "probably" in his answer. What that really meant was "probably not."

"How are things with you?"

"I might have saved Frank's girlfriend's job."

"Marcia? I'm not sure I'd call her a girlfriend. Things are sort of unsettled there."

"I'm sorry to hear that."

"What did you do?"

"Councilman Roberts was determined to shut down Wayne County Receiving, but I think I outmaneuvered him."

"How?"

"He's got interests in the Brush Park area. I made a case for closing that, razing the whole neighborhood and turning it into open space or urban farmland. Once I lined up enough support for the idea, I did some horse trading."

"And it worked?"

"I'm not positive yet, but I think so. We'll know after tomorrow's special session."

"I'm proud of you, Wendy," Richie said. "You're like a regular politician!"

"Is that really something to be proud of? But it feels good, just the same, to have maybe made a difference. And it feels especially good to one-up that asshole Roberts."

"Now you know why I liked police work. It was all about making a difference."

"You didn't like police work," she reminded him. "You liked the idea of police work."

"Okay, maybe."

"Seriously, Richie, I hate to think you're chasing your tail out there. Are you really helping anybody?"

"I don't know," Richie said. "But as long as there's a chance that I am, I have to keep trying."

"I don't want to see our credit card bill when it shows up."

"I don't either," Richie admitted. "Frank's paying for a lot of it, but there are still expenses. It'll be bad."

"I hope you know what you're doing."

He answered in the affirmative, as she had known he would. More and more, she was beginning to question his judgment.

o o o

She had given Richie the opening he needed, and he hadn't taken it. He had discussed the issue with Frank the night before, during their wide-ranging phone call. Tell Wendy, or not? He thought he should, and Frank had said, "If it's gonna keep happening, then hell, yeah, you owe it to her to tell her. But if it's a one-time thing, over and out, then I don't see what's to be gained by flapping your grill. Plenty to be lost, though. It was me—of course, I wouldn't be in that position, but if I was, if this was a once-in-a-lifetime fuckup, then I wouldn't say another word about it to anyone. Including me. And I'd make sure I knocked it the fuck off from now on."

"Sounds like a deal," Richie said. "Thanks for the advice."

Richie had been honest, to a point. He did miss Wendy, and he wanted to go home. But he also wanted Jarod Morton behind bars, where he couldn't get at any more little girls, ever. That was the most important thing. Finding Morton. Keeping him away from children. The idea of giving up had started to skate away when Richie contemplated the nightmare, and fled altogether when he found the posts on the *Freep* site. Richie decided he was willing to make some more sacrifices, if they might lead to Morton. And the more he dug, the more he believed Morton was still out there.

Richie remained online, but he needed a break from the tedious work. Although he wouldn't know for a while if what he'd found on the *Freep's* site would actually pay dividends, at least he seemed to have accomplished something.

For a change of pace, he surfed one of his regular internet stops, a site that amassed crime news from all across the country, gathering it from police reports, private citizens, and various media sources. It was a grim hobby, but it was what he had. With his tongue, he plumbed the hole where a tooth had been.

The third headline down caught his interest, and Richie clicked through to the story. A photograph accompanied it—dark, under-exposed, but horrific just the same. A naked woman hanging from a swing set.

This hadn't come from any mainstream media. They would have pixilated the exposed breasts and pubic area, at the very least.

He read the story, which was long on supposition and short on fact. A sheriff's office in rural Stanislaus County, California, had been called after an early morning dog walker had noticed the body through a fence in a town called Oakwood. The sheriff had come and secured the scene, but obviously not before someone had snapped pictures. That someone had posted them online, and this one had been linked to the story. The victim's identity was not yet known, or not released. The sheriff, Kate Dunning, wasn't commenting, using the old "ongoing investigation" dodge.

Richie stared at the picture. He hadn't made it out at first, but when he enlarged the image on his laptop screen, he saw it. The dead woman wasn't just hanging from swings wrapped around her armpits. The flesh of her back had actually been cut and suspended, giving her the appearance of having wings.

Angel wings.

He did some quick searching, and discovered that the nearest sizable city to Oakwood was Modesto. Next, he searched for portrait photographers in Modesto. Sure enough, one there used an angel-child image in its promotional material. "Precious Memories Photography," the business was called. That name hadn't turned up before.

But it fit. The little girl with the angel wings, the memories Jarod Morton must have of Kayley and his other victims, the fact that he took photos to keep those memories fresh. The young victim, slender-framed, who could almost have passed for barely pubescent. It all made a horrible kind of sense.

If this was Morton's work—and Richie couldn't help believing it was—then it dramatically altered his two-bit psychological assessment of Morton. Up until now, Morton had been the very picture of an organized offender. He had kept his life together, run a business, stayed out of prison, and committed his crimes without leaving enough evidence to point law enforcement toward him. Even when he killed his own wife, he had removed her head and hands and buried her body in another state. He was careful. It had been a fluke that had tipped Richie and Frank off to him in the first place.

But this: posing a body, leaving it where it was certain to draw attention. The butchery he had performed on it. These things spoke of a killer who was rapidly devolving. Decompensation, the psychologists called it. Morton was under enormous stress, and not handling it well. It connected, Richie supposed, to the seemingly urgent message at the *Freep* site asking to move up the date of the transfer.

If in fact Morton had been tipped off to the fact that he was being hunted, after all these years, then that stress made sense. But the reaction—Richie swallowed hard—the reaction, he should have been able to anticipate. The man had become used to getting away with it. Suddenly he was a target. *Of course* he was panicking.

It only made him more dangerous than ever.

He had to be found, and soon.

Richie had lied to Wendy after all. He'd said he would hurry home, but it looked like he was heading to California. He picked up the phone to try Frank again.

45

Frank didn't care for coincidences. They happened in life, that much he knew. He wasn't interested in conspiracy theories or divine providence, and sometimes those were the only other ways to explain what could easily be understood by accepting that coincidences occurred. But he didn't like them, he didn't trust them, and when it was possible to find an equally reasonable explanation—not one of those far-out ones, but something that made sense—he tended to gravitate toward it.

Such was the case with Otis Parrott.

He had a few facts in hand. He wasn't sure yet how they fit together, but he had a feeling they did. Wil Fowler had tried to break into what Frank still thought of as the Morton house, from which Angela Morton, AKA Kayley Ann Carrington, had disappeared. Jarod Morton, Frank now believed, was a pedophile, had been for some time, and if he was still alive, probably continued to be. Clinton Gray, Wil Fowler's stepfather, was in prison, where he was often visited by Otis Parrott. Otis Parrott was also a convicted pedophile. Was it coincidence that a pedophile visited Wil's stepfather in prison, and Wil had been trying to break into another pedophile's former home? It might have been. Maybe it was coincidence that Maynard had seem him doing it, although since Maynard lived close by and drove past that house all the time, the chances of that encounter were good. Maybe it was a coincidence that Frank had seen Maynard in the house, but again, since Frank had a habit of sitting outside the house, staring at it, not overly far-fetched.

But the pedophiles thing, that made Frank wonder if there was a reason Wil had been breaking into that particular house, beyond all the non-reasons the boy had offered up so far. The arithmetic suggested a connection between Otis Parrott and Jarod Morton.

He wouldn't find the answer sitting at his desk. Nor, since he didn't have his hands on Jarod Morton, would he find it by asking him. Wil Fowler wasn't saying anything. That left only one person to ask: Otis Parrott.

O   O   O

Frank's usual routine before paying a visit to someone who had a record was to read through his jacket twice. The first time, beginning to end, gave him an overall sense of the individual and his crimes. The second time, he read more slowly, page by page, making notes, familiarizing himself with details that might help his own investigation.

Otis Parrott's jacket, he read three times. His mind wandered, knocked off course by the various issues with his father, with Marcia, with Maynard's bad behavior. Maynard may have messed up with that woman in Omaha, but at least he still had Wendy. Frank was on the verge of losing Marcia, *would* lose her if he wasn't careful. These thoughts wouldn't let him alone.

But he was also distracted because he couldn't stand to think that Parrott had been allowed to interact with children, to work at an elementary school, for so long. He hadn't been caught for years, and even when he finally was, the prosecution had only been able to prove some relatively minor crimes. Exposing himself, possession of small amounts of child pornography disguised as nudist magazines. He lost his job with that first conviction, but he hadn't spent nearly enough time in prison.

After the third pass, Frank thought he'd read all he could stand, and all he needed. He drove to Parrott's house in Oak Park. It was a small detached home with big trees in the front yard, still dripping from the recent rains, shading a two-track driveway that led to a converted carriage house garage. The garage doors were closed, as were all the curtains. He couldn't be sure anyone was home.

The doorbell button was lifeless under his fingertip. He pounded on the door, and after a minute heard shuffling sounds inside. A door opened and Otis Parrott stood looking at him, thirty pounds heavier than in his most recent mug shot, but otherwise the same unappealing excuse for a human being.

Parrott was only five-five, but he seemed even shorter in person. His hair was long and thin, drooping in greasy strands, like the tails of dozens of rats. He was in need of a shave. He had undersized eyes that made him seem to be squinting or blinking, and a wide mouth with rubbery lips. His breath was foul, even from three feet away, as if the rot inside his soul had a physical presence. He wore a gray T-shirt with Popeye on it, holding a can of spinach, and red sweat pants. Because they were comfortable, Frank guessed, not because he was anything resembling athletic.

Parrot's Popeye shirt couldn't contain his gut, which bulged out from beneath it like a beach ball. It stretched the waistband of his sweat pants so the drawstring wouldn't tie. His arms were flabby, his feet bare, his toenails yellow. He was, all in all, one of the most unattractive men Frank had ever laid eyes on.

"Yes?" Parrott asked. He had a slight lisp, his *s* sounds coming out just this side of a *th*.

Frank showed his badge. "You're Otis Parrott."

"Perhaps."

"I wasn't asking you a question. There can't be two people as ugly as you in Detroit."

"Fine," Otis said. "What is it?"

"I'm coming in."

"Have you got a warrant?"

"Fuck that, I'm coming in."

Otis started to slam the door, but Frank caught it with the palm of his hand, shoved it. Otis squealed but backed away, letting Frank enter.

"I would like to get your badge number," Otis said. "I'll be filing a report."

"File whatever you want."

"What is this about? Am I suspected of something?"

"Look, Otis, you and I both know what you are, so there's no need to get cute here."

"I admit I've been an unwell man, but I've been getting psychological counseling."

"You're a sick motherfucker, all right, and you're up to something," Frank interrupted. "Tell me what it is."

"I don't have any idea what you mean. Perhaps you could explain."

"I'm here to talk about Wil Fowler."

"Who?"

Frank was losing patience fast. Just being in the same room with this creep made him want to throw punches. A brief mental image of Parrott's ruined face on the ground, Frank's knuckles skinned and stinging, flashed through his head. He liked it. He took a sudden step toward Otis, who backed away fast.

"All right. Handsome kid. He's a little old for me, though, don't you think? At least his stepfather brought him up right."

"Save that shit, I don't want to hear it. You've been visiting Clinton Gray up at Macomb."

"I might have been."

"It's a public record, Otis."

"Okay, I have. What about it?"

"What about it is I want to know why."

"That is not public record," Otis protested. "That is my own business."

"Otis, I don't want to listen to your fucking lisp any longer than I have to. So you're going to start answering my questions or you're going to be lisping with fewer teeth in your mouth. Am I making myself clear?"

"Quite clear, yes." *Yeth.* It got worse as he became more anxious. "Detective, I know I've been in trouble. Like I said, I'm getting counseling. I really don't know what you want from me here."

"I want to know what your connection is to all this," Frank said.

"All what? Look, I used to be connected to the community. I ran a BBS, a bulletin board system. People with a certain … appetite, communicated with each other over it. That's a long time ago, now. More than a decade. The Internet's a big, wild place, and nobody uses BBSs anymore. Now there are websites, forums, chat rooms.

Social media. You name it. It's easy for people to share their common interests."

"Was Clinton Gray part of your BBS community?"

"Nobody went by their real names on there. It was all screen names. I really couldn't tell you."

"How about Jarod Morton?"

Otis shrugged without hesitation. "Never heard the name."

Frank chuckled, and Otis shrank from the sound as if he'd been slapped. "You've never heard of Jarod Morton. You, who were running a pedophile bulletin board at the time that his eleven-year-old daughter was abducted?"

Otis rubbed the side of his nose. "Oh, maybe something back in the day. In the newspapers, on TV." He shrugged again. "Now that you put it in context. That's all, though."

"Was he part of your BBS?"

"I really couldn't say."

Frank was almost sorry that Parrott was cooperating, or seeming to. He had been hoping for trouble, hoping Parrott would give him an excuse to get physical. Maynard had admitted that he'd been looking for a fight. Frank knew the sensation. A dark spot at the center of his being swelled to fill Frank, blotting everything else, filling him with a terrible black rage. He embraced it. He wanted to beat Otis Parrott to a bloody pulp. But if he did, he would lose his access to the man, and the freedom he had been given to pursue this case. Frustrated and furious, he clenched his fists, letting them hang at his sides. He seemed no closer to Jarod Morton than he had when this whole thing had started.

Turning away from Parrott, he crossed to a bookcase of DVD and VHS recordings. He pulled DVDs and videotapes off the shelves at random, tearing them open, looking at the labels, tossing them aside. If Otis Parrott was hiding porn, this would be the easiest way to do it.

"Stop that! Those are mine!"

"Put it in your complaint."

"What are you doing? You're awful!"

Frank kept opening, comparing labels. So far everything looked above-board. "Looking for kiddie porn."

"There's nothing like that in the house!" *Houth.*

"Where do you keep it? The garage? You got a storage unit?"

"No! I told you!"

"I don't believe you."

"I'm telling you the truth."

"Then you don't mind if I look."

"You're infringing my civil liberties!"

"Ain't that a shame?"

Otis stood with his arms cocked, fists pressed against the flesh swelling up from his sweat pants. "You're a very mean man."

"Damn straight." Frank opened some more DVD cases. Parrott had a lot of children's TV shows—*Spongebob, Dora the Explorer, Blue's Clues.* Some Frank had enjoyed on occasion, but he would never be able to watch them again. To Parrott, they were nothing but bait.

He was convinced that Otis Parrott was still a pedophile, but he couldn't prove it. He had no evidence to support a warrant request, and even if he had, the way he had barged in and abused the man made it impossible to try for one. It had been a gamble, Frank counting on his intimidating presence to shake something loose, instead of doing the appropriate detective work, following the legal straight and narrow. In the end, the gamble hadn't paid off.

"You got a computer here?"

"Of course."

"Maybe I'll check that."

"Feel free. You won't find anything. Haven't you heard, detective? It's all about the cloud now. Nobody stores anything on their own drive. It's just out there, in the atmosphere, and when you need it you go look."

"You've got e-mails, other—"

"You are dreadfully behind. Anyone with anything to hide—not that I have anything like that—would use relays, proxies. If I knew that someone in Chicago, say, had some video of his ... his new kitten, I would send an e-mail. It would go to a computer in Vietnam, and from there to Spain, to Paraguay, to Russia. By the time it got to Chicago it would have lit in a dozen places. There would be no connection between me and the person in Chicago, ever. It's all just strings of numbers, out there in the ether. Out there on the cloud."

Maybe Parrott was right. Frank needed to get up to speed, if creeps like this were so far ahead of him technologically. "Okay,

Otis," he said. "I'm going now. But I might come back at any time. *Any* time. I'm watching you, and you'll never know when I'm there. I want you to think long and hard about trying anything. When you're ready to talk about Wil Fowler and Clinton Gray, or Jarod Morton, why, you reach out, and I'll be there. Until then, keep looking over your shoulder."

"Okay, fine," Parrott said. "You want to waste your time, be my guest."

"I'll do that." Frank let himself out. When he sat down behind the wheel of his car, trembling overtook him. He sat there for a very long time, clenching the wheel, until he recovered enough to drive.

46

Richie got lucky with flights, and although he had to pay full fare, with the time zones in his favor he was in Modesto by mid-afternoon. An hour later, he was sitting across the desk from Katherine Dunning, who everyone in her department seemed to call Sheriff Kate. She was trim, with rusty gray hair trending toward gray, and sympathetic eyes that appraised him as he took his chair. "You look like you lost an argument with the back end of a mule."

It had been just long enough for his bruises to settle into a Technicolor nightmare of blacks, purples, blues and reds. "You think I look bad? You should see how I feel."

"I can imagine. What brings you to Waterton?"

He started from the beginning, with the house, and told her everything. He had briefly considered making up a story, but he was done with telling lies. There was no percentage in it. Occasionally, she raised objections about the involvement of a private citizen in such matters. He shot those down, pointing out that he had Frank's blessing. The authorities hadn't been able to do anything, he reminded her. He, at least, had made real progress.

At one point, near the end of the story, she took a tissue from a box on her desk and dabbed at her eyes. "I'm sorry. It's been a very emotional day."

"I'm sure it has. I'm sorry I laid on this on you now, considering how your day started. But you understand why I think there's a connection, right?"

"I understand that you think there's a connection. I'm not saying I'm convinced."

"It has to be," Richie said. "The photo studio, the angel picture. He's been moving progressively farther west from Virginia: Detroit, Indianapolis, Omaha, Tucson. Now California."

"A lot of people move to California. And you said another photographer told you that wasn't an unusual gimmick."

"Other people have done it. It's not absolutely unique. But it's not common, and the proximity of that studio and the body, mutilated to make her look like she has angel wings? It's got to be him."

"Let me ask you something. Do the names ..." She stopped, mid-sentence, as if trying to recall something she'd heard only once, a long time ago. "Rachel. Susie. Jessie, no, Jenny ... do those mean anything to you?"

"No, I don't think so. What's the context?"

Kate didn't answer the question. When she spoke again, though, Richie barely noticed the lack. "I suppose it wouldn't hurt for me to pay a visit to this photographer of yours."

"I'm coming with you."

"No. Absolutely not. This is a police matter."

"He's very skilled at changing his identity, Sheriff," Richie said. "I would recognize him. You wouldn't. If he convinces you that he's not Jarod Morton, then he's gone. We'll never find him again."

Kate fixed him with a stern gaze.

"I've been a cop," Richie reminded her. "I know the rules. I'll keep out of the way. But you have to let me see him."

"I'm not taking you there," she said. "Period. But if you have your own vehicle, I suppose I couldn't prevent you from following. You do what I say, and you hang back."

"I will," Richie promised.

Sheriff Kate summoned a subordinate and asked for everything he could find on the owner of the photo studio in Modesto. She and Richie chatted for ten minutes or so, until the officer returned with the details. The photographer's name was Jerry Morrison. He had been in business there for four years, during which time he hadn't been in trouble with the law. He paid his rent and his taxes. As soon as Richie heard the name, he nodded. "That's him."

Kate shot a shushing look at him, so Richie held his tongue until the other officer had finished and left. "That's definitely Jarod Morton," he told her. He ran through the other aliases. Morton apparently didn't want to change his initials, probably in order to easily remember each new name.

They had him.

Given the time of day, they would go to the photo studio, which closed at six. Kate had mentioned calling the Modesto PD before they left, to make sure Morrison was there. "Where else is he going to be?" Richie asked.

"You know him better than I. Anyway, I said I *should* call Modesto. But all I have to go on is your word, and I'm not totally convinced you're right about this. If he's there, if I have to make an arrest, then I'll notify them. But you'd better not be wrong."

"I'm not wrong," Richie declared. "This is the guy. He's been molesting little girls for years, and he killed that woman last night."

"You're convinced, but you don't have any evidence. In my line—"

"I understand police work," Richie said. "We just need to get him off the street. Once we do, if he doesn't confess right away, we'll put together enough to get an indictment."

Kate took the slip of paper and headed for her SUV, a white Yukon, its lower panels smeared with mud-brown plumes. Richie followed, dashing for the rental he had parked in the lot. Every nerve in his body seemed alive, prickly with expectation.

○ ○ ○

Precious Memories Photography was on the fringes of downtown Modesto, sandwiched between a Thai restaurant and a beauty parlor. A large, framed color picture of a young blond girl with angel wings sat in the front window. Richie, already pretty sure he was right, became absolutely positive.

But the studio was closed up tight, the door locked, the electric OPEN sign turned off. Kate hammered on the door anyway. Nobody came.

She went into the beauty parlor, Richie trailing behind. "I'm looking for the photographer next door," Kate said. "You seen him today?"

A Latina hairdresser looked up from her customer, scissors in her hand. "Hasn't been there all day," she said.

Another hairdresser sat in one of the chairs, legs crossed, reading a magazine. "He hasn't been around much lately," she added. "Kind of a queer duck, you ask me." She caught herself and gave an abashed grin. "I don't mean in a homo way. Just odd, is all."

"Thanks," Kate said. Back on the sidewalk, she shook her head at Richie. "'Middle of the afternoon,' you said. 'Where else would he be?'"

"I was wrong. About that. Not about who he is. That picture in the window, that angel—"

"Creepy as hell," Kate said. "Doesn't make him a killer, but if I could arrest someone on charges of bad taste, he'd be the guy."

"You've got his home address, right?" Richie knew she did; he had been sitting there when the officer read it off and then handed it to her on a sheet of paper.

"I guess that's our next stop. Should have gone there first. He's outside Red Bank. That's most of the way back to Waterton."

The drive into Modesto had taken almost forty minutes, fifteen of which had been once they reached the city limits and had to deal with traffic and stoplights. Richie didn't like having to backtrack, but it was worth burning some gas if Jarod Morton was at the end of the trail.

"I wouldn't have expected him to take the day off," Richie said.

"After what you claim he did last night, he's probably pretty tired."

"Yes, but he would want to be all business as usual today, to make sure he didn't arouse any suspicions."

"Whatever he does, it's been working for him for a long time. I guess we can't expect him to change now."

"That's not necessarily true," Richie pointed out. "He's already changed, in a big way. He's going to keep on changing, getting more dangerous all the time."

She gave a nod, giving in without really agreeing, and climbed into her Yukon. Richie got back into his rental compact and followed again, out into the country. Most of the trip was familiar, the same roads going the other direction. She pulled off Highway 108 in Oakwood, and when Richie saw the sign at the edge of town, he recognized it as the place in which the woman's body had been found. That had been just this morning, early. So much had happened Richie felt like days had passed.

Oakwood looked peaceful: a small country town with a feed store, a gas station, an independent grocery store and a few other businesses, a little smaller than Waterton, where Sheriff Kate was headquartered. They were through it in a flash, and once again passed by cultivated fields dotted with live oaks, and neatly kept farmhouses.

When Kate stopped again it was shortly after an intersection with a handful of businesses tucked around it, homes scattered around those, growing thinner as they got farther from the intersection. It wasn't big enough to be a town or even a village, but Richie supposed it had some kind of name. Most places did, he had learned. That was what people did, they named where they stood.

The houses were on plenty of land, an acre or two. Not farms, but rural just the same. Chickens moved *en masse* in one yard, and a couple of horses grazed in another. Kate pulled into the driveway of a property on the edge of the little cluster, with fields reaching away beyond it. The house wasn't much, wood-sided, shingle-roofed, dense willows bearing the brilliant green leaves of spring blocking most of it from the road. A few wispy clouds feathered the cobalt sky.

He parked on the road and hurried to catch Kate. She waved him off. "You stay back. This is me."

"Okay." He had promised, and apparently she meant to hold him to it. He stayed a dozen paces behind and watched her knock on the front door. His mouth was parched, desert dry, and he couldn't come up with enough spit to swallow. His hands were shaking so much he stuffed them into his pockets. He wished Kate would draw her weapon. Morton might not come easily.

The door opened, but whoever was inside stood where Richie couldn't see him. "Are you Jerry Morrison?" Kate asked.

"Yeah."

"You own a photo studio in Modesto?"

"That's right. Is something wrong?"

"Can I see some ID?"

"Hang on." The door moved but Kate caught it with her foot, holding it open. In a moment, the man returned. Richie saw a hand pass over a card, a driver's license, probably. Kate studied it, gave it back.

Kate beckoned Richie, and he stepped closer. Finally, he got a good look at Jerry Morrison, standing inside the house.

The man was lean and stringy, with hair like tarnished copper and the jaundiced complexion of a lifelong smoker. His eyes were rheumy, his teeth stained, his skinny, yellowish arms heavily freckled.

"That's not him," Richie said.

"What?"

"It's not him." He didn't know how to make it plainer. "I'm sorry. It's not him."

"What's this all about?" Morrison demanded.

"Never mind, sir," Kate said. "I'm sorry to have bothered you." When she reached Richie, she took his arm in a grip so tight it hurt and walked him back to the Yukon. "What the hell is going on?"

"Look, Kate, I don't know how it happened, okay? Every sign points to it being him, but I know what Jarod Morton looks like. That's not Morton."

"Well, it's Jerry Morrison. I held his driver's license in my hand."

"I don't know what to tell you, Sheriff. I'm really sorry. I got carried away."

Her gaze bore into him, death rays shooting from her eyes. "Yeah, maybe you did. I should send you a bill for wasting my time. Today, of all damn days."

He had apologized up and down. Nothing he could say would calm her. He had been utterly convinced. He wasn't some yahoo, trying to make things difficult for the cops. He didn't jump to conclusions, not that kind. He had been right. He *knew* he was right.

But that wasn't Jarod Morton.

Kate got into her Yukon and drove off without looking back. Richie sat behind the wheel of his rental, trying to figure out where he had gone wrong.

He had allowed himself to be driven by his impulses. Those impulses got him into fights, landed him in the wrong woman's arms, and now they had pulled a sheriff away from her job on a very difficult day, in the most critical hours of a murder investigation. They had cost him the only job he'd ever wanted, and if he wasn't careful they could cost him his wife, too. Everybody had them, urges they couldn't necessarily explain or even define. The primal lizard brain, wanting what it wanted, without consideration of the other factors in a person's life. He had to learn to control them, though, or they would keep controlling him. So far, they weren't doing a very good job of steering his life in a direction he wanted to go. More like off the pavement and into a deep ditch.

He put the key in the ignition, turned it, and pulled away from the house. He drove through the California countryside, not seeing it. He figured he would find a motel on the fringes of Modesto someplace, where he could try to reason out what had gone wrong. This hadn't been just about lizard impulses. He had been *certain*. Jarod Morton had killed that woman on the playground.

47

Richie drove for more than twenty minutes, mentally grasping the bits of the story that he knew and fumbling for those he didn't. No matter how many ways he tried rearranging the pieces, the picture always came out the same. He had missed something. But maybe that had happened here, not before.

He needed a closer look at Jerry Morrison.

With Modesto already in view before him, he pulled off the road, turned around, and headed back to Morrison's place.

The willows flanked the house on both sides. Richie got out of the car and closed the door softly, hoping the sheriff's visit hadn't spooked Morrison too much. Richie couldn't tell from the road if Morrison was still inside, but had to assume he was. He started down the driveway, then ducked into the trees, taking advantage of the cover that they provided the rest of the property. A wooden fence, mostly hidden, surrounded the backyard. Richie went to the gate and peered through a gap, looking for Morrison, or watchdogs. Seeing neither, he reached over the gate, worked the latch, and slipped inside, pulling it to behind him.

There were trees in the back, too, but they weren't thick enough to hide a series of outbuildings butted up against each other. The structures were shabby, sheds really, poorly constructed, with peeling paint and shuttered windows. But the doors were bolted on the outside, and the hardware looked new. Whatever was in those buildings, Morrison wanted to keep. He hadn't locked them, though, had just thrown those bolts.

Richie went to the first one, nearest the house and larger than the rest. Next to it was a scrap heap: unused two-by-fours, rusted-out pipes, a piece of roof gutter, and more. Richie's intention was to take a quick peek inside, probably at lawnmowers, rakes, garbage cans and the like, then turn his attention to the house. He wished there was a way to get Morrison out, so he could go in and look around. Maybe he could hide in back somewhere until Morrison did leave. He'd already wet his feet at the breaking and entering business, back at the Morton house in Detroit. Going into a home someone lived in was a more serious violation, but if he could find something that would explain why all indications of Morton pointed Morrison's way, it would be worth the risk.

He turned his attention to the bolted door on the largest shed. He drew back the bolt and pulled open the door. Instead of the lawn care equipment he had expected, the first thing he saw was a woman. She was crying, holding a wad of toilet paper to her nose, her eyes rimmed with red. "Oh!" she said. "You're not—"

Richie cut her off. "You're not what I was expecting, either. Who are you?"

She might have been in her mid-twenties, with long blond hair that looked like she cut it herself, hacked off straight across her forehead, hanging to the middle of her back. She was slender and pretty, dressed in a freebie promotional T-shirt advertising cigarettes, the kind tobacco companies gave out at bars sometimes, and snug denim shorts. She had been sitting on lawn furniture that had been arranged inside the shed in a kind of living room setup. In one corner was a single bed, and in another a small refrigerator, a microwave oven and a table with a hot plate. There was kitchen equipment in plastic baskets, and clothing and personal items in similar ones stacked near the bed.

"You shouldn't be in here," she said, her tone urgent. "Does Jerry know you're here?"

Richie's mind raced, trying to figure out the best way to answer. "Don't worry about that," he finally said. "Just tell me who you are."

"I'm Rhonda." Spoken with a kind of implied "duh" at the end of it, as if he should have known all along.

"Rhonda who?"

"Rhonda Morrison."

"You're related to Jerry?"

"I'm his wife."

"But you live in here? In this garden shed?"

"It's not so bad," Rhonda said. "He lets me come in the house a lot. Only …" She blew her nose into the toilet paper. "Only, he took my baby away."

"Jerry did?"

"Yes."

"He took your baby."

"That's what I said."

"When?"

"Just today. A little while, I don't know."

Richie didn't see any clocks in the place. Even the microwave was unplugged, so if it had a clock it wasn't working. "I'm just trying to get this straight. You're Rhonda Morrison, Jerry's wife. And Jerry took your child."

"That's right."

"Where did he take it? Him, her, whatever."

"Her. He gave her to some friend of his, I think. I don't know for sure."

Richie was trying to wrap his head around her story, and finding it difficult. He didn't see any baby furniture in the little space. "Does your daughter live in here, too?"

"Her name's Sherri. Her room's back there." She pointed toward the back wall of the shed. A blue plastic tarp covered part of it, and Richie realized that the seemingly adjacent sheds actually adjoined.

"Can I see?" he asked.

"If it's okay with Jerry."

"I told you not to worry about him. Just show me." He spoke with commanding authority, having reached the conclusion that she was used to following orders.

She went to the wall and pulled aside the tarp. Richie ducked through an opening sawed between the two buildings. On the other side was a small room, not unlike the first one. It had a single bed, some children's clothes in plastic baskets, and a few books. It didn't look like an infant's room. Or an infant's *shed*, given the surroundings. "How old is the baby?"

"I call her my baby, but she's five-and-a-half."

"Five-and-a-half," Richie repeated.

"That's right. Well, almost. She's very big on half-birthdays, and hers would have been coming up in just over a month."

Richie gripped Rhonda's arms and looked into her deep green eyes. She didn't resist. He couldn't shake the feeling that she was familiar, and yet strange at the same time. They had never met, he was sure. He'd have remembered that.

And then, looking into her eyes, he knew.

"Are you Kayley Ann Carrington?" he asked her. Kayley Ann had been taken at the age of six. "Is that your name?"

She considered, pressing her right index finger against her lower lip. "I don't think I've ever heard that name."

"How about Angela Morton?"

She brightened for an instant, flashing the briefest of smiles. "Yes! Yes, that was one of my names, before."

"Before what?"

"Before I came to live with Jerry. When we got married I changed my name."

"You got married at the age of eleven?"

"He said he loved me."

"I'm sure he did." Richie was appalled, but somehow not surprised. He had found Angela Morton. That had been the goal all along. He hadn't found her with Jarod Morton, but he had never expected them to still be together. There had been the trade, after all. The one-for-one.

Still, there were pieces that didn't fit.

"What do you remember about your life before you were Angela Morton? That's when you were Kayley."

Again with the lip pressing. "Not much. Nothing, I guess. Not really."

The trauma of abduction, and her subsequent treatment at Morton's hands, might have driven those memories from her. Maybe they could be restored, in time. But not here, not now. "Okay," he said. "We need to get out of here," he said.

"Why?"

"You don't belong here."

"Of course I do. I mean … maybe what you say is true, about before. But I've been married to Jerry for a long time. This is my life."

"This isn't how people live. Doesn't he let you read books, watch TV? Have you seen anyone else who lives like this?"

"There's a TV in the house. Sometimes he lets me watch. Jerry says those things are all made up."

She had him there. "That's not the point."

"Jerry takes care of me."

"I bet. Do you have any other children?"

"Just Sherri. We've tried before, but she's the only one I've ever been able to have. I guess I'm not much of a mother."

"Don't say that." Richie used the commanding tone again, then softened it. "Does she look like you? Pretty, long blond hair?"

"Yes."

Great, Richie thought. Just Morton's type. "You said Angela Morton was one of your names, and then you went to live with Jerry. Did you have other names?"

"I was always Rhonda, after that. But I wasn't always Rhonda Morrison."

"What was before that?"

"When I married him, Jerry was Charles. Charles Welker. So I was Rhonda Welker."

"And then what?"

"Then Rhonda Morrison. But only for the last couple of years. Since Sherri was about four."

"So he's only been Jerry Morrison for about two years."

"That's right. A little less, since it's not her birthday yet. Maybe a year and a half."

The timing was vague, and Richie was having a hard time plotting it out. But maybe he was looking for a plan where there wasn't one. "We have to go. Now. I'm working with the police, Rhonda. I'll make sure you're safe. But we need to get out of here, so if there's anything you need, grab it quick."

"I don't need anything except Sherri."

"We'll get Sherri back. But we have to go."

"Do you promise?"

"I promise."

"All right."

She was far too trusting. Naïve. Like so many promises he had made, Richie had no idea how he would go about keeping this one. But circumstances demanded, so he made it, hoping he could follow through. Having grown up a prisoner of Jarod Morton and then Charles Welker/Jerry Morrison, she probably lacked the real-world experience to make decisions for herself, to be wary of strangers. She didn't question Richie, just went along with what he said.

There was a lot more he wanted to know from her, but they had to get off this property first, get her someplace where Morrison couldn't find her. "Come on," he said. "Let's go." She grabbed her roll of toilet paper off the table and followed. Didn't even go for a purse, but Jerry probably didn't allow her to have ID of any kind, or money.

When Richie pushed the door open, Jerry Morrison was standing six feet away, pointing what looked like a .38 caliber revolver. "Who the fuck are you?" Morrison demanded.

48

That's the first thing I asked him, Jerry," Rhonda said from behind Richie. "I thought you knew him."

Richie hoped she didn't mention what he'd said about working with the police. "That's not important," Richie said. "What's important is that you recognize that this is over. You've had your fun, but you knew it would come to an end someday."

"Bull *shit.*" Morrison said it like that, as two separate words.

"You said we would get Sherri back, Jerry," Rhonda said. "I want my baby girl."

"We'll get her back, Rhonda, like I told you. A few years, five or six, she'll be back with us. In the meantime, you and I are gonna work on having another."

"Do you mean it?" Richie didn't dare shift his gaze away from Morrison, but Rhonda sounded thrilled.

"Sure, I told you before."

"Yes, but you also said I could keep Sherri until she was six, and then you took her, and I got mad at you. I don't believe you anymore."

"Things changed, that's all. But you got to believe me, baby. We got to stick together, always."

This was so many layers of wrong Richie didn't know where to start. He'd have felt a lot more comfortable if the first step involved

Morrison getting rid of the weapon. "You can put that gun away, Jerry," he attempted. "You don't need that."

"Like hell. You think you can come in here and fuck up my life?"

"That's already done, Jerry. It's finished."

"I saw you with that bitch sheriff. She's gone, and you're still here. I'm guessing she don't know that."

"You're wrong. She's coming back, with help. Should be here any minute. So just put the gun down and don't make things any worse."

"Time she gets back, you won't be here."

Richie was about out of plays. He couldn't get to Morrison, not before the man pulled the trigger. And he didn't know how good a shot Morrison was. He knew nothing about him, except that he had made some kind of terrible bargain with Jarod Morton, thirteen years earlier.

He didn't have much to lose, though.

Morrison couldn't let him live.

He took a half-step toward Morrison, then brought his right foot down on a two-by-four resting on the scrap heap. It flipped up, catapulting the section of gutter.

Startled, Morrison jerked his trigger. The shot went wide, carving into the shed wall. Morrison wasn't ready for the weapon's kick, either. His right arm flew up.

Richie grabbed the two-by-four and charged, holding it like a lance. He slammed it into Morrison's gut, and the man doubled around it. Richie drew back, shifted his grip, and swung the board again. Morrison was still holding the gun, in motion, and Richie missed his target. Instead of contacting the man's chin, the two-by went low, crashing into Morrison's throat.

Morrison went down on his knees, left hand clutching at his neck, the gun seemingly forgotten in his right. Richie swung again, and the two-by hit Morrison's hand. The gun flew from his grip and he sank lower, going down on his stomach, arms propping up his head and neck. Richie brought the board back around and swung it like Phil Mickelson driving off a par five tee. The board caught the side of Morrison's head, tearing and furrowing skin.

Richie didn't drop the board until he picked up the gun, but he didn't need either. Morrison's arms had buckled. Blood bubbled up from his mouth and dripped to the grass, and more flowed from the head wound. His breathing was shallow, labored, with a loud wheezing sound every time he inhaled. His face was kind of purple.

Rhonda screamed, fists clenched and drawn up tight against her chin. "What did you do?" she cried through her tears. "You hurt him!"

That much seemed apparent. Richie might have done serious damage, especially with that shot to the throat. He pulled his phone from his pocket, wincing at the effort. His palms were riddled with splinters. While he had been fighting off Morrison he hadn't paid attention to his earlier injuries, but now they flared up. He briefly considered calling 911, but realized that he didn't know the address, and he doubted that Rhonda would. Anyway, she was barely coherent. Instead, he called Kate Dunning, who already had the address.

"Sheriff," he said, "you'd better get back over here."

"Back where?"

"Jerry Morrison's house."

"Are you still there? Krebbs, I told you—"

"I know. But I found her. I found Kayley Ann Carrington. Angela Morton."

"Do I hear screaming?"

"She's a little upset is all."

"If you're screwing with me again …"

"I'm not, Sheriff. She's here. She's been held here by Jerry Morrison, who gave her daughter away today. I believe he gave her to Jarod Morton."

"You don't give up, do you?"

"Just come, Sheriff. She'll explain it when you get here. And you'd better send an ambulance, too."

"An ambulance?"

"Morrison pulled a gun on us. I think I hurt him bad. He might be dying."

"Don't go anywhere, Krebbs. I'm on my way."

"I'll be here." Richie closed the phone.

"You think … he's dying?" Rhonda was letting out great, hitching sobs, on her knees next to Morrison, but she had brought the screams under control. Richie was thankful for that.

"Rhonda, I know this is hard for you to understand. Jerry is not a good man. The things he did to you aren't good either. You're young, you don't have to be a prisoner for the rest of your life. And you need your daughter back. That's the most important thing, right? Sherri?"

"Yes! I want my baby back. He said I didn't have to give her up until her birthday."

Richie needed to keep her focused on that goal. "We're going to get her. But I need your help, so stay calm, stay with me." He flipped open the phone again and dialed Frank. For a change, Frank picked up right away.

"What up, Maynard?"

"I've got her, Frank."

"Got who?"

"Angela Morton. Kayley Ann Carrington. She's called Rhonda Morrison now, and she's here with me."

"No shit?"

"I'm telling you, man."

"What about Morton?"

"No. She's with someone named Jerry Morrison. And Frank, she's got a six-year-old daughter named Sherri, who Morrison just gave away. Not quite six, actually."

"Fuck me."

"One for one, Frank."

"I know."

"Only, I think it goes deeper than we ever imagined."

"Meaning what?"

"What'd you say Jerry's name was before?" Richie asked Rhonda. "Charles something?"

"Welker," she said.

"That's right." To Frank, he said, "Jerry Morrison, until two years ago, was Charles Welker. He's had Angela—Rhonda—since she was eleven. Is that right, Rhonda?"

She sniffled. "That's when we got married, yes."

"Did she say *married*?" Frank asked.

"Yeah, that's how it is here. Anyway, since Angela Morton vanished, she's been with him."

"Who did he give the kid to?"

"I don't know. *She* doesn't know."

"Ask him."

"He's not in any condition to talk." Richie paused, trying to assemble it all in his mind. Frank was quiet, patient, and that helped. The pieces started falling into place. Jerry Morrison's photo studio, his name, the timing of the change from Welker to Morrison. When Sherri was four, old enough to speak and ask questions, becoming aware that people had identities beyond *Mommy* and *Daddy*, but not old enough to keep secrets. They'd want to make the transition easy for her. She would have heard the name Charles Welker since infancy, maybe even seen Morton a few times, so she'd be used to him.

"Do you remember what Charles Welker did for a living?" he asked Rhonda. "Before he became Morrison and opened a photo studio?"

She looked puzzled. "I think he had some sort of printing thing."

A quick-print type business would be almost as good as a photo studio for finding victims, Richie thought. There would always be birthday invitations, fliers for various children's activities, birth announcements, plenty of jobs involving kids.

"Here's what I think the deal is, Frank," Richie cupped his hand over his mouth. "I think the deal was that Morton kept Angela until she was too old for him. Maybe she was his first—at least, the first he had ever dared to take, to keep. Something about her was ideal to him. His fantasy angel. But she wouldn't stop getting older. When she was too old for him, starting to look more like a young woman than a little girl, he passed her on to this guy Welker. Welker likes them young, but not that young. Mostly what he wanted was a willing subject."

"Like a, what, like a sex slave?" Frank asked.

"I think so. Someone he could raise from pubescence to do exactly what he wanted, when he wanted. Who better for that than someone who had spent years being abused, whose sense of self had already been stolen away from her? Who was used to providing for a man, sexually?"

He checked on Rhonda, to see if she was listening, but she was on her knees beside Morrison, stroking his arm as he writhed on the ground, gagging on his own blood. Apparently he hadn't allowed her any first aid training, either, and she didn't have a clue how to help him.

"He took her in," he told Frank, "raised her, and kept her in a shed behind his house. She had a baby with him. That little girl is going on six now, so she went back to Morton. Morrison said Sherri would be back in five or six years, and meanwhile he and Rhonda would have another baby."

"So they just want to keep cycling through the kids?" Frank asked.

"That's what I think. When Sherri comes back from Morton, she'll be old enough for Morrison. She'll be his next. By then, that next baby would be old enough for Morton."

"These fuckers are even more twisted than I thought," Frank said. "And I thought they were subhuman to begin with. Who would do that to a person?"

"Josef Fritzl kept his own daughter in a dungeon he built under his house," Richie said, "for something like twenty-four years, and fathered seven children with her. His wife and the rest of the family never knew she was down there. When one of the babies died, he tossed it in the incinerator. No matter where you think the limits of human behavior are, somebody's always going to push them.

"Anyway, these guys are twisted, all right, but there's a certain elegance to it, too. It took a long time for Morton to get a return on his investment. It looks like they moved up the process, though—Kayley Ann says Morrison told her she could keep Sherri until she was six, but then he took her seven months early. Something screwed up their timeline."

"Maybe us," Frank said.

"Exactly. If Morton's sister told him that we were asking about him in Virginia, he got spooked. Anyway, if I'm right, now that he's got Sherri he's going to realize it's not really the same as having Angela back. Sherri's a different person. She might look a lot like her mom, but she's been raised differently. Nothing's going to live up to his memories, his fantasy of what he once had. I think he's been taking girls all along, and when they fell short, probably killing them." He cupped the phone again, lowered his voice. "No matter what Sherri does, she's doomed if we don't get her back."

"So Morton has Sherri now."

"I'm pretty sure."

"You think he took her back to his place?"

"I don't know. He might have. Wherever that is."

"If he's close by, I don't see him sticking around," Frank said.

"Not when he finds out we've got Morrison," Richie agreed. "That's for sure."

"He'll find someplace to hide, hunker down like a cornered animal."

"Someplace," Richie said. "But where?"

"You figure that out, you're the real detective here."

"I'll work on it," Richie said. "Just in case, I want to try his place here, if he has one. But I've got to get moving. Sheriff's expecting me to be here when she arrives. She'll make me answer a million questions, and she won't do anything on my say-so again without a lot of convincing." He took the phone away from his ear. "Rhonda, I'm going to leave you my phone."

She shot him a frantic look. "You're going?"

"Yes. The sheriff's on her way. You'll be fine. She'll take care of you, I promise."

"But you said—"

"I said I'd get your daughter back, and I will. I'm going to give you this phone, but I don't want you to answer it unless you see the name Robey on the screen." He spelled it for her.

"Okay."

Chances were, she had never used a mobile phone. He carried it to where she crouched beside Morrison, and pointed to Frank's name. "See?"

"I see."

"That's Frank. He's a friend of mine. He's helping us. Don't answer for anyone but Frank. I'll pick up a new phone someplace, and when I have it I'll give Frank the number. He'll call you and give it to you, so you'll know when I'm calling you. You can answer my calls. My name is Richie, Richie Krebbs, but that won't show up on the phone, just the number. You can call Frank, and once you have my number, you can call me. Nobody else. *Nobody.* Do you understand?"

"I guess so."

"I'm just trying to keep you safe and out of trouble. We don't want anything to get in the way of getting Sherri back, so I have to get going."

"Okay."

"Don't tell the sheriff where I've gone. Tell her who you are, what Jerry Morrison did to you, what Jarod Morton did to you before that. Tell her how they used you. The things they did to you shouldn't be done to anybody."

"Okay," Rhonda said once more.

"You're a good girl, Rhonda." He was talking to her like she was still eleven, but he didn't think she had been allowed to grow up much since then. "You're not in any trouble, but I have to go. And you have to cover for me. Don't tell her where I am."

"Okay."

"You all right?"

"I guess so."

"There's help on the way for Jerry. Not that he deserves it. He's a bad man, Rhonda. He deserves plenty of pain. But he'll get better and he'll go to jail."

"Okay."

He didn't think he had to worry about her disobeying. She was so accustomed to following orders, she would wait for Sheriff Kate instead of running away or hiding. She had been caged so long that freedom was probably the most terrifying prospect of all. "I'm going, Frank," he said into the phone, "I'm leaving my phone with Rhonda."

"I heard."

"I'll call you as soon as I have a new phone."

"Travel safe, Maynard."

Richie ended the call and handed the phone to Rhonda. She looked at it like it was a piece of alien technology. Richie gave her a crash course in how to make and answer calls. "Put it away," he said. "You might want to turn it off until you're not with the sheriff anymore." He showed her how. "She's kind of mad at me."

"Because of what you did to Jerry?"

"Because of a lot of things. Don't worry, she's not mad at you. You're a special case, Rhonda. She'll be glad she met you. I already am."

With that, he left her in the backyard and sprinted to the rental car. He could hear sirens closing in. He knew which way Kate Dunning would come, so he drove out another way, then looped back to the highway toward Modesto.

49

Richie was most of the way to the city before he spotted a fast food place with free Wi-Fi. He went in, bought a pop, and fired up his computer. A quick search for a Charles Welker in Stanislaus County turned up only one, here in Modesto. He mapped the address. It didn't look too far away. He left the drink where it was, barely touched, and ran back to the car.

Rush hour was under way, and he had to contend with traffic. There was nothing to do about that, he only knew the route he had memorized from the web. Getting lost would slow him down more.

When he turned onto Welker's street, a flurry of pigeons burst into the air, their wings catching the rays of the late afternoon sun, flashing like small silver beacons and then disappearing in the sky. Charles Welker's home and business were combined in a single building, a medium-sized stucco home, painted pink with cheerful green trim. Chaz Welker's Speedee-Print, a sign outside said. The place looked as if it had been painted by a candy manufacturer. Or, Richie thought, intended to entice young girls through the door.

The business was in front, with its own entrance. The front section looked like an add-on, and it had swallowed up most of the yard. What remained had been paved. A sign warned that parking was only for customers of Chaz Welker's, and oil drips stained the concrete slab. There was another door halfway down.

Richie parked on the slab. A paper sign hanging in the front window was turned to CLOSED and the door was locked. Richie went down the empty driveway, tried that door. Also locked. He pounded on the door, but no one answered. There was yet another door in back, solid wood at the bottom, with six small panes of glass above the knob. Richie used his elbow to smash out the lower right pane, shoved out the remaining shards, and reached through. He unlocked the door and stepped into a kitchen.

The place was empty, but still held the lingering odors of life; this morning's eggs and bacon, an inch of stale tea in a ceramic pot, at once floral and smoky, trash left too long under the sink. He moved rapidly through the other rooms, noting a gap in the bedroom closet where some clothes had been removed, a dresser drawer left open. A second bedroom was decked out for a little girl, with walls that matched the exterior, a white canopy bed and dresser, a shelf holding a line of dolls and others jammed with stuffed animals and books, and a closet full of small, frilly clothing. As in the other room, there were some empty hangers.

And as in Detroit, the door and window were both fitted with hasps. The window faced into a backyard completely surrounded by a ten-foot-tall wooden fence. The window was padlocked shut.

The rest of the house didn't offer any clues as to Morton's destination, but it convinced him that Charles Welker was indeed Jarod Morton. A set of narrow stairs led from the kitchen into an unfinished attic. At the top, Richie tugged on a string hanging from a bare bulb. Harsh light fell on framed walls, most without wallboard. There was only one door, painted blue and locked with two big combination padlocks. In Richie's battered condition, he thought it might kill him, but he lashed out with two quick kicks close to the doorknob. The door swung open, the locks holding but the jamb splintering.

Behind the blue door was another playroom, less elaborate than the one in Detroit. It had a bed, a little stand that held a pitcher of water (still there, the water at room temperature), and a full-length mirror on one wall. The mirror was standard, not two-way glass. On another wall was a closet that had been converted into a camera station, with a hole drilled through the door. Richie supposed that without having a full-time, live-in playmate, Morton hadn't bothered fixing it up more. Maybe he had always intended to leave town once he claimed Kayley's daughter.

Back upstairs, Richie found a door into the print shop. Inside was printing equipment, computers, and a wide variety of paper types. A desk was littered with paperwork, but underneath that the desk's surface was covered in writing. Ballpoint pen had worn grooves in the wood. Phone numbers, dates, what might have been sizes or printing specs. Old habits died hard.

And deeper, practically carved into the desk, was a double-sided, nearly symmetrical composition that Richie could only imagine represented a pair of angel wings.

Morton was gone, but he hadn't been for long. Once again, Richie was too late.

This time, though, Richie thought he knew where Morton was headed.

He fled the house, back to the rental for one last trip to the airport. On the way, he stopped at a convenience store and bought a prepaid phone.

O O O

At the airport, waiting for a flight to Detroit, he found a quiet spot, called Frank. "Call Kayley for me," he said. "Give her my number."

"I will, Maynard."

"Being in that place was bizarre. The house is different from his Detroit house. Completely different structure. But the vibe I got there? Exactly the same. He padlocked the door and window of a child's bedroom. He's got the playroom. He recreated the old house, and he's probably done the same everywhere he goes."

"He's one fucked up dude."

"Yeah. So I was thinking—"

"Good."

"—thinking that he's going back to Detroit."

Frank was silent for a long moment.

"You there?" Richie asked.

"I think you're right."

"You do?" Being inside the house had been as illuminating as if someone had flipped a light switch, but Richie had expected to have to convince Frank.

"There's some weird shit going down here, Maynard. This pedophile named Otis Parrott has been visiting Wil Fowler's stepfather, Clinton Gray, in prison. Then right after he visits, Wil's mother does. Parrott has been making them do things, working through the stepfather. Stealing those coins, for instance—I don't know if Wil took them or his mother did, but Wil had an attack of conscience and tried to give them back."

"I'm not following you."

"Maybe Parrott's trying to finance Jarod Morton's return. I think Wil's stepfather was part of that pedophile ring all along, with Parrott and Morton and this guy Welker. Maybe Gray used the rape room in Morton's basement, and got his picture taken. Pictures like that turned up in the joint, they could make things very difficult for him. Maybe Morton has pictures of Parrott, too. So Morton presses Parrott, Parrott presses Gray, and Gray presses the family to do what Parrott wants."

"You could be right," Richie said. "But how does it connect now?"

"What if Parrott's still in touch with Morton? What if that night you saw Wil heading for the Morton house, it was because Morton wanted to know if the house was safe to come back to?"

The final puzzle piece clicked into place. "Because to have everything just like it was in his memory, he'd want to be in the same house. He wouldn't have the same friends, he doesn't have Barbara, but none of that is as important as being with Angela again. In his mind, that's who Sherri is. She's Angela. He's been trying to relive that experience for the last thirteen years, and now he thinks he is."

"Wonder how much of a head start they got," Frank said.

"Couple hours, I think."

"I'll keep an eye on the house."

"Yeah, good. I'm on my way there. I'll call you when I land," Richie said. He started to say goodbye. His flight would begin boarding soon. But he caught himself. "Wait."

"What?"

"You said maybe Wil was scoping the house out, to see if it was safe to return to."

"Right."

"And I busted him. Right outside the house. So it's *not* safe. That'd be the message he got."

"Shit, you're right."

"If the theory is correct."

"I think it is. In broad strokes, anyway. But I need to do some more checking."

"Good, you do that. Meanwhile, I'm heading your way. Maybe you should watch the airport?"

"I could do that. But they might be driving, taking the bus, anything."

"True. If I had just abducted a girl, I'd drive."

"Except she was handed to him. Probably since Kayley's not about to say anything, Morrison was going to give him a breather before he reported her missing."

"Kid's been living in a shed, Frank. She's probably never been to preschool or anything. He might *never* have reported it if I hadn't shown up."

"Good point. Anyway, if he drugged her—"

"She could be asleep for the whole flight. Yeah, there's no way to know."

"I'll make some calls, see if he's booked on any flights under the Welker name or any others we know about. Then I'll go home and get some rest. Call me when you're on the ground."

"Okay, go ahead and call Kayley, and let her know I'll call her right away."

"I will. Give me three minutes."

"You got it."

Richie spent the three minutes watching people mill about the airport, wondering if in fact Morton and Sherri weren't out of town yet. They could be on his flight. When the time was up, he kept an eye on the waiting area as he dialed his own phone number.

"Hello?"

"Rhonda, it's Richie. Richie Krebbs."

"Hi." She sounded anxious, but at least she wasn't crying anymore.

"Is everything okay there?"

"I guess. The sheriff took me to her office. I'm there now. There are a lot of other police here. They're nice, but they kind of scare me."

"It'll be all right, Rhonda. They'll take good care of you."

"Okay."

"Did they take Jerry to the hospital?"

"Yes."

"He's hurt bad?"

"I think so. They wouldn't tell me. Sheriff Kate is mad at you."

"I know. Listen, I need you to do something for me."

"What?"

"I need you to try to remember when you were back in Detroit, with Jarod Morton. When you were Angela."

"Sometimes it's fuzzy."

"It was a long time ago, but try. I need you to try to think of someplace that Jarod Morton would have felt safe and comfortable. Someplace besides the house you lived in there."

"I'll try."

"Okay. Let me know what you come up with."

"I will."

Richie heard another voice in the background, over the phone. "Who is that? Is that Krebbs?"

"Call me later, Rhonda," Richie said quickly. He recognized Kate Dunning's voice, and she was just about the last person he wanted to talk to at the moment. He ended the call and switched off the phone.

His flight was being announced, anyway.

50

The houses on Wil Fowler's block were mostly dark, though a familiar blue glow emanated from some, a symptom of America's common addiction as definitive as track marks on a junkie's arm.

Frank parked in front of the Wil's house, still and silver-tinged in the moonlight. No way to avoid Carlotta this time; he just hoped Wil was home and not out getting into trouble.

He rapped on the door and announced himself loudly, hoping it would keep any neighbors from pointing shotguns at him. "Police, Wil! It's Frank Robey, open up!"

Swearing sounded from the inside. Carlotta Gray made it to the door first. She looked even angrier and scarier than the first time he'd met her. He'd faced gun-wielding thugs who were less intimidating than this five-foot-tall woman wearing a polka-dotted nightgown and showing him teeth and gums and fists. "The fuck you doin' comin' 'round here this time of night?"

"I need to see Wil."

"He's sleepin', like everybody should be."

"It's okay, Moms, I'm here." Wil appeared from the hallway, clad in boxer shorts, scratching his bare chest.

"It ain't okay."

"No, ma'am, it's not," Frank offered. "I'm very sorry to intrude, and I wouldn't have if it weren't an emergency."

"Such a big emergency it can't wait for the sun to come up?"

"I'm afraid not."

"I said it's okay," Wil repeated.

"Can we go in your room, son?" Frank asked.

"He ain't your son."

"No, ma'am, he's not. It's just an expression."

"Sound like somethin' else."

Frank was losing patience, and with it his deference to the woman's not unjustified anger. "All due respect, ma'am, I'm here on police business. And I need to talk to Wil for a minute. Sooner you get out of the way, sooner I can leave."

"Let's go, Mr. Robey," Wil said.

Frank shouldered past her and trailed Wil to his room. "'S'up?" the boy asked as he shut the door.

"I think I know what's going on, Wil." Frank leaned against the desk, careful not to damage any of Wil's art.

"Yeah?"

"I think your stepfather's being blackmailed. I think you and your mom are helping him, to keep him out of trouble. Maybe Otis Parrott is being blackmailed, too, or maybe he's just buddies with Jarod Morton. Either way, this cat Morton is bad news. He's a pedophile and a murderer, and he's just taken another little girl who has never had a shot at a decent life."

"What's that got to do with me?"

"I think the reason your stepfather is being blackmailed is because of things he used to do. Including maybe things he did to you. If he did, you got to understand that it wasn't your fault, that you didn't do anything wrong, but he did."

"Yeah, I got that."

"So he did?"

Wil offered his usual shrug.

"Okay, let it be that way. Here's something else I think. I don't think you stole those coins at all. I think your mother did. You were trying to protect her by taking them back, and then by keeping your mouth shut about it. You don't have to answer, because I doubt you will. But I want you to think hard about whether you want to go into the joint to keep her out. More than that, I want you to think about whether or not you want to protect people who prey on children, because in the long run that's what you're doing. You don't owe your stepfather anything, and you sure as hell don't owe Otis Parrott or Jarod Morton. They're scum, Wil. They're the dogshit you scrape off your shoes before you go in the house."

Shrug.

"The second best thing you and your mother could do is to stop playing along. Don't do anything for your stepfather. When Parrott and Morton find out they can't control you anymore, they'll leave him alone. They have no reason to fuck with him if they can't get anything out of him. And if they don't understand that, too bad. He did what he did and he ought to pay the price."

"You said second best."

Frank nodded, glad the young man was listening. "That's right. The best thing would be if you have any information on Parrott that you can testify to in court, so he can be put in a cage like the animal he is."

Wil's expression was blank. Frank expected a shrug, but it didn't come, so he continued. "That's what I think. Here's what I need from you. Besides that house where Richie found you, have you been sent to check out anyplace else? Anyplace Morton might take a little girl?"

"No, only that one." Wil said it with an unexpected catch in his voice.

Frank didn't know whether or not to believe him, but it was an answer instead of a shrug or an evasion, so he decided to take Wil at his word. "All right."

Wil started to give another of his patented shrugs, but before he was halfway through it, his face fell apart. His lower lip quivered, then his mouth dropped open and a thick, wet sound escaped him. He curled onto his bed, throwing an arm over his face, but not before Frank saw tears glistening on his cheeks. Wil started spasming on the bed, sobs wrenching his back. Frank wanted to go to him, to put a comforting hand on the young man's shoulders, but he figured that would be absolutely the wrong thing to do.

"Wil," he said instead, trying to keep his voice soft. He felt like someone who had walked into the wrong funeral and didn't know the way out. "I know this is hard, man. Maybe you've never told anybody about it, I don't know. But it's not something you need to be ashamed of. It's a crime that was committed against you, dig? It's nothing you did."

He couldn't tell if Wil heard him. Just in case, he kept talking, in the same vein, trying to reassure the young man that he hadn't done anything wrong. Wil's mother pounded on the door and shrieked at them, but she left when Frank shooed her.

After a few minutes, Wil's shuddering began to lessen. Frank waited, not speaking. He flipped through some of Wil's art boards again, impressed anew by his talent. One he hadn't seen before showed an event he recognized from the news, the accidental shooting of a seven-year-old girl by police, during a raid on a home. The whole thing had been videotaped. The raid netted a murder suspect, but the cost was unbearably high.

When Wil was finally still, Frank excused himself, went into the bathroom, and returned with a box of tissues. He put it next to Wil, nudging him with the box. Wil pawed one free and drew it to his face, blew his nose, and tossed it onto the floor. With the second tissue, Wil sat up again. "You still here?"

"I can't stay, Wil. Just need to know you're okay. Like I said, there's a dangerous man out there with a little girl."

"So go."

"Are you okay?"

"What it look like to you?"

"Looks like you're messed up. And will be for a long time. But talking about it can help, or that's what I hear. Talk to a counselor, a priest. Me. Anyone."

"Got nothing to say."

"That's fine. You don't have to do it tonight. The offer's there, Wil, that's all."

Wil caught his gaze, looking out over a wadded up tissue. "Thanks," he said.

That was a first.

"Yeah, no problem. Think on that other thing, too, okay. About testifying. See if we can lock Otis Parrott up for anything."

"I will."

"I got to go, Wil. You know how to reach me."

"Yeah."

"Okay. You holler at me anytime."

Wil gave him a solemn nod. Frank guessed that was the best he would get. He felt for the kid. While he was sorry he'd had to push, he thought in the long run holding the secret close would do more harm than exposing it to the air.

To his surprise, Carlotta was sitting up in the living room, watching TV. She eyed him as he headed for the door.

"You upset him."

"He's upset. I didn't do the hurt to him."

"I didn't either."

"Did you know?"

"Not while it was happenin'."

"But you didn't do anything when you found out. Turn in Clinton."

"Family's got to eat. That's terrible, what he done. But it ain't the whole world."

"Might be, to your son."

"He like to eat too."

"He'll be needing you."

"I'm here."

"See that you are." Frank let himself out the door.

She wasn't much of a mother, that woman.

But if she was there for Wil now, that could make up for something.

O O O

The flight seemed to take forever.

Morton wasn't on it. Not many people were, at least on the second leg. From San Francisco to Detroit, there were more empty seats than Richie had seen on an airplane in a long time. He had three to himself, and he was able to put his feet up and get some sleep, his back against the wall. The drone of the big engines muffled the quiet conversation of the few passengers who weren't similarly slumbering. It wasn't comfortable, and every inch of him was starting to hurt again, but he was tired enough to make it work.

He awoke as the descent started, sorry he hadn't put more effort into trying to figure out Morton's next move, but feeling more or less human again. He called Frank as soon as he reached the parking structure. "I'm on the ground," he said. "Where are you?"

Frank let out a low, groggy growl. "I'm at home. Got here, went to sleep like a fucking rock."

"Lucky man."

"Your car's at the airport, right?"

"I'll be there in a minute, unless it got towed."

"Cool."

"Hate to think what the parking fee's going to be."

"I'll reimburse you, Maynard."

"Where should I go?"

"I was hoping you'd figured that out."

"Not yet. No word from Kayley, either."

"You could swing by the Morton house, I guess. Just in case."

"Okay." He spotted his ancient Tempo, looking like an abandoned vehicle at this miserable hour of the morning. A few other travelers dragged themselves through the garage. "My wheels are here, such as they are."

"Good."

"Do me a favor, Frank?"

"Name it."

Richie unlocked the door. The interior smelled musty, as if he had left something damp inside. "I'm glad we found Kayley, but I can't get Sherri out of my mind. They could be anywhere. We picked Detroit, but he could have taken her to Tucson or Omaha or someplace he's never been."

"I know."

Richie settled in behind the wheel and let out a sigh. "Read me some Superman."

"Son, I thought you'd never ask. I got just the thing, was reading it myself a little while ago."

"Lay it on me."

"It's *Action Comics*, issue number eight forty-four. From 2007."

"I thought you liked the old ones." Richie cranked the key, stepped on the gas. The car responded as it always did, like it would rather be anywhere else. Any*thing* else.

"Mostly I do. But this is a good one, for modern times. Story's a collaboration between Geoff Johns, who's one of the top comics writers these days, and Richard Donner, the filmmaker who made the only decent Superman movie, the first Christopher Reeve one."

"That's kind of cool." Richie backed from the parking spot and started toward the exit.

"The cover's a somber thing by Adam Kubert. Tight shot on Superman, from the chest up. Monochromatic. He looks sad."

"Sounds like a downer. I told you I needed to be cheered up, right?"

"I think this is a good issue for us right now. It's the first part of a story arc called 'Last Son.'"

"What's it about?"

"I don't want to spoil it."

"Frank …"

"Oh, all right. It's about a Kryptonian boy who comes to Earth. He's found, and Clark Kent and Lois Lane adopt him as their son. It's about a lost kid who gets found. I thought it would resonate."

"Superman has a kid?"

"For a while, anyway. And I'm not counting that stupid last movie. You gonna let me read, or what?"

"Fine, read. Read!"

"You know, that Wil Fowler is a decent kid."

"I thought I told you that."

"I wasn't sure, at first. But I think he is. And he's one hell of a talented artist."

"What's this got to do with Superman's kid?"

"It has nothing to do with Christopher Kent. Just with how he came to be Christopher Kent."

"Meaning what?"

"Meaning, maybe you and Wendy should think about adopting Wil."

"He has a mother, right?"

"If you can call her that."

"She does."

"I don't think it would take much to get her to let him go."

"What, I'm supposed to buy him? I thought that went out in 1864."

"Sixty-two and sixty-three, if you go by the dates on the Emancipation Proclamation. Sixty-five, if you're counting when all the slaves were actually freed."

"I didn't call for a history lesson, Frank. Or adoption advice."

"Okay," Frank said. "I'm reading. Page one ..."

O   O   O

As he listened, Richie's thoughts meandered. He remembered his own household, growing up, a working class home thick with strife and anger and worries over making the mortgage and car payments. At the same time, though, his parents seemed to take great joy in their children, in their own perception of themselves as a family. They made family trips to the Upper Peninsula, Chicago, the shores of Lake Michigan, even Florida. Sundays they went to Belle Isle or Lake Huron. They ate at family restaurants, played family games, watched family movies. When they were all together, Richie and his parents and his older brother Sean, before the car accident on I-75 that scraped Sean across a hundred feet of pavement, his parents' worries and woes seemed to vanish. Even after Sean died, when Richie was only twelve, having their remaining son around seemed to lend his parents a strength they didn't have otherwise, whether by themselves or with each other. As a couple they weren't much, but as a family they had been a formidable unit.

Or so Richie had thought. But then came the morning that he and his mother woke up to an empty house. His father, never happy since his midlife career change, had packed a few things during the night and left without a goodbye or a note. Richie had waited for years, certain that one day a letter would come, a postcard or a phone call. His mother was less optimistic; she had seen things in the man that Richie hadn't, what she described as an emptiness as vast as the Grand Canyon—she had never seen it, but she was never one to let facts get in the way of a good story—and his departure did not come as a shock to her, though she expected he would at least tell her he was leaving.

She lived for six years after that, saw Richie through college, then faded quickly, through one illness after another, until the day she left, too. Her leaving was as sudden but less mysterious—a bottle of prescription pills and two bottles of gin. She tried calling a friend, after swallowing it all, but paramedics arrived too late. Richie heard about it well after the fact, and the guilt, when he realized how desperately sad and lonely she had become, felt like it would kill him too.

In the end, it hadn't. He had recovered, mostly. But he found himself suspicious of families, wanting to recreate what he'd known as a young boy, but terrified of how they ended up.

51

lied to you. Before.”

"About what?”

It was Kayley. Richie had been sitting in the Tempo, most of the block down from the Morton house. Only a couple of blocks from his own house, from his wife and their warm bed. He had called Wendy to tell her he was back in Detroit, and would be home as soon as possible. Dense branches shaded the car from the only working streetlamp on the block and kept some of the rain off, and he sat in the dark watching the house, the occasional vehicle passing by. Back where it all began, he had been thinking. A few nights ago, and thirteen years before that. Then the phone rang and he heard the voice of someone who might as well have been a ghost.

"When I told you I didn't remember about before,” Kayley said. "Before Jerry. I do.”

"What do you remember?”

"You asked me about places that he might feel safe.”

"And?”

"So I've been thinking about him, trying to remember. I remembered when I first went to live with them. Their names were Jarod and Barbara, right?”

"That's right.”

"They said they were my new mommy and daddy. They told me that my other parents didn't want me anymore. Because I had been disobedient. I cried for days. I had done something—I can't even remember what, something stupid—that I hid from them. I thought they must have known anyway, and that's why they got rid of me."

"You were Kayley Ann Carrington, and you lived in Virginia. Your parents never wanted to get rid of you. Jarod Morton abducted you and lied to you, and your parents never did stop looking for you." He stopped himself from going further. What he had learned about the Carringtons was from old newspaper accounts and from Carl Mueller, that retired Centreville cop, and he didn't know how much stock to put in his words. Besides, burdening her with it might not be productive. "Were you able to think of anyplace that Jarod might have felt safe? Someplace he might take Sherri?"

"I don't remember enough about him. Most of my memories are of him in the house."

Richie tried to hide his disappointment. "Okay."

"But I thought of one place where *I* felt safe. The only place. I liked it there, and when I had to go home then I got scared and worried. I thought maybe he would want to take Sherri there."

"Maybe," Richie said. "Where was it?"

"My school. When I was with the other kids, and the teachers. I didn't have many friends there, but nobody hurt me or touched me."

"And he knew that? Jarod?"

"I think so. He used to complain about it sometimes. It was the only place I was allowed to be without them, and he would threaten to make me stay home if I was naughty."

"Okay, Rhonda, thanks."

"I don't know if it means anything. I just want Sherri back."

"It's worth a shot. And Rhonda?"

"Yes?"

"Is it okay if I start calling you Kayley?"

"I guess so. I don't think of myself as a Kayley."

"You don't yet, but you will soon."

"Okay."

"I've got to go. Call me if you need me."

Richie ended that call and dialed Frank. "The school," he said, when Frank answered.

"What school?"

"Madison Elementary. The one Angela Morton attended. That's the only place in Detroit Angela felt safe."

"So if he's deluded enough—"

"In his fantasy, Angela and Sherri are one and the same. If he couldn't take her home, that's where he'd go."

"I'll meet you there."

"I'm twenty minutes out, Maynard. Don't go in without me."

"I won't."

"I mean it."

"I hear you, Frank."

The connection went dead. Richie was only blocks from the school, a mile at the outside. He switched on headlights and pulled away from the curb.

O O O

Frank had promised twenty minutes. He made it in sixteen.

Richie waited in the car until he saw Frank screech to a stop in front of the school building. Just Frank. No sirens, no SWAT. Richie met him on the sidewalk. "Where's the rest of the assault team?"

Frank flashed teeth, and raindrops splashed off his broad face. Even though it was not quite five in the morning, his silk tie was knotted. "Just us, Maynard."

"That's a big school."

"Yeah, and we don't know that he's in there. All we have is your hunch, and Kayley's. That ain't much to go on. Besides, we don't even know if he's in town yet. If he pulled up and saw lights and trucks and assault gear, he'd just turn around and we'd never see him again."

"I guess that's true."

"Plus, like you say, it's a big place. We storm the place, make a lot of noise, he'll kill her. We've got to go in quiet."

"Okay," Richie said. "You've sold me, already."

"Just saying."

"Less talking and more moving would be good."

Frank regarded the building. Richie had been studying it since he had arrived. Four stories, red brick with white molding, in a sort of

U shape. The schoolyard was cracked concrete slab with growth bubbling up from underneath. At least half of the white-painted windows were broken, and the eight-foot iron fence around it was thick with spray-painted graffiti, as were the lower sections of the building. Richie had already identified two spots where the fence had been pulled or cut away enough to allow entry.

He pointed them out. "We can go in there, or there."

"Yeah," Frank said. He indicated a spot on the building, half-hidden in shadow. "Looks like a door busted open there, see the way it's hanging?"

"Go in that way?"

"Good as any." Frank ducked back into his car, came out with two flashlights and a gun. "Here."

"I'll take the flashlight," Richie said.

"What about the piece?"

Richie hesitated. He was still in bad shape from the beating. But he'd been having power trip fantasies, thinking about fighting people and actually getting into a brawl. Before that he'd had passing thoughts of suicide. The combination of his brain and a gun was probably a bad idea. "You've got yours, right?"

Frank patted his hip. "Never without."

"Then we're good."

Frank gave him a puzzled face, but put the second gun back in his glove box and closed the car door. "Let's do this."

○ ○ ○

Frank led the way. He squeezed through the gap in the fence, the iron bars brushing against his suit. "Guess there's a trip to the dry cleaner's in my future."

"If you'd wear regular clothes …" Richie grumbled.

"These *are* my regular clothes." Frank drew the gun from his hip. "Quiet, now."

They crossed the broken concrete. The moon had long since set, and light from the streetlamps barely penetrated the gloom, offering just enough for them to see the door that Frank had picked out. As they neared it, he saw that his night vision was still solid: The steel door hung at an awkward angle, only its top hinge still functional. He tugged, drawing a high-pitched moan from it and making a space big enough for them both to slide through.

Inside, the flashlights went on. The building was utter darkness, any light that penetrated the painted-over windows failing to reach the interior corridors. Frank shined his toward the floor, which was an ocean of trash: newspapers, fast food containers, bottles and cans, condoms, cigarette packages, even some plastic toys and a broken blue wading pool. It looked like the city was using the place for landfill.

The smell was worse. Blending with the stink of trash was an ammoniac undercurrent of urine, enveloping them as they entered the building. Ankle-deep, Frank thought: forget dry cleaning, this suit'll have to be burned. It was soaked, anyway.

The inside walls were covered with even more graffiti than the exterior ones. Gang symbols, names, dates, and drawings of various acts, most of them sexual or excretory. Frank was astonished at the effort that had gone into some of them, which must have taken hours, if not days. He had seen plenty of elaborate street art around Detroit; Michelangelo would have been a tagger today. In the protected confines of the deserted school, graffiti artists had leeway to exercise their creativity.

Richie grabbed Frank's arm. Frank started, but he was carrying his weapon with his finger outside the trigger guard so didn't actually shoot anything. "What the hell is that?" Richie asked. He beamed his light toward a place about ten yards ahead of them, where the trash seemed to be moving of its own accord.

"Rat, most likely."

"Most likely?" Richie sounded nervous, his voice reaching an elevated pitch. "What else could it be?"

"Snake? An exceedingly short leprechaun? I don't know, Maynard. Rat's the reasonable guess. Now keep your voice down, you don't wanna let Morton know we're here."

"Sorry."

They had entered a back hallway, but soon came to a corner and made the turn into a wide corridor lined with classroom doors. Here the trash was shallower, and in spots the tile floor peeked through. As with the outside windows, the glass in many of the windowed doors had been shattered. Frank heard soft scrabbling on the floors, a distant knocking. From some upper floor, mad laughter drifted down.

He tried each door on the right side of the hall while Richie worked the left, pushing them open if they weren't locked or wedged shut, shining lights inside. Most of the rooms were empty, though in some, dust-caked shards of glass weakly reflected the flashlight's beam from the grimy floor. Others had captured spillover litter from the hall.

As he peered into the classrooms, Frank thought about what had taken place here in happier times. Children hushed during story time while the teacher read to them. Anxious students holding their hands up, waving their arms eagerly, wanting to be called on, while others sat on their fingers hoping to avoid that fate. Intense young faces, tongues at the corners of their mouths, looking down while they wrote on lined paper. Finger-painted artwork hanging on the walls. A school was a kind of promised land, each classroom a doorway to a world of limitless possibilities and dreams not yet corroded by the world beyond the walls.

His own school experience was decades back, and he was certain things had changed since then, but imagined that the emotional peaks and valleys were similar. He would never have children, not now, but maybe he could be a godparent to Maynard's, if the man got his shit together. That would be the next best thing. Not just him, though—the mental image was fleeting, but when Frank pictured it, he saw himself and Marcia in that role, together.

Through one of the open doors, about a third of the way down the hall, orange light flickered. Richie sniffed the air, and when he did, Frank smelled it too.

"It's a fire."

"Squatters, probably," Frank said.

"What, there aren't enough empty houses in this town?"

"They might have more freedom here. No landlord coming around, no police rousting 'em."

"You're police."

"They don't know that. Listen, Maynard, most squatters are just people down at the heels, got to have a roof over their heads. But some are mentally ill, or criminals, and potentially dangerous. We're not here to hassle them, and we don't confront them if we can avoid it."

"I hear you."

"You want to go back to the car for that gun?"

Richie looked over his shoulder, shook his head. "I'm good."

They couldn't move silently through the building, but they did their best, trying not to kick the largest of the fallen cups and flattened boxes and sheets of newspaper. Through the half-open door, Frank glimpsed three people crouched around a coffee can, one of them holding something on a stick over the fire. He hoped it wasn't one of the rats, but didn't really want to know. They were engaged in a spirited conversation and didn't notice the men in the hall.

Richie had said the school was big, and he was right. If Morton was somewhere inside, it could take hours to find him. And if he wasn't, then those hours were wasted while he had time with Sherri, someplace else.

Frank desperately hoped they had made the right call.

52

The school's basement was a frightening place.

His angel had started to awaken near the end of the flight, but he'd convinced her to drink some juice, slipping a little more Ambien into it. She had gone right back to sleep, and he had carried her out through the airport and into a rented car he had arranged by phone from California.

She woke up again in the basement. This time, he let her. He yearned for her company; if he had wanted a lifeless lump he could have stayed home with his dolls. As she came around, she began to fuss, crying for her mother. He let her roam just far enough for the darkness and the huge pipes and ductwork running through the basement to terrify her, and then she came back to him, because as scared as she was, at least he was more familiar than that place.

That was all he needed. He soothed her, comforted her, stroked her fine, golden hair, and embraced her. In time, she relaxed again, not drugged but content.

"Do you like our new home, sweetheart?" he asked her. He had put out a booby trap to help ensure their privacy, then had spread the things from the one suitcase he'd had time to pack, to soften the floor. That done, he had taken out his ballpoint pen and scratched J+A in big letters on the wall, encircled by a heart.

She mumbled something, her mouth pressed against his arm. He ran his fingers through her hair, traced them down her back. "We'll be so happy here, my darling angel," he said. "The world can fuss and blunder and blow itself apart outside, but we'll be here, just Jarod and Angela, together forever in our happy home."

"No," she said.

"Shh, it's okay, little one. It's fine."

And it would be, he was certain. The time of chaos was gone, the time of searching over. He was home, in the only place he had ever been truly happy, with his angel, his Angela of the golden locks and tender kisses. So much time had passed but she had waited for him, as he had known she must. Now they were reunited, safe and finally once again in one another's arms. He felt her small back rise and fall under his hands.

But he had been awake for too long, not daring to sleep on the flight or at the airport, and holding her warm, compact body against his, his eyes closed.

He awoke with the sick, sudden realization that she was gone. Not much time had passed, he was sure. Minutes. Less.

"Angela?"

His own voice bounced off the pipes and walls, taunting him with her name. He listened, but didn't hear her. "Angela?" he asked again, his voice quieter.

Listening.

The place was so dark, and all he had was a penlight he had bought at an airport store. He should have thought of that before. He turned it this way and that, looking beneath the big steel ductworks, and up pipes laddering the walls. "Angela, come on out," he said. "Playtime's over."

He heard a sound behind him, the scuff of a shoe. He spun, bringing the light around in a crazy arc. He had passed an intersection, and something flashed through it, small and golden. "Angela!" he shouted.

Then her footsteps exploded and he could hear her gasping breath, the rustle of her clothing, and he stepped toward the intersection, skidded on the cool, dry concrete floor, caught himself, and gave chase.

53

Richie had his head in a doorway, craning his neck to see around a pile of desks covered in transparent plastic sheeting that had long since been smothered by dust and brittled with age, when he heard Frank's yelp. Richie whirled around. His flashlight beam landed on a man bursting from a door across the hall, a man with dark skin and filthy clothes and a pipe in his fist that caught the light and painted a moving stripe in the darkness.

Frank was bringing up his gun, but not fast enough. He'd been taken by surprise, his strangled cry evidence of that. He squeezed off a shot, but too late. The man's pipe flashed and Richie heard a sickening thud. Frank collapsed against the wall. His flashlight clattered to the floor, rolled, and blinked out.

Richie lunged. The pipe swung out again, slamming into his upper arm. Richie let out a grunt and went to one knee. He grabbed for the man again, but took a kick to the chest and went down. The man raced into the darkness and was gone.

It wasn't Morton, so Richie didn't follow.

He pointed his light at Frank, who was trying to rise, the wall at his back. There was a red smear above his right eye. His mouth was working, as he tried to speak, but he sank down again without getting any words out.

"Frank, are you—?" Richie didn't bother finishing. Frank wasn't okay, not at all. The pipe had torn a deep gash in his skull; Richie had to aim the flashlight away because he couldn't take the sight of red and pink and white tissue showing through Frank's dark skin. Blood flecked the edges of his mouth, and his eyes were rolled back in his head.

"Frank, you need a doctor, an ambulance. We've got to—"

Frank shook his head vigorously, spraying Richie with hot droplets. "No time," Frank managed to croak. "Morton."

"How? Alone? Me?"

"Gun," Frank said weakly.

Frank had hung onto it. He tried to hand it over to Richie, but the weight was too much for him. Richie took it from his hand. It was warm to the touch. Richie didn't like it.

He drew his new cell phone from his pocket, pushed a key. The No Signal legend showed on the screen. The phone hadn't cost much, and it was apparently worth just what he'd paid. "I can't leave you here like this," Richie said.

He knew what Frank's response would be, but he had to say it anyway.

Frank focused his gaze on Richie, pressing the hand with the gun in it. "Kill that motherfucker," he said.

Richie hadn't held a gun since the day he was booted from the cops. He had never once fired on the job, except at a shooting range. He clicked off the safety, put his finger inside the trigger guard. Frank could afford to be cautious, but he couldn't, or he wouldn't be able to use the weapon if he needed to.

"Stay here."

What a stupid thing to say, Richie thought. If Frank could move, he'd be going with Richie, not sprawled where wall met floor.

Richie didn't know how he would find Morton alone, though. The two of them, working together in an orderly fashion, still had not even covered the first floor. And now the report of a gun had echoed throughout the building.

He was alone, in hostile territory. He heard the squeal of hinges, the thunder of footsteps, shrieks and cries. Feeling the weight of urgency, he kicked doors open, aiming light and gun into each room. "Morton!" he screamed. "I know you're in here!"

Turning the last corner of the ground floor, he saw, silhouetted against moonlight streaming through shattered windows, a little girl stepping out of a doorway, a man looming behind her, reaching for her. Richie raised the gun, felt the cool steel trigger against the pad of his finger. "Freeze, Morton!" he shouted, his cop training swelling to the fore. He sighted on the man's midsection, sure he could make the shot, the girl was short enough not to be at risk—

—and a woman emerged from the doorway, slender and angular, coming out behind the others. Richie fixed them in the flashlight's beam; a black family, young, man and woman both with the look of working people fallen on tough times. The girl mirrored both her father and mother, the way children could.

"Jesus," Richie said. "I almost shot you."

"No call for that, bro," the man said.

"I know, I'm sorry. I won't."

"We're just tryin' to stay dry is all. Stay covered."

"Sorry," Richie said again. "Have you seen a white man in here, with a little blond girl?"

"We ain't seen nothing," the woman said.

The girl hid behind her father's legs, her eyes huge, and Richie realized he was still pointing the gun at them. He lowered it and apologized once again. All they wanted was to keep their child safe. That was what parents did.

"Yeah, we'll find someplace else," the man said.

"Go outside and call an ambulance, please," Richie said. "There's an injured police officer here. A good man who needs help."

The family disappeared down the hall without answering. "Please!" Richie called after them.

Richie had to dial it back a few notches before he accidentally did shoot somebody. The stress, the hallucinatory surroundings, the weapon in his hand: a recipe for disaster.

He had passed a staircase earlier, and he doubled back toward it.

Before he reached it, he saw a small form darting out of an open door, halfway down the hall. He aimed the flashlight, catching streaming, flaxen hair.

He took a chance.

"Sherri? Is that you?"

She stopped, turned, green eyes catching the light.

And an arm snaked from the darkness, caught her by the shoulder, and yanked her away.

54

Sherri!" Richie cried. "Morton, give it up!"

The girl shrieked, but her cry was cut short.

Richie raced to the doorway, hit it hard. He was shaking so much he didn't want to have to make any difficult shots now. But he had to catch Morton, had to save Sherri.

He aimed the light through the door and saw another staircase, not a wide one like the one that led up but narrower, with concrete steps and steel banisters, angling down into pitch blackness.

"Morton! You're surrounded! Come on up and you won't get hurt!"

Silence answered.

He took a moment, trying to gather himself.

Everything he had worked toward, fought for—he and Frank both, Frank who was presumably still on the floor, bleeding and in need of aid—was down those stairs.

Richie had found Angela Morton. Kayley Ann Carrington. She had been horribly mistreated, but she was safe now, though her past would never completely release her. But the prey had always been Morton, and Morton had another girl's life in his hands. The fact that she was Kayley's daughter was almost beside the point. Any girl deserved better than Jarod Morton.

Richie had to go down those stairs. Morton would be watching, waiting for him. He could be choking Sherri's life from her at this moment.

Richie had never been so terrified.

He started down the stairs, unable to use the railing because of the flashlight and gun. It was like descending into murky waters, the darkness rising to swallow him whole.

There were boilers downstairs, pipes and ducts, what looked like miles of concrete and steel extending in every direction. It was a maze, a nightmare. How could he find one little girl in all of that?

"Morton!" he shouted. The man knew he was there, so why not announce himself? "Morton, this can end two ways. You can give up and live or you can hide and fight and die."

Morton didn't reply. Sherri got off a brief cry that ended in a strangled choke. Echoes bounced around the basement, making it impossible to isolate her direction.

He realized he didn't know if Morton had a gun. If he did, then carrying the flashlight through the darkness was a terrible idea.

He clicked it off.

Absolute blackness engulfed him. That was no good either; he could fall down the stairs and break his neck.

He turned it back on, holding it away from his body, half-expecting a bullet to tear into him.

It didn't come. The silence was total, as if he had been suddenly struck deaf. He dinged the flashlight against the rail, just to hear a sound.

Then he thought, screw it. He knows I'm coming. If he's got another exit, he'll use it, and if he doesn't, the fucker is mine.

"I'm coming for you, Morton," he said. His voice was loud, authoritative. His cop voice; he recognized it, like a high school friend he hadn't seen in years.

Nobody shot him, and he became bolder.

By the time Richie noticed the glint of wire stretched across the steps, tied to the banisters, it was too late. His leg snagged it and he had a sickening moment of dizziness, flashlight beam whirling around, nothing but black below. He pitched forward, flinging his arms out to stop his fall. They found no purchase. He slammed into the hard concrete stairs and kept going, each new bump shooting agony through his already battered body.

Somewhere along the way, the flashlight wrenched free of his grip and flew over the side, landing hard and going out. He held onto the gun, but accidentally jerked the trigger. The weapon went off, so close to his head that the report was deafening, the muzzle flash bright enough to leave retinal burn that glowed green in the darkness. Sharp smoke seared his nostrils.

His skid ended at the bottom of the stairs. While he was on the ground, fighting to stay conscious, he was dimly aware of someone moving past him in the dark, heading up the stairs. Morton, he was sure; he heard a muffled cry that could only be Sherri. He reached for the man but missed, his hand colliding with the cool steel of the railing, sending a shock wave up to his shoulder.

Trying to gain his feet, to chase Morton, a wave of nausea gripped him. Richie froze, willing it to pass. He swallowed a couple of times, then started up. Morton had already cleared the doorway, carrying Sherri, Richie guessed. The door at the top of the stairs shut with a clang, cutting off the faint light that had followed Richie in. He burst forward, hoping it wasn't locked from the other side.

It wasn't. He found the wire and stepped over it, reached the door. He pushed and it swung open. Richie emerged into the faint light of the school hallway. Morton and Sherri were already out of sight. Richie went still, listening, trying to separate the gunshot's ringing in his ears from the sounds of the building. Finally, he isolated a rising shuffle and another muffled squeal. They were going upstairs.

The inner staircase wasn't far away. Richie raced to it and climbed, three steps at a time. He could hear Morton above, still ascending. "Morton!" Richie cried. "Give it up!"

Morton didn't respond, just kept rising. Richie wasted his breath, calling out once more. "Morton, let the girl go!"

Still no response. Richie pushed himself harder. Adrenaline dulled the pain. As he neared the top of the steps, the building's moldering ceiling visible above, he caught a glimpse of Morton, Sherri in his arms, bolting through the doorway.

Richie followed. In the fourth-floor corridor, Morton had paused. Probably not sure of where to go, what his options were. Most of the doors lining the hallway were closed. At the end of the hall was a big window, painted over and with only one pane cracked. Light glimmered through.

Richie pointed the gun. Morton barely registered its presence, or his. "You're suffering a delusion, Jarod," Richie declared. "You need help. You need counseling, psychiatric care. You think you're reliving a time long since past. You're confused, Morton. This girl isn't Angela, and this isn't thirteen years ago."

Morton turned. Sherri struggled in his arms, but he crushed her against his chest, far stronger than she was. He looked much like the pictures Richie had seen, although older, the bags under his eyes and the pouches of his cheeks sagging with age. He had a thick mustache, drooping around the sides of his mouth. His brown hair was shorter than in the photographs, revealing the way his ears melded with his head. Richie couldn't see the webbing between his fingers, not from here, but he was sure it was there.

"That's Sherri," Richie said. "She hasn't been damaged yet, hasn't been ruined like you ruined Kayley, and however many others. She's clean, Jarod. She doesn't deserve to be treated the way you treat children. Nobody does. That's sick, Jarod, it's twisted and it's wrong."

"She belongs with me."

"She doesn't."

"You don't know anything. You don't understand, none of you understand."

"That's because it's wrong, it's evil. You've got to stop."

Richie held the gun on the man, his hand surprisingly steady. He was certain, now, certain at last that he had done the right thing, made the right choices.

"You can't have her!" Morton said. His hands tightened on Sherri's throat. Her eyes bulged, her face turning florid. "Drop that gun and kick it over here, or I'll kill her. Nobody can have her but me. She's mine."

Surrender his weapon? Never. "She's a human being," Richie corrected. "She doesn't belong to anybody. You least of all."

"She's mine!" Morton said. His hand contracted, his arms shaking with effort and rage.

He was going to do it, to kill her right in front of Richie. And Richie wasn't a good enough shot to take a chance. Sherri's body was between him and Morton, her legs dangling, kicking. Richie might be able to take out a knee, but the way Sherri writhed, he had as much chance of hitting her.

Still, if wounding her would save her life …

His finger pressed against the trigger. He blew out his breath, willing his hand not to quiver.

And Morton spun around, breaking into a sprint.

"You can save us!" he shouted. His words echoed in the quiet, tiled hallway. "Spread your wings, my angel, and fly!"

Richie was confused. What the hell did he mean? He was trapped, nowhere to go but into one of the classrooms, where he'd easily be cornered.

But he wasn't slowing at any of the doors, and as he neared the window, his meaning became clear.

Morton's insanity had ratcheted up yet again.

He meant to go through the window, taking Sherri with him.

But she was no angel. Wings would not sprout from her back. She was a child, and Morton a madman.

Richie pulled the trigger.

The bullet tore into Morton's upper right shoulder and punched a hole out the other side. He lurched forward, spilling Sherri to the floor. Her screams were unending. Blood fountained from Morton's wounds. Momentum carried him into the window.

It cracked, but held.

55

Richie stepped past Sherri and trained the gun on Morton, who twisted on the ground, one foot twitching uncontrollably. He meant to shoot the man in the heart or the brain, delivering righteous vengeance. But before he pulled the trigger, he decided that he didn't want Morton to die believing he was in the right. He would rather see Morton go to trial, go to prison, live for years, decades, knowing that he had done wrong and been caught and punished.

Morton was bleeding. A lot. But he would live.

Richie turned back to Sherri. The girl was terrified, crying, shaking uncontrollably. "It's okay, Sherri," Richie kept saying. "Your mommy sent me to look for you. She wants you back, she didn't want this man to take you away. Your mommy loves you, Sherri. I'm going to get you back to her."

"Do you mean it?" she asked. She sniffled back tears. "Really?"

"Absolutely."

She took a hesitant, stiff-legged step toward him, then another, and he lowered himself to her level, and she came solemnly into his arms, giving him a genuine hug. A child's hug. The kind kids were supposed to give.

Richie returned it, then shoved the gun into the back of his waistband and lifted Sherri into his arms. She weighed almost nothing, but her weight was at the same time comforting, affirming. He carried her down the stairs and through the door and into the hallway, where light from the rising sun streamed in through broken windows and open doors. At the end of the corridor, his head a bloody, pulpy mess, stood Frank, one hand out to brace himself against a wall. He looked at them, at Richie and Sherri, and he laughed.

"Maynard," he said, "you fucking did it!"

And Richie said, "Language, Frank. There's a kid here."

O   O   O

Before they reached the door they heard sirens, then brakes and shouts and vehicle doors. Frank was moving slowly, unsteady on his feet, his face ashen and slick with blood and perspiration. But then they emerged from the same door they had used going in, and there were police outside, ambulances, even a fire truck, and more coming. A news van with WWJ-TV emblazoned on the side and a corkscrew satellite transmitter drew to a stop beside them. The people Richie had encountered must have called after all, or neighbors had. Across the street, residents spilled from their homes to view the commotion. The vacant houses looked especially lonely by contrast.

Frank managed to hold up his badge case. "He's on the job!" Richie shouted. A patrol officer recognized Frank, and word spread. Paramedics rushed to Frank, sparing glances at Richie but determining that his worst wounds were past history, not current drama. "Leave me be," Frank insisted. "There's a man hurt upstairs, shot."

"He's a murderer and a pedophile," Richie warned them. "He's alive, and he's still potentially dangerous."

"A couple of you cops go with the EMTs," Frank suggested. "Cuff the motherfucker and bring him out here. I want to arrest his ass myself."

Vehicles kept coming. News crews exited their vans, retrieved cameras, unspooled cable, and well-groomed reporters arranged themselves before the school for their stand-ups. Richie and Frank tried to avoid the spotlight, but even though they declined interview requests, cameras were soon pointing their way.

After a while, a familiar Chevy Cavalier pulled up outside the lines, and Wendy got out. She was wearing bright green, a good color on her, and Richie didn't think he had ever seen such a beautiful sight. By then, he and Frank had told their story at least three times, to detectives and Frank's Lieutenant Jackson, and Sherri was being interviewed gently by a female detective, blocked by official vehicles from the ever-hungry eye of the media. Morton had been led out with his hands cuffed behind his back, scowling, still claiming that "Angela" was his beloved, and they were meant to be together. Frank had made the arrest official, and then Morton was put into an ambulance and taken for medical care.

Richie started toward Wendy, telling the cops to let her through the barrier of yellow tape they had erected. She dashed across the broken concrete to him and they embraced in the middle, heedless of the cameras. Richie hugged her hard, and she returned the embrace until he winced.

"You look like shit," she said.

"You look incredible." He led her toward the police vehicles.

"Oh, I'm just—I turned on the news before I left for work, and I saw all this a few blocks away, and somehow I knew you'd be in the middle of it."

"Well, you were right. It'll be a while before I can get home."

"Whenever. I'll call in, take the day off."

"I'd like that."

She nodded toward where Sherri and the detective talked quietly. "Is that the little girl? The one this was all about?"

"One of them," Richie replied. "She's the one I was able to save."

"You didn't just save her, Richie. What about all the ones that would have come after?"

That's true, Richie thought. By getting Jarod Morton and Charles Welker off the streets, and possibly Otis Parrott as well, they had potentially prevented the abuse of dozens more children. Maybe hundreds, over the years to come. "Yeah, you're right."

"She's adorable."

"She is, isn't she?"

"What'll happen to her?"

"Her grandparents in Virginia have been notified," Richie told her. He had provided their names to the Detroit authorities. If

Kayley Ann Carrington could get back on her feet, he thought, then *anything* could be borne, any trauma overcome. She would need a lot of help, of course. He would do whatever he could to see that she got it. Whatever small favors he might do for her would be nothing compared to the gift she had given him. She had, almost literally, saved his life. "They'll come here, and her mother will be brought in from California to meet them. I hope they all go back to Virginia together. The mother doesn't have the tools to raise her right, not yet, anyway. And the grandparents deserve another shot."

"I'm not following you."

"I'll explain later," Richie said. He was unspeakably weary, all of a sudden. He wanted to sleep for a week, ideally in Wendy's arms. "But I was thinking, earlier. We should talk about adopting."

A hesitant smile crept across Wendy's face. "You think?"

"Hey, it's good enough for Superman."

"And again, not following."

"Again, I'll explain later."

"Whatever. You did a good thing, Richie Krebbs. You should be proud."

"I am." She was right about that, too. He had achieved the goal he'd set for himself after the discovery in the Morton house and his breakfast with Frank. He was pretty sure he had found what he was meant to do. And he was good at it. He didn't know if it could pay him a living wage; so far, all it had done was cost him money he didn't have, and the only job available to him. But it was a start, anyway. It was a step in the right direction, a foot on a path. He would take the next step, and the one after that, and keep going. He had to.

Frank was holding court in the open rear of an ambulance, laughing with cops and paramedics. His wound had been treated and bandaged, and he had refused all attempts to get him to go to the hospital. Wendy looked at him. "Is that Frank Robey? He's hurt."

"He'll be okay. You want to meet him?"

"I'd love to."

"Come on." He led her to where Frank sat. The cops and paramedics drifted away. "Frank," Richie said. "This is Wendy."

"It's a pleasure," Frank said. "Heard a lot about you. You're way too pretty for Maynard."

"Maynard? Oh, right. From some old TV show."

"Dobie Gray," Richie said.

Frank laughed. "*The Many Loves of Dobie Gillis.*"

"Apparently it's not out on DVD," Richie said.

"And that's a damn shame," Frank said.

"I'm sure it is. I've heard quite a bit about you, Frank."

"Yeah, well, Maynard's a known liar, so don't hold those things against me."

"He's only said nice things."

"Like I said."

"Anyway, I just wanted to say hello, and thanks for sending my husband on a coast-to-coast excursion and getting him all beat to hell."

Frank touched the bandage on his head. "Occupational hazard."

"I can see that."

"Thanks for loaning him out to me. He made all the difference." He caught Richie's gaze. "I mean that."

"Thanks," Richie said.

"He does that for me too," Wendy said.

Richie kissed Wendy one more time, holding it for several long moments. "Go home," he said. "I'll be there as soon as I can."

"I'll be waiting."

They watched her walk off. When she was gone, Frank gave Richie an anxious look. "Listen, man, I gotta get to the hospital."

"What's up? Is there news about your dad?"

"No. He probably won't hear me, but I want to tell him we got that fucker."

"Okay," Richie said. "Come on, I'll drive."

"In your piece of shit car? No way. We'll take mine."

"Doesn't matter. I'm still driving. While we're there you can get your head examined. It's way overdue."

"Paramedics cleared me, Maynard. No concussion."

"Yeah, I'm not talking about that. Think like an astrophysicist, my ass. Let's go."

He put a hand out. Frank took it, and Richie helped tug him to his feet. The man's big hand felt comfortable in his. Right.

When Frank was steady on his feet, they walked together through the cops, past the reporters and the onlookers, to his waiting car.

Richie headed for the driver's door. Frank grinned and tossed him the keys. "Careful," Frank said. "You hit anything, I have to do the department paperwork."

"I'll be careful," Richie promised.

"Thanks, brother."

Richie slid inside, behind the wheel, Frank's bulk beside him. "Buckle up," Richie said. "It's the law."

Frank gave his deep chuckle, but he buckled up, and Richie started the car.

56

Marcia drove toward Frank's house. She'd heard all about it on the news, what he and Richie Krebbs had done. He had even been to the hospital, according to his family, seen that his father was breathing on his own, more all the time. But she hadn't seen him for days, hadn't heard from him, until he had called her during the afternoon and asked her to stop by after work. "I got something I want you to see," he had said.

"What is it?"

"I can't tell you that, you just got to see it for yourself."

"Frank …"

"It's not that far out of your way, Marcia."

"All right. I'm off at nine."

"See you then," Frank had said.

The night was cool, with a steady drizzle that wouldn't turn into real rain but still required that she run the wipers. It had been a long day, a hard day, and she was tired. Cranky. Whatever Frank wanted to show her, it had better be damn good. She thought maybe it was his precious comic book art, which he had said he wouldn't hang on his walls until the Morton girl had been found.

As she neared his block, she saw a disturbing glow. Was someone's house on fire? She didn't hear sirens or see any flashing lights. Her phone was in her purse, on the empty seat next to her, and she reached for it in case she had to call 911.

Then she turned onto Frank's street.

Every light in the block was turned on. Lights burned on porches, in windows. Even that old bastard McNabb had his houselights glowing. Every tree was wrapped with strings of Christmas lights, even though the holidays had been over for months. What the hell? she wondered.

Then her own words came back to her. That night in the cafeteria. "When you're ready to get serious, leave a light on," she had said. Something to that effect, anyway.

She dabbed at her eyes, suddenly moist.

Frank doesn't believe in half-measures, she thought. That son-of-a-bitch.

I guess he must be ready.

About the Author

Jeffrey J. Mariotte is the award-winning author of more than fifty novels, including supernatural thrillers *Season of the Wolf*, *Missing White Girl*, *River Runs Red*, and *Cold Black Hearts*, and as Jeff Mariotte, *The Slab*, the Dark Vengeance teen horror quartet. He also writes comic books and graphic novels, including the long-running horror/Western comic book series Desperadoes, original graphic novel *Zombie Cop*, and the bestselling biographical comic about Barack Obama, *Presidential Material*. He has worked in virtually every aspect of publishing and bookselling, and lives in southeastern Arizona's high desert. For more information, please visit him at:

www.jeffmariotte.com.

Other WordFire Press Titles

Our list of other WordFire Press authors and titles is always growing. To find out more and to see our selection of titles, visit us at:

wordfirepress.com